ENTHRALLED

LORA LEIGH
ALYSSA DAY
MELJEAN BROOK
LUCY MONROE

BERKLEY SENSATION, NEW YORK

THE BERKLEY PUBLISHING GROUP
Published by the Penguin Group
Penguin Group (USA) Inc.
375 Hudson Street, New York, New York 10014, USA

USA | Canada | UK | Ireland | Australia | New Zealand | India | South Africa | China

Penguin Books Ltd., Registered Offices: 80 Strand, London WC2R 0RL, England
For more information about the Penguin Group, visit penguin.com.

ENTHRALLED

This book is an original publication of The Berkley Publishing Group.

Berkley Sensation trade paperback ISBN: 978-0-425-25331-1

An application to register this book for cataloging has been submitted to the Library of Congress.

PUBLISHING HISTORY
Berkley Sensation trade paperback edition / July 2013

PRINTED IN THE UNITED STATES OF AMERICA

10 9 8 7 6 5 4 3 2 1

Cover art by S. Miroque.
Cover design by Rita Frangie.
Interior text design by Laura K. Corless.

Contents

THE DEVIL'S DUE

LORA LEIGH

In loving memory of the greatest aunt a niece could have.

Dorothy "Sugar Babe" Few Lucas. You are missed.

Not just for your laughter, your witty replies,

and generous spirit.

You are missed, just because you were you.

I love you, Aunt Sugie.

There was Death, and she faded into the shadows.

There was Slaughter, and he disappeared as dust into the wind.

There was the Lyon, who sought vengeance in the darkness, then found the light of love.

There was the Jaguar, who was the darkness, but found the heart that saved his soul.

There were so many.

There were all who knew vengeance, who knew retribution, and they succumbed to the greatest weakness man or beast could ever know.

They succumbed to the hearts they should have never possessed.

And now, the forces of man's greatest ally and his most cherished creator have looked down upon a heart that all have claimed to be black, to be without mercy or compassion, and felt Himself soften.

For mercy resides in quantities that are vast while compassion slices His soul with each act of justice he's forced to mete out.

The one they call "Devil." The one they say is the darkest of all Breeds created.

The one his creator has guided to ensure his hand had dealt the blow of justice needed to ensure the existence of the Breeds. The one for whom his creator has planned the most cherished of all gifts.

The Lyon now guides his Pride.

Slaughter now slays only the demons that risk his love.

The Jaguar now prowls only the darkness of his own lair while the bogeyman of the Breeds, the warrior Warrant, is the champion of love.

Each has received the truest gift of all, that gift of love.

Now the Devil will receive his as well.

The creator lifted his hand, his smile gentle, compassion and mercy guiding his actions as he brought revelations, hid from the Devil's enemies those secrets that would have harmed the coming gift, and laid in place each emotion, each hunger, each separate hormone and cell, the qualities needed to ensure a match none could have expected.

A mating.

A priceless, unending love.

It's now time to give the Devil his due.

PROLOGUE

Barrett O'Sullivan stared at the tiny—too, too tiny—form of the child that his best friend had followed him into hell to save.

So tiny.

A little scrap of flesh and bones that was all of nine years of age, but he swore she could be barely four if she was a day.

Now Jorn Langer, the friend who had uncovered the secret of these labs, the secret of this child, lay on the cement floor next to her, his blood staining the icy stone below.

God, it was so cold.

Barrett could feel the chill surrounding him seeping into his soul, into that place within his heart, within his consciousness, that brought the realization that once again, his life was changing.

Surrounded by that cold, his naked child lay, her skin nearly blue. The wealth of long, Irish red ringlets cascaded on the floor around her to mix with the blood of her rescuer. Irish cream flesh shadowed by the tint of freezing blue glistened beneath the ringlets.

Echoing screams, shouted orders, bestial growls and animalistic snarls were like a hellish symphony invading the lab where Jorn's greatest battle had been fought. The battle to save the child Barrett hadn't even known existed until days before.

"Fuck me, Bar," Jorn whispered weakly, his accent thickened by pain as thick Norse white blond lashes lifted to stare up at Barrett blearily. "I'm gonna die, lad. Helluva way to go."

"The hell you are." Kneeling quickly, Barrett checked the wound to his chest and knew his friend wasn't lying. He was dying.

God help him. This man was as much his brother as any blood could be, and he was dying.

"Don't you die on me, Jorn," he whispered, suddenly desperate.

All their lives it had been Jorn who had gotten Barrett's ass out of trouble, and who had gotten his ass into trouble. This was the man who had watched over him, laughed with him, fought with him.

"Got no choice, boyo," Jorn wheezed, his ruddy face pale now, the blood spilling too quickly from his chest.

"Your daughter, Bar." Jorn nodded to the child next to him.

Her breathing was slow and easy, but she was so stiff with cold.

Barrett all but tore his jacket off and quickly wrapped it around the girl's nude body, wondering why he hadn't done so the moment he stepped into the room.

She lay against Jorn's bleeding chest, her weight so slight she couldn't have increased the rate of blood loss, but still, Barrett moved to lift her from her resting place.

"No!" Jorn's arm tightened around her slight form. "Not yet. Let me hold this little angel for a moment. She reminds me of Khileen. My sweet, little Khileen."

His daughter. She was barely five, and she was the light of Jorn's life.

They both stared at the fall of hair. There was so much hair and so little child.

"Hide her," Jorn whispered, turning back to Barrett. "Remember the file I found, Bar. Don't let anyone know. They can't know she's yours and Kella's. Swear it, Bar."

"I swear it."

No one could know. It would mean more than just his and his wife, Kella's, life. It could mean their child's as well. A child created from the sperm and ova he and his wife had given at a fertility clinic in the hopes of a child that Kella would carry. A child she would nurture within her body and one they would raise from first birth.

Yet, as he stared at the child Jorn held close, Barrett realized no love could be greater than the love he felt for this child, at this moment.

Damn, his hands were shaking, he realized as he reached out to brush her hair back from her face.

Blinking fiercely at the tears that would have fallen, his gaze moved to Jorn's once again.

"Kella's lass," Jorn whispered, his accent thicker now as death neared. "She's her wee miniature, Bar."

"How do I hide her child?" Desperation began to fill him. "Fuck you, Bar. Don't you leave me to protect this child and Khileen alone. Don't you do this to me."

Jorn's rakish smile tugged at his pale lips. "I wish . . ."

"No, God, Jorn, don't you do this." How the fuck was he supposed to do what he had to do without Jorn's help?

"Stick closest to the truth," Jorn was wheezing now. "Found her here. Contact Lyons in the US. Virginia. Meet. Show him the truth. He'll give you the care of her."

The other man struggled for breath as a trail of blood began to seep from his nostrils. "Tell no one but Lyons."

Jorn suddenly gripped the sleeve of Barrett's jacket. "Swear it. Not even Kella can know. None but Lyons can know the truth."

"None but Lyons," Barrett agreed, knowing it was a secret he would have to break. There were no secrets from Kella, from his heart. What he knew, his Kella always knew.

"What Kella knows, she'll tell my lovely Jess. Jess will tell her momma—" He began coughing, blood spraying from between his parted lips.

"I'll hold the secret, Jorn. No one will threaten my child."

"My Khi," Jorn wheezed again, his blue eyes desperate and filled with such aching sadness and fury that for a moment, Barrett was certain sheer will would hold his friend to earth.

Then his eyes closed.

"I swear Khileen as well, Jorn. I'll protect her as I would protect my own. I swear it."

A tear slipped free—how could it not, now?—this was his dearest friend, the brother he'd never known until Jorn came into his life.

A peaceful expression filled Jorn's face then. "Aye then, I can go now," he whispered. "I can go."

"Jorn, please God, not yet—"

And just that quickly—

Barrett clenched his teeth, baring them in a snarl of naked agony before quickly gathering his daughter to his chest and rising to his feet.

He and Jorn had practiced this escape a million times over the past days. Getting in, getting the child, then getting out. They'd practiced getting out together, and they'd practiced escaping alone.

Had Jorn somehow known they'd never escape together?

Holding his daughter close to the warmth of his body, Barrett ran quickly for the other side of the room and the steel wall. Once there, he quickly pressed his hand against the Genetics Council symbol emblazoned on the wall and waited impatiently for the entire wall to move and reveal the hidden exit.

Sliding through the narrow opening, he pressed his hand against the matching emblem on the other side, waited for the door to close, then rushed through the hidden tunnel.

All the while, the child he carried slept deeply, untouched by the horror that echoed in blood-curdling screams on the other side of the room. Or the snarls and animalistic fury that caused them. All that mattered was getting his child out of there, and hiding her. Hiding her secret.

A recessive Wolf Breed.

Perfect human looks, straight, perfectly human canines, her animal genetics so deeply recessed that even the most advanced genetic testing hadn't picked up the fact that she was a creature of science rather than of nature.

The files Jorn had found had been stamped TOP SECRET, SINGLE COPY. There were no duplicates. Hopefully, there were truly no other copies, no other information to label her as a Breed rather than a human.

As far as the world would know, she was the daughter of Kella's cousin. Orphaned, alone in the world, and now adopted by the O'Sullivans.

His child.

His and Kella's.

Rushing into the dreary rain and fog that surrounded the underground labs, Barrett ran to the ground-hugging all-terrain vehicle he and Jorn had hidden the night before.

The armored Sergeants Dragoon sat low to the ground. It was built for speed and agility, with minimal onboard weapons. It was parked exactly where they had left it, buried beneath the natural hearty evergreen boughs of the Lawson's Cypress they'd covered it with.

Throwing open the back passenger door and hurriedly lifting the seat to reveal the padded hiding space beneath, Barrett placed his daughter inside before replacing the cover. Closing the door quietly, he moved to the driver's seat, slid inside and started the vehicle.

Before pulling out, his gaze slid to the hidden back entrance of the labs and for the briefest moment, he could have sworn he saw Jorn.

Just as quickly, the shadow of his friend was gone, the fog parting to reveal the straggled growth of a bare tree instead.

It wasn't Jorn.

His boyhood friend was gone forever.

"They escaped."

The young woman standing next to him bore most of his weight, her strength all that kept him on his feet.

"I'm dyin', lass. Let me go in peace," he whispered, regret piercing him as he stared into the wild neon color of those incredible amber eyes. This wee lass who had risked her own life, her own secrets, to tell him of the child they had ordered to be terminated. The child of the man he owed so much to.

And now he'd done gone and done it, as his wee Khileen was wont to say. Aye, he'd done gone and done it. For good this time.

God, the pain was hell. His chest felt as though it were split open, his heart exposed, a raw gaping wound and now exposed to air.

"I can't do that," she whispered, all but dragging him along a worn path until he stumbled, nearly taking her to the ground with him.

Suddenly, stronger, broader hands caught him, dragging him into a sheltering darkness before laying him out on a padded floor.

Jorn stared around at the Breeds—he knew they were Breeds. Breeds unlike any he'd ever seen before. These Breeds, they were the stuff of rumor, of horrifying tales of slow, agonizing deaths. They were the ones whose genetics had never fully progressed past the animal state.

"Nephilim," he whispered.

Men who were animals.

Animals who were men.

There was no true description of these men. The myth of the Breed Nephilim was that they were the product of experiments gone awry that the Genetics Council had studied, experimented upon, then lost control of.

They were crouched around him as he felt whatever they had dragged him into suddenly moving. Lifting?

"Why?" he whispered, directing his question to the one he knew was the leader. There were such legends of these creatures. Greater even than those of the winged breeds in the Americas that groups of soldiers and scientists hunted with such dedication.

One of the creatures gripped his arm, turned it palm outward, while another pushed an old-fashioned syringe into the vein. He could feel the burn of whatever medication was shot into his system as it began to speed through his veins. He tracked it. Through his arm, his shoulder—

"What are you doing? Why are you doing this?" he rasped, directing his question to the leader as he crouched at Jorn's side.

Nephilim, he thought again. The true terror of the Breeds.

In Europe, the Nephilim were spoken of with the same fear as vampires and werewolves had been in centuries past.

Pale, his face marked with the stripes of a white tiger, his white blond hair flowing to his shoulders, their leader gave a mocking snort as he nodded to Jorn's side. "She would leave me no peace should I allow you to die."

Jorn turned his head slowly to the wee lass that had dragged him from the labs.

Barely five three, tawny brown hair, long, thick matching lashes with sharp cheekbones, lips formed nearly like a cat's, and her eyes—

Cat's eyes.

And so young. So tiny. Surely no more in age than his wee Khileen.

"Why?" he asked her now as he felt himself drifting, lifting, becoming light as air.

"Because I'm yours," she whispered, her eyes glowing like amber fire. "And you are all I can claim as mine. How could I allow death to take you in such a way?"

What could she possibly mean? God, he needed to know what she meant. He needed to know—

Agony pierced his chest, his guts. It lifted his body as a scream tore from him as the jagged, serrated teeth of death's demon bit deep and shredded his insides like a dog shredded meat from a bone. The pain was horrifying. Brutal.

Darkness closed around him.

He prayed death took him.

Katie at 16

She was all wild Irish red hair, big emerald eyes and soft peaches-and-cream skin.

Many Irish girls were now freckled, as their American counterparts were. The world was much smaller than it had ever been, and pure Irish blood was all but nonexistent.

As Devil Black watched Katie Sullivan maneuver through the obstacles set up on the training course, admiration surged through him.

Sixteen years old and pure human, yet she could outrun, outclimb and outlast a third of the young Breed females on the course with her.

Mary Katherine "Katie" O'Sullivan was the reason he'd been called to the Breed Protection Network's training center by the center's operator, Gilliam Finneghea. A former American special forces soldier and United Nations undercover intelligence officer, Gilliam had not just trained some of the top covert agents the United Nations have ever employed, but he had also gone against some of the best, and had come out of each battle alive.

Sometimes only barely living, but alive.

Jonas would have sworn nothing could really impress Gilliam, because the man had already seen the best.

Until Katie O'Sullivan had entered the network.

"You're certain she's not recessed?" Devil asked, the Ireland showing in his accent. It only happened when he stepped out on Irish soil; no matter how he tried, the Irish blood he'd begun with couldn't be hidden.

Gilliam snorted. "She's adopted on Irish soil, Devil. Do ya think she's recessed and got away with it? This ain't America, my friend."

Testing in Europe, Ireland and Scotland was far more in-depth and done far more often on adopted children and adults than in any other countries. With the tests becoming more painful every year after the age of twenty-five, many adopted adults were opting to move to countries with less stringent testing laws. Some of Europe's Breeds continued to hide or escape the European countries to avoid the required one-to-five-year testing requirements for all Breeds, no matter how recessed their genetics were. Many of the Breeds forced into the testing facilities were so radically different, with no scientific reason for the change once they were released, that questions were beginning to be asked.

This girl was tested yearly as well. During the last genetic screening she had been forced to do, it was reported that she had punched one of the techs when he had been too rough drawing the genetic sample from her liver and spleen.

She was tough as hell, but she looked as delicate as a red rose.

Crossing one arm over his chest and propping his elbow on his forearm, Devil stroked his jaw thoughtfully. He was there to watch the girl go through training maneuvers. He would be there tomorrow to watch her in the control room of the underground command center the network had established a decade before.

It had been hidden at first, to protect the Breeds from the labs they escaped from. If they could make it to a predestined pickup point without being spotted or followed, then they were taken to a safe house overnight. Eventually, several days, underground tunnels and church basements later, they made it here.

"Okay, so she's not a Breed." Devil scratched at his jaw, his eyes narrowed, his body more tense than it should have been as he watched her go through the network's bruising maneuvers.

"Yeah, she's not a Breed," Gilliam retorted, a question in his voice as he watched Devil. "You act like it's news."

Devil shrugged. She had all the qualities of a Breed female. Beautiful. A delicate, fragile appearance.

An underlying strength.

"Okay then, I'm interested." Giving a decisive nod without looking away from the girl, Devil made his decision quickly. "I'll let Tiberian know and we'll check her out in five years."

In five years she would be twenty-one and beyond the requirement that the network reveal any underage workers. And at twenty-one, her body would be mature enough, strong enough, to train for the Bureau of Breed Affairs as a human agent.

The Bureau had been built from the ground up by Breeds, and only in the past years had they begun accepting humans into their ranks. But it was Devil's hope that rather than joining the Bureau, she would instead join Lobo Reever's security team in the New Mexico desert.

As he watched, he couldn't help but allow his curiosity to grow. A human that moved like a Breed. He was always of the opinion . . .

If it looked like . . .

If it acted like . . .

If it sounded like . . .

He wasn't a great believer in coincidences either.

At that moment, her head lifted from where she watched another trainee slipping around the form of a deserted building. Their eyes met. And in that brief moment, in that connection, Devil swore he saw a hell of a lot more than a human.

Yet, she wasn't a Breed?

ONE

Katie—8 years later

Mary Kathleen O'Sullivan, Katie to friends and family, had no idea so many reporters could exist in one place.

Standing behind one of the protective filters that now covered each of her windows, she stared at the crowd of journalists vying for position, watching her home closely, microphones and notepads held ready.

"The guardians of the masses," her father had once called journalists. He now called them "those sons of bitches," despite the fact that they were doing no more now than they had been when he'd made the first comment.

"Katie, please come away from the window," her mother requested, her soft, lilting voice heavy with concern.

Katie, her parents had always called her. She guessed it beat "Fido," or "Precious," as several tabloids' writers had dubbed her.

Turning, she did as her mother asked, glancing at the other woman from beneath the veil of her lashes.

Kella O'Sullivan had aged a bit in the past weeks. There were fine worry lines now etched in her once smooth forehead, while her emerald green eyes reflected a fear that hadn't been there before.

Her long, red gold ringlets were caught at her nape with a heavy silver clasp, displaying the family pearls she wore at her neck.

Katie had often reflected on how alike she and her mother looked. The high cheekbones and slightly tilted eyes. Small, though sensually curved lips and the thick, unusually long red gold lashes that framed their deep green eyes. Eyes that Katie had never seen so clouded with worry and fear.

Or had they been?

Katie had always sensed the well-hidden concern that rode her parents, though she'd never truly believed she was the root of it. She'd always assumed the stress came from her father's job as assistant chief constable of Northern Ireland, rather than from the freak of science their daughter was.

Maintaining her poise, she returned to the wingback chair beside the gas fireplace her father had just installed in the three-story home she'd lived in all her life. That chair had been turned to face their "guests," rather like an interviewee's chair would face some emissary of power, such as the men sitting across from her.

Callan Lyons, the Feline Breed Pride leader, was accompanied by Jonas Wyatt, the director of the Bureau of Breed Affairs, Wolfe Gunnar and Dash Sinclair, the Wolf Breed Pack leaders, Del-Rey Delgado, the Coyote Breed Pack leader, as well as the often elusive Dylan Killato, the European Wolf Pack leader determined to pull the hidden Breeds on his side of the world together, watched her, as she imagined the scientists that created her most likely had watched her: with detached curiosity.

"Katie, I know you're frightened." Dylan leaned forward, the shifting silver and amber colors of his gaze cool and calculating as the heavy Scots brogue offered to wrap her in a false sense of security. "And I hope you know our only concerns at this time are for your safety and security."

Katie could have rolled her eyes. Killato used his dark, savage good looks, the old-fashioned brogue and unusual color of his eyes to full advantage whenever he needed to.

The American emissaries still sat quiet, watchful, offering neither advice nor countering Killato's claims.

"You're becoming a sensation among the paparazzi as well as the scientists tasked by many countries to break the hidden genetic codes the Council scientists used to create us. You're both a weakness as well as a possible answer for the Breed communities as a whole. This makes you a highly sought-after prize by many opponents as well as proponents of the Breed community."

Katie turned her gaze to the still silent American group. "Do the Breeds have proponents?" she asked as her gaze connected with that of Jonas Wyatt.

One black brow lifted over a silver mercury eye. "Not in that group," he assured her as he nodded to the door and the crowds outside.

Killato shot the director of the Bureau of Breed Affairs a chilling look that had Katie wondering at the animosity she could sense emanating from him.

"I can understand why you're here, Mr. Killato," she assured the European leader. "Building and pulling together the European Packs is a daunting task, I realize." She turned back to his American counterparts. "But why are the rest of you here? How can I profit or aid the American Breeds?"

"Katie," her father scolded her gently. "They could be concerned with your welfare, lass."

Katie shook her head. "I find that very hard to believe, Da. Why risk their lives as well as their very busy schedules over just another Breed that the world has learned of?"

"But you're not just another Breed, Mary Katherine," Jonas assured her, a hint of mocking amusement filling his gaze as he leaned forward slightly, his arms crossing and bracing on the table between them. "Unlike Pack Leader Killato, I'm not going to assure you that nothing more than your safety matters. That's not true of any Breed. We're all a danger to ourselves as well as our Packs and Prides. But you are more so for the very fact that your genetics were so well hidden until this past year. With the surge of your Breed genetics coupled with the fact that your grandfather was one of the most notorious lab overseers in Europe, it makes you a sensation. Breed opponents want you silenced before scientists can use your genetics to possibly hide other Breeds among society, while proponents hope you can do the opposite; and both sides admit to the very high profitability of either answer. You are quite literally worth your weight in gold."

"I wouldn't be quite so extreme," Killato argued.

"Dylan, you know damned good and well that her father's position as Ireland's assistant chief constable, her grandfather's secrets into the Genetics Council, as well as her own genetics make her a prize that scientists from among the Breeds, as well as the more acceptable scientific societies assigned to research the Breed genetics, would kill to claim. Even if it meant killing her," Dash Sinclair argued, the gleam of worry in his eyes as he glanced at her rather surprising.

"So then?" she asked Sinclair. "How do I profit the American Breeds?"

"You ensure that you're not taken by the wrong groups and used against us." It was Sinclair's young daughter, Cassandra, who spoke from her position in the far corner of the room, rather than her father, who answered that question.

"That's a bit harsh, Ms. Sinclair," Killato growled, his gaze filled with a latent sexual intensity as he turned and glared at her.

Cassandra rose to her full height from the chair she sat in, a very false height of five-eight, thanks to the heels she wore. Elegantly graceful, dressed in white slacks and a white vest-style blouse that revealed a hint of cleavage, she moved closer to the group, entirely comfortable in the five-inch heels she wore.

Cassandra gave a small, lilting laugh. "Your greed doesn't become you, Dylan," she murmured as she walked to stand beside her father. "Neither does your need to use Ms. O'Sullivan and her family to your own ends."

"Something the lot of you have no intention of doing?" Killato bared his teeth at her in an obvious display of primal superiority.

That display gained him no less than three harsh warning glares in his direction.

"What would it gain us?" Cassandra shrugged her delicate shoulders. "As assistant chief constable, Mr. O'Sullivan has nothing that could benefit either Packs or Prides in America. His connections don't affect us. Our teams were the ones responsible for capturing her grandfather, Walter O'Sullivan, the overseer responsible for many of the labs here in Europe, when he disappeared after the news broke of his true identity, so we have no need to use her to that end. And our laws forbid, in every way, the forced induction of any Breed into a scientific study, something your European laws do not ban. It's no wonder the Breeds that have scattered across Britain, Scotland and Ireland refuse to heed your demands to reveal themselves."

It was Katie's nightmare. Already her father had had to file countless stays of the Breed scientific mandates that would have forced her into a facility of Breed study for a period not less than one year, but no more than five.

When Breeds disappeared behind the walls of those facilities, they were rarely the same once they exited, she'd read.

"How do I benefit you then?" Katie asked her, more inclined

to believe this young woman than any of the men seated in front of her.

"By ensuring we're not forced to rescue you from one of those facilities as we have been forced to rescue others," she stated without hesitation, her brilliant blue eyes glowing in the peaches-and-cream complexion surrounding them. "The Bureau of Breed Affairs is already dealing with more than a dozen official demands of restitution as well as extradition of Breeds who have fled Europe or been rescued from scientific facilities whose inhumane experiments your country claims to have no knowledge of despite the fact that they fund them."

It was no more than the truth. Her father, Barrett O'Sullivan, had closed down two such facilities and had been summarily berated publicly as well as professionally for not doing more to track down and identify Breeds hiding in Ireland, and enforcing the mandatory one year of research imposed on Breeds in Europe several years before.

Even Dylan couldn't counter Cassandra's statement, though Katie could glimpse his furious need to do so.

"Katie, they won't let you alone," Cassandra promised softly as she nodded to the door and the murmur of the journalists on the street beyond. "Your father's position can't save you from the mandatory testing, and no matter Dylan's claims, he can't hide you from the testing. In less than forty-eight hours you've become a worldwide sensation for the very fact that despite the advanced testing for Breeds, you passed each stage of that testing that the European countries have ordered conducted on all adopted children, no matter their age. You passed each test with not so much as a blip on the DNA screenings from the age of nine until your genetics kicked in last month."

"Kicked in." Now, there was a phrase.

Her genetics had kicked her ass. A fever of one hundred and

seven should have killed her. She'd lain nearly comatose for twenty-four hours before she'd begun convulsing so violently that her fiancé had rushed her to the ER, where the doctors there realized they were dealing with a phenomenon only spoken of in the fifteen years since the revelation of the Breeds.

Genetic Flaming. A sudden, "flaming" awakening of once hidden Breed genetics after a lifetime of the Breed DNA she possessed lying dormant.

Well, they weren't dormant any longer.

"The Feline Breed community of Sanctuary, as well as the Wolf Breed communities of Haven and Avalon, and Del-Rey's Coyote Packs of the Citadel offer you haven, Ms. Sullivan," Dash Sinclair spoke again, his gaze once again holding hers with the compassion and integrity all four of these men were known for.

"Their protection far exceeds what I can offer you, Katie," Dylan sighed, frustration evident in his voice. "Until Europe's Breeds become the force America's have, then we simply don't have the strength. But I offer what little we have, and I would protect you and your right to freedom with my life," Killato swore sincerely.

In that moment, she knew he would do just that. For whatever reason, whether selfish or selfless, Dylan would have done all he could to hide her. If he couldn't hide her, then he would have died to defend her.

Katie lifted her gaze to Cassandra's once again.

"I'm scared," she finally admitted, forced to fight back the tears and the horror building inside her.

From the corner of her eye she glimpsed the tears slipping from her mother's own eyes as she hurriedly tried to cover them. She watched her strong, prideful Da's throat work convulsively as he stared up at the ceiling, blinking furiously at her admission.

She could feel her skin crawling, her muscles tensing and bunching as though battling themselves. Sensations were too extreme, others' emotions sometimes bombarded her, and the sense of betrayal she felt that her parents had kept this horrifying secret from her was tearing her apart inside.

She'd always wondered why she couldn't remember her life before she'd awakened in her "adoptive" parents' home. The amnesia was the result of a drug she had been given the day the labs she was in had been attacked. The nurse that had given it to her had done so in case the Breed child she was responsible for was rescued. It was a common practice among the European labs, she had learned, to inject the children of possible rescues with the amnesia drug that had often caused older Breeds to revert to a primal state. The genetics scientists had hoped to ensure that those Breed youths would have less of a chance of being adopted into human homes.

"Katie, lass," her father whispered as her mother covered her trembling lips with her fingers. "I'd give my life for your forgiveness if I weren't terrified that you would have need of me later."

"And you think that's what I want, Da?" she demanded, the anger and tears trapped in her chest as she stared back at him desperately.

She hated the anger inside her. Hated the sense of dread and betrayal assailing her. "How much worse could my existence become if I ever felt you or Mother had done such a thing?"

He shook his dark, graying head as her mother's fingers tightened on his arm resting against his leg.

"We were terrified for you," her mother protested.

"So you hid what I was, even from me, no matter how often I asked you about a childhood I couldn't remember," she reminded them both. "The one person who should have been prepared for it was the one most surprised. Had I known, Mam, I would have never allowed Douglas to take me to the ER. I would have called you or Da the moment I felt ill and I wouldn't feel as though everyone I ever trusted cared more for the secrets they carried than they cared for the welfare of the secret itself."

She couldn't remain here. She couldn't stare into her father's pain-filled eyes or watch the tears fill her mother's gaze one more time.

Each time she did, that battle raging through her body seemed to intensify to the point that she wanted to tear into her flesh and rip from her bones the very muscles that clenched and spasmed beneath her skin as though trying to reform, or to somehow burrow from beneath her skin.

She rose slowly to her feet, her gaze locking with Dash Sinclair's.

"Mr. Sinclair—"

"Get down!" Cassie suddenly screamed.

Breeds were reacting before the words were even fully formed.

Dash Sinclair jerked his daughter from behind the chair and shoved her beneath the table as he followed her to the floor. Jonas Wyatt rolled across the table so quickly he was a blur before toppling Katie to the floor, while Wolfe Gunnar and Dylan Killato did likewise with her parents. A volley of automatic gunfire shattered the windows and tore chunks of wood and plaster from the ancient home that had been in her father's family for nearly five hundred years.

Sirens were wailing in the distance, and the gunfire sliced through the room again while cries of shock and fear could be heard from the journalists outside.

"Is this what you want?" Jonas suddenly hissed at her ear. "No matter where you go or what you do, unless you leave Europe, your father will remain at your back until he takes a bullet for you. And I promise you, it will come sooner rather than later. Now, stay put."

He suddenly jumped from her, pushed her toward Dylan and her parents as he ignored his Pride leader's furious snarl of his name and rushed from the room.

"Bastard's going to get himself killed," Dylan snapped as they all huddled beneath the large dining room table her mother's family had kept pristine since the eleven hundreds.

It was now riddled with deep gouges in the wood, no doubt from the bullets that had skipped across the top of it.

"More than likely, someone's going to be missing a throat instead," Callan sighed. "It's not Jonas I'm worried about, it's the prey he's chasing." Amber eyes locked with hers. "Get ready, we're about to be hustled out of here."

Even as he spoke, the door to the room flew open and Breeds began pouring in.

American Breeds.

Strong, silent, there were no shouted orders or codes being barked around her. She was lifted from the floor, her arms shoved into a heavy, protective vest while the bodies surrounding her rushed her from her father's house and into a waiting vehicle in her mother's precious back garden.

The fence surrounding the back of the house had simply been mowed down by the half-dozen vehicles surrounding it. Armed, hard-eyed, savage-faced Breeds stood tense and prepared, weapons held ready.

They were but a blur to Katie as she was pushed into the back floorboard of an armored Dragoon Elite, a low-slung SUV built for speed and agility in more populated areas. Rather distantly she remembered it had replaced the Sergeants model Dragoon that her father kept in a garage on the O'Sullivan estate on the outskirts of Dublin.

"Carrier three en route." Quiet, assured and confident, the unfamiliar dark voice above her had her craning her neck to try to identify it.

Unfortunately, he was all but reclined on top of her, which kept her from maneuvering enough to see much of anything.

"Carrier three affirmative," a voice responded. "Heli-jet is prepped and running. ETA thirty."

ETA thirty what? Minutes? Hours? What the hell was that supposed to mean?

"Carrier three now in blackout. Update at thirteen hundred."

Thirteen hundred hours?

"Get off!" she demanded, trying to drive her elbow upward. "You're smothering me!"

"Beats the alternative." The male grunt above her wasn't comforting.

It was harsh, almost broken. His voice was low, deep, sending shivers racing up her back as the too-active muscles beneath her skin bunched harder, tighter, determined to tear past her bones, push through her flesh, and relish the heat above her.

The response was immediate, frightening and painful.

Geez, if she got any hotter, she was going to melt into the floor of the Dragoon.

The vehicle was supposed to be temperature controlled to more than fifty feet below water. At the moment, it was sweltering, however.

The heat wasn't coming from the floor though. It was coming from the male Breed above her. It sank into her flesh, washed through her system and clenched her teeth with an arousal so white-hot and sudden she could barely control the need.

The sexual need.

The need to have those hard, broad hands push her dress over her ass, grip her hips and push inside her with a heavy, deep, bruising thrust.

She wanted all of him at once.

Her vagina clenched, rippling with hunger. It ached, flushed with heat and demanded his possession.

She wanted him.

She wanted to be touched.

Taken.

Oh God, she wanted him fucking her and she wanted it now before she was forced to scream with a need so painful it terrified her.

Horrified her.

Because she was going to demand it. Her lips were parting, a cry building in her throat when he suddenly lifted just enough to flip her to her back before wedging his thighs between hers, the hard length of his cock pressing against her sex as his fingers covered her lips.

"We are not alone," he mouthed as her eyes widened in dawning terror. "And this isn't the time for this."

Of course it wasn't.

The time would never come.

He was the Devil. The Grim Reaper of the Breeds and he'd come to drag her away and make certain she never became a danger to the species again.

Everyone had lied to her. She was a liability. A secret they didn't want to risk. She knew that now.

She knew it, because the Breed pinning her to the floor with the strength of his hips and his very aroused cock was not a potential lover.

He was a killer.

He was the Devil, and he would have no other reason to be there other than—

To kill her.

TWO

Terror.

Anger.

Injustice.

Fascination.

So many emotions.

Katie couldn't seem to settle on just one, or to figure which was uppermost. But the resounding regret, she finally realized, was the emotion that seemed to beat harder at her brain.

Why did her body pick this moment, this man, to become sexual? She was twenty-three years old and she'd berated her sexuality as well as her heart for so many years for being unable to react to the opposite sex as other women did.

She had dated. She'd tried to force a need, an arousal for some of the more appealing prospects she'd known as potential lovers, yet she'd never been able to work up enough interest to actually join one in bed. Even Douglas, the fiancé who had informed her that he had no intention of allowing Breed genetics into any children he would eventually bring into the world. And besides, he'd sneered, he'd never been into fucking animals.

He'd slipped the engagement ring off her finger while she was too weak to fight, even had she wanted to, and he had walked away without even saying good-bye. But in his gaze she had glimpsed the pure disgust he'd felt at the thought of her.

Now, in the middle of attempting to escape a situation she didn't understand, that sexuality had kicked into overdrive with the Breed known for being seen only when someone was such a liability to the Breed community that they were marked for termination.

Termination.

As though she weren't human—

Oh yeah, she wasn't human, she thought half hysterically.

She wasn't human, she wasn't an animal. She was a Breed.

She was something in-between, and that wasn't something she had expected.

Why had the Breed leaders, the very same ones that had sat in her father's living room such a short time ago and appeared so compassionate, marked her for death?

"Why?" she whispered, needing to know, to understand why she had to die by this man's hand when she would so much prefer to be stroked by it.

The hard, savage smile that pulled at his lips was accompanied by a flash of white-hot lust in the odd, amber-speckled eyes staring down at her.

"Orders, baby." A shiver raced through her at the hard rasp of his voice.

Orders? Just because of orders?

He was going to kill her despite the fact that he was iron hard and hot between her thighs, the erect length of his cock pressing firmly against her sex.

He was going to kill her despite the fact that he was the only man she'd ever felt her body grow hot and moist for?

"Damn," she whispered. "This really sucks."

Why the hell did she think he was there? Devil questioned silently. Hell, wasn't she the one that requested asylum while her grandfather Walter O'Sullivan was under investigation for having overseen one of the most notorious Breed labs in Ireland? Hell, it was even the Breeds who had managed to track him down. Then, once he disappeared, it was Breeds that found him once again, and took him into custody.

It wasn't as though he had volunteered.

It sure as hell wasn't as though he wanted to be right here, right now, his body strung so tight, his dick so hard, that he was amazed he could still breathe.

Or could he?

He felt lightheaded, as though he couldn't quite pull in enough oxygen, couldn't convince his body that he was drawing in air.

What the hell was she doing.

Trying to push him away?

Before she could push against his chest with her dainty little hands, he caught both her wrists, pulled them above her head and pressed them into the floorboard firmly.

Hell no she wasn't pushing him off her. He liked the position they were in just fine. With her pretty legs spread, her thighs gripping his hips as though she had no intention of ever letting him go, and all the while her hot little pussy was pressed just as tight against his cock as possible.

Damn, she was pretty too. The pictures he'd seen the night before hadn't done her justice.

Forget pretty, she was fucking gorgeous.

Pure creamy flesh with the lightest scattering of freckles over those high, aristocratic cheekbones. Emerald eyes blinked up at him in confusion and in pain. Irish eyes. Damned pretty Irish eyes. The prettiest he'd ever seen in his life.

And he'd seen a lot of Irish eyes.

"You don't have to . . ." her breath caught, lashes fluttering as he chose that moment to grind himself against her, to feel the moist heat through the barrier of her panties and his denim.

He was going to end up fucking her here and now if she wasn't careful, despite the fact that their driver, Flint McCain, would hear every hungry, pleading gasp he'd draw from her.

"Orders. It's all your own fault, dammit." Her fault he was hornier than he'd ever been in his life, and it was her fault he was less than a breath from screwing them both into ecstasy.

"My fault?" Feminine outrage and hunger scented the air around him. "How is it my fault?"

She was acting as though she had never made the damned request of the Breed Protection Network to help her escape from Ireland and find a secure place to hide until the furor had died down a little.

"Well it's sure as hell not my fault," Devil growled down at her, wondering if he could pull back if he actually allowed himself to lower his head and kiss those pretty, pouty lips. Because he really did want to kiss them.

"Well you're the one doing it!" Petite nostrils flared, and the hint of those cute dimples he'd seen in her pictures completely disappeared as she frowned up at him.

She'd had dimples in the pictures he'd seen.

"You're the one that asked for it," he snarled down at her, unable to resist using his free hand to slide beneath her body, grip the rounded curve of her ass and hold her to him.

"Me?" She stared back at him in surprise for a second before comprehension slowly dawned. "Wait, you're with the Breed Protection Network?"

Had Lobo sent him to rescue a madwoman?

He was beginning to think the other man might have done just that, because she was now staring up at him as though she'd believed something entirely different to this point.

"Why the hell did you think I was here?"

She blinked back at him before those bright emerald eyes as they darkened with uncertainty. "You're the Devil. You only come after Breeds marked to die. Right?"

Hell.

Sometimes, having a killer reputation could be a hell of an inconvenience.

"I'm not going to kill you." Unless he ended up fucking them both to death.

As long as she wasn't a threat, personally, to the Reevers—or to those he'd sworn to protect. He doubted she represented much of a threat to anything or anyone, let alone the family he'd sworn his loyalty to.

She glanced down their bodies, her breath catching as her gaze locked at where they were all but joined.

Her scent wrapped around him. A hint of fascination, wariness, but there was also something more—something he didn't like at all.

The scent of pure, exquisite, lust-filled arousal and feminine liquid heat spilling from her body.

Sweet, with a hint of spice. Clean, with a tempting freshness that made him wonder if she had ever been touched by another man in any way.

Of course, there was no such thing as a virgin Breed female of this age. Unfortunately, most of their females had lost that innocence before they were even old enough to understand what it was.

At that thought, he realized she hadn't responded to his statement that he had no intention of killing her. Instead, her gaze was focused on his lips, much as his was on hers. The emerald color darkened, her pupils dilating as his head lowered, his lips moving slowly closer to hers.

He was going to kiss her.

Katie could feel it coming.

Adrenaline was racing through her body, the urge to rub her hips against his, to feel the roughness of denim scratching against the lace of her panties was overwhelming.

And she wanted his kiss. She wanted it so desperately that the wild, stormy taste she imagined it held began to tease her senses relentlessly.

"Boss, we're heading to the primary pick up point and the heli-jet's landing," the Breed racing the SUV toward that "primary" point, wherever that may be, informed Devil imperatively. "We still have two vehicles on our asses and plenty of cameras hanging out the windows."

Devil grimaced as smoldering anger flashed in his gaze.

"Get us as close to the entrance as possible," he growled, lifting his head to glare at the Breed who dared to interrupt them.

Then he was moving. Ignoring her sharp intake of air as he lifted himself from her body before quickly pulling her into a sitting position on the floor of the vehicle.

"Get ready to move." Restrained, clipped and cold, his voice did nothing to dilute the arousal raging through her.

Get ready to move?

She stared ahead of them at the huge black raptor-looking heli-jet settling on the ground ahead of them as the Dragoon raced toward it. Turning to glance behind them, she winced at the sight of the quickly moving SUVs following them.

If they made it before the rapidly focusing cameras mounted on the roof of the SUVs that were controlled by the photographers inside, then they'd be damned lucky.

"Put it on." Black material was suddenly shoved over her head.

"What are you doing?" For a second, the world was black until Devil quickly righted the fabric and pulled the narrow eye slits into position.

Her hair was shoved down the back of her dress, black material draping over her shoulders as she stared up at the black mask he now wore as well.

"Three vehicles left at the same time and were picked up in a heli-jet in three different locations, while all occupants were masked before disappearing into the jets." His lips curved beneath the silky material. "You're about to lose your tails, cupcake. Get ready to run."

Brace!" Flint called back as he lifted one hand from the wheel long enough to jerk his mask from the top of his head into place.

Devil wrapped one arm around his charge, his free hand clenched on the brace bar above him as the Breed suddenly threw the vehicle into a slight turn, skidding sideways until the passenger side of the vehicle was almost kissing the heli-jet awaiting them.

The doors were thrown open by the Breeds rushing from the craft, and as he lifted Mary Katherine O'Sullivan and pushed her quickly into their waiting grasp, he wondered just exactly what he was supposed to do now.

She was the sweetest heat he'd ever scented. The purest hunger he'd ever been touched by. Equally sweet and tempting, she called to him on a level he had never known existed. A level so fucking primal he wanted nothing more than to mark her.

To mark her delicate body with his touch, to claim the sweet heat of her pussy. To push himself inside her, hard, deep, full length until she was crying for mercy. Until she was screaming in orgasm.

And, he realized, there was actually very little that existed beyond that.

Which made her excessively dangerous as well.

Reever Ranch

Cassandra Sinclair glanced up from the stack of papers she was slowly committing to memory and stared around the room. What had disturbed her? Rarely could anything pull her from her research into Breed Law, especially when confronted with the questions that the mating laws never failed to cause. If she didn't prepare just the right argument, using just the right phrasing, then some smart-ass lawyer, likely female, would end up ripping her apart at some point. The Breeds depended on her to rationalize and explain the Breed law, even as she justified actions that arose from mating heat, without actually letting anyone suspect that it was mating heat. Ah yes, the trials and tribulations of completing the language begun within the Rights of Breed Freedoms that had originally been signed into law. And now, something was making it even more difficult than normal to form those arguments. Rising from her chair, she moved to the balcony doors, opened them, then stepped outside.

That's what it was.

Pausing, she looked around slowly, silently marveling over the beauty of the desert landscape before her. Then her gaze stopped on the butte rising from the land in the distance.

Spears of stone that looked as though they had been shoved through the desert floor came together and reached into the sky. It was there that the problem hid.

He was there, hiding. Waiting.

She could feel him.

He was there watching her, waiting for her, certain his time would come.

Shadowed, broad and high, the stone wasn't quite a mountain, but still, it was more than a hill, as she'd heard it been called. It was there that he hid.

The sights of his rifle were trained on her, though he never took them from her face.

She could feel his eyes watching her, baiting her. He had every intention of coming for her. Soon. Just not yet.

She could feel his intent though. It hung heavy in the air around her, assuring her that he was still there.

He had been with her for more than a year now. No matter where she traveled, no matter how she tried to hide, she could feel him there somewhere, if not watching her, then searching for her. Since the day she had dared him to pull that infernal trigger, he had followed her. As though the very fact that she would defy him had somehow made him pause in pulling the trigger, made him take the time to figure something out about her instead.

What?

And always, it was the sights of his gun she felt caressing her face.

Would he kill her? Was this the reason why he watched, waited, why he kept the sights of his gun trained upon her?

"Cassandra, my dear, you stare into the evening sky as though awaiting a lover."

She jerked to the side, her eyes widening as Dane Vanderale, the hybrid Breed offspring of the one they called the First Leo, leaned his back against the adobe wall of the balcony, lifted a slim cigar to his lips, then lit it lazily, his gaze trained on her face, assessing, always curious.

For the barest second, the light from the match shadowed the hard, savage contours of his expression and caused the emerald green of his gaze to flare with pinpoints of reddened light.

He was a Lion Breed among a small Pack of Wolves hiding in the New Mexico desert, and seemed just as comfortably at ease as he did in the drawing room of his parents' estate in the sheltered jungles of the Congo.

"Dane, you sneak around far too much," she told him as he gave a quick jerk of his wrist to extinguish the match.

"Those of us who hide in the shadows to watch those who prefer to hide as well, learn well the value of the ability to slip in and out of the light so effectively," he told her quietly. "I do wonder though, why, my dear, do you tempt the gun sights that even I can feel caressing your very pretty head?"

He may question it, but he didn't seem overly concerned by the thought. Actually, he seemed rather amused by it.

She rolled her eyes at him. "Are you always so amused by the idiosyncrasies of the rest of these mortals, or just me?" There wasn't so much as a quiver in her voice, she made certain of it. She turned completely to rest her back against the railing that surrounded her balcony.

"I spread my amusement around," he informed her. "I seem forever tempted by the actions of those of you who admit to mortality though. I really can't seem to help it. Now, why not amuse me further and satisfy my curiosity?"

She shrugged. She liked Dane, despite his sarcasm and apparent cynicism.

"Who says I'm frightened of him?" she inquired rather than answering him. "Do I appear concerned?"

She may be many things, but at the moment, frightened wasn't one of them.

"Ah, you await him." Dane nodded slowly then, as though serious. Anyone who didn't know him wouldn't have caught the pure mockery that almost tugged at his lips. "If this is so, then why doesn't he come to you?"

And now he was baiting her.

"I don't know. Nor do I care." Frustration filled her voice now. The bastard was driving her crazy.

"Perhaps he knows he's not good enough for you." He stared into the darkness himself as his voice lowered, the South African accent most women found so charming making little impact on her.

"Why would he? Remember, it's his gun sights I feel, Dane, not the stroke of his hand. He doesn't make sense."

She rather doubted he felt the need to touch her anyway. After all, he'd simply watched her, took pictures occasionally, yet never really attempted to harm her.

"Ah, my dear, for all their simplicity, men can be the most complicated of animals."

"And here I thought it was us women who held that distinction," she contradicted him easily.

"Women are the most complicated of all creatures, no matter their race or species," he retorted. "Breed males though, and their human counterparts, are the most complicated of animals. I would never dare to call one so lovely as you an animal."

"Even if I were a creature rather than an animal, it wouldn't make sense to watch me as he does."

To kill her?

Or did he have other plans? Plans Cassie feared would destroy her, her family, or the Breeds she fought to protect.

"Come, my dear," Dane urged her. "Back inside, before the shadows trap you within them and hold you forever."

Hold her forever? She rather doubted that.

She could only get so lucky. "Dane, do you ever wonder if perhaps not all Breeds really have a mate chosen for them?" she asked him as he escorted her back into her room, pausing as he closed the balcony doors and then turned to her slowly.

He really was quite handsome, she thought. Far older than he appeared; at least sixty, she'd heard whispered in the past few years, though he refused to tell anyone his true age.

His dark blond head tilted to the side, dark green eyes with tiny specks of amber that were rarely visible, now glinting within the iris. "I believe there's a mate perfectly suited to each and every Breed, whether they were born or created," he finally answered softly as he leaned indolently against the wall, sliding his hands into the pockets of the dun-colored slacks he wore. "What would make you ask such a question, Cassie?"

She shrugged. It wasn't always easy to explain her own feelings, her own fears.

She was a Breed, a tri-species, she'd heard herself called.

Human, Wolf, and the still feared Coyote. The Coyote DNA was the one she feared the most, just, she suspected, as her parents did. As many of the Breeds did. They all seemed to. She could sense it, feel it. At times, God, she could even smell their fear.

"Surely you're not frightened that there's no such future for yourself?" The South African accent was almost mesmerizing. Cassie often found herself concentrating on the cadence of it, rather than the meaning behind whatever questions he was asking her.

"It could prove difficult." Tucking her hands into the back pockets of her jeans, she wandered to the wide, shaded glass of the bay window on the far side of her room and stared at the place where she knew her assassin hid. "I'm not human, nor am I a Wolf Breed or Coyote. So far, no Breed has mated outside his or her own species with the exception of the human pairings. Wouldn't that make it rather hard for me to find a mate?"

He watched her closely. Too closely.

He had that habit. Dane wasn't a man one could often hide things from. Nor was he man that anyone would want to try to lie to or in any way deceive.

He could be a brutal enemy.

"What do your guides tell you, Cassie?" he asked her softly, the question causing her to freeze as a hard chill raked down her spine.

Dane was the only one to have ever, at any time, acknowledged that more than just intuition had guided her throughout the years.

How could he know? Could he know? Could he sense that the beautiful, once comforting presence that had followed her throughout her life had now deserted her?

She turned to him slowly, their gazes locking as she stared back at a Breed that none could read, not even the most intuitive of their species. Even she, the one who seemed to draw the inner demons and broken spirits of the Breeds from their hiding places, had never convinced the protective spirit that always hovered close to him to reveal itself. Or to reveal his secrets.

"She doesn't visit as often as she once did," Cassie finally admitted softly.

"And you're not yet confident enough in yourself to use what she taught you." He nodded.

Cassie could only shake her head. Her father had asked her that same question.

Perhaps she just hadn't been smart enough to learn.

As she considered the subject, a brief knock at her door had her turning away from the hybrid to glance at the barrier before turning back to Dane.

A grin tugged at her lips.

Just that quickly, Dane was gone.

Back to his own room, no doubt, where she had no hesitation in guessing he was plotting world dominion. And if he were, he would succeed.

Breathing out wearily, she answered the summons with a brief, "Yes?"

The door opened several inches as one of the Reevers' maids peered around the door. "Ma'am, your father and Mr. Reever asked that I let you know Mr. Reever is putting steaks and ribs on the grill for the evening meal. He says you're especially fond of them."

The tall, buxom brunette watched her warily. The scent of the other woman's fear caused only regret to shift through Cassie's senses. It didn't hurt as it once had.

"I'll be there soon," she informed the other woman.

The maid nodded, and closed the door, and Cassie could sense her moving slowly away from the room. If she closed her eyes, Cassie thought, then she would sense much more than that from the maid. Not just her fears, but her hatreds, her self-importance, her pride—

Cassie didn't close her eyes. She just didn't want to know.

THREE

Katie hadn't expected to get so lucky as to be reunited with her dearest friend, and within hours had realized why. She and Khileen had never failed to find adventure and excitement in Ireland together. It was one of the reasons Katie's father had worried about their friendship so often.

When Khileen's mother, Jessica, had met and married Lobo Reever, it had seemed Breeds in general had drawn an easier breath though. Lobo was considered a lone Wolf, one that too many independent Wolves had longed to follow.

Lobo had no alliance pacts, had sworn no loyalties nor had he professed any. Yet, he had banded with more than two dozen of the strongest, darkest, most exactingly created Wolf Breeds that the Genetics Council had kept files on.

It was rumored there were another half dozen the Council hadn't even recorded that followed the Lobo.

With his marriage, or "mating" as she'd heard it called several times, and Reever's move to the American deserts, the Breeds' fears that Lobo would somehow upset the balance of Packs and Prides had eased.

They were a strange and often difficult lot on the best of days, but never more so than when they felt threatened.

"Cassandra Sinclair flew in last night," Khileen Langer said, her voice low as they walked through the stables several days after Devil Black had brought her to the Reever Ranch.

"What do you think she wants?" Katie frowned as they stopped at one of the stalls to pet one of Lobo Reever's prized mares.

Having Cassie Sinclair in residence couldn't be comfortable. Katie had heard quite a bit about the young woman, and couldn't imagine being comfortable around her.

"I'm not certain." Khileen shook her head, her expression concerned. "I know Lobo's been in negotiations with the Packs and Prides, but I'm not certain why."

"I thought Tiberian was his negotiator? How are any negotiations being discussed without him?"

Tiberian was Lobo's younger brother and, Katie knew, one of the Breeds the Council had destroyed records of.

Khileen looked away. "Tiberian left the night of Mother's death. I've not seen him since."

Jessica Reever's death six months before in a fall from her horse had devastated the family. She knew it had devastated Khileen.

Tiberian's disappearance was interesting though.

The fact that Cassandra Sinclair, a young mixed-Breed female becoming known as the Breeds' highest legal advisor, was at the ranch at the same time that their negotiator was missing was bad enough. Adding that to the rumors that a rogue Bengal Breed was in the area searching for a young female the Genetics Council had experimented on. The situation was causing havoc with the Navajo nation, and must have Lobo pulling his hair out by the roots.

"And with all this, he offered his protection to me?" Leaning against the side of the stall, she stared back at Khileen in surprise.

Khileen shrugged, disrupting the long black, spiral curls that had fallen over her shoulder as her bright blue eyes dimmed for a moment.

"I saw the news report when your grandfather's estate was seized," she revealed. "I know you, Katie. You would have needed to run. You would have felt it was the only way to protect your family. I asked Lobo to check with the Network to see if you had sent out a request and if you did, if he would help."

"They're threatening to investigate Da as well," Katie revealed. "He and Mam are destroyed by the revelations. They didn't know Grandfather had overseen those labs or had even been involved with them."

Her parents had gone to a fertility clinic to attempt to conceive the child they wanted so desperately, only to be told that their initial tests revealed a rare genetic incompatibility between them. The clinic had decided there was no way to help them and had claimed to have disposed of the samples they'd taken.

Those samples had then been sent to the Genetics Council, which funded the clinic, and Katie had been "created." A Wolf Breed, created to seduce and kill. The genetics her parents possessed had been exceptional, her files had stated. The potential ability to excel in numerous areas they considered fundamentally essential in the army they were building had marked her as a prized specimen.

They'd never known how her grandfather had maneuvered to ensure Barrett's best friend, Jorn Langer, Khileen's father, had learned of the labs. Once Jorn had found the lab, he'd learned that the overseer had acquired samples from the fertility clinic the O'Sullivan's had gone to in order to create a Breed. Then it had been as simple as ensuring Jorn was contacted by a group of Breeds he'd aided in escaping from several labs he'd overseen.

From there, her rescue by her father and his best friend had been planned to the last detail. Her parents had then adopted her after procuring birth records "proving" she was adopted from a recently widowed cousin of Kella O'Sullivan's.

Katie hadn't known how she was found by her father and Jorn. She hadn't known how she had been rescued or the calculated risks her family had taken to attempt to hide her, until she'd become ill, just before her grandfather's arrest. Later, when Walter O'Sullivan had escaped the Breeds and shown up at the O'Sullivan estate where she and her family had initially gone to attempt to figure out what to do, they had learned how her grandfather had used that position to ensure his son had the child he and his wife had longed for.

The genetic incompatibility had been eradicated, but only with the introduction of the Breed DNA.

All of his maneuvering had been in vain, but because of his position, he'd ensured his son had his child and that she was rescued before her Breed training had begun in earnest.

"Lobo highly respects your father, though I know he never cared for your grandfather." Khileen stepped from the stall before looking around silently for a long moment.

When her gaze returned to Katie's, the amusement in it should have warned her what was coming.

"So," Khileen drawled. "What did you think of Devil?"

There was the blush.

Katie felt it surfacing beneath her flesh, filling her face and revealing, she feared, far more interest than she wanted Khileen to realize.

"Oh, you definitely like him." Khileen laughed. "I knew there was something there when I heard him raging to Lobo over you."

"Raging?" Oh, that was just wrong. "What could he have to rage over? I didn't do anything."

Irritation flared through her at the thought of him doing such a thing. It wasn't as though she had thrown him in a vehicle, plastered him to the floorboards and held him there, teasing him with the press of her body against his.

"Devil can rage over everything, never mention your name, yet make it excessively clear that you're the object of his displeasure." Khileen rolled her expressive eyes as she propped her hands on her hips, then faced Katie curiously. "I have to say though, I've never heard Devil rage over a woman simply to be raging. They usually have to actually do something to him personally. What did you do to him?"

"Not a damned thing." The nerve of him!

Unclenching her fists slowly as she realized what she was doing, Katie shoved her hands into the pockets of the gauzy skirt she'd worn with a thin, sleeveless silk top and sandals.

Her body heated immediately at the thought though. All she'd actually done was let him know exactly how turned on she had been. Was she supposed to hide it?

Hiding it would have been impossible. Her senses had flared too bright, too receptive to his touch. Even now, her nipples were already tightly beaded, her clit throbbing in anticipation.

She'd been on the Reever ranch three days now. The two nights she'd spent in the guest room tossing and turning, her body aching for him, had been miserable. It had taken hours to fall asleep.

"Come on, Katie." Dropping her arms from her hips, Khileen chided her with friendly disbelief. "Something happened. I know Devil. He's followed Lobo as long as I've known him. He doesn't get upset over nothing."

"He had no reason whatsoever to be upset with me," Katie repeated as a flare of anger lit her senses. "I didn't even attempt to bother him, Khi."

Damn him. It wasn't her fault she'd wanted him. He was the one that had been rubbing his hard cock between her thighs and making her ache for him.

She didn't know what the hell his problem was, but she intended to find out. She refused to allow him to spoil the haven she'd found on the Reever ranch. If he wanted to bitch about *her* to others, then he could begin with telling her what *his* bitch was, exactly.

"Wow, you're as defensive over him as he was over you when Lobo questioned him at his irritation. What's up with you two?" Khileen moved quickly to draw beside her as Katie headed for the house.

"There's absolutely nothing *up* with us," Katie bit out furiously before giving a muttered little "yet."

Why was Devil Black so determined to get rid of her? He was one of Lobo Reever's most trusted men, second only to the missing Tiberian, which now made him the most influential of those surrounding Lobo. If he told Lobo she was a danger to have here, then he may well have her removed.

She couldn't afford to be sent away. If she were, then the Irish authorities could well send a team to have her collected and forced into testing.

There was a reason why Breeds hid in Europe now. A reason why they were loath to allow their government to know who they were, or where they were.

Because there were those who had come out of the facilities so changed, so traumatized that they simply were not the same. And none of them could remember what had caused the trauma to their minds, or why they may have forgotten certain passages of time during their stay.

That was what awaited her if Devil had her removed from Lobo's protection. She would be without resources, and unable to reach her family. A sitting duck, so to speak, for those determined to destroy her.

"No, Katie, I'm certain Devil doesn't mean any harm," Khileen argued behind her as they reached the house. "Maybe he just likes you. I bet as a little Breed he pulled the pretty little Breed girls' ponytails just to get their attention."

"Stop defending him," Katie demanded. "I'll deal with him myself rather than following his example by going to others."

"He's in his study. I saw him go there earlier," Khileen informed her with all apparent helpfulness as she headed into the house. "He might have mentioned paperwork at breakfast this morning."

She had missed breakfast, Katie thought furiously, because she'd been up half the night aching for a man who didn't even care that she had no place else to run to.

"Well, be careful," Khileen advised as Katie strode angrily toward the hall leading to Devil and Reever's offices. "He has a mean bite, I hear."

"Well so do I." Especially since she'd begun allowing her fangs to grow and shape correctly after the news of her genetics had been revealed.

She was only barely aware of Khileen stepping back as she neared Devil's office. She'd finished focusing on her friend. Nothing mattered now but the man who was becoming a threat to her existence and the need burning inside her that was threatening her control.

This couldn't continue. She could easily stay the hell away from him if her arousal offended him. It would hurt, but her family's safety was more important. If she were taken and forced into the testing facilities, then her parents would do anything to have her released. No matter what it did to their lives or their safety.

And that she simply couldn't allow.

Her own safety aside, she refused to see her family threatened because some damned Breed male was offended by her lust for him.

A lust he caused.

She wouldn't have it.

"How did it go?" Cassandra Sinclair opened the door to her guest suite to allow Khileen Langer into the room.

She was one of the few women Cassie had met that she actually identified with. Perhaps it was the black hair, blue eyes and similar features.

They could have passed for family members.

Khileen was also generous natured and loving, though, attributes Cassie found she herself didn't possess in quite the same quantity.

"Just as you said it would." Smiling, Khileen propped her delicate hands on her hips as she braced her legs apart.

Dressed in jodhpurs, a cool white sleeveless top and riding boots, the other girl looked ready to enjoy a day riding across the desert. In no way did she look the part she played so often, that of Cassie's confidante, and one of a few rare friends. But, Cassie had found, Khileen tended to give in to the same lovingly placed manipulations and gentle nudges that Cassie herself often found hard to resist.

"Excellent." Cassie moved to her desk where she shifted through several papers until she found the small wireless mic and receiver she'd hidden there earlier.

Flipping the antenna down to connect with her father, she waited until he answered the call.

"Cassie?" There was concern in his voice. It was rare that he didn't worry whenever Cassie convinced him to accompany her on one of her little "adventures."

"When is your meeting with Mr. Reever?" she asked him.

"I'm waiting outside on the patio attached to his office," he answered her, the growl in his tone attesting to his irritation.

"Keep him out of the office. Ms. O'Sullivan is at the Devil's doorstep at the moment."

"You have to be related to Jonas Wyatt," he all but snarled.

"Well, he did help a bit in raising me," she reminded him with a fond smile. "And you know, I'm prone to adapt to certain instruction quite well."

There were many instances when she'd been forced to stay at the Lion Breed compound in Virginia while her parents fought to ensure her and her brother's safety over the years.

"Don't remind me," he retorted, though she could both hear and feel the love he held for her. "Lobo isn't so happy at the moment, either, that we're questioning his protection of this girl."

"As long as we get the desired results, then he'll be okay with it later," she promised.

If they didn't accomplish what she had come here to do, then there would be problems. It was those problems that had convinced her father to do as she asked.

"Let's hope," he grunted. "I have to go, he's stepping into the office."

They disconnected.

Turning back to Khileen, she saw the other girl watching her, a frown tugging at her brow.

"Do you ever get tired, Cassie?" she asked softly, with far more compassion than Cassie thought she had the right to.

"Tired?"

"Of trying so hard to hide from what you're trying to hide from?"

"And what do you think I'm trying to hide from?" She had to force the amusement and unconcern into her tone. What had this woman seen that no other ever had?

"Yourself," Khileen answered softly, surprising her. "You're hiding from yourself, Cassie. I was just wondering if you were tired of it yet."

Khileen turned and left the room then, not bothering to wait for an answer. It was a good thing, Cassie thought, because she didn't have one.

FOUR

Devil narrowed his eyes on the young woman that stepped into his office before closing the door with careful emphasis behind her.

The long spiral red curls that fell around her head and down her lithe, toned body should have reminded him far too much of Lobo's stepdaughter for the reaction that immediately knifed through his body.

He'd never had a sexual interest in Khileen, no matter her harmless flirtation at times. If only he could feel the same brotherly affection toward her Irish friend.

Emerald eyes flashed with fiery anger, immediately rousing the animal instincts that surged through him. As though all the human and animal dominant qualities he possessed were immediately awakened, his body tightened, tautened until he was all but jumping from his chair and dragging her to the floor to fuck them both into exhaustion.

And doing so wouldn't take a lot of effort. Push the gauzy little skirt she wore over her hips, tear what was sure to be sexy, silken panties from her body—all could be accomplished in less than a second. In the next heartbeat, he could be buried, full length, inside her.

"Why do you dislike me?" Delicate hands curved over her hips defiantly as she glared across the room at him. "What have I ever done to you to make you want to see me dead?"

His brow lifted. "Little girl, if I wanted to see you dead, it would be easy enough to accomplish," he informed her.

Dead wasn't exactly what he wanted, and that was what pissed him off.

"Little girl?" her eyes widened then narrowed suspiciously. "Are you so terrified of seeing me as a woman that you can't even acknowledge the fact that I am one?"

Bingo. Give the girl a prize for getting the answer on the first try.

But he snorted instead before resuming his seat behind the wide desk scattered with files and reports.

"Why don't you go plan a party or a shopping trip with Khileen," he suggested, injecting just enough mockery in his tone to piss her off further. "The adults on this ranch have to actually work."

That was a little low, he admitted, but God help him, he had to get her out of his office before his cock managed to burst past his zipper and the instincts driving him to possess her overcame his determination not to.

Shifting the files around, he picked one from the desk, any one, he wasn't even certain what he was staring at, waiting for her to leave.

Instead, her scent moved closer.

"Why are you allowing Lobo Reever to know that you're displeased over his decision to allow me to stay here?"

She stomped to the desk, but she didn't stop at the front of it as she should have. Hell no, she moved right beside it.

Her pretty hands braced against the top of the desk within his sight, her delicate, oval nails drawing his gaze.

"You haven't answered me," she reminded him.

"I don't owe you any answers." But he laid the file aside before leaning back in his chair and staring back up at her. "You should leave this office now."

"Should I?" she snapped. "Not before I know what your problem is."

She wanted to know what his problem was? Did she really want to know?"

Before he could stop himself, before she could avoid him, he came out of his chair in a surge of motion, gripped her arm and jerked her to him before wrapping his arm below her ass and lifting her to the table.

In the space of a second he had her legs spread, the denim covered length of his cock pressing against her sex as he leaned closer, and he was slowly forcing her to lean back on the desk.

"This is why," he snapped, staring into her widening, darkening gaze. "Because all I can think about is fucking you. That makes you a danger to this ranch and everyone in it."

"No, it makes you a danger." She had to force the words past her lips.

"But I'm not just visiting," he reminded her. "You are."

Her lips parted to argue, to say more; rather than allowing her to do so, he shut her up in the only manner at his disposal.

His lips covered hers.

His tongue pushed past her lips, tangled with hers, and the swollen heat that filled it began to throb, pulse and fill both of them with a heady, spicy taste.

What the fuck—

It was supposed to be a rumor.

The swollen tongue and the earthy spice of a mating aphrodisiac that filled the kiss—

The inability to stay away, to resist the taste he could give them both, the pleasure that could be had—

Fuck.

Shock filled him, wrapped around his senses, but did little to dim the flames searing his flesh and the hunger raging between them. Nothing else mattered. Nothing mattered but touching her, feeling her, holding her to him with his hands and the addictive taste of his kiss.

And she did like that taste of their kiss.

Her lips surrounded his tongue with each stroke between them as he mimicked the act he was desperate for.

Groaning under his kiss, crying out with each taste of the mating hormone spilling onto her tongue, she met his hunger with her own, then forced the flames higher.

And only then, as his tongue pressed against hers, daring her to take a deeper taste of him, did he realize that the addictive taste of spicy heat wasn't just coming from him, but from this too delicate, far too tempting little Breed as well.

Leaning into her, feeling her slender knees grip his hips, nothing began to matter but touching more of her. Of jerking her top over her head and ridding her soft flesh of it.

Tasting her again, and tasting more of her. Kissing her deeper, harder, locking her to him in ways that would ensure she never attempted to escape.

As though reading his intent, her arms lifted from his shoulders just long enough for him to pull the top over her head and toss it somewhere beyond them.

God, was he really going to fuck her here? On his desk?

Could he think of any better place and time than here and now?

Jerking back from her, breaking the rising hunger of his kiss, Devil stared down at her, shocked at his own actions, his own thoughts.

He'd never, not at any time, taken a woman without first ensuring both their comfort and their pleasure.

"Please." The soft plea that fell from her lips stopped him from pulling away from her.

Breathing roughly, forcefully, Devil stared into the darkening green of her eyes and her flushed, pleasure-filled expression before he allowed his gaze to drop to the lace-covered, hard-tipped curves of her breasts.

God, what was he doing?

Smoothing along the side of her body, his hand moved to where her skirt had fallen back from her flesh to pool at her hips. Once there, he did the unthinkable. Did exactly what he was certain he could keep himself from doing.

His fingers curled into the lace band of her panties and pulled them down her thighs.

The scent of her feminine flesh tore past his veil of control and left him helpless against the hunger clouding his brain.

Easing his body back, forcing his hips from the soft flesh of her pussy, he pulled the panties from her legs before dropping them to the floor. He hooked his arm beneath her back and eased her upward into his embrace.

"You shouldn't have come here." The groan surprised him, the words tearing unbidden from him.

Loosening the snap of the bra at her back, he eased the straps down her arms before dropping it, forgotten, to the floor as well.

"This is why you want me to leave," she accused him, staring back at him with hurt, emerald eyes.

God yes, this was exactly why he wanted her to leave. Because he couldn't keep his damned hands off her.

"Fucking dangerous," he groaned, lowering his lips to her shoulder and licking the fragrant flesh there.

Damn, she tasted good. So fucking good.

It was all he could do to keep from raking his teeth across that tender flesh, from marking it, staking his claim in a way no man or Breed could mistake.

Licking, kissing his way down as he laid her back along the desk, Devil came to the firm, rising mounds of her breasts, to the ripe, pebble-hard tips of her nipples.

He couldn't resist them.

He didn't want to resist them.

And he was within a second of tasting them—

"Hey, Devil, you in there?"

Katie froze.

Her eyes flew open, her gaze meeting Devil's as horror began to wash over her.

What was she doing?

"Just a minute, Graeme," he called back, his body taut, tight with lust as he seemed poised on an edge of control and teetering her way.

"This is important, Dev," the faceless Graeme called back. "One of the mares is acting freaky and there's some dude out here asking about some Irish girl. Have you seen an Irish girl?" Just enough mockery filled his voice to assure them that Graeme had denied knowledge of her but was concerned.

Who the hell was Graeme?

Devil jerked away from her as though it had taken the last measure of strength he had. And in the next breath he was lifting her from the desk.

"Get dressed," he ordered, his voice low. "Get to your room.

Don't let anyone outside the house see you and don't make any calls until I find you."

Katie nodded, though she doubted he saw her as he quickly straightened his clothes before striding to the door.

Jerking it open, Devil stepped into the hall, opening the door no farther than necessary as she quickly dressed. Seconds later, Katie slipped out as well and raced to the guest room she'd been given.

Stepping inside, she could see that the curtains had been drawn, blocking so much as a hint of the late afternoon sun or anyone brave enough, or lucky enough, to get a view.

Closing the door behind her, Katie curled into the large wing-back chair next to the door, wrapped her arms across her breasts and stared into the darkness of the room.

Would this be her life from now on? Running? Hiding? Always searching for safety and never being certain it existed?

She couldn't imagine such a life for herself. Because that life would mean leaving the Reever ranch and leaving the Breed whose eyes seemed to stare straight to her soul and whose touch could make her forget everything but her need for him.

She'd never known a connection to another person as she felt with this Breed. She had never wanted to be with another person, not just sexually, but just near him, as she did with Devil.

For the first time since she'd learned exactly what she was and how she had come to be, Katie began to regret it. Because the very fact of her creation could very well be exactly why Devil was fighting the desire between them so hard.

Perhaps he simply didn't want a woman whose life, whose very existence came with the kind of problems that hers would come with. He could want a nice, normal woman who would present no problems and no additional dangers to his own existence.

She could understand that.

The hell she could.

No nice, normal woman could ever tolerate a Breed male. They were arrogant, dominant, forceful, and so damned aggravating they made a woman want to kill at times. She knew exactly what they were like. She'd been dealing with them since she was sixteen years old during her first training year with the Breed Security Network.

Breed males were always certain they were right. They rarely, no, they never, at any time accepted that a woman, whether she was Breed or human, could survive without a male's protection, and they were prone to prove it in a variety of ways.

They were peculiar, particular and perverse.

And she had a very bad feeling she might well be falling in love with one.

Graeme, secure the grounds," Devil ordered quietly as he watched the Jeep rumble from view, the high-range camera mounted on the top pointing back at the grounds.

It had been pointing forward when the vehicle stopped at the gates.

"They're secured," he answered, and Devil knew if Graeme said they were secured, then they were damned well secured.

The Lion Breed was one of the few recessive Breeds Devil had known with actual Breed traits. He'd arrived six months before with nothing more than a change of clothes in a small pack, a knife and a sense of security weaknesses that had immediately found favor on the estate.

Tall, broad, laid-back and rarely displaying a temper, Devil was beginning to rely on the exacting precision in which the Breed did everything he set out to do.

"The girl's still in her room," Graeme reported as he consulted the wireless electronic security monitor he carried. "She left your office just after you and went straight to her bedroom."

Devil glanced at the other man briefly. "You knew she was there."

"It would be damned hard to miss the smell of her need," Graeme agreed. "I have no doubt Mr. Reever and Mr. Sinclair were well aware of her presence there as well. Speaking of, Mr. Reever has requested a report immediately. I'd be prepared for questions regarding your activities in your office if I were you."

Devil came to an abrupt stop, not really surprised that Graeme managed to stop the instant he did as well.

"Do you have a problem with the activities in my office, Graeme?" he asked the other Breed, knowing that the continued mention of it meant that Breed likely did have a problem with it.

Impassive, his expressive gaze showed little-to-no emotion at the best of times, were it not for the glitter of life in the dark brown of his eyes.

"I have no problems with them at all, Mr. Black," Graeme assured him. "But, I'd expect questions from Mr. Reever as well as Mr. Sinclair, because they definitely seemed to have an opinion on it before the reporters showed up."

Great, just what he needed, not just Lobo questioning, but also Dash Sinclair.

Lobo was bad enough.

"I'll deal with Lobo and Sinclair," he growled. "You deal with security and we'll continue to get along, Graeme. Otherwise, your nosiness may cause you quite a bit of trouble."

More than the feline would want to deal with, and Devil would make damned certain of it.

But first, he needed to deal with Lobo and Sinclair. Because any dealings he had with the sumptuous Ms. O'Sullivan was his business and no one else's.

No one else's at all.

FIVE

Stepping from a cold shower, and it wasn't the first she had taken in the past twenty-four hours, Katie quickly dried the water from her body before donning a loose robe and belting it in irritation.

She had no idea what was wrong with her.

She was too young for hot flashes, right?

She didn't have flu symptoms. She wasn't running a fever. But she was too warm, her body aching, and the remembered taste of Devil's kiss teased her senses with the persistence of an addiction. Or at least, what she'd always heard an addiction could be like.

But, it wasn't really possible to be addicted to a kiss, was it?

To the wild, heated taste of a man's lips on hers, his tongue stroking against hers as flames swept through her body and tension pounded at her clitoris and the clenched, untried depths of her sex.

Her breasts were swollen, her nipples hard and tortured, dragging an irritated moan from her lips as she stomped back into her bedroom, only to come to a sudden stop.

She hadn't heard him enter the room. She hadn't even suspected he would be there, and she could normally anticipate most people's actions.

"Did you get rid of the reporters?" she asked before clearing her throat while drawing the edges of the robe above her breasts tightly together.

Narrowed, intense, his gaze swept over her body.

"For the time being," he assured her. "But I'd like for you to stay within the inner grounds for a few days; the walls surrounding the house are equipped with special diffusers to ensure no cameras or other tracking equipment can penetrate it."

She nodded nervously, watching as he moved to the windows and slid the curtains back several inches to catch the rays of the setting sun.

"The windows are also specially made to diffuse images in any optical equipment. As long as you keep them closed you'll be safe with the curtains open."

"I didn't close them," she said, wincing at the slight nervous quiver she couldn't halt. "They were closed when I came into my room."

He nodded before turning back. "It was probably one of the maids. They're unaware of the windows' properties, and we like to keep knowledge of it limited. It helps during those times when we key the electronics built into the windows to show the images we want seen. If everyone knew about it, then it would be less effective."

Then why tell her? She wasn't exactly a member of the family.

"How did you know the problem was reporters?" he asked her then.

"It really wasn't that hard," she told him, her expression pulled tight with the fear that glittered in her eyes. "There was, after all, a camera mounted on top of the vehicle they drove. I glimpsed that much as I peeked from my curtains."

Katie twisted her hands together to keep from reaching out to touch him again as he crossed his arms over his chest and stared down at her with a frown. "What I'd like to know is how they managed to find you here?" he growled. "I've sent one of my men out to learn as much as possible. Though, with those bastards, it's hard telling."

She had to agree with him on that one, of course. But that didn't explain the question uppermost in her mind at the moment.

"Why are *you* here, in my room, Devil?" she asked instead. "You didn't seem particularly upset that you were drawn away earlier."

"Taking a virgin on my desk wouldn't exactly be a testament to my maturity and experience either." The rumble of a growl was accompanied by a flash of pure lust in his black and amber eyes.

"And you've decided I'm a virgin, how?"

She was, but it wasn't exactly something she advertised.

"How the hell you made it to twenty-four years of age without taking a lover I haven't figured out yet." The low pitch of the rumbled words rasped over her senses as he began moving slowly toward her. "Tell me, Katie, were the men in Ireland completely stupid?"

"I was completely not interested," she corrected him, though speaking past the harsh beat of her heart wasn't exactly easy.

"You were engaged," he reminded her, his expression shifting, tightening as though the knowledge displeased him in some way. "How could you be 'uninterested' in sex and be contemplating marriage?"

How *could* she be?

"He wasn't exactly interested himself," she sighed, regretting the friend she had lost when the news of her genetics had been revealed. "And I was tired of being alone and questioned regarding the fact that I had no lover or lovers. I was beginning to feel somehow inferior to others because that desire wasn't there."

Until him.

Now, she couldn't seem to get rid of the need.

"And now you're interested. Doesn't that confuse you a bit? Perhaps cause you to question why it's happened so suddenly?" Stopping in front of her, he reached out, his fingers circling her wrist and drawing her hand slowly from the material of her robe.

"Should I?" Her senses were in shambles as he smoothed the edges of the robe over the swell of her breasts, the calloused tips stroking against her skin and causing her to draw in a hard, sharp breath.

She didn't want to question anything except why he wasn't kissing her yet.

"You're going to hate me later," he told her, his head lowering, his lips brushing against hers sensually.

"Of course I will." There was no denying that. He was too powerful, too dominant to ever understand the value of dealing with her in a straightforward manner. He was a man she could trust with her life, but not with her heart.

Unfortunately, her heart may have already made the choice.

"You know you'll hate me?" He paused, his lips still within a breath of hers.

"I think it was destined," she sighed. "But if you don't kiss me, I'm going to hate you now rather than later. How's that?"

His lips almost twitched.

Was lightning actually going to strike? Katie had sworn it would before Devil Black actually smiled.

Whether he intended to or not, before he could, his lips settled on hers, parted them, as he drew her close, showed her exactly how little she had known about kissing.

For instance, as his tongue pressed between her lips, Katie had never imagined the spicy taste of his kiss would have her lips closing around it, drawing around it as it pressed in, pulled back, thrusting against her as a sweet heat began to infuse her senses.

Katie was only barely aware of the belt of her robe loosening, falling from her shoulders to the floor a second before he pulled back just enough to jerk his shirt over his head and toss it to the floor as well.

Then his lips were on hers again, taking hard, forceful kisses as he swung her into his arms and turned to the bed.

Had she imagined she would feel like this?

That pleasure would rush through her body like wildfire, burning across her flesh and searing her senses with so many sensations that she could barely breathe for the heat and rapid fire bursts of hunger exploding inside her?

Had she ever suspected that a man's touch could do what Devil's was doing to her?

God, she hadn't.

His hands stroked over her arms, moved to her waist, her breasts as he spread those insanely heated kisses from her lips, down her neck and shoulder, then on a blazing path to the peaked tips of her breasts.

Her nipples throbbed. They were so tightly swollen they ached with the need to be touched. Then his lips were covering them, drawing them into the heat of his mouth and wringing a cry from her lips.

Oh God, the rasp of his tongue was too much. Brutal, ecstatic as he licked against the agonized tip, his teeth rasping over it as her nails bit into the bare warmth of his shoulders. Each touch, each heated lick and caress was like a shard of sensation racing to her womb and exploding into fiery fingers of heat that surrounded her clit and exploded in the depths of her pussy.

And she had no idea how to control it.

Katie couldn't help herself. She couldn't fight the hunger raging through her for the taste, the touch of this Breed. She had no idea how to process each sensation or how to survive the destructive results.

"God! Katie." His hand stroked over her hip, parted her thighs.

Calloused, excitingly roughened, his palm stroked up her inner thigh, the tips of his fingers finding the naturally bare flesh between her thighs.

A Breed female had no curls to shelter her there. Nothing to filter the heat and pleasure from her lover's caress or to hide the slick response of her arousal. Her mother had told her it was simply a genetic trait she'd inherited from a distant grandparent.

God, she should have known better, but at the moment, all she could do was revel in the exquisite sensations it allowed her to experience as his touch stroked over the sensitized flesh.

Lifting her hips to him, her fingers clenching in the sheets beneath her, she fought to breathe as his kisses moved from her breasts to the skin beneath. Each lick, each press of his lips against her flesh stoking the excitement and pleasure higher.

She needed . . .

"Please, Dev." Arching to him, feeling the stroke of his fingers against the slick flesh between her thighs, Katie fought back a scream of agonizing need. "Please touch me."

Yet, he was touching her.

Touching her in so many ways, stroking not just her flesh but also a part of her she didn't know existed. A need she hadn't known filled her.

God help him.

Devil fought for strength, for just the smallest measure of control as his lips moved unerringly to the sweet flesh between Katie's thighs.

Never in his life had he ached to taste a woman as he did this one. Never had hunger, need, protectiveness and overwhelming emotion surged through him in such waves of uncontrolled impulses as they did now.

Pressing her thighs farther apart with one hand and brushing his lips against the petal-soft flesh between her thighs, there was no holding back another growl—a demand.

Her hips lifted to him.

Sheened with moisture, slick and tempting, the little bud of her clit peeked from between her folds, drawing his tongue and his hunger.

Sweet virgin.

How had he, the Devil of the Breeds, ever deserved a woman untouched, untutored and so hungry for *him*. It wasn't just touch or sex, desire or release she ached for. She ached for him.

She *was* his.

From this moment on, tied not just by the emotions that would have arisen in time but were now flooding both their senses in overwhelming waves, but also by a heat neither of them could ever resist.

A sensual, sexual heat—a bond of ever-increasing pleasure—

For a moment, just a moment, Katie was certain she was finding a pace with the pleasure that she could process. Riding the waves of sensations, forcing air into her lungs, out again, she was able to actually make sense of some of the emotions tearing through her.

She could feel her heart racing, adrenaline infusing it as some hidden part of her senses seemed to open and reach out to him.

She'd never done that. She'd never opened herself to anyone but her parents. And never in her life had she opened herself as she was now. Reaching out to another and *feeling* him. She could feel him.

Not just physically, not just his touch, his kiss, the lick of his tongue over her hip.

She could feel the darkness inside him struggling with a compassion and a hunger that so matched the hunger she'd known herself for years. A need to know another to the very depths of their soul.

A hunger to touch another's soul as she was touching his now.

Then, his lips moved from her hip, down the bend of her thigh. They brushed against her mound, his breath feathering over the swollen, desperately aching bud of her clit.

Following the brush of air, his tongue sent her reeling.

Pressing between the plump folds of her flesh, it curled around the bud, stroked it, then his lips were drawing it inside and the thought of anything but surrendering to the crashing waves of fiery pleasure, rising emotions, and sheer desperation was a thing of the past.

"Look at me, Kate." The demand was a harsh, primal growl that brought her eyes open, instantly meeting his as he stared up at her from between her thighs.

He hadn't called her Katie, just Kate. Staring into his eyes, she realized that where others may not see or acknowledge the woman she was, this Breed could, at the very least, sense it.

She hadn't been Katie, at least in her own mind, for a very long time.

As their eyes met, white-hot sensation lanced her clit, dragging her back from any personal revelations to a place where only the pleasure mattered.

His tongue licked as his cheeks hollowed, suckling it deeper inside his mouth as he seemed to find just the right spot with his tongue where the slightest stroke and just the right pressure began to amplify the tension now pouring through her body.

The pleasure was agonizing.

It drew her body tight, shortened her breath. Each pulse of sensation throbbed through her clit, intensifying the pleasure and the rising need. It tore through her. It stroked across sensitive nerve endings, tightened in her vagina, burned through her senses, then suddenly imploded through her in a surge of such exquisite, ecstatic pleasure that she became lost in the sensations.

She became lost in her Devil.

As she reached the pinnacle of sensation and began easing back, Kate became aware of him rising between her thighs and coming over her as the heated width of his cock pressed into the swollen folds of her sex.

The intensity of her orgasm had been shocking enough, but as the crest of his erection pressed inside her, a sudden spurt of heat moisture ejaculating from him into the clenched depths of her pussy had her lashes opening wide, her gaze meeting his. And if she was surprised at the feel of it, then the shock in his gaze assured her he was even more so.

"Did you finish?" she whispered, suddenly terrified he had.

If he'd finished, how then would she ease the painful need clenching at her flesh?

"Fuck. No, babe . . ." He tightened, a hard grimace pulling at his expression as it happened again, though this time, it seemed hotter, her inner flesh more sensitive to the sudden pulse of . . . whatever it was.

His jaw clenched, his eyes glowing with his own pleasure as he eased back, then forward again, rocking his hips between her thighs, stroking her in slow, stretching degrees.

"Dev." Gripping his tight biceps, desperate for some part of him to hold on to as she watched the amber in his eyes burn as the next spurt of pre-cum was like a stroke of near ecstasy inside her.

The tension she believed had to have evaporated with the orgasm that washed through her was ratcheting higher with a suddenness that left her reeling.

The aching demand that centered in the depths of her sex became unbearable, the need to be filled, to be taken, overriding everything in the space of a heartbeat.

"I have you, Kate." His lips brushed across hers, his voice gentle despite the primal rasp that filled it and sent a frisson of sensation racing down her spine. "Just hold on to me, mate. Hold me."

His lips brushed against hers again, settled and pressed hers open as the pressure, the stretching pleasure-pain and amplified desperation increased as the head of his cock worked past her once untouched entrance.

"God, Kate." Lifting his lips, panting for air he stared down at her once again. "Ah, mate. I can't wait."

Had she asked him to wait?

"Then don't." She could barely breathe, let alone speak.

Lifting her head, moving against him, she relished each sharp sensation tightening the tension in the clenched muscles of her pussy.

"Don't want to hurt you." His teeth were clenched, the restraint he was using evident on his savage features.

Hurt her? It simply wasn't possible that pain could penetrate the hunger raging through her.

Lifting her hips higher, feeling the thick weight lodge deeper, she smiled up at him, arched more firmly into the penetration and whispered, "Take me, Devil. Just like you want to."

It was that smile.

Wild. Reckless. This was the smile she had used in the photos and vids the Breed Protection Network had on her. Filled with confidence, daring anyone to defy her.

God help him, she'd stolen his heart before he'd ever been called out to pull her out of Ireland.

With the tight heat of her pussy enveloping the head of his cock as he worked himself to the veil of her innocence, Devil could feel not just his physical possession of her, but so much more.

Their gazes were locked. Thickly lashed, sensual, the emerald of her eyes glittered with such arousal and need that it was like staring into pools of pure emotional magic. They glistened and gleamed with wonder, pleasure, hunger.

"It's not enough." Her panting whisper had his stomach clenching, his hips gathering to push past the thin barrier. "Please, Dev. Please, take me now."

"Hold me, Kate," he urged her again. "Hold me tight, mate."

His mate.

Sweet God, all his. Created for him. Gifted to him.

His woman.

The surging thrust shocked him.

Devil was unaware of the quick tightening of his hips as he pulled back. It was only as he pushed inside her once again, moving in a quick, rapid push he was unable to halt, that the motion sent him tearing past the thin barrier of her innocence.

Her eyes widened, lips parting on a soundless cry as he thrust his shaft and burrowed hard and fast inside her.

The steady tightening of her slick pussy, the reflexive clench of stretching tissue struggling to adjust to the width filling her, each hard, never-before-felt spurt of the mating pre-cum, then the rush of slick, heated feminine need easing him deeper tore a snarl of pure pleasure from his throat.

Fiery, clenching and fist-tight, her pussy milked over the furiously engorged flesh of his cock. Tugging and stroking, tightening and sucking at the engorged head until nothing mattered but feeling more and more of her. Devil was powerless to halt his own response.

Moving against her, thrusting inside her, his hips worked against her, powering the engorged length of his dick inside the steadily pulsing flesh, he gave himself to the possession of her, only to realize he was being possessed by her.

The heart he believed had withered and died before he even realized what emotion was pounded with a strength and response to her that surprised him. She possessed the soul that had never known the need for another's touch until her. She possessed the man, his dreams, his hopes, his battles and his failures.

That first stroke of lightning-bright pain gave way to a steadily increasing inferno of pleasure Kate couldn't fight and had no desire to escape.

Tightening her fingers on his powerful arms, she held on to him, held him. He was her only safety in the cataclysm of white-hot sensations. Each thrust pushed through the depths of her pussy, drove her higher, deeper inside a storm that refused to ease, that only deepened with each touch of his lips as they lowered to the rise of her breasts, each stroke of his tongue as he strung kisses to the tender flesh of her neck.

Katie writhed beneath him, lifting into each stroke, gathering herself for the next. Her knees tightened on his thrusting hips, her head lifted from the pillow to allow her lips to press to his chest, her tongue to stroke against his oversensitive skin.

They were flying. Flying through such pleasure, such a building sense of exquisite sensation, that Kate gave up on attempting to control, or to process. All she could do was fly within it, experience it, relish it.

Each stroke of his cock burying inside her pushed her deeper into the storm. The rake of his teeth at the bend of shoulder and neck had her crying out, the muscles of her vagina tightening, clenching furiously as that gathering tension began to ignite with ecstatic flares of pleasure.

It was rushing around her, through her.

Each stroke of his cock came faster, penetrating her, fucking her with increasing need and hunger until the convergence of sensations barreled headlong into each other and exploded with furious ecstasy.

Her teeth sank into the powerful pectoral muscle beneath her lips as she felt his sharper, longer canines pierce the flesh just beneath her neck, at the bend of her shoulder.

Her tongue, swollen and hot, licked at the slight wound she made, stroking over it madly as her body shuddered and jerked within a release so powerful it exploded within her soul.

The feel of his tongue doing the same at her neck was an additional pleasure, fiery pinpoints of sensations that merged and mixed in a release so intense that at first, she was unaware of the significance of the heavy tightening in her vagina.

Clenched, spasming around the heavy shaft filling her, the inner muscles began struggling to accommodate the heavy width of his cock. Stretching, flaring with sensation that mixed with the crash of her orgasm and began driving her higher, the thickening of his cock at the juncture of the tightening muscles of her vagina shocked her.

Her eyes flared open, meeting his as his head lifted from the bite he'd left at her neck.

"I have you," he groaned, ecstasy clenching his teeth and tightening his expression as the amber in his eyes burned like fire. "I have you, Kate."

The rush of pleasure filling her system exploded again, drawing a harsh cry from her lips as she jerked against each rush of rapturous pleasure.

She couldn't survive it.

The orgasmic explosions were destructive. The waves of shuddering ecstasy crashed through her senses with each tug of the thickened flesh against her inner muscles as he locked inside her.

Heated spurts of his release filled the too sensitive depths of her pussy. More sensation. More pleasure.

It built. Amassed. One ever-deepening release after another charging through her body until the ecstasy exploded in a powerful surge so intense she felt each pinpoint of sensation as it released inside her.

Exhausted, wrung out by the pleasure and the force of a release she could never have imagined, Katie collapsed beneath him, wilting like a flower as the caress of the sun eased into night.

As sleep claimed her, she felt the slow easing of the swollen flesh held captive inside her as Devil gave one last shudder of release. But as he withdrew and rolled from her, it wasn't to leave her. Rather, he pulled her into his embrace, cushioned her head on his shoulder and allowed sleep to claim her.

A full, deep, blessedly dreamless sleep.

SIX

Devil brushed his mate's hair back from her face as he finished cleaning the perspiration and remnants of their release from her thighs, along her belly and from her breasts.

It was an act he'd never done for another woman.

The lovers he'd known in the past had always jumped from bed and run straight to the shower as though they were somehow dirty and had to wash the filth from their bodies.

Kate had slipped immediately into sleep instead. Her body completely relaxed, exhausted from the force of pleasure that had exploded between them.

Picking up a long, sun-kissed curl from her shoulder and drawing it to his face, he brushed the silky softness against his cheek and let a smile tug at his lips. Those curls completely fascinated him. It was as though they had a warmth and life of their own as they flowed around her body.

Hell, the woman herself fascinated him. In the week since he'd taken her from Ireland, he'd become so entranced by her that he'd begun to wonder if he was losing his mind.

It wasn't his mind he was losing. It was his heart—at breakneck speed with no hope of slowing down.

Spurred by a phenomenon known as mating heat—a physical and emotional convergence of hormonal shifts that occurred once a Breed came into contact with his destined mate, the heart he believed he didn't have was suddenly alive. The one he would have been destined to love had he been born as human.

Unlike humans, though, there was no choice in whether to accept or reject the male or female that perfectly complemented him physically, mentally, and emotionally as well as hormonally.

Once the body, mind and heart established that this person was the one that best fit the hungers and needs inside them, then the animal took over.

Hormones gathered and built beneath the tongue, spilled to that first kiss and established a bond born of a sexual heat so intense that there was no denying it. Speeding through their bodies, spurring their emotions, each response was driven at warp speed to bind the pair together in a mating that the Breed scientists suspected would endure a lifetime.

Mating heat actually existed.

The gossip rags hadn't printed the insanity of fear-driven drivel as they usually had. For once, they'd at least partially gotten it right.

Returning the curl alongside the others that spilled over her shoulder, Devil pulled the sheet over Kate's slumbering body before collecting his shirt from the bottom of the bed and pulling it on.

Dressed, he slipped from her room and made his way silently downstairs.

Stepping into the foyer, he stopped as Lobo and Dash Sinclair stepped from the library on the far end of the entryway and headed for the door.

"There you are," Lobo growled, his dark gaze fierce as savagery flashed in his gaze. "Where's Graeme?"

"I sent him into town to check on the whereabouts of the reporters that were here," Devil answered, tensing at the ready violence that hummed around Lobo. "Why?"

"There's a fucking Bureau agent at the gates with two Irish and American Immigration agents with a warrant to search the premises for Katie. I want to know how the hell they found out she was here."

"Like hell." A flash of red filled his vision for the briefest moment before he turned to Dash. "Cassie knows Breed Law; have her send them back to the holes they crawled out of."

Dash grimaced. "She's going over the language now, but she doesn't just pull these arguments out her ass, Dev. She needs time."

"Then buy her the time she needs," he demanded. "This isn't American land, it's Navajo land." He turned back to Lobo. "American Immigration has no rights on this land, nor does the Bureau of Breed Affairs. Ignore them."

"We can't just ignore them," Lobo argued, his thumbs hooking in the belt that cinched his hips and held the weapon he carried at all times since his wife's death. "That's a Bureau agent out there, Dev. We signed an agreement with the Bureau of Breed Affairs that negates any desire we have to tell them to kiss our asses."

"They can't take a mate," he reminded the other male, suddenly remembering several of the laws he himself had read when he had been given the Breed mandates. "It's an exception to all other laws. No matter the crime, the act or the situation at hand, no mate can be taken, claimed or incarcerated unless a crime is committed after the mating."

He'd always wondered about the wording. It was explained that a mating was simply Breed language detailing a committed relationship between a Breed and a lover chosen as a life partner. He knew now exactly what it meant and why the wording had been so precise.

"You've mated her?" Dash's eyes narrowed, his nostrils suddenly flaring as amusement lit his gaze. "That's why the scent of lust was so strong coming from your office earlier. The mating scent was on you when we met, so I assumed you'd already mated."

Devil grinned. "Not until that bit of Irish got hold of me. Hell, I met her when she was sixteen and training with the Breed Protection Network in Ireland. I was there to train their agents in computer security. I saw her for a few brief seconds, and couldn't figure out why I couldn't forget her." He turned to Dash then. "Now, tell me where we stand."

"We stand strong." It was Cassie who answered that question.

Standing at the top of the stairs, her hair pulled tightly from her face and hanging down her back in masses of wicked black curls, she was dressed in a dark gray skirt, silk shell and jacket paired with plain, though obviously expensive, black high heels.

She was no longer the precocious, mischievous young woman Devil had met before being sent to Ireland to rescue Kate. The woman stepping confidently down the curved staircase was superior in every way to each and every one of them, and her very bearing emphasized it.

Cool blue eyes. She wore no makeup, no artifice. In one hand she carried a leather briefcase as the other trailed down the stair bannister.

"The laws are quite clear in this situation," she stated as she stepped into the foyer to join them. "No matter the situation, the circumstance or any previous laws, mating heat trumps it. Especially in a case of any scientific laws that should be created after Breed Law, demanded or mandated. At no time, and in no way without both mates as well as the director of the Bureau of Breed Affairs and three-quarters of the Breed Ruling Cabinet's express and written agreement can any scientific research, experimentation or study be conducted on a mated pair, no matter the justification, reasoning or country that signed the mandates of Breed Law." She smiled in triumph. "And the leaders of each section of Europe, including Ireland, signed each and every mandate of the laws presented to them before President Marion took it before the United Nations, where every delegate there signed each mandate as well." From the leather case she withdrew a folder and handed it to Dash Sinclair. "Father, as a member of the Breed Ruling Cabinet, this is the order of a stay of exemption to be presented to the Immigration officials signed by Director Wyatt and wired to me five minutes ago. Director Wyatt is currently on the line with the Bureau agent outside our gates. He'll need the signed orders before he and the men with him can force the Immigration officials back to Ireland."

Devil stared back at Cassie with narrowed suspicion. "Why are they so intent to take her? I've lost count of the European Breeds who had escaped to America, and the officials there haven't sent so much as a protest. Now, they're sending immigration officials after one lone female?"

"Mary Katherine O'Sullivan was taken from the lab her grandfather is accused of having overseen during his tenure with the Genetics Council until the liberation of that particular lab. One of the scientists that worked there was captured several months ago by MI-6 and revealed Wallace O'Sullivan conspired to have his son's and daughter-in-law's samples from a fertility clinic sent to the lab he was in charge of. From there, he had the scientists insert the Wolf Breed genetics into not just the sperm, but also the mother's ova, before fertilization. A process that was outlawed by the Council itself early in the genetic experimentations, for reasons we've yet to find explanations for."

Devil inhaled slowly, carefully.

"It was outlawed because it allowed the Breeds to conceive. It created Breed males with a mix of both human-compatible as well as Breed-compatible sperm, and in Breed females. In females, the ova could be fertilized by either species with no complications. They allowed one of these births, but terminated the Breed somewhere around twelve years of age for reasons we were unaware of."

Cassie frowned up at him. "Surely there were rumors why the Breed was terminated."

Devil stared down at her, remembering those rumors and the concern in the scientists that ran the lab he was assigned to.

"Rumor was that the Breed created by that pairing could not be identified as a Breed by any testing, nor by Breed senses. The animal instincts were so completely merged with the human psyche in cunning and in response that the Breed was so superior that they feared the result of allowing it to live. At twelve, the Breed already had the loyalty of every other Breed in the labs, and the scientists only learned later that an uprising had been only days away from the time they terminated his life."

"It was a male then?" Cassie asked curiously.

Devil shrugged. "They always referred to the Breed as the 'specimen,' 'project' or an 'it.' I assigned the sex myself out of respect for the life taken, nothing more."

She nodded thoughtfully before turning to her father. "Director Wyatt should have contacted his agent by now. You and I can take that file—" She stopped.

The instant tension that filled her body had Devil as well as Lobo and Dash instantly on guard as Cassie turned back and looked up the stairs.

Devil didn't wait to ask questions. Instead, he turned and raced up the stairs, aware of the two Breeds moving quickly behind him. Every animal sense inside his body, honed by years of training, instinct and the shadowed war being fought for Breed survival was screaming in alarm. And it was screaming his mate's name.

SEVEN

The second the door clicked shut behind Devil, Katie came instantly awake.

Regret at his departure joined the subtle ache for his touch as she rose from the bed and quickly dressed, determined to find Khileen and see if she had heard of anything resembling the pleasure she'd found with Devil.

She knew it wasn't normal. She'd had friends all her life until the world had found out she was actually a Breed, and those friends had had sex often. With more than one man. Some with women. Never had she heard of anything like the pleasure she had just experienced.

Moving into the bathroom, she quickly tamed the wild mass of curls with a detangling comb before tying it back at the nape of her neck.

As she drew her hands back, she glimpsed the mark Devil had left at the bend of her neck and shoulder. His teeth had pierced the skin, though she'd felt none of the pain she would have expected to feel.

Reaching up, she brushed her fingers over the reddened area, the light caress sending a bold shudder to race over her flesh. A sensation of intense pleasure had her thighs tightening and a sense of amazement filling her.

That was no ordinary hickey.

"Wow," she breathed out, rather impressed now. "Definitely weird."

As she considered the sensation, her nose wrinkled at the odd scent that teased at it.

That had been happening more and more often. Scents that were out of place, impressions and instincts she wasn't familiar with.

Shaking her head, she gave a quick glance at the jeans, sleeveless camisole top and sneakers she'd donned to be sure she looked presentable before turning and leaving the bathroom. Closing the door behind her, she stilled, her head turning quickly to the balcony doors.

"Eh. Let's not attempt to run," the tall male standing inside her room aimed the barrel of a laser gun at her chest and smiled coolly. "I'd hate to have to dispose of you. The price on your head isn't worth nearly as much if you're not alive."

Her senses began exploding then. The impression of Devil, Lobo and Dash quickly nearing her room, fury surging through them as they raced for her.

Devil's scent was clear, sharp and acrid with his rage. Lobo was determined and definitely furious, but his scent was more calculating. Dash Sinclair's was icy cold, and all three men were intent on murder.

She stood still, and she waited.

"Rather impressive, mating with the Devil," the dark-haired stranger drawled. "Perhaps you've already conceived."

She shook her head slowly. She would know if she had.

"You're too soon," she said softly. "It's the wrong time of the month. Besides, Wolf Breeds don't conceive easily. Remember?"

To that, he gave a muted chuckle. "Most don't. You, on the other hand, as exceptional as you are, can definitely conceive easily, as I hear it. Now, why don't you just walk on over here, nice and slow, so I can cuff you and catch our ride out of the ranch."

She could hear the muffled sound of a covert helicopter moving in on the house. No doubt every Breed in the place could hear it as well. It was quiet, she gave him that. Likely completely silent to him. Someone had definitely done their homework in attempting to hide it. But, they hadn't quite gotten it right.

"I'd rather die than leave with you." She shrugged as though unconcerned and prepared herself to move. "And what did you say, the price wasn't nearly as high if I'm dead?"

He frowned back at her. "I hear the Devil's besotted with you. From that mark on your neck, I can see that he's mated you. Do you really want to chance leaving him to a life where he can never have another woman, another lover or a family if I kill you? Wouldn't you prefer to at least give him the chance to rescue you?"

She shook her head. "I wouldn't be worth finding." She smiled then. "Besides, I'm a greedy bitch. I want him to remember me forever."

That clearly threw him off.

Devil and the others were at the top of the stairs now, racing furiously for her room. She was at the end of the hall. With a running go, Devil would take her door down instantly, surprising her would-be kidnapper and drawing his attention against his will.

Using the force he'd enter with, Devil would evade the shot that may possibly go off, and knowing Lobo and Dash, she'd be anticipating the quick trigger finger with calculating assurance.

At the most, the mirror on the dresser would shatter about one second before Devil took this man's head off his shoulders.

"Don't be difficult, bitch," he snapped out, his brown eyes narrowing furiously.

"But it's what I live for."

She dove for the floor at the same second that Devil exploded against the door.

The shot went off, glass exploded.

Lunging to her feet, Kate jumped for the mercenary, or the Council soldier, whatever he was. The only chance he had of living was if she got to him first.

Shock held him for that extra second she needed to kick the weapon from his hand, ram her knee into his crotch, then slam her elbow into his neck with enough force to knock him to the floor, unconscious, before slamming the balcony door against the sound of the helicopter circling the side of the house to pick the bastard up.

As the door closed she swung around, knelt in front of the fallen soldier and met her mate's furious scowl as he crouched in front of her, prepared to leap for an enemy that was no longer in position for the killing blow he would have made.

Devil's black and amber gaze flickered to the unconscious soldier, then to Kate as she stared back at him, determination narrowing her eyes.

"Mate, why are you protecting garbage?" he asked with lazy curiosity as he sensed both Lobo and Dash quickly reassessing the situation and relaxing their primal rush for blood.

"One man's trash." She shrugged with a suggestive smile. "Another's treasure?"

Was that jealousy striking at his brain and bringing the taste of blood to his senses?

"Is he your treasure then?" He nodded to the fallen form.

Katie grimaced. What an awful description.

"Perhaps not him," she admitted as she rose slowly from her

crouch and faced the man she'd been told was her "mate." "But, the information he might have is something else entirely."

She looked down at him again, remembering where she had seen him and the significance of the information he may well hold.

"What information could a mercenary possibly hold?" Devil asked as he took the two steps toward her, gripped her arm and unceremoniously dragged her away from the "garbage."

"I've seen him before," she admitted, turning to stare down at him as well. "Da has a picture of him in his study alongside four other men who were at the labs the night he found me. They were assigned to the labs, and one of them shot Da's best friend, Jorn Langer. When Da was forced to leave the body to hide me, he then went back during the cleanup phase of the liberation. Jorn's body was missing and this man as well as his three cohorts were seen dragging the body away."

"Langer's alive then?" Lobo questioned, the significance of the information drawing a frown to his brow.

She shook her head. "Da's certain he was dead. Khileen's mother had him officially declared dead before your marriage to her, so it wouldn't affect you or Khileen legally in any way. Da wants to fulfill a promise he and his friend made to each other as young men, a promise to make certain that if one went before the other, the surviving one would ensure the other was buried in their family cemetery in Ireland. And he wants to know why they took his body." That more than anything tormented her father, Kate knew.

"I couldn't let you kill him, Dev," she said softly. "Da's searched for these men since the night Jorn disappeared. He left him to save me. Jorn died to help Da rescue me before anyone else knew of my existence there. I couldn't let him die."

Hell, this woman would probably surprise him until the day

he drew his last breath. She was a wonder he had no idea how to decipher, and no way of understanding how he had deserved her.

"Get the garbage out of here," he ordered Graeme as the other man rushed into the room. He'd clearly not followed Devil's orders to go into town. "Then find those reporters as I told you to do."

"I sent Flint to follow the reporters," Graeme stated, his tone flat with disgust. "I delegate, Devil. There's too much damned excitement around here for me to be gone for long. Why the hell didn't you call me before rushing up here? If I hadn't heard that damned copter, I'd have never known we had trouble."

Devil's brow lifted as he stared back at the other man, waiting.

"Do I look stupid today?" the other man demanded arrogantly. "Our heli was in the air instantly, and the team aboard it just reported they've taken the pilot into custody." He tapped the earbud he wore securely in his ear.

Yeah, he was going to have to start using his, Devil decided as he turned back to his mate.

She had turned and rested on her haunches several feet back from the unconscious man, her head tipped sideways as she studied him.

Now he knew exactly why the European Breed Protection Network had so hated losing her. As she stared at the man, senses she wasn't aware she had, senses that were so much a natural part of her, were assessing him, committing each feature to memory, each scent, and drawing in every bit of knowledge that her primal senses could pick up on.

"Kate?" he questioned her softly.

Not Kate.

Katie was the girl she had been, Kate was the woman who had come to that bed with him and broken down the barriers he'd built to keep her out of his heart. Kate was the mature, instinctive, highly adept Breed female the animal inside him had known she was.

No wonder his own primal instincts had rushed to claim her as soon as possible. The animal part of him had known no other woman could match him as fully as this woman did.

"He hasn't bathed in several days," she murmured. "He's been on the estate, watching and waiting." She tipped her head to the other side and Devil swore he could feel her assessing things she wasn't even aware she had the senses to assess.

"He wasn't alone. I can smell several others' scents on him. Not just one, so he and the pilot aren't the extent of the team sent out to capture me. But the other scents aren't as strong. He's not been around them in a few days."

Devil gave Graeme a speaking look, to which the other Breed gave a quick nod.

He wanted those men, each and every one of them. He'd send a message to whoever had sent them out. Kate was his, and the Devil did not tolerate anyone at any time striking against what belonged to him.

Moving to her side, Devil watched her face then, seeing the frown that creased her brow and the look of confusion that filled her gaze. Bending down as well, he drew in the scents that covered the male and tried to find what was confusing her.

As she said, the soldier was working with at least two others. Their scents were too much a part of the soldier, yet not strong enough to indicate that he'd been in their presence for several days. They were likely awaiting him somewhere with transportation to spirit Kate out of the States and back to Europe.

He had definitely been on the estate for several days. The land around them held a unique scent, just as all places did. A combination of the ground, the movement on it and the plants that grew within it. The scent he carried was definitely that of the grounds within the secured stone wall Lobo had erected around four acres that the house sat in the center of.

Then, he found the scent confusing her. It was subtle, so subtle that even he couldn't filter it enough to identify it, but it was definitely one he'd known before. One that was unique, and teased his senses as one well known.

Known to not just Kate, evidently, but to himself as well.

"Have you figured it out yet?" she asked him softly.

He shook his head. "It's too weak."

She nodded, then slowly rose to her feet and moved back as Lobo took her place.

If the scent was well known to Devil, then it was possible, highly possible, it was known to Lobo as well.

"Familiar," Lobo muttered. "But I can't get enough of it to identify it."

"My problem as well." Devil grimaced before rising and moving to Kate.

His arm went around her possessively, drawing her to his side as he turned to Graeme and gave the other man a nod.

Flicking his fingers to the Breeds behind him, Graeme moved aside to allow them to haul the soldier to his feet as he groaned weakly.

"Lock him in the cells," Graeme ordered harshly. "I'll be in later to question him."

The cells were just as stated. Iron cells, secure and impossible to escape once locked. They were buried beneath the stables with only one way in and only one way out. Once they had him down there, he was at their mercy. And Devil knew there was little, if any, mercy in Graeme for anyone besides himself.

Graeme knew loyalty. He understood compassion. Mercy to the enemy was something else entirely. That didn't exist in Graeme's little world. And he sure as hell didn't apologize for it.

"Call Da, let him know he's here."

Devil looked down at her, then back to Graeme, and read the other Breed's instinctive rejection of the request.

Well, not a request exactly, Devil admitted with a small grain of amusement.

"I'll call him personally." It was Lobo who agreed to the demand voiced at the last minute, as a request, Devil thought as he hid his smile and nodded to the man he'd followed since his liberation from the Council lab.

"Lilith, get Jonas out here. Now." Lobo turned to the small female Breed who had entered the room silently.

Lobo's personal assistant was a quiet, submissive little Wolf Breed who always seemed rather painfully shy.

Pushing a pair of glasses up her nose, Lilith made a quick note on the small electronic pad she carried.

"And I want a team together now! By God I want to know where that bastard was hiding and why he wasn't detected before he got into my fucking house." He stared around the room then, his face darkening. "And find my fucking stepdaughter now."

The throttled fury that lit his voice had everyone moving. Only Kate remained in place, her hold on Devil's arm tightening as he moved to search for Khileen.

"She's in her room," she stated softly, though Lobo clearly heard her.

He turned back to her slowly. "How do you know where she is? Even I can't catch her scent from that distance."

Kate grimaced then before a small smile tugged at her lips.

"I kind of put this in before leaving the bathroom." She removed the small earbud communication device with a slight shrug. "She just woke up from her nap and activated her side. Give her a minute to figure out something's going on—"

"Oh my God! And you let me sleep through it? You fucking bitch!" Khileen screeched across the line.

A second later her bedroom door slammed farther up the hall as she came racing to Kate's room.

She came to a full stop at the doorway, eyes wide, shocked, looking around as though searching for some remnants of whatever she missed.

Then her gaze lit on Kate with Devil's arm wrapped around her. It dropped to her friend's neck, her lips parting, eyes narrowing.

"So fucking not fair," she muttered then.

"Your language is deteriorating, Khi," Lobo chastised her gently, warningly.

"Yeah, well the Big Bad Wolf's not exactly here," she grumbled before turning back to Kate and shaking her head in disappointment. "So not fair, Katie," she repeated. "You were supposed to tell me if it happened."

"It happened." The laughter in Kate's voice had Devil wanting to smile.

He swore he could feel something akin to, or perhaps far surpassing, happiness, as it exploded inside him.

Kate's arm tightened around his back as the other moved to circle his hips and hug him close.

"Bitch," Khileen sighed again before giving Lobo a defiant look.

"While I have you here, could you please do something about the acoustics in this damned place. If it happens outside my bedroom, then it may as well not even be happening," she accused him with no small amount of anger. "And I simply don't like it."

She turned and stalked back to her room. Evidently, this time, she left the door open.

Lobo shook his head. "One of these days, remind me to kill Tiberian. Slowly," he muttered of his brother. "Very slowly."

He left the room, throwing his hand up in a silent farewell and heading, Devil knew, for the cells.

Where he was heading himself.

Turning to his mate and lifting her chin with his fingers, he placed a quick kiss to her waiting lips. "I won't be long," he promised.

"Better not be," she warned him. "Because I think I want to bite you again."

He paused, turning back to her quickly, hunger gleaming in his gaze as Kate stared up at him with definite interest.

"One hour," he promised.

"You have forty-five minutes," she decided.

His gaze narrowed.

"Want to try for forty?"

A manly grunt and a snarl, and he was quickly striding from the room, definitely intent on making the most of his forty minutes.

Which was forty minutes longer than she should have had to wait, she decided with a smile as she stared around the destruction littering her bedroom floor. Ah well, it would give her time to move into his bedroom. She liked it better anyway.

EIGHT

There wasn't much left of the human to question.

The Breed known as Graeme stared down at the bloodied face, split lips, the swollen eyes, and had to force himself not to rip the bastard's head off.

But, he had the information he wanted.

He'd had the information he wanted hours ago though. It had really taken no more than flexing the feline claws his nails became and raking the sharpened tips, normally hidden in a groove at the top of his finger, over the man's chest. There were now four bloody furrows that would need stitches soon.

If Graeme decided to allow him to live longer.

The pilot wasn't in much better shape, though he'd had less information. A fly-by-night pilot that hired his services out for a paltry amount, considering the risk he'd taken this time.

This one, he'd simply turn over to the Bureau of Breed Affairs agent being sent to collect him.

The other, Graeme wanted to keep just a while longer. He had a feeling his friends might come looking for him. Sometimes there was a sense of loyalty among humans that made men do stupid things. Things like attempting to rescue friends who had made decidedly poor choices.

Besides, Devil's woman wanted certain information for her father. Information Lobo Reever wouldn't mind having as well. There were several questions regarding his wife's death that had yet to be answered. Questions he knew the Wolf Breed needed before bringing his brother, Tiberian, back to the States.

Until then, he could simply have fun and take his aggressions out on the human for a while. After all, a Breed that had been driven slowly insane over the years, only to find that sanity rather abruptly once again, needed something to amuse himself with until he had his own plans in place.

"Just kill me," the soldier pleaded as he struggled to open eyes swollen shut. "Please just kill me."

The stench of the man's urine, spilled in weakening terror, offended Graeme's senses.

"Do you deserve to die?" he asked, flexing then retracting his claws as he fought to keep from giving him exactly what he was begging for. "I don't think you deserve to die yet. You haven't given me enough information to pay for such mercy."

The soldier whimpered as Graeme rolled his eyes in disgust.

Reaching up to rub at his jaw thoughtfully, he pulled back at the last second with a grimace. The last thing he needed was to risk messing up the disguise he'd created. He couldn't afford to allow his identity to be revealed just yet.

He needed just a little more time before he could shed the Graeme appearance and return to claim what was his.

"I don't know anything more." The soldier disturbed Graeme's thoughts as he sobbed the declaration. "I swear, I don't know anything more."

Graeme grunted at the vow. "You stink of a liar."

Cutting the ropes that bound him to the chair, he dragged the moaning soldier to a cell and tossed him to the cot on the floor. Agony resounded in the human's moans as he lay completely still.

Maybe he'd cracked a rib, Graeme decided in unconcern. He'd mention it to the medic he'd requested to check the bastard out.

"I was merciful," he told the man as he locked the cell doors. "Ever been skinned alive? Or dissected alive? I could show you how it feels if you'd like. I know exactly how it's done."

And how it felt. How it ripped through the mind because the drugs refused to allow mercy and kept the subject conscious. What it felt like to have some bastard handle his guts with uncaring hands—

He forced the memory back as the killing rage and dark insanity tempted the animal instincts that were far too close to the surface.

The soldier had pissed himself again.

"Damn, son, at least I held my water until they actually began slicing me open," he muttered. "Show a little courage why don't you."

He'd have fared far better had he not screamed like a little girl as Graeme flashed the wicked canines at the side of his mouth in a vicious snarl no more than an inch from his face.

"Medic will be here in a bit," he called back. "We'll get you something to eat later, a drink maybe. Then we'll see what your skin looks like hanging on the wall to dry."

Hell, how much water was the bastard's kidneys holding anyway? If he pissed himself much more, then he was going to dehydrate for sure.

"Graeme, stop terrorizing the prisoner," Lobo ordered as Graeme stepped into the control room and locked the door behind him.

"Boss." Graeme nodded. "Surprised to see you here."

Hell, this fucking Wolf was like a ghost or something. He was one of the few men that could slip into the control room and watch him without Graeme sensing his presence.

"Yes, I would imagine you are," Lobo answered, his hooded gaze watching him carefully. "You know, the Bureau of Breed Affairs has an APB out on a Bengal Breed that was once dissected and skinned alive. Wouldn't know anything about that, would you?"

Graeme blinked back at him in surprise. "I don't know about the Bengal part, but I could produce a Lion Breed that's been up close and personal with it," he grunted, biting back his fury. "Fuckers damned near drove me crazy."

They had stolen his mind. Hell, they might have stolen his soul.

"Still claiming Lion status are you?" Lobo questioned lazily.

"Registered and everything," Graeme growled back at him. "Do you have a problem with me, boss?"

"No, no problem at all." Lobo shook his head. "But, perhaps you have a problem with me."

That one stopped him.

"What kind of problem?" Graeme asked carefully, allowing his suspicion to show rather than hiding it behind a wall of stoicism as he would have before coming to the Reever lands.

"A problem concerning my loyalty to those who give me theirs," he stated softly. "You've proven yourself more than once, and I've expressed several times that loyalty goes both ways here. I'm not a man you have to lie to, unless you're out to deceive me."

"I'll spread the word, boss." Graeme nodded, staring back at Reever as though uncertain where he was going with the chastisement. "I'll assure each of them, of my own personal belief that you mean every word you're saying too."

Yeah, right. This man and Jonas Wyatt were rumored to be

thick as fucking thieves. And Wyatt was overturning every fucking stone in New Mexico searching for the Bengal he had that APB on. That would be one stupid fucker if he trusted Lobo with his identity.

Lobo's lips quirked in amusement. "You do that, Graeme," he murmured. "You do that." Then he turned back to the security glass and stared at the prisoner as he crossed his arms over his chest and stroked his jaw thoughtfully. "Have you called the medic?"

"Yep. He'll be here soon." Graeme leaned against the wall, his lips curling in amusement as he glanced at the prisoner himself. "I think he's going to need rehydration soon though. The bastard keeps pissing himself."

Lobo grunted at that. "Coward."

"Now, boss, maybe he just doesn't have very strong kidneys, ya know? What do they call that? Inconsistency or some shit?"

"Incontinence," Lobo snorted.

"Or something." He shrugged. "I'll have the medic strap an IV to his ass and rehydrate him so we can help him relieve himself again."

"We're keeping him?" Lobo asked, neither agreeing nor disagreeing with Graeme's intent.

"Why not," Graeme drawled. "The boy has friends. Long-association-type friends. Those kinds of friends come looking for you when you're missing."

"Loyalty," Lobo murmured then, still staring at the prisoner.

"Stupidity," Graeme retorted. "But, I can work with that kind of stupidity if given a chance."

Lobo nodded. "Very well, see what you can do with it. You have three days to draw his friends out, then I want him stitched up, patched up and ready to fly out to Haven to appear before the Wolf Breed Tribunal for sentencing. He struck against a Wolf Breed and conspired to kidnap one to turn her over to research. That's a capital offense and only the Tribunal can sentence him for it."

"Only if he survives the transfer." Graeme smiled coldly. "Stupid bastards like that try to escape, get killed and save the Tribunal hours of needless debate and months of protests by humans."

Lobo chuckled at that. "Yeah, but hell, they like their little amusements as well." The look he gave Graeme was one he assumed brooked no refusal.

Graeme let him keep thinking that. For the moment.

"Gotcha, save him for Tribunal amusement. Check." He tipped his fingers to his forehead in a careless salute.

"And you let me know if that Bengal with the APB out on him needs a friend," Lobo reminded him as he turned to leave. "I make a hell of a friend, Graeme. A bad enemy to make, but a hell of a friend."

With one last glance over his shoulder, Lobo left the room and closed the door behind him.

Whew.

Now that was what a Breed could consider a damned good close call.

Especially a Breed with an APB out on his ass and a Bureau director determined to reel him in like a fish on a hook.

Graeme had never considered himself reelable. Or hookable.

He grinned at the image before taking his seat and releasing the electronic lock to the door the medic used to access the cells.

"Be careful of that one, Doc," he spoke into the mic as the medic made his way across the cement floor. "He likes to water his cot a bit."

"You terrorizing the prisoners again, Graeme?" the Breed chuckled.

It wasn't their first prisoner, or the first one Graeme had caused to piss himself.

"It's getting too damned easy to do it, Doc," he answered. "We need to find prisoners made of sterner stuff. Why don't you put out a memo to all those weak-assed soldiers the Council keeps sending. We need someone tougher to play with."

"Right. Memo. Send sterner stuff," the medic laughed as Graeme opened the cell and watched the medic and two Wolf Breed guards enter the barred enclosure.

"Yeah," Graeme murmured. "Send sterner stuff. At least give me a fucking challenge."

He snorted at that.

That wasn't possible. It wasn't possible because the best they'd had to offer at any given time had already had their playdates with him. He was alive, they were dead. Every last one of them.

Screams echoed in his head, agony sliced through his veins. A scream of rage built in his throat as the memories surged through his head and tempted the beast he'd managed to chain.

His claws flexed and his body tensed to jump from the chair as the insane rage that had festered in him for so many years threatened to slip free once again.

At the last second, he managed one last rational thought.

His lifeline.

Gentle eyes. The scent of moonlight and shy laughter.

"Who are you?" she whispered, her head tilting to the side as the colors of the desert shaded her head and brushed across her shoulders in the silken strands. "If you're here to kill me, why not just do it and get it over with."

Oh, he was there to kill her.

The animal could taste her blood, salivated for it as the insanity the man lived within relished the moment.

"What makes you think I'm here to kill you? Can't I enjoy the night as well? Besides, I was here first. You're the one that found me, not the other way around."

He felt her surprise. Hell, it was no less than his own. He imagined the animal snarled at him in complete shock, questioning the seemingly rational tone of voice he used.

"Did I find you?" She smiled. Right there, staring into the shadows where he hid, the faintest little smile as her arms relaxed just a bit where they were crossed over her breasts.

"What do you call it?" he asked her as he leaned against the rough stone of the cliff at his side. "I was standing here minding my own business when you sneaked up on me. I call that finding me."

What the hell was happening to him?

He could smell her, he knew her for who she was rather than who others thought her to be. Her scent was just as sweet as it had ever been, unmarred by the filth of male possession or the acrid stink of lies and deceptions.

There was just the smell of the woman, the moonlight, regret, a hint of fear, and perhaps, hell, there was the faintest scent of weariness and desire.

She shook her head, her confusion scenting the air between them. "I didn't even know you were here. I used to come out here all the time just to enjoy the night."

"So why did you stop? Better yet, why return the minute I decided to enjoy the view here? Maybe I should be scared of you." How the hell was he so calm? How had he managed to remember what it was like to tease her so gently and watch that shy pleasure as it began to warm her gaze?

"Yeah, I'm really scary." She rolled her eyes at the thought, her expression betraying her belief that nothing could be further from the truth.

"You could be some kind of assassin. One of those seductresses the Genetics Council sends out to lure innocent male Breeds back to the labs," he pointed out.

She tipped her head to the side and watched his shadow in interest now.

"No." She shook her head. "Not a seductress."

He had her complete attention. It was focused entirely on him and the subtle scent of feminine attraction mixed with something deeper, something stronger that he knew he should recognize but couldn't.

"Hmm, assassin then?" He let her see a grin, a teasing curve of his lips as he shifted just enough to allow the moonlight to reveal it while keeping the rest of his face hidden. "Are you here to kill me? I'm just a helpless Breed slipping away for a few hours before I have to save the world again."

That was what Rule Breaker had muttered that morning as he strode through the predawn light to join the team heading into the desert for patrol: Out to save the fucking world again. Give me a break.

"I'm definitely no assassin," she promised him, that shy little smile teasing him again. "I'm just a secretary that enjoys the night. A chance meeting in the dark, never to be repeated."

"Never?" The thought of that had forced the animal to step back another pace and allow one more inch of sanity to curl about its neck in restraint. "Don't tell me that, you may break my heart."

"I'm no heartbreaker either," she sighed, stepping back. "I better go."

"Promise you'll come back." Go? She was leaving him alone? Again?

The animal strained against the bonds that were far too weak to hold it if it became insistent.

She paused. "I shouldn't come back."

But she wanted to. He could feel it. Taste it on the air around them.

"I'll be here tomorrow," he promised. "Just for a few minutes. I promise. Just to talk a minute. I won't keep you long."

He should be pouncing on her. He should be tasting her terror and her blood as she stared into his eyes and realized she was about to pay for her crimes. Pay for the hell she'd sent him to.

She looked out at the darkened landscape for long moments before giving a resigned little sigh.

"What the hell," she finally breathed out wearily. "It beats the nightmares."

She turned and moved away from him, a slight shadow amid the darkness, blending with it for a moment before stepping into the moonlight once again and returning to the safety of the house and the protection of the Breeds she'd slipped away from.

It beat the nightmares.

She had no idea, he realized. Just as the other hadn't known the past that endangered her, neither did this one.

The only thing left of the person she had been was that slight scent of shy, hungry need. Not a sexual need, at least, not then, all those years ago. But a need for warmth, for caring.

Everything else had changed, and he suddenly wanted to know why.

Why was the girl she had been so overshadowed that even her scent had been altered in ways?

And what was that fucking taste—

It hit him then.

Just enough rational thought had filtered through the fury and insanity to drag the animal back long enough for him to make sense of a lifetime of hell.

Her blood had saved his life, but it had turned him into an enraged animal.

When the soldiers had caught him again, that added quality in his blood had spurred them into experiments so horrendous it had broken what little sanity he'd still possessed.

It had been the blood that had transfused him.

The scent of what the Breeds called mating heat, the taste of it in his mouth, the small glands swelling beneath his tongue each time he came near her.

This was why finding her had driven him that last short step into insanity.

She was his mate and he had finally found her.

That didn't mean she didn't have to pay for running from him.

It didn't mean Judd wouldn't pay for helping her.

It didn't mean he was sane by any stretch of the imagination.

But with her, he might have a shot at finding his sanity.

At least enough of it to claim what was his.

He's stitched up, Graeme," the medic announced as he left the cell, the guards with him securing the locks as Graeme reached out and secured the electronic safeguards as well.

"Thanks, Doc." Graeme cleared his throat as he pushed back the memories. "I'll try to keep him nice and quiet while his scratches heal."

The medic laughed as he and the guards left the cells and left Graeme to his thoughts.

His fantasies.

NINE

Two weeks later

Devil Black, shame is thy middle name," Kate laughed in merriment as she stalked into the bedroom, closing the door loudly behind her before locking it securely and facing the Breed that had stolen her heart with merciless intent. Mating heat may have begun it, but his heart had completed it.

"Council didn't give us middle names, darlin'," he reminded her as he lounged back on their bed, the hard, corded strength of his naked body displayed to her hungry gaze. "They concentrated their talents on a few more important aspects instead."

Broad, lean, his hand lowered, long fingers circling the engorged width of his cock.

Ah yes, she had to admit, some enterprising scientist had definitely shown a bit of imagination in programming the DNA of certain aspects of the Wolf Breed's male form.

Tall, lean and powerful, savagely hewn features emphasized by the unusual amber-striated black eyes and thick lashes.

She couldn't look at him and not want him.

He was the embodiment of her teenage fantasy, and now he was the lover who never failed to send her flying into ecstasy.

Toeing her sandals slowly from her feet, her fingers flipped the button holding her skirt at her hips. Chiffon and silk slid down her thighs, over her legs to pool carelessly at her feet as she stepped over it.

As a growl rumbled in his chest, Kate moved slowly closer, wearing only white silk bikini panties and the snug black cami covering her breasts.

Braless, she could feel the sensitive, hard tips of her nipples rasping against the fabric, creating a heated ache impossible to ignore for long.

Between her thighs her clit swelled and pulsed in demand, the slick essence of feminine need coating the bare folds of her pussy and dampening her panties as she drew closer to him.

The amber flared in his gaze brighter, hotter as her hand lifted, fingers stroking against the flesh bared between the elastic band of her panties and the hem of the top where it ended just below her navel.

Mating heat was a flame that refused to allow them apart for long, but it was also a key to emotions that a hardened, battle-scarred Breed might never have allowed free. The key to a sensuality that a wary, uncertain Breed female may have fought, at least for a while.

Now, there was no fighting, no hiding, no denying.

Bracing her knee on the mattress, her palms flat against the blankets, Kate lifted herself to the bed, crawling slowly between those long, powerful legs to the male awaiting her.

Watching her move to him, sensuality washing over her expression, flushing her face, tightening her breasts, her nipples, sending the sweet scent of her need to fill his senses.

Long, silken curls fell around her like twining spirals of flames as her green eyes gleamed with emerald hunger between long, sun-kissed lashes.

Damn, his balls were tight, the engorged length of his cock throbbing with steadily increasing hunger as she bypassed it only to straddle his thighs. The silk of her panties, heated and damp from the arousal building in her, pressed against the iron-hard length as her lips brushed against his.

With each passing second the heat building between them rose, overwhelming their senses as the need to touch, to taste, became imperative.

His fingers speared into the curls at the back of her head, holding her in place as his lips covered hers, his tongue licking against them, parting them until she met his kiss with a fiery heat of her own.

Spicy and sweet, the mating hormone spilling from the tiny glands beneath their tongues sent their pulses racing as the need amplified and surged through their systems.

Devil couldn't imagine a high greater than this. The pleasure of his mate's kiss, her touch, the hunger and need rising between them like hungry flames licking at their flesh.

Hooking his fingers into the elastic at her hips, it was incredibly easy to snap the stretchy lace from the silk and remove them entirely.

The feel of her flesh, slick and hot against the engorged length of his dick, had every muscle in his body tensing, tightening in a need so primal it was impossible to deny.

Holding her lips to his with his hand behind her head as he wrapped his free arm around her rear to lift her in place, he couldn't hold back the desperate growl that rumbled from his throat.

He loved to have her ride him. Loved watching her, feeling her take him. But the primal instincts tearing through him now were impossible to deny.

* * *

"Dev," Kate protested the suddenly cessation of his kiss as her eyes widened, surprise flaring through her as he suddenly lifted her from his body.

"What—?"

Before she could do more than gasp the question, he had her on her knees, one big hand pressing her shoulders down as he came behind her.

Catching herself on her elbows and swiping her hair back from her eyes, she was suddenly confronted with her own image in the full-length mirror against the wall. Bent before her mate, his hands gripping her hips, lifting her into place as he removed one hand to grip his fierce erection.

She watched him, watched as his gaze narrowed on the point where their bodies met, and felt the wide crest part the swollen lips of her pussy.

That first pulse of silky pre-seminal fluid shot inside her, the unique hormones contained within it instantly sinking, stroking against her flesh and awakening sensations she wouldn't have known otherwise.

His head fell back as he pressed the flared head inside the clenched entrance until it was lodged fully inside the milking flesh of her vagina.

The next spurt had a moan falling from her lips as she felt his cock head flex, felt the heat of the release inside her. Because she knew within seconds what would happen.

That rush of sharp, fiery sensation as her pussy clenched tight and hard, an involuntary response to the stimulation of the hormones spilling inside her. The sweeping fire clenching her womb, spasming through it with a pleasure-pain that dragged a broken cry from her lips.

A heartbeat later, as tightly as her flesh was gripped around him, flexing and milking the heavy length deeper still, her pussy wept for more. The silky slide of her juices mixed with the next hot spurt of fluid to increase the spikes of building sensation as he pushed deeper inside her.

It was agonizing pleasure, the sweetest pain she could imagine. With each shallow thrust of his hips, each backward glide of the thick erection, the sensations only mounted. And Kate couldn't help but watch. Just as he watched the penetration of her body.

"Fuck. So good," he growled, his chest heaving as a trickle of perspiration eased down his temple.

Lifting his now amber gaze, the burning flames that lit the depths dragged a sharp breath of surprise from her.

"So sweet, Kate," he growled, his gaze moving to where he was pumping in shallow thrusts, his hips moving rhythmically as he fucked deeper, deeper inside her with each movement until in one final surge, he was buried to the hilt.

A final spurt of fluid shot against her inner walls, the thick head pulsing with the release, caressing the sensitive flesh he filled so fully.

"Dev, please." The desperate cry wailed from her lips as he held her hips in place, refusing to allow her to thrust back against him, to work him inside her until the sharp bursts of painful pleasure eased.

"Let me feel it," he groaned. "The feel of your sweet pussy gripping me so tight and hot. Fuck, Kate, it's like fucking electricity surrounding my cock."

She whimpered at the pleasure that filled his voice as the little bursts of sensation continued to flare through her pussy.

Pleasure and pain.

And it didn't end. It wouldn't end until he began moving. Until the broad length of his cock was shafting hard and deep inside her.

Until then, the fluid he'd pumped inside her would keep clenching and tightening her flesh while spikes of pleasure demanded more of her heated juices to spill inside her and ease the ecstatic torture.

"Please, Dev." Breathless, riding a wave of sensation so powerful it was stealing her breath, Kate pleaded with him to ease the clenching demand building between her thighs.

Her clit was throbbing, pulsing in time to each rippling shudder that worked through her pussy, until in desperation she lowered her hand between her thighs, her fingers finding the nerve-rich center and rubbing it with quickening strokes of her fingers.

"Yeah, play with that pretty clit," he crooned, coming over her, his knees bracing hers apart, his hips moving just enough to cause the head of his cock to stroke the inner muscles, just enough to send screaming shards of pleasure to race through her nerve endings.

"Let me feel you come like this," he demanded, his gaze meeting hers in the mirror. "Let me feel that hot little pussy tighten, mate. Milk my cock, sweetheart. Suck my release straight out of my—"

A harsh groan filled her ears as his lips moved to the mating mark at her neck.

Because she was tightening around him. Impossibly tight in long, rippling contractions as the clitoral stimulation began electrifying her senses, pushing her closer, driving her harder.

Inside the heat channel, Devil worked the head of his cock, stroking hidden nerve centers as the broad shaft stretched her, seared her flesh. The pulsing throb of his erection stroked each inch of flesh it stretched, burning against the shuddering and clenching muscles wrapped around it.

Her fingers moved faster, a whimpering cry leaving her lips as he found a nipple with the fingers of one hand and gripped the tight point erotically, pulling at it, applying just enough pressure—

Oh God, she was so close.

A sizzle of brutal sensation shot from her nipple to her clit. Her pussy tightened again, clenched, as his hips moved against her rear, faster, the tiny thrusts stroking, rubbing until in one blinding second she spiraled into an ecstasy that consumed her soul.

She screamed as she felt the first spurt of his release jetting inside her. In the next heartbeat, the thickening in his cock locked him in place as his hips began to move against her, tugging at the grip her flesh had on him with each convulsive spurt of his seed inside her.

It was like flying through pure, rich sensation. All she could do was feel the sharp spikes of pleasure driving into not just her body, but also her soul. It wrung a desperate cry from her throat as his teeth pierced the mating mark once again, his tongue licking against it to ease any pain, and filling it with heat and pleasure instead.

Gasping, shuddering with each explosive starburst erupting inside her, she prayed it never ended, but she knew she wouldn't survive if it wasn't over soon.

"I love you, Kate," he suddenly groaned at her ear. "God help me, mate, I'll love you past death."

He loved her.

In the two weeks since the flames of mating heat had wrapped them together, he hadn't spoke the words. She'd given him her love, whispered it nightly, but never with expectation.

She had never thought he would love her. They were mated. He was a man of realism, of practicality. Love wouldn't fit into the life he saw before him.

But he'd placed love in it.

Holding her close, his release filling her as she gave a final shudder of pleasure, he whispered the words again.

"I love you, mate."

"I love you, mate," she whispered in return. "Forever."

* * *

Holding her close, his face buried against her neck, his body shuddering in the aftermath of pure rapture, Devil felt that final barrier inside his soul give way beneath the emotions pounding against it.

He loved her.

With all his heart, with his scarred soul and the darkness that would likely too often return, he loved her.

And he deserved her.

By God, he deserved this woman, this tiny, Irish flame that had burned through his resistance and stolen his heart.

Just as it was whispered around the estate and in the outlying towns. She was the Devil's due.

The Devil's soul.

And every dream he'd ever known.

THE CURSE OF THE BLACK SWAN

A League of the Black Swan Novella

ALYSSA DAY

This is for everyone who knows the pain of losing a parent.
Dad, you left us far too soon.
I hope somebody up there told you
that I've made my writing dreams come true.

Also, thank you to awesome reader
Jen Cash-Cook for Brynn's name.

THE CURSE OF THE BLACK SWAN

A thousand years ago, on the edge of the Fae lands, a beautiful young peasant woman was bathing in a stream, singing a song of gratitude for the golden sunshine and the magnificent day. However, unlike many who play in the daylight, the girl also sang her thanks to the moon, who rested in diurnal slumber and yet heard the lilting melody of the girl's voice and was pleased.

But others with darker purpose heard the girl's wondrous song, too. The king of the land, a cold, hard man who beat his hounds, his children, and his wife with equal fervor, followed the melody to the stream and found the girl, innocent and glorious in her nudity, and he determined to attack her with his rapacious lust.

The girl pleaded with the barbarian king, which availed her nothing. So then she ran, and she fought, as her father the woodsman had taught her, and she managed to keep the king at bay until the sun dipped below twilight's horizon, when her strength finally gave out. The king, enraged by her defiance, stabbed her through the heart and left her to die. As the girl bled to death on the bank of the silvery stream, the night wind whispered in her ear that the moon, who had appreciated the gift of the girl's song, had taken pity on her.

"I will save you from this king, but you must agree never to leave me, and to become a black swan and sing to me every third night for the rest of your life, and swear also that your daughters and their daughters will continue to fulfill this promise."

The girl, who had lost all hope as her blood pooled near her body and then slipped into the moonlit stream, parted her lips, barely able to speak. "And if I agree, will this gift—this curse—never end?"

The moon reigned alone over the dark night, and thus had her own measure of cruelty, but she knew well that mortals needed the promise of hope to survive, and so she offered this version of the truth in return:

"You and each generation's eldest daughter will be released from your vow when you meet your one true love and bear him a daughter."

The girl's tears flowed as her blood had done mere moments before, when she agreed, and the moon caused a magnificent fountain to appear on that very spot. In the center of the fountain, a perfect black marble statue of the beautiful young woman, one hand held out to a swan, now stood as eternal monument to the vow.

From that day until this one, a black swan swims in the fountain and sings her songs of loss and longing every third night, while the moon smiles her icy smile. This woman who is also a swan plots and plans for how to avoid falling in love and how to never, ever bear a daughter who would be forced to carry the curse. But the moon's pull is strong, and she is determined not to lose the lovely swan song, so these plans have never succeeded.

Not yet.

ONE

Bordertown, a place where the Fae, demon, and human worlds intersect, hidden in the heart of New York

Sean O'Malley ran into the burning building, dodging and weaving around the rest of his colleagues who were running and limping out of the inferno before it exploded or completely collapsed, either of which was due to happen any minute.

"O'Malley, get your ass back here," his boss, the new Bordertown fire chief, shouted.

Sean ignored him, just as he'd ignored the previous fire chief. He'd heard something in that building. Maybe it was only a cat, and no matter how much it tore him up inside when he found evidence that a helpless animal had lost its life in a fire, he knew the rules: Firefighters didn't risk their lives for pets. Not that he usually gave a rat's ass for rules, and he'd certainly bent a few to save pets in the past. They all had.

But it hadn't sounded like a cat. It had sounded like a baby.

Zach, the closest thing to a friend Sean had on the crew, planted himself in front of Sean, blocking his path to the door.

"Not this time," Zach shouted.

They had to be loud to be heard over the roar of the flames that were greedily consuming the old building. Too much rotten wood, too little upkeep—it would be easy to blame that, if this hadn't been the fourth building in as many nights hit in exactly the same way. They had a serial arsonist on their hands.

"I heard a baby. Get out of my way, or I'll go through you," Sean said, deadly calm and deadly serious.

He didn't have time to delay. There was no way he was taking a chance on giving up on a baby who needed him. Not now and not ever—not *ever*, but especially not today, after his mom's bombshell.

Zach was a couple of inches over six feet tall, but Sean was bigger by a few inches and probably by forty pounds of muscle, not to mention his extra abilities. Zach didn't hesitate; he moved out of Sean's way, fast, as soon as he heard the word *baby*. None of them understood how Sean could hear things that nobody else could, but they knew it was true. Enhanced hearing was one of his super powers, they liked to joke.

They also all knew that he could withstand temperatures that would have fried most of them alive. They didn't joke about that one. He'd caught more than one of his colleagues watching him warily after they'd fought fires, their expressions similar to how he imagined he'd watch a feral wolf. They weren't all that far off.

They knew he was different, but they didn't know *how* different. Sean didn't tell *anybody* he was half fire demon. Life was easier that way. Even in Bordertown, where demons were as common as low-caste Fae or shady humans, fire demons were considered to be the worst of the worst: crazed berserkers and the most terrifying of predators. His abilities already isolated him enough from the rest of the tightly knit crew. He didn't need to add to it.

All of this ran through his mind in the few seconds it took for him to hit the building doorway running. He burst into the conflagration, head down and racing for the spot where the sound had originated. Second floor, to the left. He barely paused at the staircase, but the view was enough to make a sane man flinch. A roaring wall of orange-red flame screamed toward him, and the heat knocked him back a couple of steps. His skin felt the heat, even under his suit, and when the fabric started to melt off his body, he discovered that his protective gear wasn't rated anywhere near high enough.

Whatever accelerant the arsonist had used wasn't purely chemical; no way would a normal fire be burning that hot. Magic was involved here. In fact, it would take *black* magic to push a fire to these levels. Sean could feel his eyes flaring as his pupils contracted, and he knew that anybody watching him would see the irises turn deep blood orange in color and start to glow.

Sean analyzed the situation for options, but the stairs were the only way up; no matter that the stairwell was a tunnel of flame and probably going to explode any minute. He took them four at a time, barely clearing the last one before the explosion hit and the stairs collapsed into a burning mass of tinder. He glanced back at the fiery pit at the bottom of the stairwell and grimaced, and a falling chunk of ceiling smashed down on his helmet, nearly knocking him on his ass.

He stood there, head ringing and skull vibrating, and realized that one of these days he was going to kill himself trying to act like a big damn hero.

But not today.

The sound came again, and he still wasn't sure. Wounded animals sometimes sounded a lot like babies. It could go either way. But he'd come this far, and he'd be damned if he'd leave anybody behind. He took the first door across the hall to the left, unerringly finding the source of the sound. The front room of the apartment, cheaply furnished but neat and tidy, was only beginning to burn, and he had a moment to hope that the bedrooms were in good shape before he hit the closed inner door running. Two seconds later, about a hundred pounds of shaggy black fur smashed into his chest.

Sean barely stayed on his feet. There had been a lot of power behind that furry projectile. The beast hit the floor and immediately clamped its powerful jaws around Sean's ankle and pulled, hard. The pink collar on her neck proclaimed that the creature was named Petunia.

"Okay, Petunia, hang on," Sean said, using his most soothing voice, but the dog's whining increased in both pitch and volume, and she pulled even harder, trying to move Sean over to the corner of the room.

There was a crib, or bassinette, or whatever the hell people called the small, lace-draped wooden cradle tucked against the corner of the room. He heard the crying again, and it was definitely coming from the crib.

"I got him, girl," Sean told Petunia.

She seemed to understand, since she let go of Sean's ankle immediately and stood there, panting and making deep coughing noises. Smoke inhalation could damage dogs' lungs, too, and Sean made a mental note to have the dog looked at when they got out of there. A crash sounded in the apartment's front room, and he amended the thought.

If they got out of there.

The baby turned her startled, reddened eyes up to Sean in the instant before he swept her into his arms, and then she waved one pink-pajama'd arm at him and gurgled.

"We're out of here, princess," he told her, and then he picked up the room's only chair, a wooden rocking chair, and hurled it at the window while shielding the infant.

The glass shattered outward, as planned, and Sean crossed the room and looked out. A jump from the second story was an easy one for him to make with fire-demon strength, especially only carrying a tiny baby instead of a large, screaming adult—which he'd had to do before—so he had this one in the bag.

No sweat.

And then the dog barked, reminding Sean that Petunia was not going to make it out alive on her own. He shook his head, impatient with his stupidity. His mother's news had been blanking out everything else on his mind, and he knew better than most that distraction could be fatal at a time like this.

Sean looked down at the dog's hopeful face, hesitantly wagging tail, and big, brown eyes. Petunia had stayed in that room to protect her precious charge, and she'd even pulled a Lassie on Sean's leg to get him to find the baby.

Screw the rules. There was no way in hell he was going to leave that dog to burn to death.

"You're going to have to trust me, girl," he said, crouching down in front of the dog, but keeping an ear out for the shift in sound that would tell him that the entire apartment was about to collapse. He could somehow feel in his bones that the fire was about to take the whole thing down.

The dog's big eyes looked worried, but she lifted one paw as if to shake, and Sean took that for a *yes*. He lifted her into the arm that wasn't full of baby, took a running leap for the window, and leapt out into the comparatively cool darkness of the autumn night.

Within the next five minutes, he'd reunited the baby with her mother, who'd been missing because she'd run down to the building's laundry room while her child was napping. The exploding water heater had shaken debris loose from the basement's walls and ceiling, and a big chunk of something had hit the woman and knocked her out. Zach had knocked the debris off her and scooped her up, and by the time they roused her to consciousness, the EMTs were administering oxygen to her baby right next to her, so she'd never had to suffer even a moment's fear that her child was dead. Petunia, also wearing an oxygen mask and getting checked out, was frantically trying to wrap her furry body around her entire small family all at once.

"Good job, girl," Sean murmured, tipping a salute to the canine heroine before he moved on.

As always, he wanted to be sure to disappear before the thank-yous started and the media showed up. Bordertown's lead crime reporter, Jax Archer, was a disgraced Fae lordling who just happened to be a living, breathing lie detector, so Sean preferred to stay out of his way. Sean's old fire chief had gone along with his disappearing acts, mostly because Sean worked more hours than anybody else in the department.

The new chief wasn't clued in yet.

"Where the hell do you think you're going?" the chief shouted at him, crossing behind the hoses toward Sean while everyone else, exhausted but on the alert, watched the powerful streams of water battle the raging, magically created fire.

Sean noted that the department's witch had arrived at some point, and he was now adding his efforts to the mix. Good thing, too, because water alone wasn't going to stop that beast.

"Avoiding reporters," Sean said bluntly, too tired and worried to care about playing nice with the new boss, who was turning out to be quite an asshole.

One of the reporters Sean could actually tolerate picked that moment to round the corner behind the truck and, spotting Sean, she headed straight for him, her cameraman racing to keep up with her.

"Pierce Holland, *Bordertown Gazette*," she said unnecessarily, thrusting her microphone in Sean's face.

"I know who you are, Pierce," Sean said, but the reporter kept her game face on.

"You know the drill, O'Malley. Intro for the viewers, all hail the courageous firefighter, et cetera, et cetera," she said, lowering her microphone and grinning while the cameraman checked something on his lens.

"I'm good," the man said.

Instantly, the reporter's smile vanished and she assumed the somber air of Reporter with Serious News, as Sean thought of it. The still-burning flames cast dancing shadows across their little tableau that patterned Holland's face in a harlequin's motley of black and orange, and for a moment Sean's grandmother's voice rang in his head, talking about a goose walking over his grave.

"Do we know what caused tonight's fire? Also, I heard you brought out a baby and a dog after everybody else evacuated, O'Malley. Care to comment?"

The chief, winded and red-faced, rushed up then. A less charitable man might have thought he timed his arrival with the moment the camera turned on. Sean decided he wasn't all that charitable.

"I don't think you've met the new chief, have you, Pierce? He was the one who convinced me to go back in for that baby," Sean said, lying through his teeth. He pounded his boss on the back, only a little too hard. "Excellent instincts, this guy. Going to make a great chief."

The chief's eyes widened, but before either he or Pierce could say another word, Sean smiled at them and ducked behind the truck. By the time his overactive hearing picked up the beginning of the chief's response to the reporter, Sean was a block away and moving fast, stripping off his gear as he walked.

Another couple of blocks, and he made it to Black Swan Fountain Square, his favorite place for relaxation and quiet contemplation in the middle of the night. There wasn't much room in the rest of his life for peace *or* quiet. The family business, O'Malley's Pub, was always full of loud talk, laughter, music, and merriment.

It was enough to piss a man off.

Especially when he was sick with worry about his mother's unexplained "little tests," which had left her drained, weak, and nauseous for more than three weeks now. They knew about her cancer, but when he'd dropped by that afternoon, she'd refused to give him any specifics about the latest issue. So Sean had been having a bad damn day even *before* his fire station had gotten the call that the arsonist had struck again.

He stared blindly at the black marble sculpture of the beautiful young woman and the swan in the center of the fountain, so tired that he didn't pay much attention to the actual *live* swan floating serenely in the water until the second time it came around. When he did notice it, he blinked, and then a flurry of movement in the water boiled up into a cloud of sparkling mist that he hadn't been expecting, Bordertown or no. So he figured he could be excused for rubbing his smoke-wearied eyes when the iridescent shimmer dissipated, and the bird flapping its wings in the swan fountain turned into a beautiful woman.

A beautiful *naked* woman.

Maybe that hit he'd taken to the head had been harder than he'd thought, and now he was hallucinating. Except he didn't have the luxury of that belief for more than a few seconds, because the hallucination started talking to him.

"Really? Are you just going to sit there and stare at me?"

"Well, I was here first, before you turned naked, ah, turned human. I mean, you didn't—"

"Right. Chivalry. Dead. Insert appropriate cliché." She pushed her long masses of dark curls out of her face and stalked over to him, not the least bit embarrassed that she was incredibly and gloriously naked. When she crouched down next to him, his breath got stuck in his lungs in a way that had *nothing* to do with fire but *everything* to do with heat.

She glanced up at him while reaching under the bench with one hand, and some of what he was feeling must have shown on his face, because she grinned.

"Relax, hot stuff. I'm just getting my clothes."

TWO

Brynn raised her backpack to show him she had a purpose under that bench and wasn't trying to pounce on him, and then she walked a few feet away, ducked behind a large flowering bush, and yanked on her clothes. After that, she stopped to hyperventilate a little bit, because he'd seen her transform. Catching her naked wasn't nearly as worrying as catching her turning human, because this was Bordertown, and sometimes people who were different enough found themselves sold on the black market to collectors.

This guy, though, he'd *seen* her, and now she had to wonder why it was that she hadn't noticed him sitting there, when she was usually so very careful, why the moon magic hadn't shielded her from his view, and what the consequences might be. The only clue offering her even a little rational thought was the BTFD fire helmet sitting on top of a pile of what looked like firefighter gear next to him. Even she, self-proclaimed hermit that she was, knew the insignia of the Bordertown Fire Department. Maybe he was one of the good guys.

Or he'd killed and eaten a firefighter and stolen the guy's uniform. Again, this *was* Bordertown.

The man was seriously beautiful. Even in the dim light from the decorative lanterns lining the square, she could see that he was an amazing specimen of sheer male virility. He had long, muscular legs and broad shoulders that tapered down to a narrow waist. He was no poster-perfect model, though. His dark hair was too long, his face was too stern ever to be called pretty, and she could have sworn his eyes had gleamed briefly with a spark of hot orange-gold, but in spite of all of that—or maybe *because* of all of that—she'd felt a bolt of interest that had registered as pure sensation the minute she'd completed her transformation and seen him sitting there.

But he'd seen her as a swan, and that was a problem. She stepped out from behind the bush and stared him down, evaluating which step to take next. None of her options were good. He sat with the perfect stillness of a hawk or a falcon, and like those creatures, he gave off the impression of leashed power that could explode into action in a fraction of a second.

It amused her that she sometimes thought in terms of other avian species, after the early years when she'd rejected everything about the curse. Defiance and stubbornness had sometimes been the only supports underpinning her hold on sanity. Curses did not travel lightly on their victims.

"Maybe we could talk," he ventured.

She realized he'd been careful not to stand, and he wasn't making any gesture or movement that might startle her, and the knowledge calmed her a little more. On the other hand, psychopaths were usually good at luring women in with a false sense of security.

A breeze coming from behind him teased her senses, and she sniffed the air. "Why do you stink like fire?"

He smiled, probably laughing at Brynn and her abrupt question, especially since the firefighter outfit was right there next to him on the bench. Normal people tended to mock her for her lack of social skills, anyway. She was better with animals. They didn't mind her shyness, her long silences, or her general inability to tell the little white lies that oiled the wheels of polite society.

Right. She didn't need another source of pain in her life, even if it happened to come from the hottest guy she'd seen in years. She wheeled around to head out.

"Stay," he said, and the word came out like a command, which freed her from indecision.

Commands were easy to ignore.

She took a step toward home, but out of the corner of her eye, she saw him lift a hand as if reaching out to her.

"Please." His voice was hoarse when he said the word, as if it were one he rarely used, and something about it made her stop when nothing else would have.

She'd been alone for so long, and part of her yearned so desperately to make a connection that it loosened her determination and left her wavering—indecisive and unsure—simply because he'd used the word *please*.

He sighed, and the mere exhalation of air carried more meaning than it should have. It told her that he, too, might be lonely, or at least sad. For some reason, she wanted to know what had caused it. She took a breath of her own and turned, clutching her backpack tightly in her hand as if it contained a weapon with which to defend herself from crazed killers or from an incredibly hot man who carried his sorrow in his deep, dark-chocolate eyes and slumped shoulders.

"I just want to talk," he said, and she could almost taste the richness of his voice.

As a woman who spent every third night singing, she was exquisitely, almost painfully attuned to nuances of tone and pitch. His voice was beautifully low and deep, a calming baritone that stood out from the symphony of cracked altos and drunken sopranos she was forced to endure every third night.

"Look at the swan!"

"Do you think it's lost?"

"Maybe it thinks the statue is its mate!"

If they knew her real story, maybe they'd quit laughing at her. But if people quit laughing, they might begin to pity her, and Brynn knew that would be worse.

"I understand if you want to go. A beautiful woman, alone in the middle of the night with a strange man," he continued, but now he'd sunk his head into his hands, and she could tell he didn't hold out much hope that she'd stay.

She should go. She *should*. Two things stopped her, though: his voice when he'd said please, and the BTFD insignia on the pile of smoke-drenched fabric next to him on the bench. She decided to conclude that he was a firefighter. If he'd killed the original owner of the uniform, there would have been less smoke and more blood.

She thought about that. Gruesome, but her logic seemed pretty sound, so she dropped down to sit on the end of his bench. "What was on fire?"

He glanced up, clearly surprised that she'd decided to stay. A glimmer of a smile crossed his face, and it transformed his face from ruggedly handsome to startlingly dark beauty. She realized that if he ever flashed a *real* smile at her, her legs might collapse out from under her. Before she could even suspect him of flirtation, sadness dropped back over his features like a dark cloak, and she realized that seduction was the last thing on his mind.

"An apartment building over by Ancient City Antiques," he said.

Brynn's heart jumped into her throat. Too much of Bordertown was built out of wood, and too much of it had been around since the 1800s. Fire in an apartment building would be devastating.

"Did—did everyone get out?"

"This time. But what about next time? We can't seem to catch him." He clenched his jaw so hard, she was surprised his teeth didn't shatter, and she was sure that she saw a gleam of orange fire briefly light up his eyes.

What he'd said, though, shocked her into stunned disbelief. "Somebody did that on purpose? To an apartment building?"

He aimed a long, measured stare at her before he finally answered. "This is Bordertown. What *haven't* you seen done on purpose around here?"

She flushed, feeling naïve and a lot like a fool, but she didn't jump up and run away, no matter that it was her first, second, and third instinctive reaction. Something about his attitude—his anger at the arsonist who'd shown so little consideration for human life—caught at her and made her want to know more about him.

Anything about him.

Like his name, for instance.

"I'm Brynn Carroll, and I can't believe you haven't asked me about being a swan. That's usually a big topic of conversation with me and new people," she said, lifting her chin and squaring her shoulders. Ready for the barrage of questions.

She could do this. She could meet a new person. She firmed her lips and then found the courage to hold out her hand. Normal people shook hands.

"Sean O'Malley, and I figured you'd tell me when and what you wanted to tell," he said, and then she caught what had only been teasing the edges of her senses before—the slightest lilt of Ireland infusing the music of his voice.

When his big, strong hand carefully enfolded hers, a gentle wave of warmth spread over her. She was glad to be sitting down, because she suddenly knew her knees would have gone weak and wobbly if she'd been standing. He was big, and he looked rough and scary and dangerous, especially here in the dark, illuminated only by the glow of the lanterns, but he'd taken her hand so carefully, as if it were something to be cherished.

As if *she* were *someone* to be cherished.

She pulled her hand away, banishing the fancies as she did. Loneliness was her only companion most nights; that didn't mean she had the time or inclination to transform a chance encounter into a romantic interlude. Not even in the privacy of her deepest yearnings.

She already knew that love never, ever would be an option for her.

"I have to go," she blurted out, jumping up and ready to run.

"Breakfast?"

As with *please*, the single word stopped her when a dozen might not have.

"In a brightly lit, public place, I promise," he said, holding his hand over his heart and smiling that almost smile again.

She started to shake her head. He was too tempting, too intriguing, too . . . too everything.

"Unless you only eat birdseed." He finally stood, stepping back so as not to loom over her, which was good, since the top of her head came to about his nose.

Her lips quirked into a smile, almost in spite of herself. "No, I don't eat birdseed. I'm more of a pumpkin pancakes girl, actually. With bacon. Lots of bacon."

He groaned, a deep noise that sounded like it came from the depths of his being, and it made her wonder what noises he'd make in the middle of lovemaking. As soon as the idea danced into her mind, she blushed so hot that she was glad for the darkness.

"Bacon. And eggs. And hashbrowns. Coffee. Lots of coffee," he said. "I think I'm going to like you, Brynn Carroll."

"I *am* very likable," she dared to say, as if she'd suddenly become a woman who knew how to flirt with an unbelievably gorgeous man. Now he'd make fun of her, surely.

Instead, he grinned, and his smile felt like a gift he'd given her to unwrap.

"Breakfast?"

"Breakfast," she agreed. "Where should we go?"

"Anywhere but O'Malley's," he said cheerfully, and she suddenly made the connection.

"You're one of *those* O'Malleys? The O'Malley's Pub O'Malleys?"

Everybody knew at least one of the O'Malleys; well, everybody except Brynn. Until now. They were big and brash; quick to anger and quicker to forgive, everybody said. They'd owned the pub for a long time, and everybody in Bordertown drank there or at the Roadhouse. O'Malley's had Irish music on the weekends, and Brynn had lingered outside the pub on occasion, listening to the lovely sound and wishing with all of her heart that she'd had the courage to step inside and join the fun.

Sean reached out to take her hand, as if it were the most natural thing in the world to hold hands with a woman he'd only met mere moments after she'd transformed from waterfowl to human.

"Yes, I'm one of *those* O'Malleys, but don't hold it against me. I like to pretend I'm adopted," he confided.

For the first time in a very long while, Brynn laughed out loud.

THREE

She was even more beautiful when she laughed.

Sean didn't know what to say or do with himself while they walked, so he held on to her hand in silence and hoped she didn't pull away. He was too big, too tall, too rough—he didn't want to intimidate or scare her, but hunching over to try to hide his size would make him look like a constipated gargoyle. Ever since his squad had rescued one of those from the roof of the Bordertown Bank & Trust, the guys had teased him about the resemblance.

"Hey, O'Malley, you sure your family is from Ireland? I saw some pictures of Notre Dame in Paris, and you look a lot like those stone dudes lining the roof!"

He'd laughed and taken it all in stride, but now, for the first time in his life, he found himself wishing he weren't so big and rough and thuglike. She probably would have run screaming if she hadn't caught sight of his gear. People usually trusted firefighters, even people who were shady enough to run from cops. In Bordertown, there was a lot of that going on. Things would get better if that wizard, Oliver, would ever take the vacant sheriff job, but O'Malley couldn't find it in his heart to blame the guy.

Who in their right mind would want to try to enforce the law—let alone the peace—in a Wild West town like Bordertown? Built on the frontier between three realms—the Fae kingdoms of Summerlands and Winter's Edge, the demon realm known as Demon Rift, and the human world—Bordertown was the place where the riffraff came to play, scheme, and eke out a sketchy kind of existence. People who lived here didn't want to settle down, follow the law, or live within the confines of civilized society in any of the three realms, but they usually knew enough about petty crime or magic to believe they could pull off minor-league rackets or that one big score.

O'Malley's Pub served drinks, hosted poker games, and offered entertainment on the weekends for all of them. One mountain troll with a sense of humor and a love of old movies had compared the place to Wyatt Earp's joint in *Tombstone*. Sean's brother Liam had punched the troll in the head, bought him a whiskey, and then agreed with him.

Brynn offered a tentative smile, and Sean's thoughts scattered like tumbleweeds in the desert. *Damn*, she was beautiful. She pulled her hand away from his, though, and he clenched his fingers against the tactile sense of loss.

"The diner? I know the cook, and he makes really great pancakes," she said, clutching her beat-up old backpack to her chest, as if still undecided whether or not to run away.

"The diner's great. Olaf still beating his pots together before he uses them?"

Olaf, who'd been kicked out of Demon Rift for *Actions Unbecoming a Demon*, or so said the proclamation framed and posted by the diner's cash register, was the best short-order cook in Bordertown. He'd never given his place a name—it was always just "the diner"—even though it was unique, since he'd built it out of a refurbished airship. Olaf's menu was a thing of beauty and sky-high cholesterol, and his Heart Attack Special was a particular favorite of the guys at the station when they got a chance to eat breakfast out as a group. Fighting fires burned up a lot of calories, and the treadmills and other workout equipment they trained on every day did the same.

Sean pretended he didn't notice that Brynn was ready to bolt, and he kept walking and chatting about nothing. Canadian bacon versus American, ham versus sausage, the best way to cook eggs. Sean was in the middle of mentioning that he liked his eggs scrambled with cheese, when it occurred to him that he was talking to a woman who turned into a *swan* about *eating eggs*.

Crap. He was a complete moron. He stopped walking, even though they were still about a half-block away from the diner.

"I'm an idiot. Eggs. I can't believe I was talking about—"

She looked bewildered, but then her eyes widened as she reached the conclusion before he had to admit to it out loud. She laughed, surprising him.

"No. It's okay. I mean, I'm not actually a swan. I don't lay eggs or fly or do anything that real swans do. I just take on swan form every third night and sing until nearly dawn, and then I'm back to being me." She laughed a little and pushed her hair away from her delicate cheekbones and out of her eyes.

He blew out a sigh of relief. "Thank goodness. That conversation was about to get seriously creepy."

"Well, I know this keeps coming up, but it *is* Bordertown. You can't live in a place where the most powerful ley lines in the world intersect without a *little* weird." She shrugged and smiled up at him—this time a full-on, dazzling smile—and he almost forgot how to talk.

Damn, but she was beautiful.

"Bacon?" She tilted her head toward the gleaming silver, red, and white exterior of the renovated but grounded airship that housed the diner.

"Bacon would be great."

He followed her into the diner, trying really, really hard not to watch her lovely round ass as it moved in those snug jeans, and failing completely. When they walked in to the brightly lit diner, he discovered that her dark mass of curls was actually a deep auburn color, and he almost groaned. Great ass *and* she was a redhead. He'd always been drawn to redheads; his family teased him that it was the Irish in him. He must have made a funny noise, because Brynn gave him a questioning look.

"Just enjoying the delicious aromas of coffee and fried everything," he said, relieved when she smiled and nodded instead of accusing him of staring at her butt.

Olaf greeted Brynn like an old friend and then scowled at Sean like he'd never met him before and yet suspected him of vast and nefarious wrongdoing. The cook was maybe five feet tall, almost as round as he was tall, and would be practically blind without his enormous glasses. His gleaming bald head, its skin darker than the French roast he served, was always visible as he stood on a box behind his counter and surveyed his domain.

"You be careful of those crazy O'Malleys, you hear me, Brynn? You're a good girl. You don't need that kind of bad boy," the cook scolded loudly, banging two of his skillets together for emphasis.

All the other patrons at the counter, and the few at booths this early in the morning, looked up with interest. Brynn's face flushed such a hot pink that Sean almost wondered if she might be part fire demon herself. In the light, he could finally see that her eyes were blue, a pale gray-blue like wintry clouds reflected in a frozen pond. He suddenly wanted to pull her into his arms and warm her up, match his fire with her ice.

Maybe Olaf was right to warn her about him. He was clearly losing it.

The cook pointed a spatula at him. "You hurt my girl, I hurt your face."

Sean stifled a smile. He knew the little demon wouldn't take well to being mocked.

"I just want to buy her a good breakfast, Olaf. Feed her up a little," he protested, trying to project wounded innocence.

Brynn was standing, mortified, only about two feet away, but nobody needed to know that the clean rain-and-grass scent of her hair was giving Sean all sorts of thoughts, few of which were entirely innocent.

"Okay, that's enough from both of you," she said, making a break for the booth the farthest from Olaf's window.

She dropped her backpack on the red leather seat and started to slide in next to it, but Sean touched her arm to stop her.

"I'm sorry, but I need to sit on that side," he said, indicating the seat and the wall behind it. "Unless you want to sit next to me?"

"But why—oh. Can't have your back to the door?" She bit her lip, but then she nodded and took the other seat.

He'd expected it, but still found himself a little disappointed that he wouldn't be able to feel the warmth of her body next to him, her legs stretched out next to his.

"Is that a firefighter thing?"

He was watching her seductive lips move as she spoke, and it took him a beat to catch up with what she'd actually said.

"No, it's an O'Malley thing. My dad drummed it into us from the time we could walk. 'Me boyos, you always scan the room for danger and protect the women and children.' I asked him once, wasn't *I* the child in the room?" He shook his head at the memory.

She leaned forward a little, resting her folded arms on the spotless Formica tabletop. "What did he say?"

Sean laughed. "He knocked me down and told me to stop asking him stupid questions. Then my four brothers jumped on me and pounded on me for a while."

Brynn tilted her head, watching him as if he were a strange, rare specimen of animal at a zoo. Which was almost funny, considering she'd been the one swimming around in a fountain wearing nothing but feathers, but he could see her point. A lot of people reacted like that when he told them anything about his rather boisterous childhood. That's why he'd quit doing it years and years ago.

So why was he suddenly telling tales about his family to a woman he'd only known for an hour?

Loneliness.

The word popped up, unbidden, from deep inside him, the place where he shoved words like that. Words like *regret* and *isolation* and *sorrow*. He'd been surrounded by beautiful, tempting women from the day he'd turned sixteen and started working in the bar, but even in a crowd, he'd always felt alone. There'd been plenty, male and female, human and not, who'd wanted to play with one of the O'Malley boys, but there'd never been anyone who wanted him for himself. His mom had always said that the perfect woman for him would come along, but now his mom was dying slowly from an enemy Sean couldn't battle, leaving him with no faith in miracles. He swallowed hard and pushed the anger and bitterness away, yet again.

"You were the only one, weren't you?" Her blue eyes held understanding and something else. Something he hoped wasn't pity. He damn sure didn't want pity from her.

"The only one who questioned the orders? The others wouldn't have pounded on you, otherwise," she continued, and he realized what that glimmer of emotion was in her eyes.

Not pity. *Compassion.*

A dizzying wave of heat swirled through him, and he looked down in case the demon glow made an appearance in his eyes. The sensation put him on guard at the same time as it threw him off balance. Rage was the emotion that catalyzed him into heat mode. Fear—terror—could do it, too. But a gentler emotion never had before, and yet he could feel his skin temperature rising way too high.

Brynn might be dangerous to him, he realized, and the thought only made him want to get closer. A *lot* closer.

"Yeah," he admitted. "I was the only one who ever questioned, at least until after Dad died. We were O'Malleys, so we would grow up in the pub, work in the pub, and take over the pub. Liam, Blake, Oscar, and Yeats—they all mostly followed the party line. Me? Not so much."

"Order up, O'Malley," Olaf shouted, banging a metal spoon against a pot.

"We didn't even order yet," Sean said, startled.

Brynn laughed. "Sometimes he's like that. You get what he feels like cooking for you. Trust me, it's always good."

Sean walked back to the counter to pick up the tray, which included a mountain of food, two mugs of steaming hot coffee, a carafe of more of the same, and, luckily for his rising temp, two glasses of ice water. Olaf refrained from threatening him again, but he did wag his finger in the vicinity of Sean's chest.

"I understand why you want to protect her, Olaf. She's definitely someone to be cherished," Sean said, not even knowing where the words were coming from, but knowing that he meant them.

The little demon's face relaxed out of its scowl, which was an improvement, at least, and Sean headed back to their table with enough food to feed an army of shapeshifters.

"Ooh, pancakes," Brynn said, all but moaning.

She proceeded to take both plates of pancakes, consolidate them into one enormous pile, and slather them with butter and enough syrup to put out a small fire, while Sean watched in awed disbelief.

"You're going to eat all that?"

"And bacon," she said, snatching a crispy piece from the platter. "Hey, I worked up an appetite swimming around in the cold and singing. We can ask for more if you want some. So, you're all named after Irish poets?"

"What else? Yeats had it the worst. People always want to call him *Yeets* when they see it written, instead of pronouncing it *Yates*. Drives him nuts."

Brynn raised an eyebrow. "And Oscar didn't get hot-dog jokes?"

"How'd you guess? He pretty much pounded everybody who tried, but *O-S-C-A-R* followed him around a lot when he was a kid," Sean said, grinning at the memory. "We'd all jump in and help, of course. Not too many wanted to take on the O'Malley boys."

"No sisters?"

Sean's smile faded as he remembered the time he'd come across his mother kneeling in the attic next to a large trunk, tears running down her face. She'd been folding a tiny pink lace nightgown. He'd been a kid then, afraid to intrude on his mom's privacy. Since he'd grown, he'd wondered sometimes if she'd miscarried the daughter she'd always wanted, but he hadn't known how to ask. Hadn't wanted to resurrect her sorrow.

"No sister," he said abruptly. "You? Brothers or sisters?"

"No. My mother didn't even want to have me," she said, frowning. "She was trying to break the curse. No daughters means no daughters have to turn feathery."

Sean took a long sip of his coffee, wondering how to ask the obvious question. Finally, he settled on the simplest way.

"Why? How?"

Brynn's face lost its happy glow, and he bitterly regretted mentioning it. "Forget it. None of my business. Let's eat, and we can talk about anything but fires or swans."

Her smile was the best reward he could have gotten. "Yes. I agree."

She took a big bite of pancake and closed her eyes in bliss. "Mmmmm."

She was absolutely glorious. Desire sparked in Sean like tinder to a blaze, and he suddenly wanted to lick maple syrup off her body, or at least spend the next month doing nothing but eating breakfast with her and watching her smile.

He lived his life surrounded by people, and yet he was always so alone. For the first time in forever, he felt a connection, and he had no intention of letting her get away before they could explore it.

"After we finish the pancakes and bacon, we can have waffles," she said, grinning like a child at Christmas, and he smiled right back at her, basking in the warmth of her obvious enjoyment.

They talked and laughed and worked their way through most of the food and several cups of coffee, and a good hour and a half had gone by before it even occurred to Sean to wonder why it was so easy for him to talk to her. They had an ease between them that felt more like the connection between good friends than the awkward getting-to-know-you stage between strangers.

Brynn picked up the last piece of toast, sighed, and put it back down. "I'd better not. I already feel like I won't want to eat again for a week."

He suddenly remembered something and looked around. "Isn't there usually a waitress here?"

Brynn pushed her plate back, apparently full at last, and nodded. "Ethel. She does synchronized swimming three mornings a week, so it's serve yourself on those days."

Sean thought about the old movies his grandmother had liked to watch, and decided Brynn must be putting him on. "Her name is Ethel, and she's a synchronized swimmer?"

"Yes, why?"

He shook his head. "Never mind."

The diner's door banged open, and Zach strode in, followed by a couple of the guys from the crew. The last thing Sean wanted to do was share Brynn with them, and he knew the moment they caught sight of him they'd come barging over.

"Hey, we might want to head out," he told her. "It's about to get pretty noisy in here."

She glanced back over her shoulder at the group just inside the door, and he could have sworn she flinched a little. "Yes, time for me to go. Breakfast was . . . nice."

She put a hand in her pocket, but he shook his head. "My treat."

"But—okay. Thank you." With that, she was up and out of the booth almost before he could react, but he couldn't let her go like that. "Wait. Brynn, how do I reach you? I'd like to do this again, or dinner, maybe, as soon as we can figure out a time."

Brynn started shaking her head before he'd even finished the sentence. By the time she replied, his heart was already sinking into his gut.

"Oh, no, you don't understand. We can never see each other again."

Before he could protest, she slipped through a door that said *Employees Only*, and she was gone.

Zach's booming voice penetrated Sean's stunned disbelief. "O'Malley, there you are. The chief wants to see you. Something about reporters and obeying orders."

Sean stood up and met Zach in the aisle. "Forget it. I'm off duty. Tell him to go talk to a mirror, like he usually does."

Zach didn't smile at the admittedly lame joke. "You're going, and I'm going with you. We've finally got a lead on the freak who's setting these fires."

Sean glanced back at the door through which Brynn had disappeared, but then made himself shake it off. No time to worry about mysterious women right now.

"Let's go get the bastard," Sean said grimly. He pulled out his wallet and left money on the cash register counter for Olaf.

"Go get him for all of us," the little cook said, and the murmurs of agreement from everyone in the diner followed them out the door.

FOUR

Sean sat in the uncomfortable metal chair in the conference room and amused himself by imagining all the ways he could crush Bordertown Fire Chief Arvin Ledbetter like the pompous little cockroach he was. He didn't know how many asses the new chief had kissed to get the job, but the windbag was clearly good at his work.

The ass-kissing part of his work. Not the fire chief part.

Zach and the guys had brought takeout breakfast for everyone, because they were all just too damn tired to cook. Nobody had said much until they'd devoured Olaf's cooking down to the crumbs. Now they were ready to listen, even though most of them looked ready to drop any minute. The shift change had come and gone, and the fresh day crew sat and leaned against the clutter of safety notices and posters lining the walls of the room, including one that Zach had artistically altered.

Sean doubted that Smokey Bear had ever performed such a lewd act on a goat.

Shift change hadn't meant a thing today. Not a single one of Sean's crew had made a move to go home. They all wanted to catch the arsonist before he could strike a fifth time.

"As I was saying, we suspect that this is the fourth fire the same perpetrator set in Bordertown," Ledbetter said, positioning himself in front of the whiteboard.

Sean groaned. "We know that. Same accelerant, same signature, same guy. Do we have any new evidence or not?"

The chief glared at him, and Sean could almost see the word *insubordinate* form in the jerk's brain. "Yes, if you'd have a little patience, O'Malley. We believe the fires are the work of a disgruntled ex-Bordertown city official who was fired from the parks and—"

"No," Sean interrupted, earning himself a death glare. "We already checked him out. Wagner, Waggoner, something like that?"

Zach nodded. "Yeah. Wagner. He had an alibi for the second fire."

"Alibis can be faked," Ledbetter pointed out.

"You're right," Sean admitted. "But that's not why it isn't him. Wagner is pure vanilla human. The arsonist used magic for the accelerant."

Sharply inhaled breaths and low, vicious cursing filled the room from every firefighter in it. They all knew how much harder it was to combat a magically enhanced blaze.

"He could have had a partner," Sue Newman pointed out, but she didn't sound convinced. Her short, blond hair stood up in spikes, and dark smudges under her eyes testified to her exhaustion. She'd been on the same shifts as Sean for the past several days.

They were all working too hard, but they didn't have a choice because, so far, the arsonist was working harder. Or smarter. Either way, the madman was at least one step ahead of them, and this time he'd almost claimed his first human victims.

Sean was pretty sure the man wasn't working with a partner, though. Arsonists were almost always loners—at least the true crazies and the ones who considered themselves experts were—and no amateur was behind this string of fires.

Ledbetter made a croaking *harrumph* sound. "What evidence do you have that magic was used? We found no proof of that."

Sean had been hoping the question wouldn't come up, because he couldn't explain it without revealing his fire demon heritage. As far as he knew, only fire demons and black magic practitioners could see the complete spectrum of colors in a fire and instantly know which were caused by magic, and there was no way in hell he was giving anybody cause to think he was either. He'd sworn an oath to his father—all the O'Malley boys had.

So he deflected. "You called us here because you had new evidence, Zach said, and since our witch was helping put out the fire, I just figured—"

The chief scowled, which unfortunately made his piggy little eyes squint and his puffy little jowls puff out even further. Sean made the mistake of glancing at Zach, who was clearly thinking the same thing, and he had to fight back the grin. It was neither the time nor the place for it, and there was damn sure nothing funny about the situation, but the man looked ridiculous when he tried to act important.

"Yes, well, you're right," Ledbetter said, pointing to the department witch, José Castilho, who was slumped at one end of the table looking no more than half-alive.

Castilho looked up when the guy next to him elbowed him, and he nodded wearily.

"Yeah. Magical accelerant. Worse than anything I've ever encountered before, too. It fought me like a living thing."

The exhausted night-shift men and women around the room nodded and made sounds of agreement.

"The fire just didn't act right. The air currents didn't affect it in a normal way," Sean improvised, when it became clear that Castilho had nothing else to say. "The smell was wrong, too. Whatever or whoever set this fire didn't even try to hide the fact that he used magic."

"The burn patterns were wrong, too," Ledbetter interjected grudgingly, as if he hated to agree with anything Sean said. "The electronic accelerant detector came up with nothing. Even the dogs—nothing. Nada. Zip."

That didn't make sense.

"You used the hellfire hounds?"

The chief shook his head. "No, O'Malley, we couldn't use them. They were on loan from Demon Rift, and they went back yesterday. I'm trying to borrow them again, but considering they're the only mated pair of hellfire hounds known to exist, the demons are understandably reluctant to let them out of their sight until the hounds throw their first litter."

Sean nodded. He understood but hated to hear it. Hellfire hounds were the best in the world at detecting fire starters and tracking them down, but even *they* had been thrown off at the first three sites. There'd been something fascinating about watching the powerful dogs race around and around the sites, but fascination had turned to empathy as the hounds grew more and more frustrated until they finally surrendered and sat down next to the truck, whimpering.

"The arson investigators are out there now, interviewing everybody and doing their best to discover motive, means, or opportunity," Ledbetter continued. "But we all know that motive is usually just sheer crazy in cases like this."

"We need to find him," Sean said, seeing that baby in his mind. "What if we don't get to the next fire in time?"

The chief's face hardened and, for a moment, Sean saw the

shadow of the firefighter the man had been before his internal politician took over. "All available resources are focused on this case, as of right now. Anything else is cancelled. All nonemergency leave is revoked."

There were a couple of halfhearted groans, but nobody made any real protest. They were all focused on the same goal; it's why they'd become firefighters in the first place.

"Pyromania plus pretty strong magical ability," Sean said. "A match made in hell."

After that, the meeting broke up, and everybody who'd worked the night shift headed out to get some sleep. Castilho stopped Sean with a look, and the witch nodded toward an empty corner of the room.

Sean ambled over to meet him, but before he could say a word, Castilho turned around and pretended to study a poster on protective eyewear.

"Look, I don't have any evidence of this, so I didn't want to put it out there," Castilho said quietly. "But since you mentioned the magic, I'm going to tell you what I suspect. I know it's going to sound crazy, because we haven't seen one around Bordertown in years, but I'm worried that there might be a fire demon behind this. They're all insane, and they have the ability to set fires magically."

Sean's gut clenched, and he schooled his face to impassivity. "I don't—"

Castilho glanced around, as if to make sure nobody was near enough to overhear. "Hey, I know it sounds nuts. I know it's all just rumors, but that's my hunch, and I wanted to tell somebody."

Before Sean could say a word, Castilho laughed a little too loudly and then clapped Sean on the shoulder.

"You're a riot, man. Smokey Bear walked into a bar. Too much," the witch said, grinning at the two guys standing across the room at the coffeepot as if he and Sean had just shared a great joke.

"Yeah, I'm a riot," Sean muttered, watching Castilho.

The witch suspected a fire demon. Of course he did. After all, *everybody* knew that fire demons were evil—devils incarnate, right? It was why the O'Malleys had kept their secret all these years. Sean was half fire demon, and his secret identity might even make him the prime suspect, if anybody found out about it.

Now he just had to make sure that nobody did.

When Sean arrived at his mom's house, Liam was walking down the steps from the front porch, frowning so hard that Sean could almost hear his brother's teeth grinding. The thunderous expression on Liam's face was the same one that often reduced even the most belligerent drunks at O'Malley's into submission.

"Didn't you buy a new car yet?" Liam said, all but growling as he studied Sean's latest piece-of-crap ride.

"No point, since they all wind up smelling like smoke, but I've told you that before, so why don't you let me in on what's really pissing you off?" Sean shoved his hands in his pockets to avoid the temptation to smack his brother in the head. Funny how the childhood roles always came back so easily at this house.

He rocked back on his heels and stared up at the pleasant front of the old Colonial. They'd grown up here, the house always full of the sounds and smells of boys. Shouts and laughter, grass-stained and mud-spattered sports uniforms. The O'Malley boys had been a formidable force on the neighborhood baseball and football teams, always ready for a pickup game, not so great about doing homework on time, except for Yeats, who'd been the studious one.

Through their childhoods and the turbulent teen years, his mother had been the center of the home, dispensing hugs, chocolate-chip cookies, and wisdom as needed. Even after their dad died, when Sean, the baby, had been only eight and Liam, the oldest, had been fourteen, she'd never faltered—or at least never where the boys could see it. She'd been strong enough for all of them, even managing to tame Blake's wild rebellion because she'd been able to see the pain where nobody else could see anything but the anger.

She was the strongest woman Sean had ever known, and now her boys needed to be strong enough for her.

"She wants us to meet with her lawyer," Liam said, biting off the words. "Get her affairs in order. What the hell is that about? She's still fine."

"We don't need to do that now," Sean said, instantly going into full-on denial right alongside his brother. "She's got plenty of time."

Liam's bleak expression was enough to call out the lie. Their mom didn't have plenty of time, and they both knew it. They'd tried doctors, Fae healers, and even wizards, but cancer didn't play by any rules but its own, and this time the O'Malley boys were on the losing team to the most merciless opponent they'd ever faced.

Liam studied the lawn. "Hedges need trimming. House could do with a coat of paint. Barbecue time?"

Sean nodded. "Day after tomorrow good? I'll have the afternoon and evening off."

"Yep. I'll spread the word."

They got together at least once a month for a barbecue, bringing all the food and manning the grill, and used the occasion to plan any and all upkeep the house needed. Their mom always baked her famous apple and pumpkin pies for them, but for the first time ever, Sean wasn't sure she'd be up for baking. Pain scorched through him at the thought, and he clenched his hands into fists at his sides but then forced them to relax.

He needed to chill. Try on a smile. Be brave for his mother, even when the eight-year-old boy inside him wanted to sit down right there on the sidewalk and howl.

"I'm going to go in and see her for a while before I head home for some sleep," Sean said.

"She's sleeping now. I got her settled into her recliner in the sunroom out back, and she threw me out so she could nap." A ghost of a smile crossed Liam's face. "She's still pretty tough for such a tiny little thing."

Sean grinned. At five feet, two inches, their mom had been rapidly outgrown by all of her boys, but there had never been a moment's doubt about who was in charge.

"I'll never forget the time she backed you up against the refrigerator and told you that you were, too, going to have the condom talk with your mother, or you were never going to go on a date as long as you lived under her roof," he told his brother.

Liam threw back his head and laughed. "Oh, man, I thought I was going to die. My face was still purple by the time she finished and I escaped to my room. 'You are *responsible* for your *actions*, Liam, and if I ever find out you're having unprotected sex, I'll beat your arse all the way down the street.' "

"She had the exact same conversation with me," Sean confided, shuddering. "That talk scared me out of the backseat of more than one car, let me tell you."

"Exactly as she planned. She had the same talk with Blake, Oscar, and Yeats, too, believe me," Liam said, his gaze trained on a pair of small boys riding their bikes at the end of the street. "Seems like not long ago, that was us."

Sean turned to watch the boys. It was less painful than staring at his childhood home and wondering how long his mother would still be able to live there. "And now we're all grown up."

"No wives or kids, though," Liam said darkly, kicking a stone off the sidewalk toward the street. It thudded softly when it hit a tire on Sean's car and bounced back. "Trust me, she brought that up, too."

Sean's mouth fell open. "She what?"

"She wants us to get married. All of us. Soon. Doesn't want us to be alone."

For some reason, the image of Brynn's face as she'd enjoyed her pancakes flashed into Sean's mind, but he pushed it away. She was obviously a complicated woman. The *last* thing he needed in his life was more complication.

"If she wanted grandchildren, she shouldn't have married a fire demon," Sean growled. "I never want to pass this heritage on, and I can't imagine any of us feel any differently."

Liam shrugged. "We managed to have a pretty damn happy childhood."

Sean, who'd started to head for his car, whirled to stare at his brother. "Yeah, until Dad *flamed on* when that drugged-up wannabe burglar broke into the house."

The druggie hadn't been alone, and his accomplice—who'd also been on drugs and who'd been scared to death by the sight of a fiery demon blazing brighter than the noontime sun over the Summerlands—had been carrying a gun.

Sean and his brothers had called 911 and used the fire extinguisher to put out the blaze while their mother kept pressure on Dad's wound, but it had been too little, too late. Their father had died in the ambulance on the way to the hospital, leaving Mom to run a pub and raise five boys on her own.

"I'm never going to subject a woman to anything like *that*."

When Liam didn't reply, Sean shrugged and headed for his car. "I've got to get some sleep. I'll check on Mom this afternoon."

"It would have to be the *right* woman," Liam said, so quietly that anybody without fire demon hearing would never have heard it.

Sean paused, but this time he didn't look back. They'd been down that road before, and he was surprised that Liam, of all of them, had even a glimmer of hope left.

"There is no such woman."

FIVE

After six hours of sleep and a quick lunch at a neighboring deli, Brynn opened her tiny shop and looked around, smiling. Scruffy's Pet Spa wasn't much of a business, but it was all hers. She tailored her hours to fit her late nights, and she wouldn't take a pet twice if the owner was a pain in the butt. The animals were never a problem for her, even though she'd once worried that dominant or aggressive dogs and cats would try to push her around, somehow sensing her inner swan.

Swans weren't exactly predators, after all.

Instead, it was as if they recognized a kindred animal spirit or were able to understand that she only wanted to help them. In five years of running the grooming salon, she'd only been attacked once, and afterward the vet had discovered a tumor the size of a lemon in the dog's brain. Poor guy hadn't been able to help his fear and aggression. She'd always have the scar on her left arm, but at least the experience hadn't left her traumatized.

Brynn, of all people, understood the dog's plight. There'd been a time when she, too, had been afraid and angry due to events beyond her control. She was never able to think back to her first several nights as a swan without shuddering.

Pushing the memory aside, she focused on preparing for her workday. She moved about in her usual routine, checking her tools, restocking her inventory of dog treats inside the glass case from the fresh shipment, and getting the cash box out of the small safe. Her cleaning service had done a terrific job as always. A brother-and-sister Fae team ran the cleaning business, and she had engaged their services on the barter system. The two Fae owned four excitable Dalmatians, and the dogs wouldn't let anyone but Brynn, whom they adored, give them baths. In turn, Brynn always got a kick out of seeing the haughty Fae brought low by a quartet of canines.

As she prepped for the hundred-pound golden retriever mix scheduled to arrive soon, she caught herself humming. She froze, automatically glancing at the giant red clock on the wall, and was shocked to realize that she'd spent at least five minutes rearranging the same three brushes on the table.

Sean.

He'd invaded her fountain, her solitude, and her dreams. She couldn't even remember the last time she'd had so much fun doing something as ordinary as eating breakfast, and the tingle of sexual attraction had added a zing to every minute. If only she could be normal for once, then maybe . . .

Maybe nothing. *Maybes* and *if onlys* were for fools. She could never have a man like Sean O'Malley, and she shouldn't even want him. She'd promised herself that she'd never fall in love, never take the chance of getting pregnant and subjecting another generation—her own daughter—to the curse of the black swan.

The bell over the door rang, and Brynn flashed her biggest smile to welcome tiny old Mrs. Mastroianni and her dog. Peaches, as far as Brynn could figure out, was golden retriever crossed with moose. The friendly dog easily outweighed his owner, and could have pulled Mrs. Mastroianni across town—or carried her on his back, if he'd wanted to do it. But he was extraordinarily gentle with his tiny owner and saved all his boisterousness for the Bordertown dog park.

"Let's trim his fur this time, dear," Mrs. M. said, patting her dog's shoulder without needing to lean down even a little. "And please use that apple-scented conditioner that leaves his coat so shiny. He's looking a little scruffy."

Brynn smiled, knowing her line. "Then he's in the right place, isn't he? We're here for all the dogs who don't want to be scruffy anymore."

Mrs. M. chuckled, as she always did, and toddled off to meet "the girls" for tea and gossip. As Brynn watched her go, a trace of worry shadowed her mood. Her favorite client was walking just a little bit slower than usual. A little bit stiffer.

"But she'll outlive us all, won't she, Peaches?" Brynn ruffled the silky fur behind the dog's ears, and Peaches, who never seemed to mind his silly name in the slightest, grinned his happy openmouthed doggy smile up at her as if agreeing.

Four hours later, Brynn, tired but content, swept up dog hair and disinfected the grooming table. In addition to Peaches, she'd bathed and groomed a pair of huskies, a chunky little pug who hated to have his nails trimmed, and a young wolverine who'd fallen into a vat of pickles. It had taken three shampoo-rinse-repeats with her special herbal shampoo for Brynn to remove the pungent aroma, and the faint scent of dill still infused the air.

Mrs. Mastroianni graciously had insisted that Brynn take a two-dollar tip, as always, and Brynn had given in, as always, never once letting on that she only charged a fraction of her usual fee for Peaches. Mrs. M. was pretty clearly on a fixed income, and it probably took a good portion of that just to keep Peaches in dog food. With her arthritis, there was no way the elderly woman would have been able to bathe and groom the enormous dog on her own, and it boosted both her pride and her dignity to add in the small tip. Brynn made sure that Mrs. M. never discovered that the shop's other clients generally tipped ten times that amount.

"Hey, it's two dollars I didn't have this morning," Brynn told the framed photograph of the original Scruffy, a two-hundred-pound Irish wolfhound who'd wandered over to the fountain one night, wounded and limping. He'd curled up at the edge of the water and watched Brynn swim around for the next several hours.

Almost as if he'd been standing guard.

As soon as she'd turned back into human form, Brynn had taken him to Dr. Black, the best vet in town. She'd said Scruffy had probably been hit by a car. After he'd recovered from his injuries enough to leave the animal hospital, Scruffy had lived with Brynn for another three years before he'd died peacefully in his sleep. He'd been the best friend she'd ever had, and although it had been several years since he'd gone, she hadn't been able to bring herself to get another dog.

The bell over the door rang just after she knelt down behind the grooming table to retrieve a nail file that Theo the pug had kicked off during his valiant struggles to escape.

"I'm sorry, but we're closed," she called out without bothering to look up.

"I've got an emergency." The man's voice was deep, rich, and a little desperate. It was also the voice that had murmured to her in her dreams a few short hours before. She slowly stood up, sure that her mind must be playing tricks on her.

It wasn't. Sean O'Malley stood, large as life—and that was

pretty darn big, considering those incredibly broad shoulders—in the middle of her shop, holding a hissing Persian cat.

"You!" Sean and Brynn said at the same time, and then they both laughed.

The cat didn't appreciate the humor, apparently, because it lashed out with one paw and scratched the back of Sean's hand. Sean didn't even flinch, and he didn't say a word of reprimand to the cat. Brynn liked him even more for that. Most creatures were jumpy when they came into a place that, no matter how clean, would always hold the scent of other animals.

"Do you work here?" Sean glanced around. "Nice place."

"It's mine."

Brynn felt a moment of fierce pride over her neat little shop. The rows of colorful dog and cat accessories behind the counter gave the place a festive air, and framed photos of happy customers and their pets lined the walls. She'd made a success of her business in spite of the challenges that came with the swan curse.

"I was just closing, but you said you had an emergency?" She let the question ring in her voice. "Must be my day for it. I had a baby wolverine with a pickle problem earlier."

He grinned. "Sounds like an interesting story."

The cat in his arms yowled and lashed out again, leaving a second red stripe next to the first on Sean's hand, and Brynn decided she'd had enough of *that*. She marched over to Sean and took the cat out of his arms before he could protest.

When the cat hissed at her and started fighting in earnest, Brynn pulled it more tightly against her chest, wrapping the squirming bundle in her arms.

"Stop it right now," she said firmly, and the cat's eyes widened at her tone, and then the tension seeped out of its body as it relaxed against her.

Sean's mouth dropped open. "What did you do? I've never seen

Barty calm down like that for a stranger. He hates most people. Well, pretty much all people except for my mother."

Brynn smoothed a hand down the cat's fur and crooned at him. "Barty isn't a bad boy, are you, my beautiful one? Just a little misunderstood."

The beautiful white Persian closed his brilliant blue eyes and began to purr, and Brynn almost laughed at Sean's stunned expression.

"It's a gift," she confided. "If animals didn't like me, I'd go out of business."

"Makes sense," he said.

His gaze swept her from head to toe and she suddenly flushed, realizing how she must look. Sweaty hair, no makeup, her Scruffy's apron covering her T-shirt and jeans; she was no fashion plate, that was for sure. Of course, she'd been wearing feathers the first time he'd seen her, so it was all relative. Sean was wearing a dark green shirt and a pair of well-worn jeans and, even though the dark shadows under his eyes told her that he hadn't slept much, he was still absolutely gorgeous.

It was entirely unfair.

"Your emergency?" she prompted.

"Oh, right. He has a big wad of gum stuck in his tail. Neighborhood kids probably dropped it on his favorite spot on the stone wall in front of the house. My mom wouldn't let me chop it out with scissors."

Sean dragged a hand through his own silky dark hair, which needed to see a pair of scissors, too, but Brynn kept that observation to herself.

"You live with your mother?" It was none of her business, but she was curious.

He laughed. "No, but we all go visit her a lot. She's rattling around in that big house by herself now, and we worry. I caught some shut-eye and then arrived just in time for the cat emergency this afternoon."

"Let's have a look," she said, carrying Barty over to the table.

The little cat started to protest again when he saw the grooming table, but Brynn took a clean, soft towel from a shelf and placed it down first, then set him on top of it.

"Nobody likes a cold metal table," she told Sean.

He was watching her again—studying her as if she were a puzzle he needed to solve—and she didn't like it.

"Don't stare at me."

"I can't help it. You're beautiful," he said, and she was caught off guard by the sincerity in his voice.

She covered up her flustered reaction by reaching for the tools she needed. A fine-toothed comb and a little oil should do it.

"I'm not beautiful. You must not get out much," she snapped, before pointing to the shelf behind him. "Please hand me that bottle of sesame oil from the shelf."

When he silently gave her the oil, she winced at the sight of the scratches on his hand.

"There's a first-aid kit under the counter. You should clean up those scratches."

"I'm fine. I'm sorry if I embarrassed you. I'm not really good at small talk," he said, his face grim as if he'd had to force out the words.

She rolled her eyes and started combing the edges of the gum out of Barty's tail. "You practically grew up in the most popular bar in Bordertown, and you have four brothers. How can you not be good at talking to people? If you'd had my childhood, I could understand it. I spent most of my time alone."

He shrugged, but she was almost sure he'd flinched a little. Interesting. Deep cat scratches didn't bother him at all, but questions about his social skills made him uncomfortable. Yet another thing they had in common.

"Please go tend to those scratches. I'll be stressed out about it until you do."

His gaze caught hers as if demanding her attention, startling her into perfect stillness. A spark of deep red-orange color pulsed in his pupils for an instant, and then was gone so fast she wasn't sure she'd really seen it. When he turned toward the counter, she exhaled a shaky breath.

Barty let out a particularly loud meow, startling Brynn into almost knocking over the uncapped bottle of oil.

"Yes, baby, I'm sorry. Let's try a little oil to work that gum out, okay?" As she started to carefully work the oil into the fur around the gum, she glanced up at Sean, who was disinfecting and bandaging his hand. "He has quite a loud meow, doesn't he?"

"That's how he got his name."

"Barty?"

Sean grinned. "Nope. Bartholomeow, if you can believe it."

"That's a good one," she had to admit. "I've heard a lot of funny pet names, as you can imagine. Today I had one of my favorite dogs in here; an enormous golden cross named Peaches. He's quite an elegant, dignified dog, so I always wonder if he's a little embarrassed by his name."

"I think I know that dog," Sean said, after he put the first-aid kit away. "Tiny little Mrs. Mastroianni?"

"That's the one. Bordertown is a small place, isn't it?"

"Mrs. M. is a friend of my mother's. They used to go for tea, before . . . before."

Brynn recognized the pain that stamped his face. She'd worn the same expression after her mom had died.

"She's gone?"

"No. She's—no. Cancer. She doesn't have much time left. Maybe three or four months, they tell us." His eyes were dry, but his voice was rough with the unshed tears that she knew must be clogging his throat.

"I'm so sorry," she said, wanting to do something—anything. Reach out to him, give him a hug, offer some comfort. But she knew better. Getting involved was dangerous.

Caring about someone was worse. Look what had happened to her mom.

She worked diligently to remove the rest of the gum, and then she washed the oil out of the beautiful Persian's fluffy tail. He was purring now, lying on his side and enjoying the attention.

"I can't get over how calm and happy he is for you," Sean said, gesturing to Barty. "He hates everybody."

Brynn gently rubbed the cat's belly, and a thought occurred to her. "Has he always been like this? Persians are one of the best-tempered of all the cat breeds. It's unusual to hear of one hating people."

"Come to think of it, he hasn't. He was a perfectly good cat for the first couple of years she had him. Cute as a button when he was a kitten, too. It's just for the past year or so—"

Brynn knew what was coming when his voice trailed off. "When did your mom get sick?"

"Right about the same time, I think, although she didn't get her diagnosis until several months ago," he said, his eyes widening. "Do you think Barty knew?"

"It's very common for animals to react when their people get sick," Brynn said. "There are even doctors who use dogs to detect cancer in humans. They can smell the tumors or the difference in the bloodstream, or something like that, I think. I'm sure cats can do the same, only I haven't heard of anyone trying to train a cat to do the job."

"I'll be damned," Sean said, lifting the now-clean and gum-free cat up off the table and staring into his eyes. "Are you just worried about Mom, Barty?"

The cat meowed plaintively and quite loudly, and Sean smiled at him. Brynn's heart stuttered in her chest at the sight of the big, masculine firefighter sharing a moment of compassionate understanding with the beautiful little creature, and the feeling rang every warning bell she had.

"Oh, boy, you should be on a poster," she muttered, going to wash her hands and drop the comb in the disinfectant.

"What was that?"

She turned around, and he was standing way too close to her, even though she hadn't heard him move.

"You," she said, almost accusingly, backing away. "You're like a movie poster. Hot guy rescues people from burning buildings and saves kittens from trees in his spare time. You don't own a spandex suit, do you?"

A slow, deliciously wicked smile spread across his face. "Hey, if you're into that kind of thing, I'll see what I can find."

SIX

Sean watched the intriguing rosy glow rise in Brynn's face, and the blood in his body rushed straight to his cock. He'd never been so glad to be holding Barty, whose fluffy sweep of a tail hung down and concealed Sean's enormous erection. Damn, but he was suddenly acting like a teenager at his first sight of cleavage, although Brynn couldn't be more covered up.

His memory, though, was happy to rush in and supply her image, in full-color detail, from the night before. Her incredibly beautiful body, naked and gleaming in the moonlight, wasn't a picture he was likely to forget anytime soon. His throat went dry, and suddenly he wanted nothing more than to pull Brynn into his arms and kiss the breath out of her. He could put poor Barty in one of the roomy crates lining the back wall—just for a few minutes, or an hour or two—and see if kissing her would quench the need that had been simmering at a slow burn ever since he'd first seen her.

His cock strained against its denim confinement, and Sean knew the answer was a resounding *no*. Kissing wouldn't do anything but make him want more and more of her. Long, slow, powerful kisses. *Naked* kisses. Long, slow, hard thrusts into her hot, wet, welcoming body, maybe right there up against the glass counter.

He groaned, and Barty hissed at him, snapping him out of the fantasy and into the reality in which Brynn was staring at him like he was a lunatic, and they were standing in front of the floor-to-ceiling glass front wall of her shop.

With people walking by outside.

So, maybe not.

Instead, he took a deep breath and told her a different truth. "It's pretty impressive that you own and run your own business, when you have to deal with the curse."

She blinked, clearly not having expected him to say that.

"I—it's—thank you. I'm very proud of my little shop, actually," she admitted, and her cheeks turned pink again.

He caught himself staring at her like an idiot, and tried to come up with something to say.

"Dinner," he finally said desperately.

"Excuse me?" Brynn looked around, probably wondering if she had a bigger pair of scissors nearby so she could use them to protect herself from the crazy man. He tried again, but this time he attempted to channel his brother Oscar, who was charming and funny and great with women.

It didn't work.

"Dinner? With me? You?"

Her lips quivered, and he realized with relief that she was trying to fight back laughter instead of yelling at him to get out of her shop.

He hoped.

"Is this a thing with you? One-word invitations to meals?" Her smile faded quickly, though. "Sean, I told you, I can't get involved. The curse—"

"It's only dinner. You have to eat, right? Eat with me."

She glanced down at Barty, who seemed to be bored with the entire conversation, and then back up at Sean's face. "Well. I do have to eat. How can I refuse an eloquent invitation like that?"

"Tomorrow? No, I have the night shift. The day after tomorrow?"

A shadow passed through her winter-blue eyes, and he remembered that she'd have to do swan duty then.

"We can eat early, if you like," he added, willing her to agree.

She bit her luscious lip, which made him go right back to wanting to kiss her, but then she nodded. "All right. But just dinner."

"Just dinner. How much do I owe you for Barty?"

Brynn smiled and shook her head. "No charge. Bring him back to me for a bath and grooming soon, though, okay? He's looking a little scruffy."

"Scruffy," he said. "Is that why the shop's name is Scruffy's?"

She nodded at a framed picture of a shaggy gray dog. "Yes and no. That's Scruffy, and I named the shop in his honor, too. A play on words. I'll tell you about it at dinner."

"I look forward to it," he said, and then he headed for the door before he could say something stupid and cause her to change her mind.

"Sean," she called after him, and he stopped with one hand on the door.

"Any progress on finding that arsonist? The business owners around here were talking about nothing else at lunchtime," she said. "We're all worried."

"We'll find him," he promised grimly. "We'll stop him."

"Be careful," she said, and he carried the words—and the concern that had been clear in her voice—with him for the rest of the day.

It was almost midnight before he remembered that, for once, he had a conflict in his schedule. He'd asked Brynn out for the same night as the one for which he and Liam had planned the family barbecue.

No problem. Surely Brynn wouldn't consider meeting his *entire family* to be "getting involved," right?

Zach shook his head when he caught Sean pounding his head against his locker. "Yeah, buddy, I've had days like that, too."

Two long, quiet nights later, Sean left work almost as tired as if he'd been fighting fires nonstop. Sometimes, the slow nights were worse than the busy ones—especially when they were all on edge, waiting for an arsonist to strike again. He was hungry, exhausted, and on edge, but he wasn't interested in food or sleep. He wanted to see Brynn. *Needed* to see her.

He started out walking, with no particular direction in mind, since he didn't know where she lived and he was pretty sure her grooming business wasn't open at six in the morning. Nobody was around at dawn except cops, firefighters, and people who'd been up misbehaving all night, like the thugs hanging out on the street corner about a dozen feet in front of him. He should sleep. He was going to see her that evening, if she hadn't changed her mind. He abruptly stopped walking and scowled so fiercely at the thought, that a couple of juvenile delinquent goblins who'd started trash-talking about him wheeled around and headed the other way. The few remaining made a point of studiously looking down at the ground when he passed by, but he barely noticed them, because his mind was still on Brynn.

Please let her not have changed her mind.

She'd attracted him with her looks, but she'd captivated him with her spirit. He'd always had a different idea of beauty from most; he liked rounded figures, not model-thin ones. Interesting, intelligent faces rather than vapid, model-perfect ones. He was drawn to a sense of humor and a great laugh as much as he was to a pair of flashing eyes and a great ass.

Hey, he was a guy. He wasn't going to deny, even to himself, that a great ass wasn't a big draw.

But Brynn. *Brynn.* She was gorgeous, no doubt, with all that curly red hair and those winter-pale eyes. Her body, that he kept seeing over and over in his memory, was incredible. She was so much more than that, though. Somehow, in spite of the tough childhood she'd mentioned, and in spite of a curse that had hijacked fully a third of her life, she'd been tough enough to start and run her own business. She was compassionate enough to calm an angry cat and diagnose Barty's fury as worry for Sean's mom.

How could a woman like that still be alone, the curse be damned? If he ever got lucky enough to have the chance to be with her, he'd never—never what?

What did he think he could do? Tell her he was a fire demon and live with her happily ever after? Who was he kidding? Was it even possible for a *worse* combination to exist than fire and feathers? Just because something about Brynn touched the soul-deep loneliness he'd been living with for so long didn't mean he had any chance with her, or even any right to try. He should call her and apologize, and then make a point to never see her again. That would be the right thing to do. The *gentlemanly* thing to do—an expression that his father had so often used.

"Screw *that*," he snarled, and a banshee hunched on top of a nearby roof screeched and took flight.

"It's only dinner," he shouted after the creature, as it winged its way off into the sunrise.

She had to eat, right?

SEVEN

After Brynn closed the shop and took a quick shower in her private restroom in the back, she dried her hair, got dressed, and wondered what she thought she was doing. She stared at her reflection in the mirror, and an unfamiliar person stared back: a woman who wore eyeliner and mascara and even a little lipstick. A woman who'd dressed to impress a man whom she had no intention of keeping.

Did she?

Unnerved by her conflicting thoughts, she put the makeup bag down, figuring she'd done the best she could, and smoothed down the skirt of her one and only little black dress. She'd spent the past two days talking herself into and out of having dinner with Sean. It wasn't the idea of the dinner date itself; she'd been out on dates before. She was a normal, healthy woman, after all. She liked men. She liked dinner. But this time was different.

Sean scared her to death.

It wasn't just that he was unbelievably hot, although he was. Tall, dark, and delicious. The muscles, the hair, the amazing cheekbones, and those melting, chocolate-brown eyes were all bad enough, but when he smiled, she wanted to rip his clothes off with her teeth. It was a little late in the day to discover the latent sex fiend lurking inside her, so she figured that her extreme reaction was all about Sean.

She'd met plenty of great-looking men, though. This was Bordertown, after all. The Fae were almost always beautiful, even the men, and water demons were a little like self-servicing plastic surgeons—they could use their powers to enhance their looks whenever they wanted. So, sure, she'd seen hot guys before, but a lot of them were so arrogant and vain that she'd been turned off by the first words out of their mouths.

Sean, on the other hand—he was anything but charming or smooth. She smiled, remembering how he'd asked her to dinner in the first place, standing there with that "deer in the path of the Wild Hunt" expression, as if he'd been sure she'd turn him down. He'd raced out of the shop, clutching poor Barty, so fast that she hadn't had a chance to get his phone number or give him hers, so she was guessing he'd show up here at the shop.

If he didn't show, she'd probably be better off, anyway. She didn't need complications.

She walked out into the shop, almost not sure which she was hoping for—that Sean would show up or that he wouldn't—but ultimately she couldn't lie to herself. She would be disappointed if he stood her up. Even a little bit devastated, maybe.

The realization scared her all over again. How had he become so important to her, so fast? What was she going to do about it?

The knock on the door jolted her out of her low-level panic, and she turned to find Sean standing there, darkly elegant in a white shirt and black pants, and all of her mental reservations fell away like dog fur beneath the shears. She wanted this. She wanted *him*.

She unlocked the door.

Sean never thought it would take so much effort to keep from swallowing his tongue. She was so damn beautiful in her simple black dress, with her curls, brushed loose and shining, hanging in a thick, luxurious mass down her back. He wanted to bury his hands in her hair and smooth the shining strands against his face. He wanted to see it spread across his pillow. His body tightened at the pillow idea, and he had to clench his teeth against the rush of desire that swept through him.

"I didn't know what to wear," she said hesitantly, and he realized he'd been standing there silently staring at her like an idiot, probably with his mouth hanging open like the fish on the wall at O'Malley's. The one that came to life, sang songs, and heckled the customers.

"You look amazing," he told her honestly, and then he realized he hadn't told her they were going to a barbecue. Women had dress codes or something for what they wore. She probably wouldn't have wanted to get so dressed up for a barbecue, but he'd be damned if he'd regret it. She looked like his own personal dream of the perfect woman, come to life just for him.

And he was ambushing her with dinner with his family.

He *was* an idiot. The *fish* was smarter than him.

"Are you okay?" She was starting to look concerned, and little wonder.

"I'm going to throw myself on your mercy," he confessed. "I ran out of here so fast the other day that I didn't get your number, because I was afraid you'd find a reason to say no if I hung around.

So I didn't have a way to call you and tell you we're actually going to a barbecue."

She raised one eyebrow as she stepped out and locked the door behind her.

"Yes, I can see the problem. So hard to look up Scruffy's in the Bordertown phone book or online," she said dryly.

The dress came down to a few inches above her knees, but there was a little discreet slit up the front that flashed her leg at him as she walked, and it distracted him completely as he opened his car door for her.

"Yeah," he said, clearing his throat and shoving away all thoughts of pinning her against the car and biting her neck until she moaned. "Yeah, that would have been a great idea, if I'd thought of it. Although honestly I would have been worried that if I called, you'd have had a chance to change your mind."

She stopped, inches in front of him, and the scent of violets and spring rain teased his senses.

"You're being very candid, Sean," she murmured. "Is it sincere or is it meant to disarm me into telling you my secrets, I wonder?"

He blinked. "You have *more* secrets?"

Brynn started laughing and then slid into the car, flashing an appealing length of bare leg. "Smooth, Sean. Very smooth."

By the time they finished discussing her day (three dogs, one cat, and a rabbit who'd encountered a skunk) and his day (no progress or news on the arson case), they were pulling up in front of Sean's family home. Brynn looked around in obvious disbelief at the residential neighborhood and then narrowed her eyes.

"When you said a barbecue, I assumed you meant Bordertown Barbecue, which was already sketchy considering the rumors of the kind of meats they put in their pulled 'pork,' " she said darkly. "It did not even occur to me that you'd be introducing me to your friends on our first date."

"I'm not," he protested.

"Not what?"

"Not introducing you to my friends. Also, I like the sound of 'first' date, because it implies there will be a second date," he said, smiling hopefully. "We don't have to stay long, but I promised I'd stop by."

She frowned at him and crossed her arms under her breasts, which did breathtaking things to her cleavage and promptly made him lose his train of thought again. So he quit talking and jumped out of the car, walked around to open her door, and held out his hand.

She met his gaze for a beat before she took his hand, so he didn't let go of her all the way to the house, just in case.

"You live here?"

"Nope."

"But you're not introducing me to your friends?" She slanted a suspicious look at him.

"Nope." He started to knock on the cheerful red door that he'd given a fresh coat of paint only the month before, but it flew open before his fist could connect.

"Sean! You brought a friend," his mother said, beaming.

"They're not friends. They're my family," he told Brynn, tightening his grip on her hand.

She smiled up at him and whispered five words through clenched teeth. "I'm going to kill you."

But she followed his mom into the house, so Sean called it a win. Whether or not he was going to end up dead later, she was all his for now.

EIGHT

Brynn's stomach clenched into a tangle worse than the one the gum had made in Barty's fur. She'd swallowed her misgivings and agreed to have dinner with the first man she'd ever met who pushed every single one of her buttons, and now she'd ended up at dinner at his mother's house. If she hadn't known about Mrs. O'Malley's illness, she would have wondered what kind of grown man took a woman home to Mom for their first date. Since she *did* know, the fact that Sean had brought her here was actually kind of touching. Mrs. O'Malley led her into a spacious family room, comfortably decorated with big, sturdy-looking furniture, lots of plants, and dozens of framed photos of Sean and his brothers at varying ages from babyhood to adulthood.

"Mom, this is Brynn. Brynn, this is my mom," Sean said, grinning at both of them.

"It's Kathleen, and you are very welcome to my home."

"Brynn Carroll. You have a lovely home, Kathleen."

Kathleen O'Malley was clearly ill. Her skin had thinned to near translucence, and she was far too thin. Wisps of close-cropped white hair feathered across her head as if she'd lost most or all of it recently and it was only just starting to grow back. Her warm smile, however, gave no hint of anything but delight.

"I heard all about you," she confided, taking Brynn's hand in her slender fingers. "You saved my dear Bartholomeow from the shame of an unsightly tail."

Kathleen's smile let Brynn know she was gently poking fun at her own "emergency."

"Sean said you were pretty," she continued, and Brynn felt her face warm up.

"Sean's kind of pretty himself," Brynn said, flashing a conspiratorial smile.

A shout of masculine laughter sounded from the entry to the kitchen, and Brynn looked over to see a slightly older, slightly less-rough-edged version of Sean leaning against the archway.

"Oh, he's pretty all right, but I'm much prettier."

Sean scowled and put a territorial arm around Brynn's waist, surprising her. "Back off, Oscar. Brynn's not interested in self-proclaimed ladies' men."

Oscar's eyes widened. "Well, well. So that's how it is," he said quietly. "Interesting."

Brynn pulled away from Sean and crossed the room to shake Oscar's hand.

"I'm happy to discuss who and what I'm interested in all by my little old self," she said lightly, slanting a glance back at Sean.

Oscar held on to her hand for a little bit too long. "It's very nice to meet you, Brynn Carroll, although you have very bad taste in men," he said, grinning. "I hope you like steaks."

"You leave Sean's girl alone and go outside with your brothers to watch the grill," Kathleen chided her son. "She's going to help me with the pies, aren't you?"

Brynn nodded and then watched, bemused, as Sean and his brother jostled and joked their way out the kitchen door and, presumably, into the backyard. She looked at Kathleen, who was maybe about five foot nothing, and then at the door through which the two big men had departed.

"You had *five* of them?"

Kathleen blinked and then started laughing, and Brynn flushed as she realized what she'd said.

"I'm so sorry. I don't really have much in the way of social skills. I spend most days mainly in the company of cats, dogs, and dill-scented wolverines," she explained, feeling painfully foolish.

"And you spend a third of your nights as a swan," Kathleen said quietly, looking up at Brynn with eyes filled with compassion and understanding.

Brynn's shoulders slumped. "He told you?"

Kathleen patted her arm. "Honey, this is Bordertown. I'd almost be worried if you were plain vanilla human. The most surprising thing about you isn't that you turn feathery a couple of times a week, anyway."

"It's not?" Brynn picked up the stack of plates Kathleen indicated, but then stopped. "What is the most surprising thing about me? I'd think with a name like O'Malley you'd be used to seeing red hair."

Kathleen smiled gently at Brynn's lame attempt at a joke. "What surprises me the most is that my Sean finally brought someone home. He's never introduced me to a woman in his life before."

Sean watched Brynn as she gradually relaxed around his family, and he wavered between wanting to drag her off so they could spend time alone, and feeling an unreasonable burst of pride that she liked his family maybe as much as they clearly liked her.

Some of them maybe liked her *too* much.

He glared at Blake, who'd leaned a little too close to Brynn, laughing at something she'd said, but Blake just grinned at him and shook his head. Liam and Yeats were at the pub, so he'd only had to contend with two of his brothers, thankfully. They'd managed to work out plans for chores and house repair over steaks and salad, and now that they'd polished off the pies, Sean was ready to escape and get Brynn away from their evil clutches. Oscar was too damn charming for his own good, and Blake had been making Brynn laugh too damn much. It all left Sean feeling like he was ready to thump their heads together like he hadn't done since they were kids.

His mom turned toward Sean and smiled, and his heart cracked open a little. She was too frail—too thin—too sick. He'd deliberately taken a job where he could save people; why the hell couldn't he save her?

She touched his arm. "She's truly delightful, Sean. I'm so glad you brought her to meet me."

"I know. She's amazing, Mom. Tough, like you." His gaze returned to Brynn. Barty lay sleeping curled up in her lap and, for the first time in his life, he was jealous of a cat. "I think we're going to head out. Spend some time alone before she has to report to the fountain."

His mother nodded. "I understand. Bring her back soon, okay?"

Sean smiled and kissed his mom on the cheek. "I'll try."

He stood up and held out a hand to Brynn, and felt a surge of fierce, possessive triumph when she took it.

"We're out of here, boys," he told his brothers. "Cleanup is on you tonight."

They didn't offer more than token protests, which made Sean suspicious, until he realized that they were on their best behavior for Brynn. Funny the effect she had on the O'Malley men.

Brynn leaned down and gave his mom a quick hug before they left, and Sean had to swallow over the lump in his throat. He didn't speak again until they were in the car, buckling up.

"Thank you for that. We needed to sort out the house chores, and my mom was thrilled to meet you," he said, looking down at the steering wheel, out the windshield—anywhere but at Brynn.

"She's amazing," Brynn said softly. "You were lucky to grow up with her and such a big family. My mom died when I was young, and I never knew my dad."

"No siblings?"

"No. Just me." Her face was tense in the pale glow of the streetlights. "My family tends to stop procreating after the one daughter."

"I'd offer you a couple of brothers, but I think they'd like it a little bit too much," he said, hoping to make her smile. "Believe me, I tried to sell them, give them away, and even pay people to take them when I was a kid."

Her peal of laughter was his reward. "Really?"

"Oh, yeah. Once, I put up a sign in the yard that said, *For sale: 4 used brothers. Cheap.* Except I spelled it wrong, *C-H-E-E-P*, and my stupid brothers followed me around making bird noises and pounding on me for a week." He grinned at the memory, and Brynn stared at him in disbelief.

"Boys have an interesting idea of fun, don't they?"

He thought back to how he'd gotten revenge for the bird noises, and how long it had taken him to find four rotten eggs, and he started laughing and put the car in gear. "Oh, yeah. Definitely interesting."

NINE

They talked about everything and nothing, sitting on Brynn's front porch, and when the time came for her to go to the fountain, Sean insisted on walking there with her. Brynn changed into jeans and a sweatshirt; easy on-and-off clothes.

"I don't like this," Sean grumbled, shoving his hands in his pockets as they walked. "It's not safe. Anybody could bother you, or hurt you, or even eat you. What if some creature passing by happens to be hungry? You can't protect yourself as a swan."

She slanted a glance at him. "It's not that I don't appreciate your concern, but I've been doing this awhile, and my ancestors before me for a thousand years, or so the legend goes. Do you think we would have lasted ten days, let alone ten centuries, if the moon didn't extend her protection?"

He blew out a breath and nodded. "Of course. Moon magic. I should have figured that out."

"She doesn't want anything to happen to her pet singers, after all," Brynn said bitterly.

"How does that work?"

"I'm not sure. It's not like laser beams shoot out of my wings or something. From the best we can figure out, the moon's magic shields us and gives off a 'you can look, but don't touch' vibe. It almost always works when I'm getting dressed and undressed, too, actually, which is why I was so surprised that you saw me. So far, nobody has ever tried to hurt me."

They turned the corner to Fountain Square, and Brynn's shoulders slumped. The last thing she wanted to do was spend the next several hours floating mindlessly in the fountain, singing, but the curse was already taking hold. She could feel the tingles in her arms and legs that preceded the change.

"Sean, I—"

Her thoughts scattered when she looked up at him. His eyes were glowing hot red-orange, and her first reaction was to be wary, but her second reaction was far more primal and erotic. She turned toward him like a flower seeking the sun, wanting nothing more than to be warmed by his heat; captured by his fire, when she'd been so cold for so long.

"Beautiful," she whispered, staring into his extraordinary eyes.

"Yes. You are," he said roughly, and then he wrapped his strong arms around her and captured her mouth with his own.

His kiss was a revelation. He claimed her with a powerful masculine dominance that weakened her knees and stole her breath from her body. His tongue pushed at the seam of her lips and she opened for him, moaning when he delved inside and plundered, taking what he wanted like a pirate come to claim his spoils. She clutched at his shoulders, dizzily wondering if she would collapse if he let her go, but he held her even more tightly.

He was relentless—demanding. He tasted like the apple pie from dinner; cinnamon had suddenly become her favorite spice. She kissed him back, taking as well as giving, riding the day's emotional roller coaster up and up and then over the crest of heat and sensation. If they hadn't been in the middle of Fountain Square, she would have started taking clothes off—his or hers, it didn't matter—and then—

Fountain Square.

The curse.

She pulled away, though everything in her rebelled against it. Her breathing was too shaky to form words for several seconds, so she rested her forehead on Sean's chest and drew in a long, deep breath.

"Never before. I've never forgotten myself and the curse like that, not even for a second. Sean, you're—"

"I'm the man who wants you in his life," he rasped, and she felt a moment of sharp pleasure that the kisses had affected him as much as they had her, but the curse's demand increased, overwhelming everything else, as it always had.

Brynn's eyes burned, and she was shocked to realize she was fighting back tears of loss and longing. Longing for the normal life she could never have.

"I *never* cry," she said, but it was too late. The warm wash of sadness overflowed, and she tried to turn away from Sean, but pushing against his hard, muscular chest was like pushing against the marble statue.

"Don't cry," he said, and his voice was almost frantic. "Damn me for a fool. Brynn, I'm sorry. I should have asked your permission or—"

"Let. Me. Go," she said urgently, and he released her, clenching his hands into fists at his sides.

She ran for "her" bench, tearing her clothes and shoes off, but she barely had time to reach her backpack before the transformation took her. The moon was jealous of her songbird, and evidently Brynn had delayed the moment for too long.

She stood, naked and shivering, while the brief agony of the shift took her, and the last sight she saw through her human eyes was Sean, pain stark in the grim lines of his face as he watched her.

Once she was a swan, she didn't care about anything except reaching the water and beginning her song, but the wisp of human consciousness that floated in the back of her brain thought that both song and water were especially icy that night; cold as the deep reaches of a solitary heart.

Sean shoved Brynn's clothes in her backpack and then tossed it on the marble bench and sat next to it, all the while cursing himself for being an overbearing buffoon. He'd rather face a raging fire without any of his safety gear than ever be forced to see Brynn crying again. His chest ached, and he didn't like it one bit. How could her tears have so much power over him that they reduced him to helplessness?

He should have asked, or warned her, or something. *Anything.* Except—she'd been kissing him *back*. Her sweet mouth had dueled with his, and she'd held tightly to him with the same ferocity he'd felt as he kissed her.

Claimed her.

Claimed? He jumped up off the bench, suddenly unable to sit still. Where had that thought come from? He'd only just met her and hardly knew anything about her. It was definitely not time to think about claiming.

His gaze arrowed to the elegant black swan floating serenely in the waters of the fountain, raising her head toward the moon, and a fierce wave of protectiveness swept through him. *Claiming* might be a good word, after all. There were other words that he'd thought of, too, when he'd looked into her silvery blue eyes.

Holding. Touching. Keeping.

Mine.

The otherworldly sound of her song wove through the strands of his consciousness, tantalizing and seducing, and it took him a few beats to realize that he'd never heard a swan actually *sing* before. It must be a side effect of the magic. There were no words, of course, but Brynn—as a swan—was singing; her song was an ethereal, plaintive melody that tugged at his heart and wound its way into his soul.

He wanted to keep her. The shock of the discovery rocked him back on his heels so hard that Sean didn't pay much attention to the tall man in the long black coat until he'd walked to the edge of the fountain and stretched out a hand toward Brynn.

"Get the hell away from that swan," he told the intruder, his voice cold and deadly.

The man turned to face Sean, who recognized him instantly and prepared for a difficult and possibly fatal disagreement.

"Luke Oliver," Sean said. "I heard you were running for sheriff. Shouldn't you be off somewhere kissing hands and shaking babies?"

Oliver bared his teeth in something that might have been called a smile. "I never shake babies in Bordertown. Who knows what they might transform into?"

Sean didn't think the man whom everyone called the Dark Wizard of Bordertown had said *transform* by coincidence. The fire demon inside him wanted to blast the wizard, but he fought back against the rage that was jacking up his body temperature to a dangerous level.

"You'll be leaving the swan alone," Sean said evenly, as he advanced on Oliver.

Oliver raised his eyebrows and then laughed. "You're as *fiery* as your grandmother was, aren't you?"

Sean abruptly stopped. "You knew my grandmother? Which one?"

None of the boys had ever met his dad's parents. They lived

deep in Demon Rift and had disowned their son for marrying a human. His mom's mother had lived in Bordertown but had died several years before.

"I wouldn't go so far as to say I *knew* her. I met your grandparents once, when I was traveling through the Firelands," Oliver said, his face shadowed with memory. "She wanted to singe my ass for me when I accidentally walked through the edge of her garden."

The corners of the wizard's mouth turned up in a wry grin. "And I mean *singe* literally, as I'm sure you know, fire demon."

Sean folded his arms across his chest, wariness replacing anger, but he didn't bother trying to lie. "So. You know. What do you want?"

Oliver studied him. "I don't want anything. I damn sure don't want to be sheriff. I have no interest in telling Bordertown about your heritage, if that's what you mean."

Something in Sean relaxed. "You mean you don't think a fire demon is behind the arson?"

"No, I do not," Oliver said grimly. "But when I find out who is, he won't be long for this world—or for any of the three realms."

The remaining traces of Sean's wariness vanished, replaced by a feeling of kinship. "If I don't find him first."

Oliver nodded and then headed off to wherever it was that wizards went at midnight. When he reached the edge of the square, he stopped and looked back at Sean.

"I was wrong. I do want something from you, O'Malley."

Sean tensed. "Of course you do. That's the way of life, isn't it? What is it?"

"Be good to Brynn," Oliver said. "I've known her since she was a baby, and I wouldn't be . . . *kind* . . . to someone who hurt her."

"Neither would I," Sean said, and the words were both a promise and a threat.

TEN

Brynn hopped up and out of the fountain, transforming back to human as she moved, and headed straight for Sean. He sat, unmoving, on the same bench where she'd dropped her clothes, and even in swan form she'd known that he'd stayed and watched over her the entire time. She was naked, but she didn't care. She needed to touch him, hold him, reassure him that it hadn't been his presumption that had caused her tears, but his passion.

"You stayed," she said, her voice breaking. "You *stayed*."

He leapt up and strode toward her, holding out his arms, and she flew into them.

"Nobody has ever stayed," she whispered. "Nobody but Scruffy, and I kept him, and now I think I have to keep you, too, because—because—"

But she didn't have time to find or articulate any reasons. Sean lifted her off her feet and fiercely captured her mouth again, branding her with his savage possession.

"Put your clothes on so I can take you somewhere and take them off again," he said, and his deep voice was a steely command coated in velvety seduction.

She laughed at his words and trembled at his touch, but within minutes she was dressed and they were sprinting toward her tiny house. She unlocked her door with shaking fingers, and then he was kicking the door shut, locking it, and stalking toward her with an almost feral determination.

"I'll be having you now," he said, his Irish lilt singing out in the words, sensuous and rich.

Her breath caught in her throat, and she raised a hand to her chest, backing away almost instinctively. He was too big, too male, too dominant. She'd never be able to control this man, and she prided herself on a life lived entirely under her control.

"You can't just tell someone you'll be having her," she said breathlessly.

He threw back his head and laughed. "Oh, my beautiful one. I will, and I did, and if you want me to leave, you'd better tell me right now, or my next move will be to rip those clothes from your body and taste every gleaming inch of your lovely skin."

He stopped moving and stood, completely still, like a predator deciding whether to pounce. "Will you be telling me to leave, then, Brynn my lovely?"

Brynn hesitated for a single heartbeat, but deep in her heart she knew that she'd already made her decision. She'd made it when she'd found him waiting for her.

"No. I don't want you to leave, because I'll be having you, too."

Triumph soared through Sean, and he didn't give her a chance to change her mind. He grasped her luscious ass and lifted her up, groaning as she instinctively lifted her legs around his hips, pressing her body against his straining cock, exactly where he needed her to be.

"Where?" He gritted out the word from between clenched teeth.

She pointed toward a short hallway and then started kissing and nibbling his neck as he walked. His vision blurred and the door to her bedroom seemed to be limned in red-gold light. He knew his eyes must be changing, and he knew he should care, should stop, should give a fiddler's damn about keeping her from seeing them, but all he could think of was getting his hands on her skin and his mouth on her sweet, round breasts.

"I want you," she whispered, and his cock twitched, growing even harder, until he wondered desperately if he'd even be able to work his way out of his pants.

He kissed her, deep, hard, and long, and then he set her down on her feet and pulled her shirt over her head in one swift motion.

"Finally," he said, covering her breasts with his hands and blowing out a deep breath. "I don't mean to sound crude, but I've wanted to get my hands on these since I first saw you."

She laughed, and the sound was high and wild and breathless. "Imagine that. A man who likes breasts. How surprising."

"Oh, but yours are spectacular," he said, leaning down to surround one taut nipple with his lips.

He sucked, hard, and she cried out, digging her fingers into his shoulders.

"Oh, Sean, *yes*," she said, and the words were kindling to his flame.

He tossed her on the bed, stripped off his clothes, and stared down at her, indulging his need to see every inch of her body, but she was still too covered up. He didn't like it.

"The pants. Take them off," he said roughly.

Her eyes widened, but she complied, and then she was beautifully, gloriously naked, and his hungry need for her burned into a conflagration. She was exactly what the lonely, lost part of his soul had been craving for so long, and she was here, and she was *his.*

He wasn't ever going to let her go.

Brynn blushed as he stared down at her, but she also reveled in the powerful desire that blazed from his fascinating, glowing eyes. She held up her arms, wordlessly enticing him to come to her, as she let her gaze wander down his hard, muscular body. His powerful chest narrowed down to the carved muscle of his abdomen, and an intriguing trail of silky hair seemed to point the way to his large, jutting erection. He was aggressively, proudly male, and he'd come to claim her like a conquering hero from a fairy tale.

Brynn, who spent every third night of her life as a living, breathing participant in a fairy tale, wondered if she'd finally become the princess instead of merely the swan. Sean was no Prince Charming, though. He was too rough—too *alpha*—to ever be considered charming. More a pirate than a prince. But now he was *hers*, unpolished edges and all.

He joined her on the bed, pulling her into his arms. She dared to touch her tongue to the edge of his ear, and he rewarded her with a long, heartfelt groan. He caught her mouth with his, invading and possessing, while his busy, clever hands stroked her sides, her bottom, and her breasts, until he drove her to the brink of insanity. Creamy heat rushed to the juncture between her thighs, and her nipples tightened until they ached from the sizzling electricity of his touch.

"Sean. I want you. Touch me everywhere," she demanded, and he lifted his head and flashed a wickedly seductive smile.

"Oh, I will, lass. Before dawn paints the sky, I will touch and taste every bit of you," he promised. Her pirate had surprised her again by turning poet.

He kissed her again and again, until she was drowning in need and want and sensation, and then he shifted slightly so his hand could reach between their bodies. He caressed her exactly where she needed and wanted him to, and she cried out from the sensation.

"You're so wet for me," he said, and his big body shuddered under her hands. "I need you, Brynn. I'm not sure I can wait—"

"I don't want you to wait," she said. "The drawer next to the bed. Hurry."

He kissed her again, long and lingering, and then opened the drawer where she kept the unopened box of condoms she'd bought a while ago in a random burst of optimism. He quickly covered himself and then he was back, positioning himself between her legs.

She wrapped her legs around his, and her arms around his neck, urging him on, and he plunged into her with one powerful thrust and then stopped, holding himself up with straining arms.

"You feel so unbelievably good, Brynn. I can't—I can't be slow about this."

"Hard. Fast. Now," she said, bucking against him.

He took her at her word, driving into her with all the power and passion she'd suspected lay just underneath his calm exterior. She was helpless to do anything but match his pace and his urgency, driven by her own need to reach the climax that rushed toward her on wings of red-gold flames.

Her body tensed, clenching around him as he took her up and over, and her mind and body exploded into sparkling waves of sensation. She clung to Sean, calling his name over and over, and it goaded him into increasing his pace, until he was thrusting into her so powerfully that a second, stronger wave of climax broke over her just before he roared out his own completion. Shuddering with the force of it, he slowly rocked to a stop, and then he turned on his side and wrapped her in his arms while still inside her.

"You belong with me," he said, and she nodded, agreeing completely, before she realized what the consequences of it all might be for the future.

"Sean—" she began, but he kissed her again, silencing her insecurities, if only for a while.

His eyes, still glowing with the color of flame, stared into hers, and he reached down with one hand and pulled the quilt over her. "Let me take care of the condom, and then we need sleep. All the rest of it can wait. *Please.*"

His penis pulsed inside her as if punctuating his request, and she gasped a little bit but then nodded. He was gone and back quickly, and he pulled her back into his embrace as if he'd missed her in even that short time.

"Okay. Let's get some sleep," she said, snuggling close, reluctant to spoil the moment with talk of curses or futures. She'd never, *ever,* felt anything like the incredible magic of Sean's lovemaking and—just this once—she wanted to forget her problems. She wanted to simply bask in the afterglow.

Serious, independent, responsible Brynn could wait until later. Sensual, decadent, feminine Brynn owned the *now.* As she lay there with her body tucked against his, she realized that he hadn't only filled her body, but her heart and soul, too, and she waited for the wave of terror to wash over her at the realization.

It didn't.

Instead, a sense of complete peace and contentment swept through her, a feeling of belonging. A feeling of *home.* She wanted this man, and she was beginning to wonder how far she would go to keep him.

ELEVEN

Sean woke to the noon sun slanting through the window shades, turning Brynn's auburn hair to a glowing coppery red. She slept in his arms, and he stayed quiet and still, not wanting to wake her, content simply to watch her sleep.

She'd turned his life upside down, this magical woman. He, the eternal loner, suddenly wanted to find a way to make room for her in his life. She'd already stolen a place in his heart. Her delicate lashes fluttered as she slowly woke, and she blushed when she glanced down and noticed that his cock was hard.

"I won't apologize," he told her. "I'm always going to be hard when I wake up next to you."

"Always? Sean, we have to talk about this."

He hated to see worry in those winter-blue eyes of hers, so he decided to do his best to replace it with passion.

"We could talk about it," he said, rolling onto his back and pulling her on top of him. "Or we could do this."

With that, he gently rocked his hips up and down, rubbing

against her sensitive clit, and he enjoyed it far too much when her eyes glazed over and she gasped.

"Oh! That feels so good," she said, almost moaning.

Then she flashed a grin and encircled his cock with one slender hand.

"But if we're going to distract each other from serious conversation, I think it's my turn," she said, gently but firmly stroking the length of his erection up and down, until he was shaking from the effort it took not to come in her hand.

After that, they spent quite a long time distracting each other, both in bed and in her shower, where Sean discovered that a wet, soapy, and slippery Brynn was very distracting indeed.

Brynn made sandwiches in her cheerful blue-and-white kitchen, casting glances from beneath her lashes at the large, utterly *male* person who'd made himself at home, in both her house and her life, in the space of only a few days.

"I've told you about the curse, at least the short version. Let me give you more than the headlines," she said, handing him the largest sandwich she'd ever made in her life.

He glanced at it and grinned. "You must think I really worked up an appetite."

"I sure did," she blurted out, and then she felt her face go scarlet. "Stop it. Eat your sandwich."

He laughed, but he picked up his sandwich. After a few bites, he glanced across the tiny kitchen table at her. "Maybe give me the full version?"

So she did, neatly folding her napkin and placing it next to her plate, and then telling him about the peasant girl, and the king, and the moon's bargain. When she finished, she waited for him to show his disappointment or, worse, his revulsion at the thought of becoming involved with a woman who was destined to doom her own daughter to the curse of the black swan.

His face was cast in hard lines, and he crumpled his own napkin into a ball in his fist. "What a bitch," he said grimly.

She blinked, utterly confused. "What? Who?"

"The moon. Or the moon goddess, depending on your beliefs. Whoever or whatever made that bargain was not playing fair. One saved life in exchange for a thousand years of servitude? I don't think so." He slammed his fist on the table, rattling the salt and pepper shakers. "We have to find a way to break the curse."

She sat back in her chair, nonplussed. Of all the reactions she'd expected, this wasn't even on the very bottom of the list. Break the curse? Nobody had even considered that, as far as she knew, in the entire history of her family.

"It's the *moon*," she said, enunciating carefully. "How do you break a curse cast by the moon?"

He shrugged. "You find a witch who's bound to the moon goddess and ask him or her. This is Bordertown. I'm sure we can figure it out."

She was already shaking her head. "I don't want you to have false hope. The moon is too powerful. I plan never to have children, because I don't want to do this to my daughter. The curse will stop with me."

"Okay," he said blandly, and then he picked up his sandwich and took a huge bite.

"Okay? What do you mean 'okay'?"

After he swallowed and took a drink of water, he grinned at her. "Okay. We'll find a way to break the curse, or we won't. Either way, I'm not planning to let you out of my life, so just deal with it."

"Deal with it?" Her voice came out sounding unnatural, and she realized she was echoing him like a stupid parrot.

"You forget, we have something that your ancestors didn't have all those years ago," he said, his rich brown eyes sparkling with humor.

"What is that?"

"Birth control."

Her mouth fell open. "I know we have birth control, you idiot. But I couldn't ask you to be content with a woman who can never give you children."

"I want you, Brynn Carroll," he told her, shoving his chair back and rounding the table to pull her up and into his arms. "We'll figure out the curse and the children later, and in the meantime we can adopt a dog or three. They'll be the cleanest, best-groomed dogs in Bordertown."

"But—"

Sean stopped her by the simple means of kissing her until she gave up and kissed him back, but his conscience prodded him with its sharp blade until he reluctantly pulled away from her.

"There's something else, though," he said, steeling himself to tell her the truth about his fire demon heritage, hoping that she could understand and accept him.

Hoping she wouldn't run screaming or throw him out of her house.

Before he could figure out a way to begin, the antique rotary phone on her counter rang, and they both looked at it as if it were an alien artifact.

"I should answer it," she said apologetically. "It's the number I give out for customer emergencies."

"Like wolverines in the pickle vat?" He grinned at her. "Skunk encounters?"

"Exactly." She picked up the phone and had a quick conversation about, from what he could decipher, a garage mechanic's dog who'd rolled around in automotive oil. The owner couldn't get it out and was worried.

"Yes, I'll be glad to come in early. I'll meet you at my shop in twenty minutes," she said, ending the call.

"You have to go," Sean said, resigned and more than a little relieved. A reprieve, then, until he had to admit that half of his DNA came from the most hated and feared species of creature in Bordertown.

"I have to go," she confirmed, already cleaning up and getting ready to leave.

He stopped her with a hand on her shoulder. "I need to tell you a secret of my own, Brynn, before we go any further."

She frowned. "If you tell me that you're married—"

He laughed. "Are you kidding? My mother would have skinned me alive if I had a wife and brought a date to her house."

"Okay, well, tell me this evening. After work," she said, a slight frown shadowing her beautiful face.

"Can't. I have to work tonight, too," he said.

"Then come by when you get done, even if it's the middle of the night," she said. "Whatever it is, it can't be worse than my curse, right?"

Her attempt at a smile faded when he didn't return it. She squared her shoulders. "Okay," she repeated. "We'll figure this out."

They finished cleaning up in silence, and then they both headed for the door and their respective days. He'd just stepped out onto the porch when she stopped.

"I forgot my keys," she said. "You go ahead, and I'll see you later."

Sean hesitated, but he did want to check up on his mom before he went to work. He pulled Brynn close and kissed her again, taking his time about it, right there on her porch.

"I'll see you tonight," he promised. "Good luck with the oil emergency."

She smiled. "Thanks. All in a day's work at Scruffy's."

Sean sauntered down the steps and headed for his car. It wasn't until he'd traveled halfway to his mother's house that he realized he was whistling. They'd figure it out. She'd be okay with his secret.

He refused to let things turn out any other way.

TWELVE

Brynn rushed to her bedroom to get her keys, but before she could make it back to the front door, it started to swing open, and sheer, effervescent joy bubbled inside her. He hadn't been able to leave without another kiss, maybe.

"Back so soon," she teased, but the large man who entered her house wasn't Sean.

She stumbled back a step, but she wasn't really worried, not yet, even though he was entering her house uninvited, because he looked familiar to her for some reason.

"Can I help you?"

The man raised a closed fist to just in front of his mouth, opened his hand, and blew. A shower of fine gray dust shot forward into Brynn's face before she could duck or dodge away.

"What—" she managed, but the rest of the sentence died away as the poison entered her system. The room spun, and her vision funneled down to black, except for sparks of light from the matches her attacker was lighting.

Matches? But why—?

Her last thought before unconsciousness claimed her: *Sean.*

THIRTEEN

Sean heard the alarm when he was still halfway down the block from the station, and he started sprinting. The arsonist had taken a few days off, but even though Sean and the rest of his crew hoped the scumbag had fallen off a cliff or, more fitting, set himself on fire and was now out of commission, nobody was relaxing. This could be him again, and—worse—he could be escalating. People could die.

Please let it be a normal, boring backyard grill out of control.

"House fire," Sue told him, when he started gearing up. "We don't know if it's him or not."

"Where is it?"

She rattled off the address and Sean dropped his helmet, whirled around, and grabbed her. "What did you say?"

She blinked and glanced quite deliberately at his hands on her shoulders. He immediately released her.

"I'm sorry, Sue, but I need to hear that address again *right now*," he demanded. Terror sliced into him with a scalpel's edge, and rage wasn't far behind.

She repeated the address.

It was Brynn's house.

He pulled out his phone and started running.

"Scruffy's Pet Spa," he snapped, and the computer handling information repeated the name and then connected him to a phone that rang and rang, six long rings, before the voicemail picked up and informed him that Brynn had gone home for the night.

She'd never reset her message today.

She wasn't answering the phone.

She might be in that house.

He ran faster.

Sean arrived before the truck and crew, and he was still too late. Brynn's tiny house was an inferno, and there was no way anyone could possibly be alive inside. He threw back his head and roared out his anguish and rage, and the heritage he'd spent so long denying rushed to answer his call.

Every inch of the surface of Sean's body blazed into flame. The fire was so intense and the temperature so high that his clothes and the gear he'd managed to don instantly disintegrated into ash. Unexpectedly, the fire didn't hurt him at all; not that he would even have felt the physical pain. The neighbors and other mindless lookyloos who always gathered at fires started screaming and running, probably to get away from the terrifying fire demon, but Sean didn't give a damn about any of it.

Not that he'd outed himself, not that he was scaring the populace, not that he didn't know if he'd survive what he was about to do. He hit the front of her house running and used his body as a battering ram to hurl himself through the front windows, not bothering with the door. He expected the lash of back draft that hit him, hard, but it didn't matter. None of it mattered.

No fire could compete with the blazing heat of a fire demon.

He shouted her name, over and over, but heard nothing in response except the roar of the fire. The *magically created* fire.

The arsonist had struck again, and this time he'd made it personal.

Sean crashed through crumbling, fire-engulfed walls until he reached the black and ruined hull of the kitchen that he'd sat in only hours before, promising Brynn that they'd find a way to be together.

Now she was gone, and the fiery monster who was all that was left of Sean could feel nothing but agony.

Could want nothing but revenge.

He finally stumbled out of the inferno. She wasn't here. There hadn't been any evidence of a . . . body.

Brynn hadn't been in the house.

Castilho was on the lawn, using his magic to combat the blaze. He saw Sean burst out of the house in full fire-demon mode and flinched, but to his credit he didn't back away.

"Sean. Is that you? What the hell? Why didn't you tell me?"

Sean slowly approached, unsure of his new abilities—he had no idea how close he could get to a human being without setting the person on fire.

"Didn't want you to fear me," he told the witch, whose eyes widened when he heard Sean's voice coming from the demon's mouth.

"Well, hell, if *you're* a fire demon, then they can't be all bad, can they?" Castilho grinned at him, and then turned his full attention back to the complicated magic he was working to help contain and extinguish the fire.

Sean didn't know how to react to the man's easy acceptance and, what's more, he didn't really care. He had to find Brynn.

Sue came running across the lawn, waving her phone at him. "Sean, it's Zach. He says he needs to talk to you."

He snarled at her. “No time. Have to find Brynn.”

Sue was paler than he’d ever seen her, and he’d been shoulder to shoulder with the veteran firefighter when she’d battled the worst of the worst blazes.

“You don’t understand, Sean. Zach says he has Brynn Carroll, and if you don’t show up within ten minutes, he’s going to set her on fire.”

FOURTEEN

Brynn had never been so afraid in her life. The man—Zach, he'd called himself—who'd knocked her out with poison powder and set her house on fire was absolutely, certifiably, insane. Worse, he was messing with black magic.

He'd slapped her face until she'd regained consciousness, and then he'd bragged to her about how he'd set more than seventeen fires in Bordertown and other places. The seventeen fires had claimed six victims so far, and he'd recited every single name, almost as if he were boasting, chanting the six names rhythmically like a prayer.

Like a curse.

When Brynn had been unable to hide her revulsion, he'd slapped her again, tied her hands behind her, shoved her over to a wooden box, and told her to sit. When she'd tried to fight him, he'd pulled out a plastic bag filled with more of the gray powder and asked her if she'd rather be conscious or unconscious when her lover arrived.

So now she sat, hands tied behind her, and fought back the

shuddering terror that Sean would run headfirst into Zach's trap and get himself killed. She didn't have time to fall apart. She needed to be able to think, plan, and fight back.

Zach was planning to kill Sean, and there was absolutely no way she was going to let that happen. She took a long, steadying breath, and forced herself to calm down, look around, and think. Unfortunately, there weren't any convenient caches of weapons or a telephone handy, because she wasn't living in a movie. Bruce Willis wasn't going to yippee-ki-yay his way into the building and save the day, but Sean—the man whom she now realized she loved—was going to try.

She believed in Sean far more than any movie hero, but if she didn't act fast, he was going to get himself killed.

The stench of mold and garbage permeated the interior of the hulking warehouse where she'd regained consciousness. The building was made of steel and concrete—harder to burn, Zach said—and it had clearly been abandoned years before. Piles of debris hunched in corners, and Brynn was sure the movement she'd seen at the edges of the cracked concrete floor was rats.

Zach took a break from his frantic pacing and followed her gaze.

"Rats! Are you afraid of rats, little girl?" He chortled like a caricature of an evil villain, and all she could do was watch him in disbelief.

"You kidnapped the wrong woman, if you wanted somebody who was afraid of rats," she said flatly. "Why don't you let me go, and I'll help you catch a few of those rats so they can eat your eyes out? Then at least you won't be able to see to set any more fires."

He turned his reptilian gaze on her, and she shuddered. "Watch your mouth, you slut. Dropped your pants for O'Malley fast enough, didn't you? That's the problem with people today. No morals."

"You're an arsonist and a *murderer*," she shouted at him. "How dare you speak to me about morals?"

He whirled and threw his hands into the air, hurling a bolt of green smoke at the rats, who squealed and scurried away. They didn't seem to be hurt, but they weren't sticking around, either, so Brynn didn't know how to judge the strength of Zach's magic.

Before she could say or do anything else, a thunderous roar sounded from just outside the door. Someone was shouting her name, and Brynn realized she was out of time.

Sean had arrived.

The warehouse door blew off its hinges and slammed down to the floor, and a creature she'd only heard about in rumors and fairy tales crashed into the room. Red-hot flames surrounded the shape of a big man, but they didn't seem to be burning him. The blaze moved with him—part of him—covering him like a second skin. Heat shimmered around his body like a warped version of a halo, and she didn't need to get any closer to confirm that her first impression had been right.

This was a fire demon in full, raging fury and, if the stories were true, its next move would be to set fire to Zach, Brynn, and everyone else within a half-mile radius of the warehouse. Despair washed through her, and she fought wildly against the rope tying her wrists behind her. She didn't care if it killed Zach, but she didn't want to die today, and she really, *really* didn't want to burn to death.

She jumped up off the box, but before she could take a single step the demon started running toward her, and she caught sight of its face.

His face.

The fire demon was Sean.

He hadn't been kidding about secrets.

Sean saw Brynn hunched over, one side of her face red and swollen, and any hope of restraint shattered. Zach had hurt her, and he was going to die badly. But Brynn was alive. She was *alive*.

He roared her name again and headed straight for her, not realizing until he saw her face that she might not welcome his approach. That she might be *afraid*.

Afraid of *him*.

The flames engulfing him must have malfunctioned in some way, because now they were searing his heart.

Before he could think of something to say to reassure her, he caught sight of movement in the corner and spun around, shielding Brynn with his body, and faced Zach.

"I knew it! I knew you were a fire demon all along, or at least I've known ever since I started to practice black magic," Zach said, smiling crazily.

"You were my *friend*," Sean said, low and deadly, rage and pain combining to intensify the flames surrounding him. "*Why*?"

Zach tilted his head. For an instant, he looked truly bewildered, as if he didn't understand, either, how he could have turned into such a monster, but then something evil took over and stared at Sean through Zach's eyes.

"Because I could," Zach sneered. "You kept blocking me, though. You, with your super hearing and your impervious skin. I wanted that baby to *die*, because the power I would have gained from sacrificing an innocent would have been incredible, but you had to play the hero and save her."

The madman who'd once been Sean's friend raised his hands into the air. "You just wouldn't leave it alone, would you? So now, *you* have to die, and then your woman will die. But since she's not an innocent, she's going to have to suffer quite a lot of pain first, to make her death worth my while."

Zach started laughing, and he hurled a wave of greenish-black smoke at Sean. "Goodbye, O'Malley," he screamed.

Sean braced for the impact of the magical attack, but it didn't hurt him—not one bit. Instead, the flames coating Sean's body reached out toward the smoke and greedily sucked it in, dissipating it completely.

As Zach stared at him, dumbfounded, Sean suddenly had an interesting thought about fire demons. Maybe, since nobody knew exactly what they were, nobody knew exactly how to hurt them. Or, at least, maybe Zach didn't.

"No! No, no, no, no, no," Zach shrieked, raising his hands for another attack.

"Now it's my turn," Sean said, and he instinctively called for an ability he'd only guessed he might possess, and he hurled a blast of scarlet fire.

Zach threw up a magical shield, though, and then he countered with a different kind of magic. This time, the attack smashed Sean back on his heels. Sean whirled around, absorbing the brunt of the attack and then countering with another, more powerful blast of fire that Zach couldn't deflect.

This one connected.

Zach screamed horribly as he died.

Sean slumped, exhausted and completely drained, and the flames surrounding him subsided and then disappeared completely. He fell to his knees on the cold concrete, shaking hard and unable even to stand up for one more moment, as his body reacted to his first use of his fire-demon powers.

"Brynn," he croaked, turning to look for her.

But she was gone.

FIFTEEN

Brynn stormed back into the warehouse with her backup in tow, but when she saw the aftermath of the battle, her heart screamed at her that she was too late. Sean, human again and completely naked, lay collapsed on the floor. Zach, or at least what was left of Zach, lay smoldering in a charred heap in the corner.

She ran to Sean, knelt down, and lifted his head onto her lap, tears running down her face.

"An ambulance is on the way, but you'd better wake up right now, Sean O'Malley. You wake up, or I'll get the moon to put a curse on you, too, and turn you into a—into a *pigeon*. A fat, stupid pigeon," she babbled, uncaring that Sean's brothers were watching her fall apart.

The four of them picked up Sean and Brynn both, ignoring her protests, and carried them out of the stinking building into the clean night air, not stopping until they arrived at a small park across the street and gently set the pair down on the soft grass. Brynn immediately wrapped her arms around Sean again, holding her breath as his eyes slowly opened. She was relieved to see that only a hint of red-orange fire remained in his pupils.

"A pigeon, hmm? Can a swan fall in love with a pigeon, lass? If so, then I won't be minding so very much," he said, his Irish lilt pronounced.

"I don't know about that, but a swan can fall in love with a fire demon, and I know one who has," she told him, laughing and crying all at the same time.

She kissed every inch of his face, over and over, until he caught her cheeks in his hands and held her still while he kissed her long and deep, right there on the grass in front of his brothers and, as they arrived, sirens blaring, the entire Bordertown Fire Department, all of whom cheered and made hooting noises.

"I love you, Brynn," Sean said, gazing into her eyes, and she started crying again.

"I love you, too. Never, ever scare me like that again."

Oscar took off his shirt and tossed it down over Sean's hips, laughing.

"Why don't we cover up the jewels, boyo? And welcome to the family, Brynn. Maybe you can knock some sense into my brother."

Brynn stared up at the four of them, suddenly realizing that they were hers now. And Kathleen was hers, too. She had a family.

She had a *family*.

Fresh tears poured down her face.

Sean's strong arms banded around her, and he murmured into her ear. "Let's go home, Brynn. My home is yours now."

At his words, she remembered that her own house had burned to the ground, taking all of her personal possessions with it, but the pain of loss wasn't nearly strong enough to match the exhilaration soaring through her heart. She'd only lost *things*. She still had her business, anyway, and—most important of all—Sean was safe.

Sean was safe, and he *loved* her.

"That's really terrific red hair. I think you're going to be a great O'Malley," one of the brothers said, and the others started laughing.

Brynn's mouth fell open. Things were suddenly moving very fast. "An O'Malley?"

"Yes," Sean said firmly. "*My* O'Malley. Forever."

SIXTEEN

Three months later

Sean's mother leaned on his arm as they walked from his car to Black Swan Fountain. She was fading rapidly now, the cancer carrying her away from them and into a world made up of pain and weakness. Too often, he and Brynn, or one of his brothers, would find her staring off into the distance at something—or someone—that only she could see.

"I'll see your father again soon," she suddenly said, as he arranged a warm blanket on the cold marble bench for her.

"Mom," he protested. "You have plenty of time left. Don't—"

"I don't, Sean, love, and you know it," she said gently. "Of all my boys, you were always the most realistic, even though you were the baby."

"Even though I fell in love with a swan?" He glanced at the fountain, reassuring himself that Brynn was there—safe—although he could already hear her lovely song.

"I fell in love with a fire demon," his mom replied, smiling a little. "Sean, I want you to know how happy I am that you found your Brynn. She's strong, and smart, and she loves you with her entire heart. I could never have asked for more for you, my beautiful boy."

He felt his eyes start to burn, but he smiled for his mother's sake and put an arm around her frail shoulders.

"A mother's love is one of the most powerful forces in the world, Sean. I carried you in my body and nurtured you as babies, and then cheered you on to independence as boys, and now I am so proud of you all as grown men. My biggest regret in all of this is that I have to leave you before you come to the next chapters of your stories. I wish I could see your brothers all find love, as you have. I wish I could see you bring your own children into the world and help you raise them."

He started to protest, but the gentle sadness on her face stopped him. She knew the truth and didn't want to hear false platitudes. Not now.

"I love Brynn as if she were my own daughter," his mother said, and he pretended not to see the tears that she tried to hide as they fell slowly down her face. Instead, he looked steadily at the fountain until she'd patted her cheeks dry with a tissue.

"She loves you, too, Mom. One day, when we break this curse, we're going to have a daughter and name her after you," he promised, even though it was tough to get the words out past the lump that had lodged itself in his throat.

"Oh, don't do that," she said. "Kathleen is so old-fashioned."

She thought about it for a moment. "Or at least only for a middle name . . ."

They shared a laugh and then sat in silence for a little while, watching Brynn and listening to her beautiful song.

"We'll find a way to break the curse and bring baby Kathleen into the world, don't worry," he said, hoping it was true.

"I have some ideas about that," his mother said, pulling a piece of paper out of her pocket and handing it to him. "That's one of the reasons I wanted to talk to you tonight—and here."

He scanned the paper, which turned out to be a short list of names, one of which he recognized. "Mrs. Mastroianni?"

His mother smiled. "Did you know that Mrs. Mastroianni is a pretty powerful moon witch? We have some thoughts about how to beat this curse . . ."

Her eyes lit up as she explained, and then they sat quietly, sharing the peace and moonlight for what Sean knew might be the very last time. When she grew tired, he gently helped her to his car, and then took her to her house, where the kind and wonderful nurse they'd hired to help with his mother's personal needs settled her in bed with a cup of herbal tea.

When the nurse indicated that his mother was ready, he went in to say good night.

"I love you, Mom," he said, kissing her cheek.

"I love you, Sean. Now go on with you and watch over that girl of yours until we can break the curse," she said, shooing him out with a smile.

Later that night, peacefully in her sleep, Sean's mother crossed the silver seas into the heaven in which she'd always believed. A few days later, her sons shared a bottle of fine Irish whiskey at O'Malley's Pub during her wake—the largest ever held in Bordertown—and agreed among themselves that, if the world held any justice at all, she'd found their father, and the two of them were spending eternity together, loving, laughing, and watching over their boys.

EPILOGUE

One year later

Brynn O'Malley, her husband Sean, and little Maeve Kathleen, snug in her father's arms, took a walk around Black Swan Fountain at midnight. Maeve was a little fussy, and nothing calmed her like a stroll in the night air.

They'd scattered Sean's mother's ashes in the fountain, at her request, and Brynn knew that each of the O'Malley men, at different times and never together, of course, came out here and brought flowers with them. She smiled as she caught sight of a bouquet of lilies wrapped with a gold ribbon.

Yeats had been here recently, then.

"Now, now, love," Sean said, soothing their daughter. "Hush, my wee lass."

He sat down on the bench she thought of as "theirs" and glanced up at Brynn. "A bit of help here?"

Brynn laughed to see her big, rough, powerful husband conquered by the tears of a tiny baby. She reached out to take her daughter and cuddled her miraculous, beautiful, wonderful child close to her heart.

"Let me tell you a story, my sweet girl. Once upon a time, more than a thousand years ago, a girl sang to the moon," she began, looking into the gently glowing red-gold eyes of her husband, the man she would love and cherish forever. "But this is not that story."

Sean leaned close and kissed her, sweetly lingering until Maeve fussed at them to pay attention to her again.

"Ours is the story of the woman who loved a fire demon," Brynn continued. "And the man who loved a swan, and how, thanks to your daddy and your grandma, the curse of the black swan will never, *ever* have anything to do with you."

SALVAGE

A Tale of the Iron Seas

MELJEAN BROOK

To Cindy, who let me save my brain by writing this story, and who miraculously hasn't killed me yet.

ONE

When Georgiana came across her good-for-nothing cheating bastard of a husband washed up on the beach with a bullet in his side, she considered leaving him for dead. Then she wrapped both hands around his iron wrist and dragged him up to the house.

Despite the tiny mechanical bugs that lived inside her body and enhanced her strength, hauling him wasn't easy. *Big Thom*, everyone in town called him. Taller and broader than any other man of her acquaintance, her husband deserved the appellation. But Georgiana had other names for him.

Always-Gone Thom. Empty-Hearted Thom. Abandon-Her-Bed Thom.

Not that his cold heart or her bed mattered now. Georgiana's hopeful expectations for their marriage and her burgeoning love had wilted the first time he'd sailed off and left her alone. All remaining affection had withered to ashes during his most recent absence, which had passed without any communication from her husband—just an occasional bit of money in an envelope stamped with his ship's seal, and no note to accompany it. Georgiana hadn't needed the funds, but there had been days when she'd have given anything for a single word from him. Now nothing he ever said could soften her heart toward him again.

If he'd sent even one message, she might have attempted to carry him up the stairs to the seaside entrance of the house. Instead she dragged his body up the steps and listened to the four solid *thunks*.

One for each year he'd been gone.

She had lit the stove before setting out on her morning walk. Georgiana usually welcomed the cozy warmth after the brisk ocean air, but while sweating and flushed with exertion, the kitchen seemed stifling and cramped. Her shoulder muscles burning, she pulled Thom through the entrance, leaving a trail of seawater, blood, and sand. Her mother's hand-knotted rugs slid across the stone floor with him, bunching under his head and shoulders. Her bottom bumped into the table before his boots cleared the door.

The big, heavy dolt. She let go of his wrist. His arm dropped to the floor, his sodden gloves and woolen coat muffling the clink of iron against stone.

Where to now? Unwrapping her scarf, she eyed the door leading to the second level. The bedchamber she'd shared with him was up there, but she'd closed that part of the house years ago. It made no sense to open the upper floors now, and her husband wasn't worth the effort of hauling him up the stairs or the expense of heating the rooms. She would put him in the single bedchamber downstairs, then send him on his way the moment he was well enough to walk out of it.

That wouldn't take long. Thom was infected by the mechanical bugs, just as she was. They'd have him on his feet within a day or two.

After shedding her coat and gloves, Georgiana bent for his arm again. The iron forearm beneath the wool sleeve was thicker and more solid than she expected. His prosthetics were of the skeletal kind, resembling metal bones. But perhaps his iron arms always felt bigger than they appeared. Georgiana didn't know. She'd only seen them once, after walking in on Thom while he'd been changing into the nightshirt he'd worn to their wedding bed. He almost always wore gloves, as well—not for warmth, but with a lightly oiled lining to prevent exposing his jointed iron fingers to the rusting effects of the salty sea air. She'd seen his hands only a few more times than his arms. And although she'd often rested her palm upon his coat sleeve, which had given her some idea of the shape beneath, she'd never had to wrap her fingers around his wrist and drag him around before.

The bedchamber stood on the opposite side of the kitchen. With her skirts swinging around her booted feet, Georgiana huffed her way past the table and stove and through the door. Once inside, she let his heavy arm drop again.

Soaked and bloody. Thom wasn't going into the bed like that. She stripped the quilts down the mattress, then covered the sheet with towels.

Thom needed to be stripped, too. She reached for his cap, damp but warm. *Too* warm. Heat radiated through the knitted wool. Tugging it off, she laid the backs of her fingers to his forehead.

Burning.

Oh, no. *No, no, no*. When she'd first found Thom on the beach and rolled him over, she'd touched his face. His skin had been cool. Not now. And the bugs wouldn't heal this—they *created* the fever. It only happened rarely, and with severe wounds. The tiny machines worked so hard to heal him that they overheated his body. Infected men and women almost never sickened or died from anything but old age, unless an injury killed a person faster than the bugs could heal him. But bug fever was often fatal.

Rushing to the window, Georgiana threw it open. Frigid air swept inside the room. She flew back to Thom's side. She needed ice, opium. His temperature had to be lowered, and the drug slowed the bugs. They wouldn't repair his wound as quickly, but the opium might keep the healing from killing him. He probably only lived now because his body had lain half-submerged in the freezing ocean water.

She tore open the buckles of his coat, her mind racing as quickly as her fingers. A few blocks of ice were stacked in the ice house, but she would have to send a wiregram to town for more. The physician could bring opium.

But she had to get Thom undressed first. She wrestled the thick coat down his arms and tossed it aside. A woolen fisherman's gansey lay beneath, the gray weave soaked in blood. She yanked the pullover up to his chest, taking his linen shirt with it and exposing the bullet hole in his side.

The small wound had stopped bleeding. Carefully, she turned him. The bullet's exit had done more damage, the injury larger and more ragged, but no blood seeped out. The edges had already healed.

Thank God. Even if the healing slowed, this wound no longer threatened his life. She just had to worry about the fever.

Gripping the hem of his gansey and shirt, she stripped them the rest of the way off, almost losing her balance in the process. His prosthetics thunked back to the floor, and—

He had new arms.

For an instant, astonishment froze Georgiana in place. No longer dull, skeletal iron. These were steel, and shaped in proportion to his body—a combination of intricate machines designed to resemble a pair of long, muscular arms.

Where on Earth had he gotten them? Who could have made such incredible devices?

But Georgiana knew. She'd heard the whispers, rumors that had flown by airship and sailed by boat across the North Sea to the small Danish town of Skagen. Yet although she herself had called him a cheating scoundrel in her mind, that was only when she'd been at her angriest, her most hurt. She hadn't believed the rumors. After all, Thom had only visited her bed three times. Three awful times that he'd seemed to enjoy even less than Georgiana had. So she hadn't believed that he'd gone to another woman's bed.

And maybe he hadn't. Perhaps there was another explanation. It hardly mattered. As soon as he was well again, she would say good riddance to him.

He would go, anyway. Thom always did. But this time, for the *first* time, Georgiana would have the satisfaction of knowing that he went after she'd told him to leave—and not after she'd asked him to stay.

By evening, the rash that signaled the worst stage of the fever began spreading over Thom's throat and chest. The doctor didn't say anything as he administered another injection of opium, but Georgiana didn't need the grim-faced man to tell her how little hope was left. Those small red dots marked the beginning of the end.

Thom would leave again. He wouldn't come back. Not because she'd told him to go, but because he'd made her a widow.

But that was *not* how this would end. She had accounts to settle with her husband before he left, so Thom could *not* go like this.

Georgiana would simply not allow it. And in recent years, she had become very good at getting her way.

The lamps flickered throughout the night, the flames dancing in the draft from the window. Accompanied by the roar of the ocean, Georgiana bathed his nude body in ice water until her fingers shriveled and ached. In the morning, the doctor pumped Thom full of opium again and helped her replenish the chunks of ice piled around his motionless form. She resumed bathing his skin, her frozen hands stiff and her mood too heavy to lift.

Exhaustion finally claimed her in the middle of the second night. She fell asleep in an armchair next to Thom's bedside and woke at dawn with a crooked neck. Her husband lay still, with only a sheet over his hips for modesty. The gray light through the window paled his skin, washing away the flush of the fever. The ice surrounding his big body had melted almost to nothing.

The dour Doctor Rasmussen stood at the vanity, snapping his black case shut. He wore his scarf and gloves, and the brim of his hat shadowed his humorless features. From outside, Georgiana heard the chattering engine of his steamcart.

She jolted upright, her back and neck protesting. "You are already leaving? But we must add more ice."

In a tone as somber as his expression, the doctor replied, "There is no need for more, Mrs. Thomas."

No need . . . ? Fear yanked Georgiana to her feet. Her gaze shot to Thom's pale, still form.

The doctor continued, "The rash receded during the night. I've administered another dose so that your husband continues to rest, but he should not need another."

Relief descended in a bone-dissolving wave, but Georgiana didn't trust it until she flattened her palm against Thom's chest. Still too warm, but not burning. His heart beat in deep, even thuds. The angry rash and the swelling in his throat had faded.

She glanced at the fresh bandage wrapped around his abdomen. "And the wound?"

"The nanoagents have sealed the skin. I removed the stitches. As long as he does not reopen it, he should be out of danger." The doctor paused. Though he only seemed to have one attitude—grim—Georgiana detected a hint of apology from him. "You will likely have a visit from the magistrate today."

Because Thom had been shot, and the physician was required to report such wounds. Well, he didn't need to be sorry for that. "I understand your duty, sir. But you might tell him to come tomorrow, after my husband has woken. I have no answers for his inquiry."

Now surprise put a faint twist in Rasmussen's lips. But he only nodded and wished her a good day, and had already quit the room when Georgiana realized that the doctor assumed *she* had shot Thom.

Which was ridiculous. Not that Thom hadn't given her reason to shoot him, because he had. But if Georgiana *had* wanted to murder him, she wouldn't have missed his heart, and she certainly wouldn't have called on a physician to heal him. Georgiana would have buried his body in the steamcoach shed, where her digging wouldn't be observed—though there was slim chance that someone would happen by her isolated home at the same moment she needed to conceal a body, it was better not to risk discovery.

Not that she had often pondered his murder—or anyone else's. But planning for unexpected events was just common sense.

She hadn't planned well for *this*, however. She didn't know who might have shot him, either. On the seas, attacks could come from any direction, but salvagers like Thom weren't usually targets for pirates or thieves. Perhaps it had been a personal matter . . . but Georgiana would not let her mind dwell on that, any more than she dwelt on how he'd obtained his new prosthetics.

Whatever the answers, they had nothing to do with her.

Georgiana set about clearing away the ice. Meltwater soaked the bed. The day maid arrived at eight o'clock full of gossip from town, of an aristocrat's airship that had flown into Skagen's harbor and of twin babies that had been born. Aware that Thom's condition would soon be more fodder for wagging tongues, Georgiana only listened with half an ear while they wrestled a mattress down the stairs. On the bed, the sodden mattress was too heavy to drag off the frame. They made a pallet on the floor and, together, she and Marta transferred Thom onto dry sheets. He didn't lie so quietly now, turning his head against the pillow and restlessly shifting his legs, as if swimming through rough dreams.

Her secretary came shortly afterward, bearing a stack of cargo receipts and inventories. The following hours were spent catching up on two days of neglected work. After lunch, Georgiana sent him back to her offices in town with the assurance that she would be in the next morning.

Perhaps with Thom in tow. She didn't know what the terms of their separation would be, but she'd make him a fair offer for his part of her shipping business. Though to her mind, *any* offer would be more than fair. His involvement in her venture had begun and ended four years ago, and only comprised an envelope containing a bit of money. All of the risks and the work had been her own.

Tired, she returned to the armchair in the bedchamber. She'd barely closed her eyes when Marta came in carrying Thom's clothing, a frown on her softly lined face.

"I patched up the holes, ma'am, but the shirt and gansey are still showing the bloodstain. Would you like me to give them another wash?"

"There's no need. Clean will do well enough."

Marta nodded and turned toward the wardrobe before abruptly turning back. Her fingers dipped into her apron pocket. "Before I forget and make a thief of myself—this fell out of Captain Thom's coat."

The maid dropped a heavy gold coin into Georgiana's palm. Not a livre, though by weight, it must have been worth as much as one of those valuable coins. A shield was stamped on one side and a crowned rose on the reverse, with a diameter as wide as her two middle fingers together. She didn't recognize the lettering along the edge.

"Do you suppose he found it while searching through those sunken ships, ma'am?"

Georgiana smiled. It was a lovely thought, but despite their depiction in popular adventure tales, salvagers rarely discovered anything of value that wasn't already claimed by the ship's owner. Most were hired to recover recent wreckage before the cargo spoiled completely. They didn't keep any of it for themselves.

Perhaps Thom had found a single coin or it had been given to him in payment. And if he'd found more than one, they were gone now, anyway. "If this is part of a treasure, Marta, it must have been cursed."

Because Thom's ship must have sunk, too. He hadn't dropped into the ocean out of the æther, and unless he'd shot himself, his ship must have come under attack. Her secretary had confirmed that *Oriana* hadn't sailed into Skagen's harbor, and Georgiana hadn't seen the old herring buss's familiar silhouette on the water the morning she'd found Thom on the sand. She'd spent too many days searching the horizon for *Oriana* to have mistaken her for any other ship.

Georgiana's smile faded. She put the gold coin on the side table where Thom could find it when he woke up. The coin and their separation settlement would easily buy him a new ship.

Then he could be off again.

A dry whisper penetrated Georgiana's sleep. She opened bleary eyes. Darkness had fallen outside. A blanket covered her legs, curled up in the armchair. From the adjoining kitchen, Marta's soft hum and the scent of roasting lamb wafted through the room.

The whisper came again from the pallet on the floor. *"Georgie."*

Thom.

She sat up. His eyes had opened. Not looking at her, though he repeated her name again on a rasping breath, as if through a parched throat. Unfocused, his pupils had dilated, his irises just a thin ring of dark blue.

Not truly awake. Still in the opium's grip.

Though not lucid yet, he could take a few sips of broth. Untangling her blanket from her skirts, she rose from the chair and retrieved a small bowl from the kitchen. She sent Marta home and returned to the bedchamber. Spoon in hand, she knelt beside his left shoulder, the mattress cushioning her knees.

That dry rasp came again. *"Georgie."*

His gaze had fixed on the ceiling. He wasn't speaking to her—or at least, not the real Georgiana. She might very well have featured in his drugged dreams.

"I'm here, Thom." Cradling the back of his head in her palm, she tipped him forward and brought the spoon to his lips. "You need to swallow this. It will help your throat."

She didn't know if he heard or if he simply swallowed in automatic response to the broth being spooned into his mouth. Not a single drop spilled, even now. He'd always been a fastidious man.

Not overly concerned by his appearance—he just preferred neatness and order in all things.

That was something Georgiana had learned about Thom before she'd ever met him. Eight years ago, her father had hired him on as chief mate of his whaling ship, and within a day, the gossip from Skagen had been laden with the complaints of the sailors taken to task for sloppy stations and berths. At the dinner table, however, her father spoke nothing but praise.

Although she'd heard much about him, five months passed before Georgiana had actually seen her father's new chief mate. And although Thom gave little thought to his appearance beyond keeping himself neat, *she* had not been able to stop thinking of it.

Not because Thom was handsome—though he was that. His dark hair held just a hint of curl, in a sensibly short style that he trimmed himself. Taken one at a time, his features were too heavy: thick slashing brows over deep-set eyes, a prominent nose, and a wide mouth. But the strong frame of his angular jaw and cheekbones prevented the boldness of his features from overwhelming his face, and complemented his height and breadth. Altogether, he made a striking figure.

But it hadn't been his face or his size that had captured her interest. It had been his stillness. It had been the intensity of his gaze when he'd looked at her in return. It had been his quiet manner, and how he used as few words as possible when he spoke, so that each one felt significant—like a promise.

So when Thom had asked what would make her happiest, Georgiana had told him. After years of watching her mother pacing in front of the window facing the sea, her gaze searching the horizon, and waiting weeks and months for Georgina's father to come home, she'd known exactly what would make her happy. *A husband who will hold me in his arms every night.* And she'd believed Thom when he'd sworn that he would.

Then the morning after they were married, he'd sailed off in the salvaging boat her father had given him as a wedding gift.

With a sigh, Georgiana put aside the empty bowl. These weren't memories that she wanted to revisit. Their wedding night had been painful enough—and she'd understood that remorse and guilt had driven him away, despite her asking him to stay. But it didn't explain the second and third time. That last visit, he had not even waited until morning to go. He had not even waited long enough to spend his seed inside her, but abandoned Georgiana in the middle of their coupling—even though it hadn't hurt that time, and he'd had nothing to be sorry for.

Nothing to be sorry for, except staying away for four years. That had been more painful than anything she'd experienced in their bed.

But those years had apparently treated him well. Despite the fever and bullet wound, he appeared healthy. Shadowed by dark hair, thick muscles carved his broad chest and strong thighs, their shape well-defined even at rest. He was just as handsome. Like many men at sea, he wore a beard to protect his face from the elements—and kept it neatly trimmed, so that even after two days' growth his whiskers didn't look unkempt.

The last time Georgiana had seen him, he'd been clean-shaven. Each night he'd taken her to bed, he'd always taken a razor to his beard first, and his skin had been smooth when he'd kissed her.

But not now. Frowning, she ran her fingers down the short, silky strands covering his jaw. He wasn't clean-shaven now, despite the rumors that he'd been in another woman's bed.

When she'd first heard the whispers, her instincts told her not to believe them. This beard told her the same. And it was hardly solid evidence that he'd been faithful during his absence—he could grow a beard within a few weeks, after all—but whispers were no more substantial. Georgiana preferred to trust her instincts over rumors.

Not that it mattered. His fidelity had never been the problem; his absence was. But believing that he'd been true to his vows hurt less than believing he hadn't been.

And she would not think about how substantial his new arms were.

Those arms moved restlessly at his sides, steel fingers clenching. He turned his cheek against her palm.

"Georgie?"

His voice didn't sound so painfully dry now, more like his own; her name was a low, deep rumble.

"I'm still here, Thom." Right where she'd been for years.

His unfocused gaze looked beyond her shoulder. "I failed you, Georgie."

"Yes." A hard little laugh escaped her. "Yes, you surely—"

"I was coming to stay. To hold you every night." A rough hitch of his breath was like a hook through her chest. "But I lost it. I lost it all."

Coming to stay? Her heart suddenly seemed pinched in a vise. She couldn't breathe.

It meant nothing. The words of a man blissed on opium. And even if they were true, he'd said them far too late.

But despite the stern reminder Georgiana gave herself, almost a minute passed before she could speak again. "You were coming to stay?"

He didn't respond. Still only seeing the Georgiana in his dream—or perhaps seeing nothing at all now.

She tried again. "What did you lose, Thom? *Oriana*? Your crew? And who shot you?"

Silence. She wanted to shake his shoulders and rouse him. To make him answer. But there would be time for answers tomorrow.

Nothing he could say would change her mind. But she would need the time to ponder what *she* would say if Thom's answer was that he'd hoped to stay.

TWO

He never should have married her.

Sitting naked on the pallet, Thom flicked the coin over in his palm. Just a small bit of gold—and all that was left of his hopes and intentions.

Almost nothing.

He'd wanted to give Georgiana so much more. He'd been arrogant enough to believe that he could. But this coin had been waiting for Thom when he'd awoken, as if to make certain he didn't spend another second fooling himself. In sleep and dreams, her face and her touch had been so close. Then he'd seen that glint of gold, and the memory of everything he'd lost had crashed through his mind like a cold wave, sweeping those dreams away.

Losing it all was the last thing he remembered: the airship flying in low over *Oriana*'s sails, the rail cannon firing a chunk out of his ship's bow, and the turned-out pirate who'd descended from the airship and asked Thom for the chest of coins—then the crack of a pistol and the stabbing pain through his side. A dim recollection of the waves and a lighthouse might have been memories or more dreams. Thom didn't know. There wasn't anything solid after the bullet, until the glint of gold.

But the room he was in now told the rest of the story. Henry Tucker's house—the bedchamber on the ground floor. Thom must have been too heavy to carry up the stairs, so Georgiana's parents had put him in their own bed. The mattress dripped water that puddled on the stone floor. Only one reason for that. He'd had a fever and they'd packed him in ice.

It would have been better if they'd left him for dead. Now he'd have to get off this pallet and look Georgiana in the eye. Tell her that he'd come home with nothing, and that he was leaving again. But Thom thought that going this time might kill him—because this time, he would be leaving for good.

She deserved more than this. He couldn't be what she needed. He couldn't make her happy. He had to let her go, give her a chance to find a man who knew how to be a husband. Who didn't return empty-handed.

Now Thom didn't even have a ship.

He dressed, his movements slow. The bullet through his side was nothing more than a twinge now, but he didn't want to hurry. From the kitchen he heard a woman's light tread and the clink of utensils. Georgiana, or her mother. Though he ached to see his wife, a step out of this room was a step closer to leaving. And if it was her mother, he dreaded the woman's cheer. He'd never seen Jane Tucker unhappy. Always simmering with joy, and a smile now would be a curving dagger through his heart.

But the delay could only last until he pushed his feet into his boots. He braced himself for whoever waited beyond the door, battening down the pain in his chest. He couldn't falter in this. Georgiana was a stubborn woman. She wouldn't give up on their marriage easily, and when she argued, Thom would be tempted to soften and give in. But he'd spent four years forcing himself to stay away. He would have to rely on that strength again.

Silently, he opened the door. At the table, Georgiana sat with her back to him—just like the first time he'd seen her. He'd been standing on the deck of her father's ship, *Sea Bloom*, returning after a five-month whaling expedition. Georgiana had been waiting at the docks with her mother, but she'd turned to greet someone, and he'd only seen her black hair, her graceful neck, and a summery yellow dress that left her arms bare.

She was just as graceful now, but her hair had changed. Instead of a long braid, she'd rolled it into a thick ball at her nape. A dress of dark blue hugged her figure, with long sleeves for winter.

Aside from the pounding of his heart, Thom had been quiet, but Georgiana must have heard him. She turned her head just slightly, so that he glimpsed the shell of her ear and the shadow behind her jaw. "You're awake and well?"

"I am."

"Sit and eat, then."

Georgiana rose and moved to the stove as she spoke. There was never any nonsense about her when a task needed to be done, even one as simple as breakfast. Always practical. Many of her father's sailors called her cold and humorless, but Thom had appreciated her steady nature from the first.

And she wasn't cold. Nor was she humorless. Just reserved. After those barriers had fallen away, he'd discovered that her teasing could be gentle or sharp, and usually at unexpected moments in their conversations. During the long walks they'd taken while courting, Thom had laughed more with Georgiana than he could recall laughing in all of the years that had come before, and he'd realized that far more went on in her head than ever came out of her mouth.

But there was nothing in his head except Georgiana. She'd made him happy. He'd wanted to do the same for her. He hadn't.

Heart heavy, Thom chose the nearest chair and sat. “As soon as I’ve finished, I’ll haul out that wet bed.”

“Thank you.”

She returned from the stove. *Oh, sweet blue heavens*. Standing close, she set his bowl and mug on the table, and the fragrance of her filled his senses, that delicate flowery scent from a bloom he didn’t know the name of, but that he always thought of as Georgiana’s. Her hair had smelled of it the first time he’d kissed her, moments after she’d accepted his hand. Her nightgown had carried the same scent on the night of their wedding, and it had taken every bit of his control not to strip it from her body and discover if she smelled the same everywhere.

It took all of his control now. He closed his eyes, fingers clenching against the urge to carry her upstairs and lose himself in her warmth. Never again. Even if he’d intended to stay, never again. He’d promised himself the last time, when she’d been under him, whimpering and squirming as she bore the pain of his raging need.

Never again.

He’d done wrong, asking her to marry him. His need had been part of that wrong, coming upon him from the moment she’d turned to face him on the docks eight years ago. He’d been fool enough to believe he had that hunger under control.

He couldn’t let such needs rule him. *He* controlled them now. He kept them in order. Marriage should have done that, too. Marriage put them both in their proper place. Wanting a wife, then having her in bed. That was a proper order. Yet his hunger had only grown, and his control had become a bare, slight thing. He’d wanted her every second—if not inside her, then just to *be* with her.

Just as he wanted her now. But her presence and that fragrance weren’t a poor substitute for the bed. They were a sweet pleasure of their own.

She moved on to her chair, and her perfume was replaced by

the scent of hot grains wafting up from his bowl. He glanced down. Some kind of porridge. It didn't matter. Everything he'd ever eaten in this house was better than what he had on his ship.

Georgiana must have read his silence as a question. "I sweetened it with honey," she told him. "No sugar."

He hadn't doubted. "Thank you."

And though she drank tea, she'd given him coffee, because two hundred years ago the Horde had slipped the bugs in through sugar and tea, then put up their towers that made slaves of an entire population. He'd only had to tell her once what he would and wouldn't eat, and she'd always provided what he needed without asking why. That was Georgiana. She hadn't pressed him to talk about memories he'd rather forget, or of the occupation in England. Thom didn't think about his arms being taken and replaced with iron, or the years on a boat, hauling up fish. He didn't think of the frenzies and the revolution. All that was done. He'd left England behind and found himself in Skagen, where he'd tried to make the sort of life that other men did, men who hadn't been born under the boot of the Horde.

He'd tried and failed. Thom was his own master now. But he would never be what other men were.

Holding her mug cupped between her hands, Georgiana watched him eat, her green eyes steady and calm. "You'll need to speak with the magistrate about the bullet wound."

Mouth full, he nodded.

"Who shot you?"

"I ran into pirates," he said between bites.

"Your crew?"

There was no crew. Thom shook his head, but his mouth was full again, and she went on before he could answer.

Her voice troubled, she asked, "And *Oriana*?"

"Stolen."

Along with his new submersible, and a fortune in gold coins. His throat closed, making it impossible to swallow.

It was time to tell her that this was done.

But he couldn't yet. He couldn't meet Georgiana's eyes now, either. His gaze dropped to the bowl. Still mostly full, but he couldn't eat. And there was one question that still had to be asked before he could leave. "It's been some years since I was here."

Just the corners of her mouth tilted upward, as they did when her humor was sharp. "Yes, it has."

"Was there a child?" He had to force it out. "The last time."

"It's difficult to conceive a child when your husband spills his seed on the way out the door."

Heat rushed to his face. He hadn't actually spent on the floor, but the way he'd rushed out of the room to escape the pain and shame of hurting her, he might as well have. "And your father, mother?"

Her smile disappeared. Her thick lashes swept down. Quietly, she said, "They're gone."

"Gone?" Thom stared at her. "Dead?"

"Yes."

When she looked up again, moisture had pooled in her eyes. She abruptly rose from the table to pace its length. No task to complete. Just upset.

"How long ago?" His voice was rough.

"A month after you came home last. The lump fever swept through town. They both caught it."

Almost four years ago. So Thom's failure was worse than he'd known. Raised in a Horde crèche, he didn't know what it was to have a mother or father. But he knew she had loved them. Losing them must have ripped her heart to shreds.

"I should have been here."

"Yes."

Her soft reply was a heavy condemnation. Thom knew he'd never stop feeling its weight. "Who's been supporting you, Georgie?"

"I have been, Thom. *Sea Bloom* came into my possession. I made use of her."

Throat thick, he nodded. He'd let it all fall out of order. Her father had told him, over and over. Thom's place as a husband was to support his wife, support any children. And not to come back until he had something worth bringing.

Go on, Thom, and make yourself a man. I'll look after her while you're gone.

But her father hadn't. And Thom shouldn't have relied on anyone to help him. He'd been so focused on trying to do what a man should, on trying to make her happy, that everything had lost its place. Georgiana had been supporting herself, while Thom had come home with nothing.

And she wouldn't be arguing with him, he realized. Not his strong, practical Georgiana. She'd see all the wrong here, too, and let him go.

With a sigh, she took her seat again. "The money you sent was appreciated."

"It wasn't much."

"It was enough." Her steady gaze held his. "What are your intentions now?"

"I'll be going again."

"Without a ship?"

Without anything. No home, no work. But he'd been there before. He'd left England with nothing, and had found everything here.

Now it had gone all wrong. Even if he found work, found a place to sleep, Thom didn't think his life would ever be right again. It didn't matter where he went, what he did.

But he had to give some kind of answer. He picked the name of the nearest town. "I'll try to find work in Fladstrand. Maybe on the docks."

"Not in Skagen?"

"No." He made himself say it, though the ache in his chest felt like it would rip open and swallow him whole. "It'll be for the best. I'm hardly a husband to you. Never bringing you anything worth having. Not doing what makes you happy."

For a long second, Georgiana didn't react. Just looked at him. Finally, she nodded. "We'll go into town and see the magistrate together, then, and set about drawing up papers of separation."

"Papers?"

"Legal papers, Thom. Marriage binds us together by law. Those ties have to be dissolved."

He hadn't even known there'd been anything official to it—he'd thought the marriage had just been a ceremony and a promise. But she'd been tied to him by law. Something as real and as solid as the emotions that were choking him. And no sooner had he learned of them, those bonds were to be broken.

The ache in his chest burrowed deeper, threatening to overwhelm his control. But he wouldn't let pain be his master.

Jaw clenched, he gave a sharp nod. "That seems sensible."

"We'll have to decide how to divide the money and property."

Thom didn't want any of it. "What I have is yours. Though it's not much. I never made much."

And when he had, he'd lost it all.

She slowly nodded. Then her gaze fell to his gloved hands. "You made enough for those arms."

Which would have cost more than Thom had earned in four years, if he'd bought them. But he hadn't paid anything for the prosthetics, except for the time he'd spent helping a blacksmith build a better diving machine.

He could imagine how it appeared to Georgiana, though. Sending her tiny bits of money, yet coming home with arms fit for a king.

"They were a gift," he said.

"From Ivy Blacksmith?"

A new note had entered her voice, something hard and trembling. No surprise, that. He'd kept notorious company when he'd helped Ivy.

"Yes. You know of her?"

"I heard rumors of your acquaintance. And Mad Machen's obsession with her is just as well-known. He came into town about three years ago, searching for her, and there weren't many people who dared leave their houses while he was here." She looked down at her cup, her thumb rubbing along the rim. "Is he the pirate who shot you?"

Why would Mad Machen have reason for that? Thom had no argument with the man.

"That wasn't him. It was some nobby gent." But even as Thom spoke, he realized what she'd been getting at. Sharp anger spit up his throat. Had people told her that he'd been carrying on with Ivy? "Whatever you heard about me and her, it wasn't anything like that. Is this why you're agreeing to the separation?"

Her gaze lifted to his. "We *have* been separated, Thom. This just makes it official."

Official. And he was suddenly desperate for her to argue, to persuade him to stay. Maybe that's what he'd wanted all along. So he could be secure knowing that he'd tried to do right by her, telling her that he'd leave—yet remaining here when she asked him to. Now he wanted to beg her not to let him go.

But this was for the best. He knew it. Now he just needed to persuade his heart of it.

Softly, she asked, "Why did you keep leaving, Thom?"

I wanted to make you happy. But he hadn't. And his throat was so rough, he could hardly speak. But this might be the last she ever asked of him. He'd give her this, at least.

"I wanted to bring something back to you." And he'd brought a little. "This is what I have left. It's yours."

He slid the gold coin across the table. She barely glanced at it before her solemn gaze returned to his.

"You should keep—"

"You'll take it, Georgie! Let me give you one damn thing worth having, then maybe I can pretend that I—" Clenching his jaw, Thom bit off the rest. He was losing control. Not with her. Abruptly he stood, chair legs scraping across stone. "I'll haul that bed out."

Georgiana gathered her coat and reticule while Thom went to fire up the steamcoach's furnace. She expected him to return to the house and wait for the boiler to heat, rather than staying out in the cold morning air, but as the minutes passed she realized that he wasn't coming. She made her way out the roadside entrance of the house and to the shed, but stopped before going in. By the trickle of steam rising from the coach's vents, she could see that the boiler wasn't ready—and neither was Thom. He stood at the side of the coach, his hands braced against the aluminum frame supporting the roof. His head hung down between his arms, eyes closed and face rigid.

Feeling as if she were intruding, Georgiana hesitated. Telling her that he wanted to separate had been hard for him. Her husband was a man of few words, but Georgiana had never seen him have any trouble finding them. Yet when he'd said he was leaving, Thom almost hadn't gotten the words out.

That difficulty had been a surprise in a morning of surprises. She'd never thought his character was a mystery. He was quiet, sturdy. Calm and controlled, not given to strong emotion. And what Georgiana had known of him, she'd loved. But she was realizing that she hadn't known her husband at all.

He was a man of few words. But he was also a man of powerful emotions.

And she shouldn't be wondering what those emotions were. They'd agreed. Separation was best. But she couldn't help wanting to look under the surface of Thom's quiet facade now that she knew much more lay beneath it.

How much had she known of him before? A substantial amount, she'd thought. She knew that he'd been born in England just over thirty years ago, when that country had still been occupied by the Horde. He'd grown up in a crèche, like an orphan, though his parents had probably still been alive. But they wouldn't have been parents as Georgiana knew them—just a man and a woman caught in a mating frenzy produced by radio signals broadcasted from the Horde's controlling tower. Thom had been taken from his mother at birth and raised with other children, and when he was a young man, his occupation had been determined for him. His arms had been replaced by skeletal iron, and hydraulic braces across his back and chest offered additional hauling power. Then he'd been sent to work on the Horde's fishing boats.

Thom had never spoken of that history. She only knew of it because, before her father had hired him on as chief mate, Thom told him that he had experience hauling nets. The arms and his braces had been self-evident. The rest of it was the same awful story shared by so many laborers during the Horde's occupation, so Georgiana assumed the same was true for him.

And because of his silence, she'd also assumed that Thom hadn't wanted to speak of his past. So she hadn't wanted to hurt him by dredging up terrible memories simply to satisfy her curiosity.

But perhaps she should have. Perhaps she would have had a better understanding of the man who would be her husband. Perhaps she would have better understood why he'd left each time. He'd wanted to bring something back to her.

And that sounded exactly like her father.

With a sigh, she glanced up at the house. Georgiana had been a young girl when her father had tired of the crowded landscape and overfished waters of Prince George Island, as well as the disapproval of his wife's well-to-do family. He'd left the English territories in the Americas and brought Georgiana and her mother here, to the very tip of the Jutland Peninsula, where the North Sea met the Baltic. He'd built their new home on a stretch of flat beach two miles from the nearest house, a home unlike any of those in town, but in the style her mother had grown up in. Three steep gables contained windows overlooking the sea. A widow's walk surrounded the chimney, and on fine days her mother had abandoned the windows of her room to search the horizon from the roof, instead.

Georgiana loved Henry Tucker. He'd been a wonderful father, a good man.

But he'd been a terrible husband.

So had Thom. Except . . . he'd obviously been trying to be a good one. They'd simply had opposite ideas about how to go about it. He'd wanted to do the right thing by her. Maybe she should have asked before they were married what he considered *right*.

But Georgiana hadn't. Not really. Theirs had been a smooth courtship. He appealed to her. She had appealed to him. And she'd liked him, in every way. Her father had approved of the match, no doubt lining Thom up as his successor. They'd known each other three years before they'd married, but they hadn't been delayed by doubts or hesitation. Thom had simply been gone—away on whaling expeditions. He'd spent months at a time on a ship with her father. There was no question how he'd formed such strong notions about a husband's duties.

Each time he'd returned, however, they hadn't spoken of that. He'd told her of the oddities and dangers he'd seen while at sea. She'd told him of the town, the people who lived there—always trying to make him laugh, and so gratified when he had. She'd asked his opinion of everyone they knew, to judge the sort of man he was, how he saw others.

But she hadn't asked Thom about himself. She hadn't asked what he wanted from their marriage or what he expected of her. He'd asked what would make her happy. She'd never asked the same question in return.

Now they were on their way to dissolve their marriage. But the fault wasn't all his. It was hers, too, for failing to ask so many questions.

Georgiana didn't like knowing that. And she wasn't sure what to do, now that she *did* know—or whether she should do anything at all. Perhaps it would still be best to continue on to the magistrate's, and be done with the wreck they'd both made of their marriage.

In the shed, Thom pushed away from the coach. The thin eddies of steam had begun to billow. He walked toward her through them, like a large ship emerging from fog. "I'd have come for you when the engine was ready."

"I thought I might enjoy a few extra moments of sun." And the way it glinted in his dark hair.

Nodding, he said, "Best enjoy it while you can. We won't have much of it today."

"That is what you said on every walk we took," she reminded him with a curve of her lips. "You were always wrong."

And they'd walked often. On the road to town, along miles of beach—close to his side, her arm occasionally brushing against his, and every part of her feeling heavy and light all at once, as if her body hadn't known how to settle when Thom was near.

"Wait and see," he said with a slight smile. "Maybe I'll prove you wrong this time."

Maybe he would, at that. "If you're right, at least we have the coach."

He glanced back at the canvas-topped vehicle. "Did you buy it?"

"Yes."

"So you don't always trust the sun."

She laughed and shook her head. "Not at all between October and March. And I go into town more often now. There is little time for leisurely walks."

Very little time at all. Her friends had urged her to move into Skagen so she wouldn't have to make that journey every day. It would have been more practical. Her offices were there, and the expense of the wiregram lines she'd installed to connect her business to her home—and the cost of repairing them after every storm—could hardly be justified. No one waited for her at the house. But Georgiana couldn't bring herself to leave it.

At first she'd worried that if Thom returned, he wouldn't know where she'd gone. But after hope for his return had faded, she'd stayed, anyway. She loved the house. She loved the beach and the constant roar of the ocean. She loved being able to leave the town behind.

She also loved driving into town, because every day, she had a purpose there. In the steamcoach, her gaze was fixed on the road ahead of her instead of on the horizon.

And not every day was a sunny one. She appreciated the roof over her head.

She frowned a little. Thom wouldn't have one.

"Where do you intend to stay tonight, Thom?"

He shook his head. "I'll figure something."

"You don't need to. Stay at the house until we have everything settled. I've room enough—and we'll avoid the gossip in that way. I'll open the upper bedrooms."

"They're not ready now?"

Not after Georgiana had become her mother, standing at the window and waiting. "No."

His gaze searched her face. "I don't want to give you trouble."

"It's no trouble. I'll leave a note for Marta."

He exhaled on a sharp breath, looked out over the sea. Debating. After a quiet moment, he said, "I'd best not stay. You'll be looking for a new husband soon. I'll be in the way."

"A new husband?" Surprise pushed a short laugh from her. "Why would I do that?"

"You have to have someone."

She frowned at him. "You sound like my father. I did well enough on my own for four years."

"You wanted children."

Yes, she did. "Perhaps I'll have those on my own, too."

He didn't respond, but his gloved hands clenched at his sides. That was the Thom she didn't know well. The one who kept so much concealed.

She gave that hidden Thom a little push into the light. "Perhaps it won't be long until I have a baby, if you stay tonight."

His head jerked around, gaze locking with hers. He took a step before stopping to stare down at her, eyes burning blue. Georgiana's breath caught. He'd looked down at her like that before. In bed, his arms braced beside her shoulders and his mouth carefully tasting her lips. Everything he'd done, so controlled—but that burning in his eyes had eventually been smothered by her tears. She'd known their lovemaking would hurt the first time, yet breaching her virginity had been even more painful and bloody than she'd expected. And the second time, she'd been so tense that his entry had hurt again, even though he'd been so careful and slow.

But the last time, he'd kissed her endlessly before finally lifting her nightgown to her waist and settling between her legs. There'd been discomfort, at first. Then just wetness and heat and Thom sliding back and forth inside her, and all of her body had been caught between the same sensation of heavy and light, but so much heavier, so much lighter. He'd been *so* slow and *so* careful, but she hadn't been able to stop herself from moving beneath him, or the little noises that had welled up, so that she'd had to bite her lips to keep herself from begging him for . . . she hadn't even known. Faster. Harder. Something *more.*

Now that same need rose inside her again—and he wasn't even touching her.

And she wasn't crying this time, but the burning in his eyes still went dark. "I don't know how to be a husband, Georgie. I know even less about being a father."

"I would be enough of a parent for any children."

"And I should abandon them?"

"You abandoned me," she pointed out, and the edges of his mouth whitened. She didn't know if it was anger or hurt.

It was anger. His face hardened, cold steel that matched his voice. "Only because you asked me to."

Georgiana gaped at him. "*What?*"

Through gritted teeth, he repeated harshly, "You *asked* me to. Don't you—"

He abruptly stopped. Not controlling his emotions again, she realized. Something had changed. His gaze had fixed behind her, a frown slowly darkening his features.

"You have your pistol, Georgie?"

Oh, dear God. Without question, she dug into her bag, spinning around to scan the beach and road. Ravenous zombies roamed the continent, but they didn't cross water. A shallow sound to the south prevented almost all of the creatures from venturing this far up the peninsula, but now and again one made it through and wandered into a town. In all of the years she'd lived here, none had come near her home or as far north as Skagen. Yet she always kept a pistol with her, nonetheless.

Nothing moved. She glanced up at Thom, saw that he'd focused on the sky—on an airship flying along the shoreline. A white balloon over a small wooden cruiser. Such airships were a common sight . . . except that it flew silently, using its sails instead of propellers. This far from town, there was little reason to stay so quiet, unless they didn't want the engines to announce their approach.

"Thom?"

"The shed." He didn't wait for her to make sense of that. His arm wrapped around her waist and he hurried her through the humid clouds of rising steam and into the shed. "You have more bullets?"

"In the coach, under the bench."

Heart pounding, she glanced at the airship again. Just a personal yacht or a small passenger ship, though by the gleam of its polished hull, a rather fine one. Why had the sight of it alarmed him? Who did he think was coming?

The clank of metal against metal turned her head. Thom had found the ammunition box, set it on the coach's boot. He shoved his sleeve up over his steel left arm. With his opposite thumb, he flicked open a small panel on the inside of his forearm, revealing a cylindrical chamber. He began loading the bullets into his arm, one by one.

Georgiana's lips parted in shock. What in the world? "Thom?"

"You hide, Georgiana. You stay in this shed, out of sight. No matter what."

"Why? Who are they?"

"The same pirates that took *Oriana*." He snapped the chamber in his arm closed and covered it with his sleeve. "Maybe they think I still have some of the coins. I don't know. I'll give them the last one and send them on their way."

And if he truly thought they'd leave so easily, would he be telling her to hide? Georgiana wasn't going to fall for that. "Thom."

His jaw clenched. "Listen to me. He aimed a rail cannon at *Oriana*'s deck and came aboard, asking for the coin chest. I offered to give it over, even though it meant I wouldn't be coming home with anything but my ship. He said he wouldn't risk anyone else having a claim on the gold and shot me. So you stay here. I'll try to stop them however I can. I won't see you hurt, too. Let me do this one thing, and protect you."

So Thom had given up the money, yet the pirate had put a bullet in him, anyway. And now he believed the pirate would kill him whether he gave the coin or not.

Georgiana wouldn't allow it to happen. "Get in the coach, Thom."

"We can't outrun them."

"No, but if we're moving too quickly for them to get a good shot at us, perhaps we'll stay out of their hands long enough to make it into town." When he shook his head and turned away from her, as if intending to leave the shed, Georgiana clamped her hands around his wrist. "*Some* chance is always better than none."

"And any risk to you is too much." But his eyes narrowed, as if he was thinking it over again. "I'll make a run in the coach alone. The airship will come after me. You send a wiregram to town, ask them to round up carts and send as many men as possible. When he sees them coming, the bastard might decide to fly off."

Not by yourself. Georgiana closed her lips against that automatic response. If the pirates caught up to Thom, she didn't want him to be alone. But she knew this was the most practical plan, and offered the best chance of keeping them both alive and safe.

Still, her throat tightened with worry and fear. "Be careful, Thom."

"I will." For a brief moment, his gloved hand cupped her jaw, his gaze softening as he looked down at her. "You wait for the airship to turn around before you come out of the shed."

Georgiana nodded. Her heart an aching hammer in her chest, she stepped aside and watched Thom climb into the coach. The driver's bench creaked under his weight. He engaged the engine and the vehicle rattled to life.

His eyes met hers through the plate-glass windshield. Then he was off on a great huff of steam, the coach quickly picking up speed. He reached the road and sped toward town, out of her sight.

Concealed by the shadows within the shed, Georgiana stood in an agony of tension, waiting for the airship's sails to furl and draw in against the sides of the wooden cruiser. It flew less than a hundred yards from the shed now, but an airship couldn't quickly turn around. It would take a few seconds to haul in the canvas.

The pirates must have realized they'd been spotted. The engines fired, breaking their silence with a heavy thrum across the sky. The propellers began a lazy spin.

Yet their heading didn't change. They weren't following Thom.

Perhaps he'd been wrong and they hadn't been coming after him. Perhaps their appearance was only a coincidence, and they were headed to some other destination.

Georgiana couldn't assume that, though. She had to prepare for the worst: that they had seen her outside earlier, and guessed that she'd remained behind.

But what sort of preparations could be made against pirates? She would be far outnumbered. She might be able to shoot one or two before they returned fire and killed her.

No, shooting meant certain death. She would only use her pistol as a last resort. If she waited, though . . . perhaps there would be some chance. Thom would alert the town. And she would fetch any pirate a healthy ransom, as long as he left her alive.

The engines became louder. Blocked by the roof, she lost sight of the airship as it neared the shed, but its oval shadow darkened the ground outside. Directly overhead now. *Keep flying on, keep flying on.* Her pulse pounded in her ears at a dizzying pace.

The rattle of chains sank her heart. The cargo platform was being lowered. Someone was coming down.

Oh, God. What to do now?

Only what she could. Straightening her shoulders and steeling her spine, Georgiana tucked her pistol into her reticule. She could reach it quickly enough. And if she was to be taken, perhaps they would assume that she only carried frivolous items and overlook the weapon.

A *clank* sounded beside the shed. The rattle of chains stopped. They'd lowered the platform to the ground out of her sight—either fearing that she'd shoot their legs as they came into view or concealing their numbers. Georgiana strained to hear anything more over the thrum of the airship's engines.

In all the noise, the man who appeared at the shed entrance could have stomped his way there and she wouldn't have heard him. Georgiana's fingers tightened on her reticule. He didn't hold a gun. That didn't mean he wasn't dangerous.

And he must have been the nobby gent whom Thom had spoken of. Tall and wiry, with lightly tanned skin and brown hair tied back in a queue, he was smartly dressed for a pirate. His black silk waistcoat and buff breeches didn't show any stains or signs of wear. His tall boots gleamed with high gloss.

He stepped into the shed and offered Georgiana a charming smile. "Mrs. Thomas, I presume."

This gent could presume all he liked. Georgiana raised her voice over the airship's thrum. "If you are seeking my husband, I must tell you he's left."

"He's abandoned someone as beautiful as you? No. He'll soon return."

The pirate spoke in English, not the trader's French commonly used with strangers. He had a Manhattan City accent—and though that city lay just across the river from Prince George Island, where her own family hailed from, each word he said marked his higher class and education.

Why would such a man resort to piracy? Georgiana couldn't imagine. And she didn't care to. She only wanted him gone.

"I've always looked the same, sir, yet my husband has managed to leave me before. He's quite adept at it. He's never been as good about returning."

The pirate only shook his head.

His condescending smile irritated her. How could he be so certain?

Georgiana tried again. "If you are looking for the last gold coin, he took it with him. He said that you already possess the remainder."

He nodded. "It's true, I *did* possess them. And that is the problem, you see. Now I require your husband's assistance, but I doubt he will gladly offer it. I need a guarantee that he will help me. So come on out, Mrs. Thomas. I prefer to have you aboard my flyer before he returns."

Georgiana hesitated. If this pirate needed Thom's help, that meant he needed her husband alive—at least for a short time. That might give them a chance to escape. Yet how could she trust the words of a pirate? She couldn't.

But he didn't leave her with any choice. The pirate drew a pistol from behind his back and leveled it at her chest. As if that were a signal, he was suddenly flanked by a pale-haired woman in trousers and a shorter man, his lips fixed in a leer. Both were armed with guns.

"Leave your reticule, Mrs. Thomas," the pirate said, gesturing at it with a wave of his barrel. "Unless you've tucked a small child in there, nothing but a weapon would weigh down the bottom so much."

Damn him. But she obeyed, dropping her satchel to the ground. If nothing else, its presence here might alert Marta or anyone who came to investigate Thom's and her disappearance.

Because they would both soon be gone. As Georgiana exited the shed, she spotted her steamcoach tearing down the road toward them, leaving a thick trail of black smoke and steam.

Oh, Thom. He shouldn't have returned. He should have continued on to Skagen and sought help. That would have been far more practical.

But Georgiana could not fault her husband for this. She would have come back for him, too.

THREE

The bastard had taken Georgiana.

Thom roared up to the shed at full steam and slammed to a stop. On the ground, a cargo platform waited to carry him up to the airship.

As if he'd bloody wait.

He grabbed the platform chain and hauled himself up, climbing hand over hand, trying to regain his control with every long pull. Not since the destruction of the Horde's tower in England twelve years ago had so much wild rage and terror laid open his heart and clawed through his mind. Senseless with it, he'd killed dozens of the Horde soldiers who'd tried to quash the laborers' rebellion with their weapons and vehicles, ripping their flesh apart with his iron hands, uncaring of the danger to himself.

Thom didn't care for his own safety now, either—and given half a chance, he would tear every damned pirate aboard this airship apart.

But he couldn't risk Georgiana being hurt.

He fought for control until his fear and anger were a cold storm inside him. With a final, powerful lunge, he swung over the gunwale and dropped to the wooden deck.

No one had a gun pointed at him. They didn't need to.

The nobby bastard held a pistol to Georgiana's side. Through the rage, relief hit Thom hard. She was all right—and she was furious. Green eyes bright with anger, her face flushed, and her mouth tightening when the pirate spoke.

"We meet again, Big Thom. As you see, I've had the pleasure of making the acquaintance of your lovely wife. I must confess that when I heard the talk in town that you'd been found on the beach with a coin in your pocket and a bullet in your side, I could hardly believe it. What healthy man could swim a full league through those waters, let alone one who is wounded? But with such an incentive to reach home, it is not so inconceivable after all."

Thom dug the coin out of his coat. He flipped it across the distance separating them. The gold hit the boards with a dull *clink* and rolled before bumping into the toe of the bastard's shining boot.

"That's all we've got," Thom said roughly. "Now let her go."

"That coin is all I have now, too." As he spoke, the nobby bastard glanced at a nearby aviator. With a slight roll of his eyes, the aviator bent to scoop up the coin, then dropped it into the bastard's open hand. "I have need of your salvaging services, Big Thom. But considering our history and the danger of what I'll be asking you to do, I want to ensure that you don't offer any resistance."

Using Georgiana to put Thom over a barrel. For her, he'd take anything. "I'll do whatever you want. Just let her go home."

"She'll be coming with us. Mrs. Winch," he spoke to a tall blond woman, "run down to the house and collect Mrs. Thomas's things. A week's worth ought to do it." He glanced back at Thom. "I suppose your belongings were on your ship?"

"Yes."

"Then you'll have an opportunity to collect them. Don't fear that we'll treat you poorly. Mr. Blade will shortly escort you to the stateroom, where you'll remain until we've reached our destination. You and your wife will be comfortable during your stay, and when you've finished your task, we'll return you both to your home."

By the bloody stars, Thom vowed to smash the teeth out of that lying bastard's smile before this was over. "What task?"

"We'll speak of it soon. Let us be on our way first. We've miles to go, and you have dangerous friends, Big Thom. We don't want your absence discovered too quickly."

We? The nobby bastard could speak for himself. Discovery couldn't come soon enough.

But Thom doubted that help would come at all. It would be up to him to get Georgiana off this damned airship, and he would do anything to make sure it happened. Even if it destroyed him.

Because losing her would, anyway.

Georgiana held tight to Thom's hand as they were escorted down the ladder to the second deck. The man showing them the way, Mr. Blade, was the same leering pirate who had come to the entrance of the shed, and as they walked, he kept prodding Thom's back with the barrel of his gun. Thom didn't react in the slightest, but only the danger of their position prevented Georgiana from whirling on the man. Fury dogged her every step along the corridor. Whatever niceties and manners the master of this airship pretended to have, the crew obviously did not share them.

Blade prodded them toward a cabin door at the far end of the passageway—toward the front of the vessel. Georgiana had never been on an airship before, but the narrow corridors and wooden bulkheads didn't appear or sound much different from a sailing ship's. The engines had been stopped while they'd waited for Thom, and from all around them came the creaking of boards and the noises of the crew. The sway was much different, however—as if they were swinging rather than rocking. Not badly enough to affect her balance, yet still disorienting.

They reached the cabin door. Blade gave Thom another prod.

"Go on through, the both of you. Lord Pinchpenny is playing captain, so he's given you the fancy room. Don't leave it unless someone's come to get you."

Lord Pinchpenny? That didn't bode well. A crew member's blatant disrespect for the master of a ship never did. But there was little here that *did* bode well.

The door closed behind them. Thom's hard arms immediately surrounded her waist, pulled Georgiana tight against his broad chest. She clung to him, his warmth and the strong beat of his heart soothing away some of her anger and fear.

Almost as quickly, he stepped back and swept his gaze from her head to her toes. "You're all right?"

"I am. Oh, Thom. Who is this man?"

He shook his head. "No idea. But he's not a pirate, as I thought."

"Not a pirate? He stole your coins and your ship."

And Georgiana wasn't surprised that Lord Pinchpenny had heard all about Thom in Skagen. She was only surprised that he'd flown there. Pirates avoided the harbor, preferring rum dives and lawless cities like Port Fallow. Georgiana could only recall one pirate coming into town—Mad Machen, in his search for Ivy Blacksmith.

"He stole them, just as a pirate would," Thom agreed. "But look at this cabin, Georgie. This isn't a pirate ship."

She'd barely had a moment to look. Turning, she saw that Thom was probably right. Roughly triangular to accommodate the shape of the bow, with a personal privy cabinet taking the point, the stateroom abounded in luxuries. Deep rugs of blue and cream covered the deck boards. Sunlight streamed through two thick glass portholes, twice the diameter of any she'd ever seen in a ship. A table large enough to seat four stood beneath one of the portholes, and a settee upholstered in blue damask lay beneath the other. A full-sized bed topped by a fine, pale blue counterpane sat flush against the port bulkhead, and there was still room enough for a wardrobe and washstand.

She glanced at the rugs again. Only someone who thought nothing of cleaning would ever put a pale color on the floor. This was a wealthy man's personal vessel. Perhaps the pirates had stolen this as well, but if so, they likely wouldn't have kept this cabin waiting for passengers.

"But what of the crew?" she wondered. A motley bunch. She hadn't seen even one liveried servant. "They don't fit here."

"They don't. Blade said that the nobby gent was playing captain." Thom strode to the starboard porthole and looked out. "I'm thinking that he put the regular crew off and hired mercenaries."

A cold slip of fear trickled down Georgiana's spine. She'd have preferred pirates. Most of them operated by a code. They would kidnap and steal and murder, but in trade for ransom, they'd usually leave most captives alive. She might have been able to negotiate that.

But mercenaries had no code except the cash they received from their employers. And anyone who kept a personal flyer probably had more at his disposal than Georgiana did.

"If he hired mercenaries," she said, "then he had a job in mind."

Eyes cold, Thom glanced back at her. "Yes."

A job that he didn't want his regular crew to be involved in . . . or to know about. Such as boarding a salvage ship and shooting her captain.

"Whatever his purpose, he needs to keep you alive for it," Georgiana said. "And he will keep *me* alive to see that you perform it. While he does that, we'll watch for a chance to escape."

As she spoke, the engines started again, the thrum humming through the airship. The boards vibrated under her feet. Flying away from home.

She fought the panic that fluttered in her belly. They *would* come back home. Alive.

As if seeing her distress, Thom returned to her side. Earlier when he'd looked down at her, his face had been gentle. Now determination hardened each bold feature. "I won't let any harm come to you. We *will* escape."

Nodding, she desperately tried to think of *how* they would. Her gaze fell to his gloved hands. "You put bullets in your arm—do they function as guns?"

His lips twitched. "Among other things."

His humor sparked her own, and she grinned up at him. Her husband was a man of surprises. Of course he couldn't shoot anyone now, just as she hadn't dared to fire her pistol. They would have to wait for the right moment. When the time came, however, hopefully these mercenaries would be surprised by her husband, as well.

A sharp knock sounded at the cabin door. Before they could respond, it opened and the pale-haired woman in trousers came through carrying a bundle of Georgiana's clothing. A mercenary, too, most likely, though it wasn't the daggers or gun tucked into her belt that made Georgiana think so. It was the flatness of her gaze and the firm set of her mouth. Georgiana had seen that look in the mirror. This was a practical woman who would do what was necessary when it needed to be done, but who never forgot her own interests. Georgiana and Thom wouldn't find any help here.

"Mrs. Winch?" Georgiana recalled that Lord Pinchpenny had said the woman's name. "Can you tell us where we're headed?"

"Out to sea." She dropped the bundle on the bed. "I won't tell you more."

That was enough for now. “Thank you.”

Out to sea. Escape might be more difficult, but it could have been worse. She looked to Thom when Mrs. Winch closed the cabin door behind her. “Well, it is better than flying to the continent and trying to salvage among zombies. You’re a good diver.”

Thom nodded, but she knew what he was thinking: the sea held dangers just as terrifying as zombies were. But he truly was a good diver. He knew to be careful beneath the waters.

She was more concerned about the dangers on this airship.

“Which of your friends does he believe will come for us?” But even as Georgiana asked, she realized the answer. Lord Pinchpenny had known about Thom washing up on the beach, so he’d obviously talked up someone in Skagen. He’d have heard the same rumors in town that she had. “Mad Machen? Lady Corsair?”

Thom shook his head. “They’re not friends of that sort. Even if they were near enough to hear that we’d been taken, I don’t imagine they’d rush to a rescue.”

“But they *are* acquaintances?”

“Yes.”

“Such company you keep, Thom.” So surprising. But as much as she would like for him to continue surprising her, they couldn’t afford to miss any opportunity to gain an advantage. Ignorance of any sort could only harm them now. “So tell me of this treasure, and why he believes that the most notorious of pirates and mercenaries would come for you.”

Thom moved to the porthole, keeping an eye on the sun’s position and trying to estimate their heading. North by northwest, for now. Nothing lay ahead of them but the sea and the gray clouds piled up on the horizon.

He glanced back at Georgie, who was waiting for him to

speak—and hanging up her dresses in the wardrobe. Even with all of this pressing on her, she did what needed to be done.

Thom was the same. But everything he'd ever done seemed like a fool's path now. Leaving England, to start. He hadn't even known what he'd wanted then—he'd only known what he *didn't* want.

He didn't want to live under the Horde's boot. He didn't want to work for nothing. He didn't want to be an animal, or anything less than his own man.

Then he'd met Georgiana, and he'd known. He wanted to be in her bed. He wanted to be her husband. He wanted to be a man for her, the only man she'd ever need.

And if Thom hadn't wanted her, if he hadn't made her his, Georgiana wouldn't be here now.

But she was. Now the only thing that needed to be done was seeing her make it safely away.

Thom wouldn't be doing it alone, though. He'd rather have her anywhere else, but he was grateful for that. Georgiana was clever and practical—and she was right. They needed to figure out exactly what advantages they had and why this bastard had come after him, so it'd be easier to spot lies that might get them killed.

So he started at the beginning of it all. "Two years ago, Mad Machen came to *Oriana* looking to borrow a diving suit. His blacksmith was going down in a submersible she'd built, retrieving a lockbox of Lady Corsair's that had ended up in the bottom of the harbor at Port Fallow. He wanted someone under the water to help out if she got into trouble."

"That was Ivy Blacksmith?"

An odd note in her voice made Thom glance back. She'd stopped beside the bed, holding a pink dress and looking at him.

"You sound fond of her," she added softly.

"I am." But he shook his head. "Whatever you've heard, it wasn't more than that."

"What was it?"

A weight settled in his chest. How much of this should he reveal? They were separating. None of it mattered now.

And he might soon be dead. Nothing mattered at all now except for Georgie.

"She was the closest I'd come to staying with you."

Her dark eyebrows pinched together. "What?"

"Ivy was like me. Born under the Horde. Given a sweeper's arms instead of a hauler's apparatus, but the same. And she left England when she could, but now she has arms of mechanical flesh."

A frown creased her forehead. "I still don't understand."

"I wanted arms like that. I couldn't afford them." Salvaging was hardly a lucrative business, and the one man who could create flesh made out of metal fibers and nanoagents charged a small fortune for each limb. "But seeing those arms on Ivy made getting them seem more possible. And that made the possibility of coming back to you seem a little closer."

"Why would you need those to come back to me?"

Anger and hurt dug into his heart, sharp and hard. "You asked me to hold you in my arms every night, Georgie. I had iron bars."

And he'd never thought much of it until leaving England. Prosthetics were as common as noses there. But not around the North Sea—and he'd known that she hadn't envisioned a man holding her in an iron cage.

Yet he'd promised. He hadn't cared if it meant getting newer, better arms. That suited him. Making her happy suited him even more. He just hadn't known it would take so long.

But Georgiana damn well shouldn't pretend that she hadn't asked him to do it.

Now she stared at him, her face absolutely still. After a long second, she whispered, "I did say that."

"You did."

"And that's why you kept leaving?"

He gave a sharp nod. "I promised to make you happy."

A wild little laugh burst from her and she sank onto the edge of the bed, clutching the pink dress to her chest. "You were hoping to earn enough for mechanical flesh."

"Yes." Because Thom hadn't known that anyone could make prosthetics like he possessed now. Though not mechanical flesh, they were just as amazing in their own way.

"So you made their acquaintance in Port Fallow. And then?"

Thom hesitated. Her voice was strained. Her face had paled, but her eyes were bright, as if she held back tears.

"Georgie?"

She shook her head. "Staying or leaving isn't so important now, Thom. How do you think the rumors began? Is there anything we can use as leverage against this man?"

Staying or leaving wasn't important. For so long, it had been all that mattered. It didn't now.

Thom pulled a chair from under the table and sat. "Ivy likes building things. I had experience diving. So about four months ago, Mad Machen sailed into Port Fallow's harbor for a few weeks' stay, and while she was there we made a trade. I'd tell her what I knew of diving in deeper waters, and she'd give me the first submersible she'd made. So we spent time together while she built a new one. But anything else?" He shook his head. "She's a fine woman. But I haven't had eyes for anyone but you, Georgie. And she doesn't have eyes for anyone but Mad Machen."

"For the pirate? But I thought he abducted her. Forced her to work on his ship." Her green eyes hardened. "Forced her into his bed."

"That's what people say, but I asked her once if she wanted help getting away. She said no. And I never saw anything that made me think he'd hurt her."

Instead, he knew exactly what the man felt when he looked at her. Thom was feeling the same now, looking at Georgiana. There was the woman he'd kill for, die for—and do both without a single regret.

"Truly?"

He nodded. "Considering what she's capable of building, Georgie, she could have gotten away a long time ago. If she'd wanted to."

Her expression thoughtful, Georgiana rose from the bed and hung up the pink dress. "He has a terrifying reputation."

"And he's earned it. He *is* a madman."

"A dangerous man." She joined him at the table, skirts swaying with each step, sweeping her flowery scent around them. "But you weren't worried?"

Thom shrugged. "After watching a megalodon swim by when I was a hundred feet below the surface, mad pirates don't seem much of a threat."

Unless they pointed a gun at Georgie. Even a giant armored shark couldn't terrify him as much as seeing her in danger.

Smiling, she took the nearest chair. The sun shining through the porthole caught the reds in her hair like sparks of fire and deepened the shadow beneath her soft bottom lip. Her gaze fell to his arms. "So they truly were a gift?"

"Yes. Ivy said it was in trade, too." Though they were worth far more than any help he'd given.

"She sounds very generous. And amiable."

"She's both."

"The rumor is that she's a little mad, too."

"Considering that she gave me these arms for nothing, I'd say there was some truth to that," he said, and her laugh in response lifted through him. "Though I never put much stock in rumors."

"I don't, either." Her smile faded. Steadily, her gaze held his. "But it's sometimes difficult to ignore them, when a rumor is the only news of your husband that you receive."

Throat suddenly thick, Thom nodded. He'd done wrong by her in that. The easy excuse had always been that he couldn't read and write, anyway. But he could have had a message sent. Thom just hadn't been able to make himself tell her that he still had nothing. And the longer he'd gone without a message, the harder it had become to send.

But that soft admonishment was all she said of it. "And these coins? How did you find them?"

"While I was in Port Fallow, working with Ivy on that submersible, I ran into Lady Corsair again. We met on Mad Machen's ship and she invited me up to her skyrunner for a dinner."

Georgiana stared at him. "You had dinner with Lady Corsair."

With a grin, Thom nodded. The disbelief in her voice wasn't that of someone wondering whether he lied. His wife was wondering whether he'd gone mad, too. Maybe for good reason. A mercenary, Lady Corsair's reputation was even more ruthless than Mad Machen's.

"And while we were eating, Archimedes Fox told me—"

"Archimedes Fox!" Now she laughed. "He's not a real man. He's a character in those adventure stories."

"All of them based on his salvaging runs." Though it wasn't the type of salvaging that Thom did. Instead of recovering recent wreckage, Fox risked the zombies in the abandoned cities of Europe, searching for treasures. That risk had paid off for him, too. "Much of it's true. Especially the bit about his colorful clothes—I nearly go blind every time I look at him."

She laughed again. "Truly?"

"Yes," he said. "His sister writes the stories. She lives in Fladstrand."

Not far from Skagen. Georgiana's eyes widened slightly. "I heard that Lady Corsair flew into that town a few times—and that

Fox's sister was kidnapped last year. But I thought it was all part of another story."

"They didn't tell me anything about that. Fox was more interested in talking about a wreck that might be worth diving. It was more than two hundred years old, and he said it was just waiting for any man who could dive deep enough for it—and that in a wreck so old, I wouldn't have to worry about anyone claiming ownership of anything I found."

He'd also said that others had died searching for it. But Thom hadn't thought there was anything to lose by trying.

He'd been wrong. Though he'd found the treasure, there'd been everything to lose.

"How deep was it?"

"Fox didn't know for certain. Just deep enough that no one had found it yet, though his research had given him a good idea of its location. But it was just over three hundred feet."

"*Three hundred feet!*" Georgiana shot out of her chair, her hands flying to her head as if to keep her brains from exploding. "Thom! What the hell were you thinking?"

She was right to be angry. That dive had hit him harder than any other, making him dizzy under the water, and feeling as if every joint in his body would snap apart after he'd come up, despite a slow ascent. In her place, he'd have been shouting, too.

But foolish or not, his answer was the same. "I was thinking that I had new arms, but that I didn't have anything else to bring back to you. It seemed worth the try."

Her lips compressed and she turned away from the table, arms crossing beneath her breasts. Those soft mounds rose and fell sharply a few times before she nodded. "Where was it?"

"Off the eastern coast of Ireland."

She glanced back at him, baffled. "Ireland?"

"It was the wreck of the *Resolution*." That was met with a blank expression. "It was the ship that the Irishmen fired on when the Horde first invaded."

Her eyes slowly rounded in realization. She knew the story, then. Thom hadn't until Archimedes Fox had told him. It was apparently common knowledge among the descendants of the Englishmen who'd fled Britain for the Americas—and a sore point between everyone living in Ireland and Manhattan City. But not in England. Those who'd lived under the Horde hadn't known anything of the incident. And truth was, Thom didn't care enough to hold a grudge now. He could see both the horror of what had been done, and he could see the sense of it, too.

Two hundred years ago, a good number of Englishmen had been infected by the Horde's sugar and tea. And when the radio signal had begun broadcasting, a good number of people suddenly had their emotions dampened. They'd become pliable, obedient.

A good number of people, but not all of them. Those who could had tried to flee, but there'd been no airships then. The only escape lay across the water—and Ireland was the nearest destination that wasn't teeming with zombies.

The people on the first ships to Dublin had been allowed to disembark. But those ships had been full of panic and rumors of infection, and the city had recently lost a large number of its population to a plague, so the Irish had set up a blockade at the mouth of the bay and began ordering new arrivals to turn away. The English refused, and soon the sea had been teeming with boats waiting for entry, some of the passengers taking the risk of rowing to shore or attempting to sail farther along the coast—until the Lord Mayor of Dublin had ordered cannons to fire on the largest ship, *Resolution*, as a warning of what would happen to them all if they didn't leave.

The drastic action had the desired effect, but that hadn't been the only ship sunk. Several dozen that left Dublin had also been lost in the North Sea and while trying to cross the Atlantic.

"Fox told me that, aside from the fishing boats, most of those who'd managed to escape England only did because they could afford to go—and that all of the valuables they took with them had likely sunk, too."

"The Irish always denied it ever happened," Georgiana said.

"But people saw it, talked about it, wrote letters about it. Some painted the scene later. Fox had studied the letters and pictures, and told me where to find it."

"And you did." Her admiring look sent heat rushing under his skin. "Were only the coins left?"

"I don't know." Thom hadn't stayed down long enough to look for anything else. "As soon as I saw the chest, I knew it would be enough. There were five thousand coins in it."

Georgiana's mouth opened. No sound came out. She plopped back into her chair, looking astounded.

Thom imagined he'd looked the same when he'd first come across the chest. "Fox had given me the name of a salvage dealer in Brighton. So I took one of the coins in. He called it a Carolus Broad—one of the last English coins minted before the invasion. He said he'd had a collector eager to know if any came in. He gave me that collector's offer, but also told me that the offer was lower than the value of the gold itself, and that, considering where I'd found them, I could take in more at auction or ask for a higher price. I wanted to bring the coins to you first, anyway, so I told the dealer to make his inquiry and send word to me in Skagen."

"So you were coming home with a chest of gold," she said softly.

"Enough to buy mechanical flesh if these arms wouldn't do."

Her chest hitched. "Oh, Thom. They would have."

But he'd been too late, either way. He'd had these arms when she'd agreed to separate. "At least it was something worth bringing home. Something I could have given you when I left."

"The gold?"

He nodded. "That's a husband's duty: earning enough to support his family."

" 'And a man doesn't deserve to come home unless he's done it.' Yes, so I've heard my father say." She rose to her feet and paced a few steps, rubbing her forehead with the tips of her fingers—a gesture Thom had seen many others make when they were frustrated or tired, though he'd never formed the habit himself. Skeletal iron fingers didn't smooth away tension well.

She faced him again, eyes narrowed. "Was this salvage dealer the only man who knew you'd found the coins?—but you met him before. So the dealer is not the same man as on this airship."

"The collector he contacted knew, too."

"You increased the price. Maybe it was more than the collector could pay—or he realized that hiring a band of mercenaries would cost far less."

That would fit. "So he came to take it rather than make another offer."

Georgiana nodded, blew out a sharp breath. He could imagine what she was thinking—the man had tried to kill him rather than make another offer, too. This task he wanted Thom to do probably wouldn't end any differently.

Her eyes met his for a long minute before she stepped closer to his chair. Her hand lifted to his face. Just a gentle touch, her fingertips sliding over his bearded jaw, but need slapped him hard, turning his body into one thick ache. Hanging at his sides, his hands clenched to fists. He wouldn't grab her, haul her onto his lap. He wouldn't take her sweet mouth with his.

But smoking hells, he wanted to. And Georgiana had to see it.

Her gaze was arrested on his face, her lips parting. Her fingers had stilled on his jaw, then her focus dropped and he felt the light brush of her thumb against the corner of his mouth.

"Georgie," he said roughly.

Her eyes closed. With a sigh, she turned her face away, her gaze sliding around the stateroom. "We need to search this cabin," she said. "Maybe we'll find something to aid in our escape."

Always practical, his Georgie. And she was right. He nodded against her hand.

"Let's look, then."

FOUR

The search needed to be done, but it was also a mindless task, and Georgiana desperately needed the time to think on everything that Thom had told her.

Her husband was such a good man. A far more fascinating man than she'd realized. And knowing why he'd stayed away left Georgiana ashamed and angry at herself now.

She *had* asked him to hold her in his arms every night. Of course, she hadn't meant it so literally—and the important part hadn't been his arms, but that he would be there every night.

She'd been so thoughtless. Cruelly and selfishly so. Why had she never imagined how such words might sound to a man whose arms had been replaced with iron? And she'd never explained what she'd meant, or why it mattered, so that he wouldn't mistake her meaning. She hadn't told him of her mother. Why had she assumed that he would know exactly what she'd wanted? As if it had been *his* responsibility to perfectly interpret her every thought and desire.

Oh, and this was the very worst time to think about whose fault it was that her marriage had fallen apart. What did any of it matter if they didn't survive this? She had to be clever and focus on their escape, not think of the past.

She had to be clever. Even a few days ago, Georgiana would have said she was. Also sensible and intelligent. Her lack of understanding of the man she'd married dealt a shattering blow to that belief. Her gaze had been so limited and narrow. Searching the horizon for his ship, but never seeing anything but herself.

With a heavy sigh, she pulled open the final drawer in the writing desk. Nothing there. Either wealthy people didn't keep anything that could be used as a weapon in their staterooms, or this cabin had already been cleared out.

Holding the mattress angled up with one hand, Thom turned away from his examination of the bed frame. "Nothing?"

"No. If I were more clever, I would know how to make an escape balloon with the lamp and the skirts cut from my dresses. I'd sew them together and we'd fly off."

"I'll be glad to take a ride under your skirts, Georgie."

"Thom!" So outrageous. And wonderful. She blushed and laughed, shaking her head.

His response was a grin that she felt down to her toes. A man of few words, but he didn't need many. He could lift her from sorrow and shame with the widening of his mouth and a laughing flash of his teeth.

Why had he never teased her in such a bold way before? Was this new—or another part of him that he'd hidden? Wherever it stemmed from, she hoped he would continue. Forever, if possible. But forever could only happen if they escaped.

And after they did, Georgiana was determined to win her husband back.

If she could. He'd wanted to stay—but he'd intended to leave her, anyway. He'd thought himself a failure as a husband. That hadn't changed. He probably still intended to leave; and maybe he would. But whether he stayed or left, Georgiana would do everything she could to prove that he hadn't failed at anything.

Thom let the mattress flop back to the frame. "There's nothing here, either. But looking at you, I don't doubt we'll figure out something."

Her determination must have been apparent on her face. As well it should. She *was* determined to get through this.

Her gaze fell to his arms. Thom and she weren't completely without weapons. And Thom wore gloves, sleeves. Lord Pinchpenny probably knew of the prosthetics, but he likely didn't know that they weren't the typical skeletal sort, or what was hidden beneath.

Even she didn't completely know. "But you have a gun?"

"Yes."

"What else?"

"Anything I might need underwater or hauling sail alone. A diving knife. Cables. Grapples. Clamps."

All useful, but Georgiana's mind couldn't work past the initial part. "Hauling sail alone? What of your crew?"

Not a large crew. Just two other men. If their trip into town had gone as planned, Thom would have given their names to the magistrate, listing them lost at sea—though they might both still be on *Oriana*. A pirate would kill a captain, but he needed someone to sail a stolen ship.

Thom shook his head. "About two years ago, I rigged her so that I could handle her alone. With no crew to pay, I could send more of my earnings to you."

And he'd thought that amount wasn't a lot, but it must have cost him so much more than the money he'd sent. The past two years, as alone on his boat as she'd been at home—but sailing and diving were far more dangerous. Anything could have happened to him and there'd have been no one to help.

Her heart twisted. She could have changed that. She'd sent out messages to Thom when her mother and father had died. Not knowing where he was, she'd sent them to towns and harbors where she knew he'd been. But when he hadn't replied, she hadn't tried again.

She could have. A few more messages, a few months later. Eventually, he'd have received one. But she'd been so angry and stubborn and hurt.

Thoughtless and cruel. Angry and stubborn. Georgiana was not liking this new view of herself at all. He had not been a failure of a husband, but she might have been a failure as a wife. And she understood why, feeling this way, he'd want to leave. Because now Georgiana wasn't certain that she deserved to keep a man like Thom, either.

But she had to try. And also try to be something that she'd thought she was: just a little bit clever. Because she wouldn't lose him again. Not like this.

The vibrations under her feet changed subtly, the thrum of the engine deepening. Frowning, Thom crossed the cabin.

"We're slowing," he said.

She joined him at the porthole, looking out. Only water. No ships. "We're going to need a boat when we escape," she said. "He said that you'd be able to retrieve your belongings. I'd hoped that meant wherever we were going, we'd see *Oriana* there."

"I did, too."

They both turned at the knock. This time, the door didn't open until Thom answered it. Blade stood in the passageway. Not leering now. Perhaps he wasn't brave enough to do it in front of her husband, just as he'd only prodded Thom in the back behind the safety of a loaded gun. If so, he was the worst kind of coward—a mean one.

"His majesty says to come on up. But the missus stays here."

Thom glanced back at her. Georgiana nodded.

"I'll be fine. You'd best find out what he wants."

A cold wind scraped across the upper deck, whistling past the cables tethering the balloon overhead. Coming off the ladder, Thom turned up the collar of his wool coat. Blade pointed him to the starboard side, where the nobby gent stood, looking down at the water. Thom started across, his gaze sweeping the deck. Near the stern, two clinker-built cutters hung on pulleys beneath the balloon. Lifeboats, capable of holding twenty. Thom only needed to seat two.

He looked south, squinting away the tears the wind whipped from his eyes. No land on the horizon.

Bundled in a thick scarf and wearing goggles, his nose red from cold, the nobby gent glanced up when Thom reached the side. "There you are. Have you settled in comfortably, then?"

Comfortable? What the hell did that matter? "What do you want with me?"

With a sudden grin, the bastard nodded. "You're a direct man. I trust that I can be as well."

He already had been. "There's nothing more direct than a bullet."

"I suppose not. But I should have taken a few moments before pulling the trigger to ask where you'd hidden the chest. I assumed—falsely, as it turns out—that I would have an opportunity to search your ship and find it. But at the time, I was more concerned with sailing your ship away from the coast, where it might be recognized." He sighed and looked down at the water again, and Thom saw a round buoy rolling on the swells. "My men didn't know how to handle your rigging. She capsized and went under right here."

He'd stolen *Oriana*, only to sink her the next day? Thom's hearty laugh rang across the deck.

"I'm not insensible of the irony, Mr. Thomas," the bastard said, still smiling. He paused. Behind the clear lenses of his goggles, his eyes narrowed. "No. It's not *Mister* Thomas, is it? Just Thomas. No one in the Horde's laboring classes knew their family names."

They didn't know any family, either. "We didn't."

"Your single name is refreshing, in truth. So many of the others take such ridiculous names. Strongarm. Screwmaster. Blade." His lip curled. "Longcock."

"I think they've earned the right to call themselves whatever they damn well please."

"Perhaps they did, at that." He regarded Thom thoughtfully. "Your wife took your name as hers. How did you earn that, I wonder? An infected man with no education, no history, no family. No arms."

"I have two right here." He'd always had arms. They just hadn't always been made of flesh and bone.

"Arms that the Horde gave you? I've seen their like."

No, he hadn't. But Thom didn't bother with an answer.

The gent smiled faintly, as if amused by Thom's silence. "You haven't asked me who I am."

Because it didn't matter. "You're the man who's holding my wife hostage in exchange for gold. That's all I need to know."

Being shot, losing *Oriana*—Thom could let those go. Not the threat to Georgiana.

"Fair enough. Especially as the name I'll have will depend on those coins." All trace of amusement fled his face. "And all that I need to know of you? You're a man who can haul and dive. I want those coins back. You're going to get them for me."

And so now Thom knew something else about the nobby bastard. This man would look at him and his arms and anyone else who'd lived under the Horde, and think they were all lower than shit. But he'd use them, anyway, if they served his purpose.

So Thom was back to being under someone's boot. But he wouldn't be working for nothing. This would be for Georgiana's life.

And it might take his own life. His gaze scanned the horizon again. No telling how far out they were. But it was farther out than he usually dove. "Did you plumb the depth?"

"Sixty-five fathoms."

"Impossible," Thom said flatly. That was almost four hundred feet.

"Not for you. The infected are less prone to the divers' disease."

"But not immune to it, and there's more than that to worry about. Any deeper than a hundred, and even men with bugs can black out, like they're swimming drunk. I've felt a bit of that myself. What you're asking is a hundred feet farther than I've ever gone, and that was deeper than I should have."

"Deeper than you should have, yet you're alive now. So you *could* have gone deeper." The bastard stepped back, his hand dropping to the pistol tucked into his belt. "I will keep it simple for you, Big Thom. Dive for the gold, or you'll watch me put a bullet in your wife's head. Then I'll put one in yours."

Rage swallowed any response Thom could have made. Only sheer will kept him in place—and fear of what would happen to Georgiana if he ripped this bastard apart where he stood. The Winch woman had been standing guard outside the stateroom door when he'd left. If Thom did anything here, he wouldn't be able to get back to Georgiana in time to save her.

"Return to your cabin now. Talk to your wife. Sleep on your decision, if you must. But at sunrise, you're going into the water.

Your only choice is whether you'll be dead or alive, and whether your wife goes with you."

There was no decision to make. Georgiana was right: some chance was better than none. And if his submersible was still bolted to *Oriana*'s deck, maybe their chances would be better yet.

"I'll dive," he said. "So let me see the equipment you've got."

Georgiana attempted to remain calm while Thom was gone, but she ended up pacing the floor until he returned. She didn't wait for him to close the door before asking, "What does he want you to do?"

"Dive."

She'd already guessed that. "Dive for what?"

"*Oriana*."

His ship? Georgiana stared at him, expecting him to tell her it was a joke. But it was even funnier if true—and his grin told her that it was. She burst into laughter, shaking her head.

He unbuckled his coat, glanced around the stateroom. "I told them to bring me the suit and hose so that I can look them over. They'll be coming with those and a tub."

To make certain everything was watertight. "How deep is the wreck?"

"One hundred feet."

Deep, though not horrifyingly so. And still dangerous. Most wrecks went down in the shallows, where giant eels and young sharks and sharp rocks threatened to tear into a man or into his air hose. The dangers of the open sea were not worse or better. Just different.

And now she watched Thom's gaze slide away from her face, as if there were something he meant to conceal. But she could imagine what it was. "Did he threaten to kill me if you didn't go down?"

His gaze snapped back to hers. "Yes. But I'll kill him before he touches you."

"I know." That had never been in question. Knowing that he was diving for *Oriana*, however, raised another one. "Was your submersible aboard? Is there room enough for two?"

"Yes. And I was thinking the same." Striding to the wardrobe, he hung his coat on a hook and dragged off his hat. His short hair stuck up every which way. He ran his gloved palm over his head once, as if to smooth down the strands. It didn't help.

Well, *she* would not help him. Georgiana rather liked this wild look. "Do you think it's a better option than a boat?"

"I do."

"What of the megalodons? Sound will carry better through a metal hull. It might attract their attention."

"She runs quiet. Just the propellers and whatever noise we make. But either way is a risk, boat or submersible. We have to decide which we like better." His expression grave, he stopped close, looking down at her. "If we took a boat, it wouldn't be anything for this airship to come after us. They'd spot us on the water and that would be the end of it. But if we're under the surface, we'd be out of their sight."

So they would have to weigh the uncertain chance of attack from an enormous shark against the certainty of being caught again. Georgiana knew which risk she'd rather take. "What of the air? Without another vessel, we couldn't use a pump or hose."

"We'd come up when we needed it, open the top hatch to let in the fresh air. Then go down again before they could catch up to us. It wouldn't take long before they'd lost us completely."

Georgiana nodded. "How will you bring it up from *Oriana*?"

"I wouldn't have to. If she's still full of air, she'll pop up to the surface as soon as I release the bolts. The question would be when to dive for her."

So that they could avoid anyone on the airship knowing they had a mode of escape. It would have to be at night—but that would make seeing anything underwater almost impossible.

A sharp knock sounded at the door. The equipment had arrived. They would have to discuss this more later.

For now, her only task would be to assist him in checking and rechecking every seal and valve, and every inch of that hose. Lord Pinchpenny would use a threat against her to make Thom go down. She would help make certain that he came back up alive.

FIVE

Lord Pinchpenny threatened their lives . . . then sent Mrs. Winch to invite them to dinner in his cabin.

Georgiana debated whether to refuse, and saw the same struggle in Thom. But in the end, refusal didn't seem worth the risk, and she told Mrs. Winch that they would join him as soon as they'd washed up. With a sigh, she rose from her kneeling position beside the tub, where she and Thom had just rolled up their sleeves and begun running the long coil of air hose through the water to check for leaking bubbles.

With shorter sleeves and a bit of lace at the scooped neckline, her pink cotton dress seemed most suitable for dinner, but she wouldn't wear it for Lord Pinchpenny's sake. She only wanted to please Thom—and she changed into the dress to please Thom, too, though she wasn't quite bold enough to face him after she unfastened the blue wool and stood in front of the wardrobe, clothed only in her chemise and stockings. Her cheeks felt as pink as her dress when she tugged everything into place, but the burning in his eyes when she turned around was worth every moment of embarrassment.

He must have watched her the entire time. When she'd left him by the tub, he'd been rolling down the right sleeve of his linen shirt. Though several minutes had passed, the left sleeve was still bunched up over his steel elbow.

She glanced at his hands. "You'd best finish covering those."

The sound he made in response might have been a *yes* but emerged more like a primitive grunt.

Smiling, she moved to the mirror and began repinning her hair. In the reflection, she watched him pull on his woven gansey, followed by the gloves. Oh, but he was such a handsome, incredible man. Every part of her felt more alive when he was near.

And though Georgiana liked his hair wild, she would like this even more. "Have a seat. You could use a good combing."

"I can do it."

"I know. But I want to."

That seemed good enough reason for Thom. But Georgiana's true reason was that it gave her an excuse to move in between his knees when he sat on the edge of the bed, and stand with her body close to his. He would only have to lean forward to pillow his cheek upon her breast. His gaze had settled there instead, his lips parted, as if the shadow of her cleavage was an entrancing thing.

Her heart pounded. She slicked the wet comb through his thick hair, trying not to think of his mouth so near to the bare expanse of skin above her neckline, unable to think of anything else. Each breath she took seemed to tighten her bodice across her breasts, and she could hardly bear the ache at their tips. Thom must see how her nipples beaded beneath the cotton. But though she yearned for him to touch her, his hands had fisted at his thighs.

Now was not the time, anyway. Desperately, she searched for something to distract her. Anything. Such as dinner with Lord

Pinchpenny. She wondered breathlessly, "Do you think that he put off his cook with the rest of the crew? He doesn't seem like a man who will tolerate poor fare at his table."

"He doesn't." Thom's voice was rough. "But he also doesn't seem a man who does anything by half."

"Then he would have had to hire another for this job. A mercenary cook. I didn't even realize there was such a thing, though I suppose all of the knives come in handy," she said, and smiled when Thom laughed. That quiet rumble counted among her favorite sounds in all the world.

When his laugh faded, she felt his hand upon her hip. But not to pull her closer. It was a small touch of apology, instead. "I won't be good company at dinner. I'd as soon kill him as talk to him."

"I won't care if you don't speak a single word, Thom. You are always good company to me." She used her fingers to smooth back a few dark strands near his temple, then sighed. "We should not delay much longer."

"No. But I'll need another minute before I'm decent."

"Oh?" Then she saw the state of his trousers, and heat flooded her cheeks. "Thom!"

He laughed again at her admonishing tone—though the truth was, she did not mind a bit.

And she could use another minute, too.

The captain's cabin also lay on the second deck, but at the stern rather than the bow. Squared off, the cabin was bigger than the triangular one, and whoever the usual captain was, that person had more sensible taste than displayed in the stateroom. A heavy brown curtain separated the main part of the room from the berth. Sturdy furnishings and dark woods gave the cabin a somber appearance. Paned windows overlooked the tall blades of the twin propellers, and beyond them, offered a view of the setting sun painting orange across the water in broad strokes.

Lord Pinchpenny was alone, reading by the glow of a small lamp. As they entered, he set the book aside and rose from his chair to greet them. "How lovely you look, Mrs. Thomas."

"Thank you." Her reply was stiff. She did indeed look well. But a single heated glance from Thom pleased her a thousand times more than flattery from this man ever could.

"Please, come and be seated. I cannot tell you how grateful I am that you're here. I've longed for civilized conversation."

He gestured to the table, a more formal setting than in their stateroom, and large enough to seat eight. Standing at the head, he pulled out the chair on his right.

Thom took it. He dragged the next seat back for Georgiana, keeping himself between her and Lord Pinchpenny.

Flattening her lips to stop her smile, Georgiana sat. Not much civilized conversation would be found with her husband—which was exactly how she liked him. Lord Pinchpenny didn't attempt to conceal his amusement. He regarded Thom with a wide grin before looking to Georgiana again.

"By your accent, I believe we must have been almost neighbors once. You lived on Prince George Island?"

Near to Manhattan City, but in many ways, she couldn't have been born any farther away from this man. They were most certainly not neighbors. But she only replied, "Not for many years. My family came to Skagen when I was a young girl."

Still standing, Lord Pinchpenny filled their glasses with red wine. "Before the revolution in England?"

"Yes."

"And you didn't return home when the tower was destroyed?"

"England was never my home, sir."

His brows rose at that. "I have always considered it mine. All of my family has. Indeed, that is how we've come to this situation now."

"The situation where you've threatened both me and my husband?" Georgiana smiled, so that he would know this conversation was still civilized. "What is it that you needed, sir? The money?"

"No." He finished pouring wine for himself and took his place at the head of the table. "I'm not a thief. This is reclamation of honor."

Through piracy and murder? "What honor do you wish to reclaim?"

"Title, lands. But above all, a good name." He leaned back in his chair and crossed his legs at the knee, the easy posture of a man utterly sure of himself. "I'm the Earl of Southampton—or rather, I *should* be."

And Georgiana had always thought she should be Queen of the North Sea. That didn't make her so. "And why aren't you?"

"Shortly before the Horde's invasion, my ancestor—Henry, the sixth Earl of Southampton—shared the fears of those who had already fled England, and sent his countess and children to the Americas. But he remained behind. My family had extensive holdings and many tenants dependent on them, and the earl was loyal to the Crown. He would not abandon either out of fear. Like every man of my line, he believed that it was his honor and duty to serve them."

Beside her, Thom drew in a long, slow breath and closed his eyes. Probably because he was rolling them toward the heavens.

Georgiana suppressed another smile. "And so he was caught in England when the tower went up?"

"No. He was among those who weren't infected by the Horde's radio signals. And you have likely heard the stories of what had happened then. Confusion and panic everywhere. No one quite knew what had happened; they only knew England was under attack of some sort, and even the king had been affected. For the security of the Crown, his ministers agreed that a portion of the treasury should be taken out of London for safekeeping until the threat was defeated. They entrusted my ancestor with some of those treasures."

It finally began to make sense. "Including the chest of gold coins?"

"Yes. Everything my ancestor took with him was documented, with the understanding that it would all be returned when the Horde had been overthrown. That documentation reached the Americas with one of the king's ministers. But my ancestor did not. The Irish fired upon his ship, instead."

"They denied it."

"Yes. So my ancestor was labeled a thief when the treasures in his keeping disappeared—and his title and lands were stripped from him and his heirs. I ought to have been next in line."

"Now you want to restore your family's good name." Along with the title and lands.

"Yes."

"And you needed the coins as proof that your ancestor didn't steal them?"

Smiling, he dipped his head in a slow nod. "Exactly right, Mrs. Thomas."

What a load of ballocks. She didn't doubt that there was some truth to his tale of being an heir and of lost titles, but the history of those coins would have been revealed when Thom put them up for auction, and Southampton's family's name would have been cleared then. So that could not be his only reason for taking such drastic measures to secure the coins—and the most probable reason was the same as the one she'd first suspected: money. Those coins were worth a fortune. A clever man could claim that he'd only recovered half their number from the wreck, return those to the

Crown as proof of his ancestor's innocence, then sell the remainder on the sly.

Georgiana didn't know what his ancestor had been, but this would-be Lord Southampton was likely nothing but a thief, after all.

But she didn't say so. "You must have been searching for these coins for some time—along with the other treasures that your ancestor took with him."

"As my father did, and his father, and *his* father. We have hoped to hear any mention of the items."

"So that is how Thom's salvage dealer knew to contact you."

Southampton nodded again. "I would not miss any opportunity to gain proof of my ancestor's innocence. My children will not be raised under the shadow of shame that I was."

Perhaps in Manhattan City, that shadow had been a painful one. But considering that he would likely try to deny Georgiana and Thom the chance of having any children at all—or a life that lasted longer than a few more days—she could not feel sympathy for him.

"Why didn't you send your own divers to Dublin, then?"

"We didn't know exactly where the items were, in truth. The weeks following the invasion were complete chaos. No one was certain which ship he'd boarded, or even if he'd made it onto a ship at all. The treasures might have shown up anywhere."

So he hadn't known much of anything until Thom had found the coins. "And what would you have done if they'd been found elsewhere?"

This time, the smile that touched his lips wasn't amused. Just determined. And a bit frightening. "The same thing I am now: make my best offer, then go about securing them any way necessary."

"And you *will* let us return home after Thom retrieves the coins for you?"

"Of course." Southampton shrugged, the coldness falling away. "Just as I said I would."

"So you did."

And Georgiana didn't believe a word of it.

Their dinner arrived shortly thereafter—fish and potatoes, and just as coarse as she would have expected from a mercenary cook—and they spent the remainder of the meal speaking of pleasant trifles. Georgiana was glad to finally return to the stateroom, where her time would be spent in a worthwhile purpose.

It was almost midnight when she and Thom finished running the air hose through the tub—at least five hundred feet of it. Probably more than would be used in a hundred-foot dive, but he would need at least some of the extra length to move around when he reached the bottom, and it was always better to have too much than too little.

She rose to her feet, rolling her shoulders to loosen stiff muscles. "Are you coming to bed?"

Shaking his head, he hauled the giant coil of hose out from the middle of the floor. "I'll make do with that big chair."

Big chair? Georgiana glanced toward the porthole. He meant the settee—but to a man of his size, it probably looked the same.

And it would be ridiculous for him to sleep there, whatever he called it.

"No, Thom. You've just spent days in a fever, recovering from a bullet wound. You *will* share the bed with me."

Once again, her husband proved himself a sensible man. He didn't argue with her. He just nodded.

Mrs. Winch hadn't brought any of her nightgowns. By the soft glow of the lamp, Georgiana unpinned her hair. She removed her dress and stockings, then quickly climbed into bed wearing only her chemise. She watched as Thom stripped down to his drawers and snuffed the lamp. Darkness filled the cabin, but the silvery moonlight through the portholes allowed her to follow his progress to the bed. She waited, holding her breath. He lifted the blankets. The bed creaked, the mattress dipped.

As soon as he settled onto his back, Georgiana turned against his side, flattening her hand over his heart. Crisp hair tickled her palm. His hard body tensed against hers before he relaxed. His fingers slid down her spine, steel whispering over cotton, and with a tightening of his arm drew her a little closer against him. Smiling, she rested her head against his biceps.

A few seconds later, she began shaking with silent laughter.

"Georgie?"

"It's harder than I realized." She sat up to the sound of his deep laugh and tucked her pillow into the crook of his arm. "Is this all right?"

"Yes."

In the faint light, she saw he was smiling. Georgiana lay down again, her cheek cushioned by down and supported by steel. In all her life, she didn't think there'd been a single moment that had been as wonderful as this.

Then she sighed, because there were less wonderful things that needed to be spoken of. "Even if you find the gold tomorrow, you should delay bringing it up."

"So that we'll have tomorrow night to bring up the submersible?"

Or to develop another plan, if that proved impossible. "Yes."

"You think he's lying about returning us home, too."

She nodded against his shoulder. "Your discovery of the coins would have been the proof he needed to clear his name. But as the salvager, you'd have had a claim on any profits—or a reward, if the Crown decided to simply take the coins back."

"He's after the money," Thom agreed. "As if he doesn't have enough."

"I don't think he does." Georgiana came up on her elbow, her breasts pressing softly against his side. Moonlight and shadows made a handsome sculpture of his features. "I *did*, but not after he told us that he'd made his best offer. That doesn't make sense. I believe that he wants to reclaim his title—that he's desperate to. So why would his best offer be so low? He'd want to be certain that no one could buy those coins before he did. So I don't think he was able to offer more."

"You think he's strapped?" Doubt colored Thom's voice.

"Very likely. In Manhattan City, it's quite common for the noble families to have all the appearance of wealth, while in truth they are living on credit and the goodwill of their relations. And if Southampton was desperate for the money as well as his title—or if he's just a greedy bastard—it would explain why he chose this route."

"Trying to kill me for it? He still could have just taken the coins when I offered them."

"But you know how many coins were found. If fewer than five thousand were returned to the Crown, you are the one person who could expose him."

"The dealer knew." Thom's body stiffened against hers. "And you know, too."

"And that's why I don't believe he'll let us live. No matter what he says. And I wouldn't lay bets on your dealer's life, either."

With a heavy sigh, Thom nodded. He reached up and drew the curtain of her hair back over her shoulder—it had been shadowing her face, she realized. She caught his hand before he lowered it back to his side.

Her fingers slipped through his. Hard, cool. Surprisingly smooth. The joints were so finely constructed, she could barely detect the seams. In brighter light, she'd seen the great number of components, as if Ivy Blacksmith had taken twenty different machines and reshaped them into his arms.

"They are truly amazing," she said softly.

"Yes."

His voice was thick. Suddenly her throat felt the same. Without letting go of his hand, she lay her head against his chest, listened to the heavy thud of his heart.

"I need to tell you, Thom. What I said—what I made you promise—it wasn't what I meant."

"What wasn't?"

"Holding me in your arms. I should have explained. My mother . . . When my father was gone, she was always looking out the window. Waiting for him. And when he wasn't home, she never even seemed alive. Like some part of her was gone, too."

"She always looked happy to me."

Georgiana came up on her elbow again, saw his confused frown. "Because you only saw her when my father was there, too. When you worked on his ship, you came home when he did. So after we married, I didn't want to be like my mother. I didn't care what sort of arms you held me with. I just wanted you home every night."

His mouth flattened into a hard line. "But I left, anyway."

Yes, he had. And that remembered hurt tightened her throat. Because she hadn't explained herself then, but he'd known she wanted him home. "I asked you to stay."

As if in frustration, he lifted his head and slammed it back against the pillow with a soft *whump*. "Your father told me you would. And that if I did as you asked, and didn't bring anything home, soon you'd be asking why I wasn't out there working and supporting you."

Georgiana frowned. Though she didn't like to think so, maybe she would have. When they'd married, she'd had no occupation for herself, aside from helping keep her father's records. What had she expected Thom to do? She'd wanted him to stay near to their home. But work was scarce, and staying close to home wasn't always an option for a laboring man.

It would be now. Her shipping interests earned enough to support them both. Thom could work anywhere he liked—or not work at all, if that was what he wanted.

And despite all the hurt of the past four years, a part of her was suddenly glad for every bit of pain. His absence had turned her into a woman who wouldn't ask her husband when he would support her.

"Did I do that to you?" His words were low and rough. "Did I make you watch at the windows, with a part of you gone?"

She shook her head. "I wouldn't let myself. I kept myself occupied. I made a business."

"Did you?" Admiration tinged his deep voice.

"Yes." Lightly, she traced her fingers down the center of his chest. "And it's partially yours. For years, my father had been selling whale oil to men who turned around and made a fortune trading it with the Horde. So I took the money you sent and used it to pay a crew to sail my father's ship to Morocco and trade directly. I might have lost everything. But I was lucky. I made enough to buy more vessels, though I don't take so many risks now. Primarily just shipping cargo around the North Sea."

"That's good, Georgie. I'm glad you did well. But I'm sorry that you had to. I should have done better."

The sudden bleakness of his expression ripped at her heart. "No, Thom. It was good of you to want to, to try to. But you're not the only one in this marriage who is responsible for my happiness and well-being. Or for yours."

He gave a slight nod. Not of agreement, she saw, but the sort of nod someone gave when they didn't believe something, yet they didn't want to argue, and there wasn't anything left for them to say. Despite her words, he still thought that he'd failed as a husband.

She would convince him otherwise. But she needed to know how to do it, and first learn more about this man she'd married. Not by assuming, but by asking.

"Was it truly such a huge difference, Thom, when the tower came down? In everything you thought and felt?"

He hesitated for a long second, then his throat worked and he said, "Like coming out of the fog into bright sun."

"But that's a good thing." Though the thickness of his voice and that hesitation made her wonder. "Isn't it?"

"It is. Now."

"But not then?"

"It was then. But it was all at once. All these things I never felt, all at once. Fear. Rage. Everything. I went mad with them."

She couldn't imagine it. Not her calm, ordered husband. But perhaps that explained why he was so controlled now. "Did being that way frighten you?"

"Yes. I was more like an animal than a man. I wanted to be a man again. The things I did, Georgie . . ." Voice strained into nothing, he shook his head.

Her heart ached with every painful word. Talking about this was clearly difficult for him. She could barely make herself ask more. But she needed to know. How could he ever think he wasn't a man? "What sort of things?"

"Killing the men trying to put us down. Rutting."

Rutting? Did he mean . . . "With women?"

"Not just. Men, too."

"Oh." Georgiana didn't know what to say. That was completely outside her experience, except as whispers and jokes. But Thom didn't seem to think one or the other any different—only his lack of control seemed to bother him. So that would be her only concern, too. "You did that during the frenzies, too?"

"It was the same. Though the tower made us feel it, then. But after it came down, that need was overwhelming in the same way. I was still trying to get ahold of myself. And all around me, others were trying to do the same. Just a look or a touch could set us off, and we'd fuck in a street." His jaw clenched. "I'm sorry, Georgie. I shouldn't have said."

"You have nothing to be sorry for. I wanted to know, Thom." Her heart hurting, she stroked her fingers down his beard. Some of what he said, the way he said it—all rough and shocking, but so had his life been. "You weren't like that with me."

"I made myself control it. I didn't want to hurt you. Back then, I only cared about what I felt. Getting into someone and spending inside them. I didn't want to be an animal with you." He met her eyes, and the torment she saw in his almost ripped her open. "But it's still in me. All of it's still in me, Georgie."

"Oh, Thom. If feeling more than you can bear and wanting someone makes you an animal, then I am one, too." She leaned over him, her fingers sliding into his thick hair. "But you're a man. The finest I know."

Without waiting for his answer, Georgiana bent her head. Her lips pressed to his. She felt the sharp catch of breath, but that was all. He didn't move. Still controlling himself.

He didn't need to, not with her. But perhaps she would never persuade him with words alone.

She softly kissed her way from the corner of his mouth to the center of his firm bottom lip. A shudder ripped through his big body. Steel hands came up to frame her face, then he kissed her back, his mouth so gentle and slow that she wanted to cry from the sweetness of it.

Her husband. Her man.

Her breath hitched. Immediately, he pulled away.

"I don't want to hurt you, Georgie," he said hoarsely.

"You won't."

Through the shadows over his eyes, she saw that he wasn't convinced. But he was not the only one responsible for their happiness. She was, too. And when necessary, she would see to a task herself.

"May I touch you, then?"

His brows drew together in a dark line. "Me?"

"Yes." Smiling, she smoothed her palm along the heavy muscles atop his shoulder, marveling at the seamless meld of hot skin to cool steel. "When you were with fever, I washed you down with ice water, and saw more of you than at any time since we've married. And I was so worried then, I didn't think of how appealing you looked—but now I cannot stop thinking of all that I saw. Of all that I'd like to touch now that you're well. And how I want to kiss you again."

Expression torn by desire and worry, his face darkened in the silvery light. But he didn't deny her. "Anything you want of me, Georgie."

His mouth, first. This time, he didn't hesitate before kissing her back, half rising to meet her. Not so sweet now, but hot, his mouth opening against hers to suck lightly at her upper lip before moving to the lower, gentle tugs that pulled at a painful need inside her. Heart racing, she couldn't seem to catch her breath, though she could feel the air coming and going through her parted lips, sharp little pants heated by Thom's mouth.

Her fingers fisting in his hair, she pushed closer. A gentle lick against her bottom lip sent pleasure bursting into a desperate ache. She whimpered low in her throat, wanting more and more.

Thom dragged his mouth away. "Am I hurting you?"

"No. You can't. Please, Thom."

Lying across his heaving chest, she pulled him back into the kiss, wanting him to feel what she had, licking and tugging at his firm lips.

With a groan, his hands gripped her hips. He hauled her fully on top of him, her thighs straddling his abdomen, her chemise sliding up past her knees. His mouth opened under hers and suddenly there was the *more* she'd wanted, in the steady pressure between her legs and the thrusting penetration of his tongue, but they didn't ease the ache, only made it sharper and harder.

Deep and hungry, each kiss drew more whimpers from her throat, started the rocking of her hips. His bare skin so hot between her thighs, and the ridged muscles of his stomach so hard, she couldn't keep herself from rubbing against him, where she felt so empty and needy and . . . wet.

Oh.

Face suddenly hot, she made herself stop moving. Thom's kiss slowed, then he eased back to look up at her.

"All right?"

"Yes." Just embarrassed. And she couldn't hide it. Her skin felt so warm that he could probably see her blush, even in the moonlight—and he had to feel the wetness all over his stomach.

But she didn't want to move. It had all been so wonderful. Was *still* so wonderful. Even though her lack of control was completely mortifying.

Thom studied her for a long second before he nodded. "Sit up, then. Let me see you."

She did, forcing herself to hold his gaze instead of turning away while he looked. It was so unnerving. Georgiana knew herself to be an attractive woman, but this wasn't like being judged and found pretty or wanting. She felt exposed. And even in her chemise, she felt bare. Nothing could be hidden. Her lips felt swollen and hot. Her stiffened nipples stood at attention beneath the cotton, the moonlight exaggerating their shapes with long shadows. Her legs were opened wide across his abdomen, her skin visible from the middle of her thighs to her feet.

She didn't know where to put her hands. To stop their trembling, she braced them against his chest.

Steel glinted in the dark. Thom's fingers hooked beneath the straps of her chemise. Slowly, he dragged them down her arms, smooth metal gliding over skin. Cool air kissed her breasts. The pink flesh around her nipples puckered and tightened.

Oh, she couldn't bear it. She squeezed her eyes closed.

They flew open again at the rough sound of his voice. "I'll never be able to stop thinking of seeing you like this, Georgie."

Just as she'd told him, only moments ago. When he'd been uncertain. When she'd been trying to persuade him that he needn't be.

Oh, God. How she loved this man.

And though she still trembled, the need to look away had gone. More exposed than she'd ever been—yet no longer wanting to hide. She only wanted him.

She found her courage again. "Are you going to touch me, Thom?"

"I am. After this."

He dragged her down for a sweet, hot kiss. Her bare breasts flattened against his hair-roughened chest, and it was such a perfect, wonderful sensation, skin against skin.

And steel against skin. His hands slid down her sides. Her breathing ragged, Georgiana sat up again, then bit her bottom lip to keep from whimpering and rocking when his palms cupped her breasts. Utterly still, she watched him touch her, his eyes burning and his face rapt as he looked.

Maybe not *just* looking. "Can you feel what you touch?"

He slowly nodded, his gaze never leaving her breasts. "Yes. Not everything. But some. Like soft and hard."

His thumbs swept across her taut nipples. Unexpected, sharp pleasure seared like fire through sensitive flesh. Georgiana gasped and arched into his palms. "Thom. Oh, Thom."

Expression stark with need, he slid his hands down. "The difference between cloth and skin."

His fingertips skimmed over the chemise bunched at her hips, down the tops of her thighs, stopping at her hem. His gaze lifted to hers. Trembling, Georgiana didn't look away from his eyes as the fingers of his right hand ventured up the delicate flesh of her inner thigh. Higher. Tension tightened her legs against his sides, pushing her away from his touch. His left hand caught her hip. Between her thighs, his fingers neared her center, slipping over skin left slick by her arousal.

"I feel heat." His voice had deepened near to a growl. "And wet."

Oh, sweet God. "Thom—"

A soft touch of steel. Georgiana froze, her hands braced against his chest and her gaze locked on Thom's, but her entire being focused on the sensation of his fingers slowly stroking her most intimate flesh, slippery with need.

Except for his fingers, Thom's body had stiffened to solid stone, his heavy muscles corded with strain. "All right, Georgie?"

Unable to speak, unable to breathe, she only nodded.

A low groan rumbled through his chest. Parting her, he delved deeper through her folds, his thumb sliding up to rub at the apex of her sex. Shock and sudden, needy pleasure jolted her hips forward. Georgiana cried out, her fingers curling against his skin.

Desperately, she rocked against his hand. "More. Again."

Her plea was met with a tortured groan. Thom reared up, catching her lips in a searing kiss. His thumb circled her slick bud, and she gave a strangled cry into his mouth.

As if propelled by that sound, Thom turned and bore her back to the bed—lips still fused to hers, his fingers still stroking through her wet heat. Overwhelmed by need, Georgiana clung to his shoulders, widening her thighs, but he didn't settle between them. He stretched out alongside her, instead, his erect length heavy against her hip. Oh, God. She needed him inside, where she was aching and empty. Hands diving into his hair, she tried to pull him on top of her. He didn't move.

Frustrated, frantic for him, she whipped her head aside, breaking the kiss. "I need you inside me, Thom. Don't leave me like this."

"I won't leave you." As rough as gravel, his reply was followed by the tight circling of his thumb. Helplessly, her hips lifted against his hand, urging a stronger touch. "But I won't risk hurting you. Let me please you like this, instead."

His mouth opened over hers again, stopping her response. Steel warmed by her skin, his big hand delved deeper between her legs, the tip of his middle finger stroking through her folds to find her entrance. With a moan of realization, Georgiana stilled. Her body shook, anticipation and need and uncertainty building into a furious storm. Thom groaned, stroking through her wetness again. His long finger began a steady penetration.

Not the same. Not as big. But still tight and full and wonderful, sliding back and forth inside her, and all of her body moving like liquid with him.

He pushed another finger alongside the first, a deep and slow invasion. She cried his name, but nothing else inside her was coherent, just a spiraling ache and tension fed by more pleasure than she'd ever known. Her head fell back. Uncontrollable moans escaped her throat. Writhing against his hand, she found his lips again, Thom, her Thom, his mouth so hot and his need as deep as hers, his tongue thrusting with the same slow rhythm as his fingers. Kissing him endlessly, though the ache became unbearable and her body didn't feel liquid anymore, but sharp and hard, until Thom groaned brokenly into her mouth, his slippery thumb rolling over that sensitive bud.

She splintered apart. Nothing that was Georgiana, just pieces of her. Her fingers, clenching hard in Thom's hair. Her mouth open under his, but no longer kissing, just open and soundless and not even taking in air, because her lungs had stiffened into iron. Her spine bowed, and her toes curled, her knees bent and locked into place, as if they'd been jerked up toward the center of her, which hadn't locked or stiffened but was clamping around Thom's fingers in tight pulls, drawing him deeper.

Refusing to let him go.

Then it was gone, and she could breathe again, her heart pounding harder than when she'd dragged him up her steps from the beach. With his back to the portholes, Thom was all in shadow, but she found his mouth again easily—and felt his smile against hers.

Still inside her, his fingers suddenly pumped deeper. Georgiana gasped as a shudder wracked her body, her inner muscles clamping around him again.

"I felt that, too," he said.

"Thom!" she cried, then laughed, though she had to hide her face against his shoulder.

Gently, he withdrew his hand. His lips pressed against her hair. "All right?"

"Wonderful." Absolutely perfect.

She knew it wouldn't have hurt if he'd entered her himself, instead of using his fingers. But this had been better than she'd ever imagined. She would eventually convince him, but for now, she could not remember ever being so satisfied, and drained, and energized all at once.

But Thom had not been satisfied, she realized.

Georgiana lifted her head. He lay on his side next to her. With a push against his shoulder, she urged him onto his back. He went, the moonlight washing over him again—all hard muscle and steel and his bold, incredible face.

"I haven't touched you yet," she told him. She hadn't done more than kissing.

His fingers stroked down her hair. "You can touch me all you like. But let me clean up first."

"Clean up?" Her gaze swept over him. His heavy erection still bulged behind his linen drawers, though not as fiercely as it had earlier. But there was no wetness. Just on his stomach, and that was . . . not all hers.

"I have two hands, Georgie. They were both busy."

Though her face blazed, she met his eyes again. "I imagine your arms are worth a fortune for that improvement alone."

His deep laugh rang through the cabin. "They are."

Grinning, she leaned over him. Her lips pressed to his. Thom caught her before she could pull away, lingering over her mouth with a sweet kiss.

He drew back, his eyes burning. "I'm going to clean up. Then I'm going to hold you all night."

Her heart filled. "I'll be waiting for you right here."

SIX

Thom woke before dawn with Georgie burrowed in against him, her dark hair spread across her pillow and her leg cocked over his stomach. For the longest time, he didn't move. Just held her, breathing in that flowery scent.

The dive today stood a good chance of killing him. But that deep water didn't scare him near as much as knowing what would happen to her if he didn't come up.

So he would. There just wasn't any other option. If Thom could have, he'd have torn through the airship now, killing everyone on it who presented a threat. But Southampton wasn't a fool. He'd be expecting that. Especially in the hours before the dive, when desperation might drive any man to attempt his escape. Thom would probably be shot the second he opened the cabin door. In the time he'd been lying awake, he'd heard the muffled voices of four mercenaries in the passageway, but no footsteps leading them away. Not a moment had passed without someone standing guard outside the stateroom, but Southampton had recently quadrupled the watch.

At his side, Georgiana stirred. Her lashes fluttered across his skin.

For the first time, his wife was waking up in his arms. Her hand slid across his chest, her fingers curving around his ribs. But though there were tasks to be done, she didn't immediately lift her head, or make any move that would take her closer to getting out of bed. She just held on to him, as if there was nothing in the world more important to do.

And if he'd known how it would feel to have her there, his heart bursting out of his chest and his throat so full and tight that he couldn't have spoken a word if he'd wanted to, Thom would never have been able to pass a single night away from her.

He didn't know how he ever would again.

Though he'd gotten into a canvas diving suit by himself a hundred times, Thom didn't protest when Georgiana insisted on helping him, checking every seam and seal in the inner and outer layers. He liked having her close. And since he'd be going up on deck in a few minutes, this would be the last time they'd speak without having Southampton or any of the mercenaries listening in.

There were a thousand things he wanted to say. But her life mattered more than all of them. "Georgie."

She glanced up from his waist, where she'd been tugging on the belt that would anchor him to the airship's tether cable. After Thom found *Oriana*, he'd hook the tether to the submersible and use the cable as a guide back to the surface—or tonight, as a guide through the dark waters. And if Thom got into trouble before he reached the bottom, they could haul him back up with it.

But not this time. "If something goes wrong—"

"It won't." She tried to stop him, shaking her head. "Don't even say it."

This *had* to be said. “If something goes wrong, I’ll unhook the tether and my hose. They won’t have a body to pull up. And after I put the brass on, between that and my arms I’m heavy enough that I won’t start floating. Then you’ve got to stay alive. You don’t cry. You don’t do anything to make them think we didn’t plan it. You tell them that I got into the submersible and I’m heading to Skagen for help. And that if you aren’t brought to town alive by sunset, I’m going to find Mad Machen and Lady Corsair, and we won’t stop until we hunt every single person on this airship down.”

Georgiana bent her head, hiding her face. Her breath shuddered. Finally she looked up, her eyes glistening. “And I’ll tell them you took the gold with you, and you’ll use it as a reward for any man who brings you Southampton’s head.”

“That’s good. You’ll turn what he hopes to use those coins for right around on him.”

Biting her lip, she nodded. Then said, “You should do it in truth.”

“Do what?”

“Take the submersible and gold. And I’ll use that as leverage to—”

“No.”

“But Thom—”

“*No.*” He couldn’t even think it. “I’ll never leave you alone again.”

She swallowed hard and looked away. After a long second, a faint smile curved her lips. “I suppose it didn’t work so well for us the last time—with the steamcoach and the shed.”

“No, it didn’t.” Leaving her had never worked well at any time. “So just get that thought out of your head.”

“It’s gone.” Georgiana sighed and tugged on his belt again, then tested the carabiner’s spring gate. “And you’ll be all right. Nothing will go wrong.”

Thom didn’t know if she was reassuring him or herself, but her tone said she wouldn't accept any other outcome. He wouldn't, either.

The knock at the door came then. The bastard Southampton stood in the passageway, smiling.

"Ah, very good. You're almost ready." He glanced deeper into the cabin. "Are you certain you wish to go up, Mrs. Thomas? It's quite brisk this morning."

"I'm certain. But I'm not only going up on deck. I'll be on the platform while he's under."

Frowning, Thom looked back. Georgiana had put on her coat. In her gloved hands, she held Thom's hat and scarf—neither of which he'd be using in the suit. But she'd still be cold and uncomfortable and wet.

He shook his head. "Georgie, no."

"Yes." Steadily, she held his gaze. "If you believe that I'll trust your air hose and pump to any other person, then you're absolutely mad."

"Taken in that light, I would prefer it, as well," Southampton said. "Accidents would not serve any of us, and no one has a more vested interest in your life and your success than your wife. I had intended for two of my crewmen to assist with the pump on the platform, Big Thom, but your wife will replace one of them."

Thom could see the sense of it. And he would feel better knowing that it was Georgie watching over his air pump. But he didn't like it.

By the bloody stars, he didn't like *any* of this.

He felt the faint pressure of canvas against steel—Georgiana had touched his arm as she passed him. Reassuring him again, as if to say everything would be well.

Southampton stepped back from the door as she left the cabin. Four mercenaries stood in the passageway behind him, parting to let Georgiana through. "If you're ready, then, I have men waiting to take the air hose up."

"I'll do it." Thom hefted the heavy coil with one arm. The bulk made it awkward to carry, but he didn't trust Southampton's men not to snag it while stumbling their way up the ladder. He tucked the brass diving helmet under his other arm and started down the passageway after Georgie.

Though cold, the wind wasn't as sharp as it had been the previous day. A few seagulls squawked around the balloon. The sea below rolled in smooth swells. Standing at the side of the airship, Thom scanned the water's surface. No dorsal fins in sight. But megalodons rarely announced their presence until it was too late.

"We did as you asked," Southampton said beside him. "No food scraps thrown over."

And her engines had been quiet since the previous evening. No sounds or scents that might attract the sharks. Thom nodded and moved to the gangway, where the hull of the ship opened to the cargo platform.

Georgie was already there, crouching on the deck with her blue skirt pooled around her, putting his brass guards in order. There was nothing unsure in her movements, no hesitation or confusion as she looked at each piece. And though she'd helped Thom with his equipment the night before and this morning, until this moment, he'd never thought how strange that was. She was a strong and capable woman, so it never surprised him when Georgiana proved herself knowledgeable. But maybe it should have. Her father had been a whaler, not a salvager. Thom had only taken it up because he'd had experience diving while working on the Horde's boats, going under to make repairs or untangle nets, and because he'd tired of the smell of whale blubber and fish guts.

Thom set the air hose on the platform and sank to his heels beside her. Softly, he asked, "Where did you learn this?"

"Learn what?"

"Diving."

"Oh." Without looking at him, she fiddled with the buckle on his chest guard. "When you left the second time, I got it into my head that if you wouldn't stay, then I'd go with you. And I didn't want to be useless while on *Oriana*."

So she'd learned what she could about his job. But the next time, he hadn't even stayed long enough for her to suggest it. He'd left in the middle of the night, after leaving her whimpering in their bed.

His heart twisted. Never had it occurred to him that she might go. Her rightful place had been at home. His rightful duty was to bring something back to her.

But it was hard to care about what was rightful now. "I'd have liked that."

"Well, I don't know if I would have." She gave him a wry glance. "On a boat for years on end? But perhaps a few months now and then."

Which would have been better than what they'd done. But he couldn't go back and change it now. He couldn't change any of it. The long years he'd been gone. Her parents dying and Georgie being alone. The messages he'd never sent and the nothing he'd brought home. Everything that had led to her agreeing to a separation. None of it had changed. And when they returned home, she'd have no real reason to change her mind about the separation.

His throat an aching knot, Thom nodded—though he couldn't even remember what he was responding to.

"But that was then." Georgie's gaze returned to the brass guards, and she gave a heavy sigh. "Now I'm just glad that I can help you."

Gruffly, he said, "I'm glad of it, too."

Standing again, he helped her position the guards that would protect his back and chest. Against a full-sized shark, his entire body wouldn't even be a mouthful. But the brass plates might prevent a bite from any smaller predators in the sea—or stop Thom from gouging himself on splintered wood and twisted iron when he found *Oriana*. Anything to keep blood out of the water.

When Georgiana picked up the brass bracers for his arms, Thom shook his head. With a faint smile, she bent to buckle a pair of long guards around his thighs.

Standing at the rail, Southampton watched with interest—and a growing frown. "You'll be able to swim back up carrying all that weight *and* the gold?"

Thom could, if necessary. But it wasn't. "I won't swim. I'll haul myself up along the tether. Did your men mark off the distance along the cable?"

"A flag every twenty feet, just as you asked. Why is it necessary?"

"So that Thom knows how quickly he's ascending," Georgie said, fastening more brass around his lower leg. "If he comes up slowly, the divers' disease might not affect him as badly."

"Yes, but *why*?"

Thom shrugged. "I don't know. I just know it's true."

"Fair enough." Southampton glanced as a bundled-up mercenary joined them at the gangway. "You've both met Mr. Blade, my chief crewman. He'll be watching over Mrs. Thomas on the platform."

The prick who'd prodded Thom's back with his pistol—and apparently the leader of this mercenary band. At his feet, he saw Georgie's mouth tighten and her tug on the strap between his shin and calf guards was a little sharper than the one before. She hadn't liked Blade any better than Thom had. None of the mercenaries had been friendly, and he wouldn't expect them to be. They were doing their job. But none of the others had gone out of their way to poke at him, either.

"That all right with you, Georgie?"

She huffed out a breath. "Does it matter?"

"Not really, no," Southampton said easily. "Mr. Blade will have the same instructions that I would give to any of my crew, which is to eliminate all obstacles that might prevent us from recovering my gold and to ensure that nothing unexpected returns from your ship with you."

Blade opened his coat, exposing the pistol at his waist. There could be no mistaking Southampton's meaning. If Thom brought up weapons from *Oriana*, Blade was under orders to kill them both.

But Thom didn't intend to bring anything up. Not yet. And he already had his weapons with him.

Finished with the brass guards, Georgie rose. Anger brightened her eyes and flattened her mouth, but she only walked onto the platform. His body weighed down by brass, every step that Thom took after her felt like wading through a current.

Blade joined them, standing in the one corner of the platform not taken up by equipment. Thom hooked the airship's tether to his belt, then pulled to make certain the cable unspooled easily. He glanced at Southampton and nodded.

With a clank and rattle, they began to descend to the water. But there was still more to do before he went in. Holding the brass helmet under his arm, Thom connected the air hose to the back of the dome. The pump sat near the front edge of the platform. Kneeling beside it, Georgie cranked the handle, testing the flow, then glanced up at him.

She spoke over the loud rattling of chains. "This fast?"

"You can go a little slower. And when you get tired, just switch over with Blade." When she began shaking her head, Thom said, "A missed second or two won't kill me, Georgie. Just speed it up a bit after the switch, so the flow in and out is equal again."

"I'll do it myself for as long as it takes." Her tone said there'd be no arguing it, and Thom wasn't a fool. But the frown pulling her brows together told him that he hadn't quite escaped. "The past two years, you didn't have a crew on *Oriana*. How did you do it alone?"

"The first time we met, Ivy gave me a pump she'd made, powered by three small automatons. I just had to wind them up, and they'd crank for two hours."

Her frown darkened. "With no backup?"

"No."

"*Thom.*"

Sweet blue, there was nothing like an admonishment from Georgie. He loved it every time, the way she only had to say his name and her voice would be full of shock or outrage or exasperation or anger, but also told him so much more: that she liked his teasing. That he made her laugh. That she cared enough to yell at him.

But he didn't want to worry her. "I'm not alone now, Georgie."

Not alone at all. And he couldn't change anything of the past, but that was something different from before—neither one of them was alone now. When they returned home, maybe she'd still want to separate. But for now, they were in this together.

"You're absolutely not alone," she said, then reached up and pulled his mouth to hers.

And even if there'd been no threat, no gold, nothing else between them, this would have been reason enough to return, simply to feel her lips pressing sweetly against his again—to feel Georgiana kissing him as if she believed he was the man he'd wanted to be.

The platform jolted to a halt, stopping two feet above the rolling water. Reluctantly, Thom lifted his head.

"Be careful," she whispered. "And please come back to me."

"I will."

He lifted the dome over his head, muffling the squawks of the seagulls. Each of his breaths was loud in his ears and fogged his view of Georgie's face. Then she disappeared, and he felt her fingers at his back, tightening the thumbnuts that fastened the helmet to the suit. She went over each one twice, then moved around front again, her expression focused as she concentrated on each bolt. Finally, she seemed satisfied and looked up at him through the fogged glass plate, her eyes glistening.

With a gloved hand, Thom cupped her face. His thumb swept across her cheek.

No tears.

Setting her jaw, Georgiana nodded. She moved to the pump and knelt beside it. A few seconds later, cool air flowed into the helmet, filling his ears with a loud, persistent hiss. The glass began to clear. Turning in the stiff suit, he found the short rope ladder dangling off the edge of the platform and into the water.

And with a few steps, lowered himself into the cold, swirling dark.

Georgiana barely breathed as water closed over the top of the brass dome. Beneath the surface, Thom stopped, hanging on to the bottom rung of the rope ladder. Bubbles from the exhaust valve trickled up through the rolling water. After a full minute, he lifted his hand, letting her know that he was getting enough air.

With her free hand, she gestured for him to go. The longer Thom was down, the more dangerous the dive would be. He released the ladder.

A few seconds later he was gone, with only bubbles to mark where he'd been. Beside her, the air hose slowly uncoiled, slipping easily over the edge. The tether cable angled down from overhead, and she measured Thom's descent with the flags as they went under the surface. Twenty feet. Forty. Sixty. Eighty.

Only a little farther—though if Thom had to walk any distance along the bottom, he would need more line.

Another flag. Then another and another. All of them were going under at the same rate as the ones before. That couldn't be right. Unless Thom was sprinting along the bottom somehow, he wouldn't be moving so quickly. The terrifying thought that he'd been snagged by a shark that was speeding away like a fish caught on a line sent her blood draining from her head and spots swimming in front of her eyes, until she forced herself to breathe deep and think sensibly. The tether wasn't being dragged in one direction or another. Judging by the angle of the cable, it still looked as if he were going straight down.

She glanced back at Mr. Blade, and found the mercenary standing closer to her than she'd realized. He must have come nearer to the edge to watch the descent—or to make certain that she didn't pull any sort of trick.

Though Georgiana didn't even want to look at him, let alone speak with him, she had to know. "How deep is he going, Mr. Blade?"

"I don't know, missus. How deep do you let him get?"

Disbelief dropped her mouth open. Had he meant . . . ? But he *did*. Because he was leering again. Of course he was. Her husband was gone. The coward could feel brave now.

Disgusting man. Coldly, she said, "Did you measure the distance to the seafloor, sir?"

Her anger seemed to please him. A smile slid across his mouth like oil. "We did. It's sixty-five fathoms."

Almost four hundred feet. Overwhelmed by sudden panic, Georgiana turned away to stare into the water, cranking the pump. But there was nothing to do. Hauling Thom back up on the tether might kill him—if Blade or Southampton didn't do it first. No doubt they'd kill *her*. Georgiana's reluctance and fear would be an obstacle to eliminate.

Another flag disappeared into the deep. How many was that

now? She'd lost count while talking to the horrible bastard behind her. However many, it was *too* many.

Four hundred feet. Oh, dear God.

Thom had lied to her. He'd known the depth. He'd known the danger. He must have feared what might happen, maybe even expected it, telling her what to do if he had to unhook his tether and air hose. Yet he'd gone anyway, to save her life.

And she wouldn't lose him to panic.

Yet it still held her in its grip as she cranked and cranked and cranked, her panic easing only a little when the flags stopped moving so steadily and a hundred feet or so of hose remained in the coil beside her.

Slowly, more hose paid out. Oh, that was Thom. Moving somewhere on the seafloor.

The danger wasn't over yet. Coming up would take longer. Anything could happen between now and then. But he was down there and moving around. Hope began to replace her fear.

Her arm began to tire and her knees began to ache but she didn't slow. She stared at the water, watching the hose, the cable, anything that offered some indication of how Thom was doing. Dimly, she was aware that Blade had moved closer—and that another noise had joined the gentle roll of the waves, the creaking of the airship, and the gulping rhythm of the pump.

She glanced over. Shock almost made her hand slip from the crank. Directly behind her shoulder, Blade had opened his coat—was *rubbing* himself through his trousers.

Revulsion and anger slapped furious heat into her cheeks. "Back away from me, sir! This moment!"

"I don't think so." His oily smile returned, but as slick as that was, his eyes were hard and mean. He held his pistol at his thigh. "You're doing a fine job there. But you've got a free hand, so you're going to give me a good pumping, too."

Rage stole every single word. Incensed, Georgiana craned her neck back and looked to the airship. No one stood at the rail. Even if they had, Blade's open coat would have blocked his disgusting actions from their sight.

"His majesty will have gone below. He doesn't like the cold. And even if my crew hears you, they won't help."

Georgiana didn't doubt that. But Blade could threaten all he liked. This cowardly bastard wouldn't shoot her. He wouldn't dare, not when he'd have to explain it to Southampton.

Shaking with anger, too sickened to look at him, she resolutely faced the water again. "This isn't the job your employer gave you, Mr. Blade. Now back away from me."

"My job, missus, was to end when Lord Pinchpenny collected his gold. And that was to be four days ago, when we caught up to that old ship. But now collecting the gold is taking longer, and his majesty isn't extending the pay, saying this is all one job. Not one of my crew is happy about it—and I'm looking for my bonus."

And *she* was supposed to pay it? Seething, Georgiana cranked. "Then go ask Southampton for a hand and leave me be."

After a short pause, Blade stepped back. Relief touched her for a brief second, then crumbled to horror. He'd moved away from her—and now stood next to the coil of Thom's air hose, the toe of his boot resting on the line.

"Don't you dare! I'll kill you if you do!"

Blade regarded her with hard amusement. "It seems to me that your husband's diving deeper than most men can. That he even told his lordship the dive was impossible. An accident wouldn't be no surprise. And then there won't be questions if you're dead next. There's no use for you if your man's not alive, and if I didn't do it here, his lordship would do it himself when we went back above. So give me your free hand, missus."

The filthy disgusting coward. Georgiana glanced around her.

There was nothing to protect herself with. And she didn't dare leave the pump.

"*Give me your hand, missus.*"

Setting her jaw, she looked down at the water. No bubbles in sight yet. No Thom coming back up.

Blade's boot pressed down, flattening the hose against the platform boards. The pump wheezed, jolting terror through her heart.

He would murder Thom.

Sick with rage and fear, Georgiana lifted her hand. Blade stepped off the hose, coming around behind her shoulder again. Hard fingers circling her wrist, he pressed the back of her gloved fist to the front of his trousers. Not demanding bare skin or her participation. He hadn't wanted her touch. He'd just wanted to force her—and to win.

But only for now. Georgiana stared ahead, briefly imagining turning her hand around and crushing Blade's organ through his trousers. She didn't dare risk it, though, when he'd likely shoot her and step on the hose again or knock over the pump in his agony. It had to be decisive. She couldn't allow him the opportunity to use his gun or react. So she watched the water, sending air to her husband and killing Blade a thousand times over in her head.

As she would in truth.

The moment he'd stepped on Thom's air hose and forced her hand, Blade's days had ended. In Skagen, or in any civilized land, she'd have had another recourse. Law and authority would have punished Blade for this. But not on the seas. Here, there would be no justice except what she took.

Blade believed she was helpless. That was the only reason a coward like him would have ever dared this. But Georgiana was just delaying her response until her husband was safe.

And she needed a weapon. Thom had knives in his arms, he'd

said. But to prevent the other mercenaries and Southampton from assuming Blade's death was an attack on the ship, it had to be done before the platform reached the top, and Thom would have to rip through his canvas suit to access the blades.

He needed that suit to dive for the submersible tonight, and a patched one wouldn't be as safe. A knife also ran the danger of spilling blood into the water.

Something blunt, instead.

Would she need to fear Southampton's retaliation? Probably not. He'd said himself that any of the other mercenaries could have fulfilled Blade's duties. Southampton wouldn't do anything to risk losing the gold. He'd kill her and Thom if they jeopardized its recovery—and he'd kill them after he received the coins. But for Blade? Georgiana didn't think so.

Beside her, Blade grunted. Georgiana yanked her hand away. Abandoning the pump for the space of a second, she ripped off her glove and tossed it into the water.

Laughing, Blade stooped to her ear. "That was good, missus. Now if your husband doesn't bring up the gold this time, he'll be going down again. And if you want him to suck on a hose when he does, then you'll suck on mine."

Sour revulsion burned in her throat. Her face froze into a mask of hate, darker and colder than any she'd ever known. She did not wonder anymore at what Thom had feared in himself when the tower had come down. It must have been like the rage she felt now—all-consuming, such fury that only love and Thom's very life prevented her from rising up and destroying the man behind her, without fear of his gun or her own death or any other pain.

But this was not an animal's rage. It was a rightful rage, and purely human.

It filled her to the brim, a furnace that pistoned her aching arm around and around, that fired hotter with each bellowing breath she took. She waited, kneeling and stiff, her body like iron, her eyes fixed on the water.

An hour passed. Bubbles popped on the surface. Then movement under the sea. Relief and joy broke through at the same time Thom did, water streaming around the brass dome. He hauled himself up the tether cable and over the platform, the air hose in a giant coil at his side—he must have been gathering it during his slow ascent. He dropped from the tether, landing with a heavy thud that rocked the platform and rattled the chains.

Georgiana flew to him, her fingers working at the thumbnuts that fastened the dome to the suit. His glass plate had already fogged again. She helped him lift the heavy helmet and at her first sight of his face, fear made her cry out.

"Thom!" Bloodshot, his eyes had more red than white. His skin was pale, and sweat plastered his thick hair to his head. "Oh, dear God. How are you feeling?"

"All right. Only a few rough minutes." Tiredly, he shook his head. "But I think it'll get worse before it gets better."

Heart thumping, she nodded. That was how the divers' disease came on—worse after he was out of the water. "We'll get you to bed. Mr. Blade! We're ready to go up."

Blade turned to clank the platform chain with the barrel of his gun, shouting up to the airship. A moment later, the platform jerked beneath them and they began to rise.

When she glanced back at him, Thom's gaze was searching her face. A frown darkened his expression. "Are *you* all right, Georgie?"

"I will be. Excuse me, please. I have something to do."

Over the rattling and the noise, he didn't hear her come. Blade was just turning away from the chain when Georgiana swung the diving dome with all of her strength. The heavy brass helmet rang dully against his skull. Jarring pain shot through her fingers and wrists. Her palms went numb.

Blade dropped in a heap. His gun clattered to the boards. She left it there.

She turned back, but Thom was already at her side, his arms coming around her.

"Georgie?"

"Oh, Thom." Fighting back sudden, hot tears, she pressed her forehead to the cold brass plate over his chest.

"I'm glad I never pissed you off that much." His arms tightened before he drew back. "What was it?"

She closed her eyes, hating the tears slipping down her cheeks, but now that it was done, something broke, and she was cold and shaking.

But not feeling an ounce of regret. "He stepped on your hose."

"Not by accident, I guess." His voice hardened. "Are you all right?"

"I am. He . . . used my hand." Simply saying it pushed the sour sickness up her throat again. "And told me tomorrow it would be my mouth."

Thom didn't respond. Just held her tighter. But she knew what was burning in him.

They were halfway up to the airship. With a deep, shuddering breath, she glanced down at the diving helmet still clutched in her hand. She'd been careful to hit Blade with the side of it, where the impact wouldn't damage the valves or the glass face plate. Blood and short hair clung to the smooth brass.

"Not even a dent. After it's cleaned, it should be fine to dive in again," she said.

Thom gave a rough laugh. "Georgie."

She set the dome on the boards, slipping her arm around him to face the airship. Their hands were empty. It was best to show everyone right away that they didn't intend to kill anyone else.

Not yet, anyway—and not unless they had to.

But hopefully not at all. "Did you find the submersible?"

"Yes. Flooded."

"Oh." They wouldn't be using it, then. She fought the weight of disappointment. "Well, we'll find another way."

He nodded. His gaze dropped to Blade, crumpled on the boards. "I'd have done it for you."

"I thought of asking. But he'd have been wary of you, and more prepared to shoot when you went for him."

"I'd still have done it." His jaw tightened, and the sudden anger on his face would have been terrifying if she'd seen it on any other man. But Thom would never harm her, so it couldn't frighten her. "I want to do it now."

"I know."

Because she wanted to do the same to the man standing at the side of the airship now. Southampton had forced Thom's hand using her life. He just had more protection than Blade. A good number of mercenaries stood behind him now. None with guns drawn, but it was clear that they *would* shoot, given a signal from their employer.

Southampton frowned down at Blade. "What is this?"

"He forced my wife to touch him," Thom said flatly.

"Ah. He deserved it, then." Face clearing, the other man raised his voice. "Remember that Big Thom and his wife are our guests! I won't tolerate such violations."

Behind him, not one of the mercenaries seemed disturbed by Blade's death. A few looked to Mrs. Winch, who was smiling faintly as she regarded Blade's still form. She glanced up at Georgiana and tipped her head, as if in thanks.

Either Winch had hated Blade as much as Georgiana did, or the woman had just been made the new chief of this mercenary band.

Perhaps both.

Southampton stepped onto the platform, his gaze holding Thom's. His voice lowered. "But I will hand your wife over to every mercenary on board if you don't find the gold. Did you?"

Thom didn't answer for a long second. Controlling himself, Georgiana realized. Wanting to destroy the man now, but knowing they'd both be killed if he did.

"I found the wreck." Teeth clenched, he finally grated the words out. "But my time was out. It's tethered off, so I can go straight to it tomorrow."

"Not today?"

Ridiculous, greedy man. Georgiana had to control her own rage. "You will kill him, sir, and end up with nothing. My husband is standing now. Within an hour, he won't be."

Southampton looked back at Thom, his gaze coming to a rest on his bloodshot eyes. "All right. Tomorrow."

A few mercenaries shifted their feet. Not one looked glad to hear it—but also not as upset as Blade had suggested.

Holding tightly to Thom's hand, Georgiana left the platform. Winch turned to follow them—would be their guard, she realized. Better than Blade.

Georgiana paused for a moment. "Will Southampton still pay Blade's share, Mrs. Winch?"

"He will. It'll be split between the rest of us."

No wonder the others hadn't looked too upset. "Like a bonus?"

Winch shrugged. "If you like."

Georgiana did.

The divers' disease hit Thom hard soon after they reached the stateroom. She managed to get him out of his suit and into the bed, but there was little she could do after the first pains started. Soon he was sweating, his body twisting up in agony. Georgiana hovered over him, massaging his joints when he could stand to be touched. He was silent through it all, jaw clenched, and she wished he would make some sound—but she was the only one who did, whispering his name through the worst of it.

But whatever was happening inside him, the mechanical bugs soon healed it. The pains passed just after noon. Too wrung out to even raise his head for a bit of soup, Thom fell into a deep sleep that lasted the remainder of the day.

It was after dark when he woke. Georgiana had dragged a chair to his bedside, and glanced up when she heard him stir.

Her heart lifted. He was awake, looking at her—and his bloodshot eyes had cleared.

"Oh, Thom. Are you well?"

"I am." His voice was a dry rasp. He swallowed. "And you, Georgie?"

"So much better now." And sitting here, smiling at him like a useless ninny, when he hadn't eaten all day. "Dinner is waiting. I told Southampton we wouldn't be joining him, so they brought it here. Would you like it in bed or at the table?"

"Not in bed."

He sat up, the muscles of his stomach rippling. Sometime soon, Georgiana vowed, she would run her hands over them when he *wasn't* sick. But not now. She waited long enough to ask whether he needed help—he laughed at that before crossing the cabin, just as strong and steady as always—then laid out their meal while he tended to the necessary and washed. He pulled on trousers, but didn't tuck his shirt before joining her.

Her neat and orderly Thom, not so orderly now. And she liked it very much.

His knee bumped into hers when he sat and pulled up his chair.

"Now eat," she told him, and he suddenly laughed before obeying and taking a bite.

She didn't know quite what had amused him, but couldn't stop herself from smiling again—smiling, even though they had no submersible. Smiling simply because he was there.

"I've spent every moment this afternoon trying to think of a clever escape. I haven't yet, though I *do* know how to avoid the guards outside this cabin."

Mouth full, he raised his dark brows.

Georgiana tapped the porthole over the table. "We're fortunate that our abductor is a rich man—or that he has the credit of a rich man. You would never find such large windows on the bow of a poor man's airship. Not when the glass has to be replaced every time they hit a goose."

Thom grinned. "That's a truth."

"I don't think we'd have to break it, either." Which would make far too much noise. She fingered a bolt in the metal frame. "Are your hands strong enough to pull these out?"

Taking another bite, he nodded.

"Then we can climb up outside the hull and onto the deck. We'll have to surprise whoever is on watch—and maybe take one of the boats." She sighed. "But I don't know what to do after that. This flyer will catch up to us. They have every advantage. Weapons. Speed. And I don't see how to turn that advantage around."

Her voice broke at the last. Oh, God. It was so hard to remain practical and unaffected when their lives were at stake.

He set his fork down. "We *will*, Georgie."

Yes, they would. Trying to gather herself, she drew a deep breath. "Do you think we can delay another day?"

He lifted his gaze to stare out the porthole. Not looking at anything, she knew. Just weighing their chances, as she had been all afternoon.

"Maybe I can bring up just a bit of it, and tell him I have to go back down the next day for the rest. Or we'll convince him to wait another day so that I can bring up the submersible. If he's after money, it's worth a bit. And we'll take our chances in the boat tomorrow night."

Her chest tightened. "How far do you think we are from shore?"

Thom was quiet for a long moment. Then he said, "I think we have a better chance in a boat than we do here."

A long distance, then. She nodded, and despite her best effort to stop them, her eyes suddenly spilled over with tears. Then Thom had her in his arms, holding her in his lap while she sobbed against his neck.

"Georgie, Georgie." His fingers stroked through her hair, her name a broken murmur in her ear. "I'd kill him again if I could."

And he knew. He knew how wrong this all was. Everything wrong, except being in his arms. Her breath shuddered against his throat. "I was so angry. *So* angry. I'd have ripped it off if it hadn't risked you."

"You should have, anyway."

"Would you have? If it was me needing that air, would you?"

His livid silence gave Georgiana the answer. He wouldn't have risked her, either—and just thinking of it infuriated him.

It did her, too. "And not just because he made me feel so disgusting. Not just because he took something that should be a gift. But that he would *dare* use your life against me like that. And his reason was that he hadn't been paid enough. But Southampton's just the same. He feels that he's owed something, and he'll use our lives to get it—and he degrades you just as much while he's at it."

Not in the same mean way that Blade had, but Southampton degraded Thom in his own manner, by treating him as less than a man. He was just more subtle about it. Georgiana didn't even know if Southampton recognized what he was doing.

Thom shook his head. "It's the same in some ways, Georgie. But not anything like what Blade did. I can ignore what Southampton says and he doesn't hurt us for it, as long as I dive. Blade didn't give you the choice to ignore what he'd done."

That was true. But both men were wrong, either way. She sat back in Thom's lap, met his eyes. "Do you want to kill him?"

"Yes." No hesitation. His gaze flattened, and the same terrifying anger hardened his expression. "If I knew of any way to do it without risking harm to you, I would. But I'll warn you, Georgie. Right now he's just full of threats. The moment I think he intends to hurt you, I'll rip him in half. I won't stop myself, no matter the danger. If you see that happen, you get to one of the boats, because I'm going to tear this ship apart and bring everyone else down with it. But for now, I'll leave him alive if that's what it takes to get you away."

"And get you away, too."

He shrugged.

Georgiana frowned. "That's not something to be dismissed, Thom."

Though he didn't argue, she saw the response in the bleakness of his eyes. As long as she got away, Thom didn't think it mattered if he did.

Or maybe he didn't think that was a possibility anymore.

But he was wrong on both counts. He would escape with her. And she would fight for him to stay with her.

Maybe that wouldn't be their future, though. It hurt so much to think it might not be. But whether he stayed or not, she needed him to know he *did* matter.

More than anything.

"Thom." Gently, she cupped his face in her hands. "I know you felt that you've never brought me anything worth having. But you did. You brought yourself back—and you're worth more to me than a hundred thousand chests full of gold."

And for the first time, he didn't quietly shake his head or insist he should have done more or apologize for not supporting her. His throat worked, but his only response was a rough whisper. "Georgie."

"Thom." Smiling, she softly pressed her lips to his, then the corner of his mouth, and the silky beard over his jaw. "Today, you were the only light I knew. While you were gone, I only felt fear and rage. But then you came back to me, and there was hope and joy again."

His eyes closed. "That's all there is when I see you. And fear when I think you might be hurt. I'd risk anything to stop it."

"As I would for you." She lightly kissed his mouth again. "And I was terrified when I discovered that you were diving four hundred feet. You didn't have to lie to me, Thom."

He looked at her again, his arms tightening around her. "I didn't want you to be afraid."

"But I was, anyway."

"I wanted to protect you from that."

"And you don't have to." Sliding her hands around the back of his head, she pushed her fingers into his thick hair, still rumpled from his long sleep. "I suspect there is much in you that you don't let me see or know, because you think I'll be frightened or you need to protect me. Please don't hide it anymore, Thom. Don't hold it back. I have no right to ask this of you. But I want to be with the man that you are, rather than the man you think you should be."

His body stiffened against hers. "No holding back?"

"Not with me. With others, do as you please." She didn't want to share him, anyway.

He stared up at her, his blue eyes slowly beginning to burn.

Georgiana's gaze fell to his mouth, and she suddenly felt every inch of her dress twisted around her legs and stretched across her breasts.

"All right." Abruptly, Thom lifted her against his chest, carried her to the bed.

And left her there.

Uncertain, Georgiana watched him move to the wardrobe. Reaching behind his neck, he dragged his shirt over his head.

Without looking at her, he said gruffly, "You'd best get that dress off."

Oh. With heat in her cheeks, she quickly unfastened the buttons at her throat. Her gaze followed Thom to the vanity. Oh, but he was a fine man—his back muscular and broad, his wide shoulders a smooth meld of flesh and steel.

Water splashed into a bowl. Thom's eyes met hers in the oval mirror hanging above the vanity, then he looked down and began lathering his beard.

Shaving.

Her breath stilled. Thom had done this every time he'd come to her bed, but she'd never watched him before. His soapy fingers moved in sure, even strokes. With his trousers hanging low on his hips, he braced his left hand against the edge of the vanity and leaned in closer to the mirror. His weight shifted to his right foot, left leg slightly bent, and his back was not just a beautiful sculpture now but the most arousing thing she'd ever seen, the muscles bunching over his left shoulder and smoothing along his ribs, and the groove of his spine the perfect width for her fingertips.

The razor scraped over his jaw, the rasp of it like a slow abrasion over her skin. Her heart thudded, as if her blood suddenly ran thick. With trembling fingers, she finished unfastening her dress and stripped it off, leaving her clad only in a chemise.

Hands lifting to her nape, she began unpinning her hair. At the vanity, the razor clinked against the bowl before swirling through water. Tipping his jaw back, Thom scraped beneath his chin. Soapy water ran in thin rivulets past the hollow of his throat, down the center of his thickly muscled chest. Her lips parting in envy, Georgiana followed the soapy path in the mirror, until the lather slipped past the bottom of the oval frame.

When she glanced back up, Thom was watching her in the reflection. Tilting his head slightly, he scraped another swath up his throat.

"You'll have me again, Georgiana?"

Have him. She clenched her thighs, trying to ease the sudden ache. "Yes."

"I promised myself I wouldn't." He glanced down. The razor clinked and swirled. "After the last time, I promised I wouldn't risk hurting you again."

And they'd both said and done and promised far too many things based on what they'd *thought* was true of each other, rather than what *was* true. "I think we should forget about all of the promises we ever made, and make new ones, instead."

He nodded. With his thumb, he pulled the skin taut at the sharp corner of his jaw. The scrape sent another delicious shiver racing across her nerves.

"And, Thom"—she waited until he glanced up—"you didn't hurt me the last time. I just didn't know how to tell you how much I was liking it."

He stared at her in the mirror for a long second, eyes narrowed. "That's truth?"

"Yes."

With a nod, he angled his chin, scraped away the last of the lather and whiskers. Water splashed. When he looked up, his strong jaw had been rinsed clean.

He turned toward her, not bothering with a towel. A swipe of his hand flicked the soapy water from his chest.

"Here's my first new promise, then." He rounded the foot of the bed, untying the front of his trousers as he walked. The thick weave strained across his heavy erection. "Tonight, I'll have you over and over again."

Oh, sweet God. Arousal pulsed through her in a thick, liquid beat. She rose up on her knees at the edge of the mattress, waiting for him. "And I'll finally touch you like I wanted to."

Passion roughened his voice to a growl. "You'll get your chance when I'm done."

All at once, Thom captured her face between his palms, and his mouth slanted over hers for a ravenous taste. With an eager moan, Georgiana wound her arms around his neck, opening to the stroke of his tongue past her lips. The scent of soap and wet, bare skin filled her senses. He clutched her to his chest, the damp linen of her chemise clinging to her breasts.

All too soon, he broke the kiss. Standing against the bed, he pushed her back to the mattress. His big hands gripped her hips and dragged her bottom almost to the edge, hooking her knees up around his sides. Her chemise slipped down, exposing her thighs. Thom stilled, staring, and with a sudden groan, shoved her hem up over her thighs, her hips, higher, as if once he'd begun to bare her skin he couldn't stop. Frantic with need, Georgiana helped him, lifting her bottom and wriggling the material free of her shoulders. He tore the chemise over her head before leaning over and taking her mouth again, hot and deep.

Cool metal slipped between her thighs. Georgiana arched up against his hand. "Inside me, Thom. Please."

"Not yet." He looked down at her, his face taut with strain. "Because I touched you last night, Georgie, but what I've dreamed of most isn't what I'll do with my hands."

His head dipped to her breast. At the same moment his fingers pushed inside her, he latched onto the throbbing tip. His cheeks hollowed, sucking her nipple to a burning point.

Georgiana cried out, her body lifting in a rigid bow. Her hands fisted against the sheets. With a hungry moan, he lifted his head and moved to her other breast. Hot and wet, his mouth closed over her nipple. Between her legs, the rhythm of his fingers quickened, his thumb relentlessly sliding over her aching knot of flesh.

"Thom!" Overwhelmed by pleasure, Georgiana rolled her hips, her thighs tightening against his sides. "Thom, please!"

"Your taste. Sweet fucking blue, Georgie." He pulled back, his hand leaving her empty. His bold features set in a mask of insatiable need, he dropped to his knees. "I need more."

His head dove between her thighs.

"Thom!"

Shocked beyond bearing, she screamed his name. Her fingers stabbed through his thick hair, tried to pull him up, but the heated swirl of his tongue twisted shock into pleasure. She keened low in her throat, rocking against his mouth. And there must have been something hidden within her, too—something wild and fierce and needy, like a storm at sea, lashing at her with every slow lick. Her head thrashed against the sheet, her body anchored only by his hands on her hips, his tongue and his lips.

And she crashed, splintering. He moaned against her, licking as she shuddered and cried his name. Then he rose up, a sheen of sweat slick over his skin, his lips wet.

Lifting her, he sat at the edge of the bed, settling her over him. Georgiana straddled his thighs, his erection a hot iron bar against her stomach.

She'd never seen him this way before. Only flaccid in fever and sleep, only as a softening bulge beneath his drawers. But he was so much thicker and longer. Looking at his arousal now, she didn't wonder why their coupling had hurt so much the first times. The only mystery was how it had ever felt so good the last time.

But it had. She remembered exactly how much.

"As slow as you need to, Georgie." His voice was hoarse, every muscle in his body as hard as his arms. "Even if you take all night to fill yourself up with my cock, I'll hold back until you tell me you're all right. And then I'll never hold back again."

Rough, explicit words, but no embarrassment or shock was left in Georgiana—only her desperate need to feel him inside her. Rising up, she braced her hands on his shoulders. Her eyes locked with his when the broad crown slid through her slick folds and lodged against her entrance.

Without hesitation she took him in, easing down over his heavy shaft. No pain at all. No discomfort. Just full. *So* full. Her head fell back on a moan, and she slowly undulated her hips, taking him deeper and deeper.

Until she couldn't take any more, stopping with her legs spread wide, her bottom against the tops of his thighs. Panting, she looked down, where their bodies melded together as seamlessly as flesh and steel.

Filled with his cock. A perfect, impossible fit.

Rigid with strain, Thom shook against her. "You're all right, Georgie?"

"Yes. Oh, Thom." No holding back. Not when he was so deep inside her. "You feel so good."

His fingers clenched on her bottom. She rose up again at the urging of his hands, then cried out as he pushed her back down, filling her again.

Fingers catching in her hair, he brought her gaze to his. "This time, you know how to tell me that you like it."

"I do. So much." She drew a shuddering breath. Every tiny movement seemed to stretch her sheath tighter around his thick shaft. "Do you?"

"Do I?" A tortured laugh rumbled through his chest, ending on a groan. "I love being in you. You're so tight, squeezing around me. So hot. I can't ever get deep enough, Georgie. But I'm going to try."

Hands locked over her hips, he surged upward. With a strangled cry, Georgiana took him deeper, pleasure searing her senses. She rose up with him, then he filled her with his cock again, just as she wanted, needed. The wild ferocity rushed over her, driving her up against him over and over, her fingers clenching in his hair, sharing his breath as she rode, faster and faster, his face the only thing in her sight.

Then she was there, her mouth feeding greedily from his as her body clenched around him, tighter and tighter, before leaving her liquid and boneless.

Groaning, Thom eased her onto her back. "Wrap your legs around me, Georgie. Tighter. Sweet blue, you're so wet I could drown in it. Pull me in deep."

Loving the heavy feel of him over her, she ran her fingers down the flexing muscles of his back. Hands braced beside her shoulders, he lowered his mouth to hers—just as he had the first time, and the second, and the third, but this was nothing like before, with no clothes between them and her hands roaming free, and Thom not slow and careful now. He drove into her, each deep plunge bringing Georgiana back with him, not liquid anymore but soon tense and frantic, writhing beneath him, his heavy thrusts wringing desperate cries of need and frustration from her lips. Not holding back but giving—all the pleasure he could, and when she came again, the clench of her sheath seemed to destroy any remaining control. Lunging forward with a broken yell, Thom held himself deep, pulsing inside her.

Then he kissed her, hot and sweet and smiling. He rolled onto his back, holding her against him—and Georgiana made her second new promise to herself.

She was never letting him go again.

SEVEN

Thom woke just after dawn with Georgie's head pillowed on his chest and her dark hair spread over his shoulder. This time, he didn't feel her wake up in his arms—her eyes were already open, her gaze fixed on the porthole.

Probably imagining their escape.

As if sensing he'd woken, she said, "I'm trying to think of something clever. Or not so clever, if stupidity will get us away just the same."

"I'll do what I can to delay and just bring up part of that gold, or convince them to wait for the submersible." Closing his eyes, he breathed in the scent of her hair. The third morning away from home, only a faint hint of flower remained. He wanted to destroy Southampton for that alone. "But if I come up and he's set on killing us, I'm going to bring the ship down and get you into that boat."

"I wish we could get into it now." She turned her head to look up at him, crooking her arm over his chest and cradling her chin against the roll of her fist. Her full lips pursed. "Or climb on top of the balloon. We could hide up there while they wonder where we went, and hang on until they fly back to some port."

Thoughtfully, Thom nodded. "We could, at that."

"I wasn't serious. That was a not-so-clever suggestion."

He knew. Between the cold, the wind, and no knowing where they were going or when they'd get food, the top of a balloon could be a death trap. "It's better than other options we have."

She sighed heavily against him, acknowledging that sad fact. "Is there anything on *Oriana* that you can bring up? Perhaps something that we could attach to the bottom of the platform—or to the tether, just below the surface—and keep it hidden until we need it?"

Offhand, he couldn't think of anything that wouldn't be noticed. "I'll look around."

"Be careful, though. It isn't worth your being trapped in a wreck." Her eyes were somber as she regarded him. After a moment, a faint smile curved her lips. "It's odd to say this, Thom, but despite not yet having an escape, and despite Southampton's threats—I am happier at this moment than I've ever been."

He was, too. "I'll be happier when we are away."

Georgie laughed and dropped a kiss to his chest, directly over his heart. "I will be, too."

And she was full of more smiles and kisses after they rose from the bed, as she helped him into his diving suit—and when he teased her, full of laughter and blushes and cries of *Thom!*

Until sunrise, when Southampton knocked at the door—and told Thom that if every single coin wasn't aboard the airship by the end of the day, he and Georgie would both be dead.

Within an hour, Georgiana was watching the sea again, endlessly cranking the pump. On the other side of the coiled air hose, Mrs. Winch sat at the edge of the platform, her bare feet dangling into the cold water and a cigarillo between her lips.

Unlike Mr. Blade, she obviously had no interest in harassing Georgiana. They'd barely exchanged any words since the platform had descended.

That suited Georgiana. Her worry for Thom kept her company—as did thoughts of escape. But she hadn't yet figured out how . . . and if they didn't delay Southampton's leaving for one more day, she and Thom would likely never find the opportunity.

Tonight would be their only chance, and the submersible was their best hope of securing that extra time. But Georgiana didn't believe the machine would tempt Southampton. Though valuable, the twenty or thirty livre it might bring at market would be nothing to a man who would soon possess thousands of gold coins.

It would be a hefty sum to mercenaries, however—probably more than Southampton had paid them for this job.

So Georgiana would try to tempt them, instead. Over the noise of the pump, she said, "I hope Thom will bring up the submersible as well. It's worth quite a sum. Not as much as the gold, of course—though if Southampton gives all the coins back to the Crown, I suppose he will walk away with nothing extra."

For a long second, Mrs. Winch studied her through a small cloud of smoke. Then she nodded and said, "I don't understand bringing the gold up at all if his lordship just gives it away."

"I suppose you would earn a larger percentage if Southampton also recovered any treasure for himself. If there was something coming up from *Oriana* that Southampton wasn't giving away, its value could make up for the additional time you've spent on this job."

Winch's eyes narrowed. "Are you trying to buy me off, Mrs. Thomas?"

Georgiana hadn't been, but she wouldn't pass up the opportunity. "Yes. Could I?"

The other woman smiled and shook her head. "In my profession, there's only two things that matter aside from the money: the job you're doing, and the next job you'll get. And anyone who gets a reputation for sinking one job when a bit of gold is flashed in front of her won't be getting another job."

"Then I suppose it would take a lot of gold to persuade you—enough that you'd never need another job."

"Yes."

Georgiana wasn't *that* well off. And giving Mrs. Winch the gold coins wouldn't secure her help. If the mercenary would betray her employer, then she would likely betray Georgiana and Thom, too.

But Mrs. Winch might extend a job by one day, if she knew there was a possibility of earning more money. Not changing Southampton's plan to kill them—just benefiting from delaying it. So Georgiana would let the knowledge that a valuable submersible waited below simmer in Mrs. Winch's head for a while.

Cranking the pump, she shrugged and sighed. "It was worth the attempt. I doubt I could have paid more than a man like Southampton. I'm sure you will be very well compensated."

"You'd think so."

Georgiana nodded, as if she hadn't detected the edge in Winch's reply. "He seems a fair man. Despite taking us against our will, he has treated us well. Thom and I have no complaints, especially as he's promised to return us home. I'm sure that Southampton is fair in his dealings with you, too."

Winch looked out over the water, her mouth tight. No doubt the mercenary knew very well that Southampton didn't intend to be fair in his dealings with Georgiana and Thom. Now she was likely wondering whether he'd show her mercenaries the same type of fairness.

"Indeed," she finally said, and took another draw from her cigarillo.

Satisfied for now, Georgiana glanced up at the airship. The polished hull gleamed in the early morning light. Not the swiftest vessel in the skies, but quick enough to chase them down in a boat.

Her gaze lifted to the balloon. As the morning passed, climbing up the cables anchoring the hydrogen-filled envelope to the wooden cruiser, and hiding atop its rounded bulk seemed less *not so clever*, and more *no other choice*. But as long as they were being foolish, she and Thom wouldn't wait until they died of exposure. They would haul one of the lifeboats up with them, start a leak in the balloon—and when the airship settled into the sea, they could row away laughing.

Georgiana's breath stopped. She turned to stare into the water again, her ears filled with the squawking of seagulls and the gasping thrust of the pump, and her mind filled with thoughts of leaking balloons.

It *was* a terrible idea. Incredibly stupid and dangerous. And it would also take away every advantage Southampton had over them. Right now, she and Thom were outgunned. But no one would dare fire a pistol on an airship with a leaking balloon. And they couldn't have escaped in the lifeboat now, because the flyer would simply catch up to them—but not if her balloon had been compromised.

Oh, but they would be taking *such* a risk. A single spark could destroy them all.

Yet some chance of escape was still much better than having no chance.

She spent the next hour weighing the risks over and over, trying to minimize every one. By the time she spotted the bubbles breaking against the surface, Georgiana knew that it would be their escape plan. Not at all clever, but it was the best they had.

As long as they could delay Southampton for a little longer. It did not even have to be until that night—just until Thom recovered from his dive.

This time, Thom didn't haul himself up the tether with the air hose coiled at his side, but gripped the edge of the platform and dragged himself out of the water, a bulging canvas sack in his left hand. He dropped it onto the boards with a heavy *thunk*—and the unmistakable clink of coins.

With his help, Georgiana worked his diving helmet off. His eyes were bloodshot again, his face pale and sweating.

The dome had not even cleared his head when he asked, "Are you all right, Georgie?"

She laughed. "That is my question to you. I'm fine, Thom. Are you?"

Beside them, Mrs. Winch crouched in front of the canvas sack. "You brought up what you were supposed to?"

"A bloody fortune," Thom said. "Five thousand gold pieces and no weapons. Open it and look."

Winch did, her eyes widening. "There's five thousand here? Southampton said it was only half that."

"He must have been mistaken," Georgiana said.

"He must have." Winch stood and clanked on the platform chain, signaling to the airship. The boards jolted under Georgiana's feet. Her heart began to pound. The gold had been retrieved. Their task for Southampton done.

"Thom still needs to haul up his air hose, Mrs. Winch!" she called over the rattling chains. "Or he won't be able to return for the submersible."

Winch glanced at her. "That'll be up to his lordship, Mrs. Thomas."

And the bastard would either be greedy enough to stay another day, or Thom would bring it all down. Georgiana clutched his hand through the wet canvas glove and tried to resist when he subtly moved her behind him, until he said quietly, "I'm covered in brass armor, Georgie. Let me protect you a bit."

That was sensible—and terrifying. She was almost dizzy with fear by the time the platform clanked against the side of the hull.

Wearing a cold little smile, Southampton stood waiting for them at the gangway, with the band of mercenaries behind him. "You didn't release the tether from the wreck, Big Thom. I hope this doesn't mean you returned empty-handed."

"It only means that my submersible is still down there. I'll go back for it tomorrow."

Southampton's gaze lit on the bulging canvas bag. "But you retrieved my gold?"

"I did. All five thousand."

Southampton looked to Mrs. Winch, whose mouth flattened as she nodded her confirmation.

Thom continued, "You don't have to worry that I'll make a claim on those coins or mention to anyone that I ever laid eyes on them. But that boat down there is all I have to support us . . . and I can sell the submersible on it for thirty livre, enough to buy another ship. That'll get my wife and me back on our feet when you return us home."

Oh, Thom. Georgiana squeezed his hand. So very clever. At their dinner, Southampton had spoken of his noble family's honor and duty, and now Thom appealed to him like a vassal appealing to his lord. If Thom had been appealing in fact, this would have been impossible for him—but her husband probably liked using Southampton's supposed honor against him.

And Southampton still wouldn't let them live, but he'd no doubt enjoy playing the generous noble until he put a bullet in their heads.

"A word, your lordship?" Mrs. Winch left the platform and drew Southampton forward along the deck. Georgiana didn't hear anything of what Winch said to him, but she could well imagine. The value of the submersible might be enough to keep her mercenaries from feeling they'd been cheated, given that the gold Southampton had was worth twice what he'd said he owed the Crown.

Relief almost knocked Georgiana's knees from under her when she saw Southampton's nod.

He returned to the gangway, a pleasant smile fixed around his mouth. "Forgive me. Of course I would never deny you the means to support your family, Big Thom—especially as you've done *my* family so great a service. We will stay until tomorrow, then."

Good enough. They only needed tonight.

The pains soon hit Thom again, though not so hard. He'd taken a longer time coming up and hadn't been down so long. Georgiana still worried every second, checking his temperature for fever and doing her best to soothe him.

As soon as he slept, she began to prepare. She rolled up two blankets and strapped them together, so they would be easy to carry on her back. When their noontime meal arrived, she requested extra bread for her sick husband, then made a satchel from the skirts of her pink dress and stuffed into it everything from their plates that wouldn't leak. Coats and hats and gloves and scarves. Thom only had one change of clothes, but she dressed in her warmest wool, with two pairs of stockings.

When he woke, she had everything ready and had settled into the chair by his bed. There were still several more hours to wait. Fewer mercenaries would be on watch late at night, and any bit of fire would be easier to spot and extinguish.

Thom sat up in the bed, his gaze searching her face. "You've thought of it."

"Yes." She drew a deep breath. "We have to cut open the balloon."

His big body tensed and he shook his head, as if in instinctive rejection. "If it catches fire, Georgie—"

"I know." That was the reason it had taken her so long to think of this plan: Cutting open a balloon was simply unthinkable. "But when we come up from the porthole and onto the deck, we'll have the advantage of surprising the watch. You're strong enough to pierce the envelope?"

Not everyone would be. The metal fabric was made to withstand weather and birds and the weight of the ship. Georgiana doubted that she could stab a knife through—the blade would just slide across the envelope's surface. But she didn't have Thom's arms.

"I can," he said.

"Just the threat of ripping through it will make them run to smother all the flames on deck and sound the alarm. And after it's leaking, not one would dare use his guns."

Thom was nodding now. "They couldn't come after us, either."

"So we could lower the boat to the water," she said. "Get in and go."

He settled back against the pillows again. Frowning, thinking it over. She waited for him to decide.

With a heavy sigh, he said, "It's a hell of a risk, Georgie."

But that response meant he would take it.

"I know," she said, and when he reached out and tugged on her fingers, she slid onto the bed and curled against him. His arms came around her, and she rested her head back against his shoulder.

Holding on to each other, while they could.

Quietly, she lay with him. His back propped by the pillows, Thom stared out the porthole, and she knew he was going over it all in his head again.

"When they sound the alarm, all the crew will come up," he said.

"Yes." She slid her hand over his chest. "But we have to make sure they sound it. Or someone might come up with a lantern."

He nodded. "I'm just thinking about you, Georgie. There's ten mercenaries, and I can handle them if they come at me. You've just got to make sure you're behind me or out of sight."

"All right." She wouldn't argue. If Thom knew she was safe, he would be safer, too. "What about Southampton?"

"That depends on him. I'd like to kill him for every threat he made toward you. But I won't go out of my way to do it. My only concern is getting you off this ship." He stroked his fingers down her arm. "When we go out, you'll have to hold on to the rail while I take care of those on deck. Can you do that?"

Hanging on to the outside of the ship. "I'm stronger than I look."

"You are." Shifting her against him, he tipped her chin up and looked down at her with narrowed eyes. "You are, Georgie. And I didn't think of it much until now. Growing up, everyone was strong, man or woman. But out here, everyone's almost always weaker. Not you, though. You're infected?"

"Yes."

"When?"

"After you left the last time. You always seemed so afraid of hurting me. It seemed practical to make certain that hurting me wouldn't be so easy."

"It wouldn't have made a difference. Hurting is still easy. Just the healing is faster." Gently, he smoothed his thumb across her bottom lip. "Most people are afraid that the tower will go up again—or that they'll be zombies. You weren't?"

"I was more afraid that you wouldn't return to my bed again." Her eyes filled suddenly, and she blinked at the tears, willing them away. "And I think it saved me when the lump fever came."

Because she hadn't caught it, though both her parents had.

"I'm sorry, Georgie." His voice thickened. "I'm sorry I wasn't there. I wish I had been."

She wished he had been, too. But she shook her head.

"If you hadn't gone, Thom, I'd never have infected myself. I probably wouldn't be alive now." And as much as she'd missed him, Georgiana liked the woman his absence had let her become. "All that matters is that you're here now."

"I am." His arms tightened around her. "I am."

"But only until tonight." She grinned up at him. "You'd better not be here after that."

They waited until after midnight—when, hopefully, whoever stood watch on deck would be half-asleep and huddled down against the cold.

Carrying the blankets and her satchel, Georgiana watched Thom pinch the head of the steel bolt that fastened the thick window to the porthole frame. He twisted and pulled.

A metallic squeal rang through the cabin.

Thom froze. Heart pounding, Georgiana stared at the cabin door, waiting for the guard to burst through and see them attempting to escape.

No one. She looked back at Thom. "Try again?"

He shook his head. "We'll need to make some other noise to cover this."

"What noise wouldn't bring them in?"

"No one came in when we were making noise last night."

"Thom!" Her blush warmed her cheeks.

He grinned.

Unable to stop herself, she laughed and looked to the bed. It would be the sort of sound that might draw attention, but wouldn't be unexpected in the cabin of a married couple. "Shall I jump on it?"

Thom shook his head again and led her to the door. Softly, he said, "That won't be loud enough. Do it here, instead."

Where? "I don't understand."

"You bang up against the door, like I'm having you against it."

She met his quiet explanation with a look of sheer disbelief.

Without a word, Thom wrapped his hands around her waist and hefted her up. With her thighs around his hips, he pushed her back against the wooden door and gently rocked between her legs.

Oh. Her fingers curled into her palms. This was actually . . . quite . . . wonderful. Despite the urgency of their situation, despite knowing a guard stood in the passageway just beyond the door, heat began to coil inside her, winding tighter with every slow thrust.

She was almost sorry that they needed to escape.

He set her down again, then pushed at her hips, her backside bumping against the wood. "Like that, Georgie, but harder," he murmured. "You make some loud noise, and I'll get those bolts out."

She nodded. "I can do that."

"Then start yelling."

Yelling? Georgiana thought she just had to bang against it. "What do I say?"

"Like this," he said softly, then raised his voice. "Going to spread you wide and fill you up, Georgie!"—his elbow thumped against the door and he gave a heavy grunt—"Going to shag your hot pussy deep and hard!"

"Thom!" she cried—scandalized and muffling her wild laughter behind her hands.

"You'll soon be screaming my name." He thumped and grunted again. "Lift your beautiful tits to my mouth now." *Thump.* "I'm going to suck on your sweet nipples until you come all over my cock!"

"Thom!" With her face ablaze, Georgiana bumped her backside against the door. "Oh, Thom!"

Grinning, Thom lowered his head, his lips against her ear. "My mouth is full, so I have reason to be quiet. Now you start shouting all those things you said last night."

He left her bumping at the door, trying to recall exactly what she'd said. Every moment had been seared into her brain, but she'd barely given a thought to most of what had been tumbling out of her mouth.

"Oh, Thom!" *Bump.* "Thom!" *Bump.* "Oh, yes, Thom!"

At the porthole, another bolt squealed. Georgiana threw her hips back harder, faster, trying to cover the sound.

"You're so deep, Thom. Oh! Oh! Don't slow down. Oh! Harder, now. Thom! I need more! *More!*"

His back to her, Thom seemed to hunch over. His shoulders were shaking so hard that when he reached for another bolt, his juddering fingers missed it—twice.

Laughing.

Oh, Georgiana always loved to see him do that. Enjoying herself now, she slammed harder and harder. "Thom! Oh! Faster! Don't stop! I feel it coming!"

And she was running out of things to shout. Remembering last night was no help. Mostly she had just moaned and cried his name.

Desperately, she called up her memories of touching his body afterward, exploring every ridge of muscle—"You're so hard, Thom!"—running her hands up his thick shaft—"And so big. So long and strong and powerful!"—circling her fingertips around the flared crown—"They should call you the King of the North Sea. Oh, Thom, make me your queen! Oh, oh, *Thoooommmmm!*"

By the time her wail faded, the glass was out of the porthole frame and her husband had collapsed into the settee with his head in his hands, tears streaming down his face and choking on his laughter. His muffled snorts likely fit quite well into their impromptu bit of theater.

Her face flushed from the exercise, Georgiana joined him. "I must say, Thom—that was quite invigorating."

Still laughing, he pushed to his feet. Catching her around the waist, he kissed her hard and far too briefly. "I love you, Georgie. Now are you ready?"

No. She wanted to stay here and bask in those words. She'd known he did. Love had never been in question between them—only whether it was enough to overcome all the other hurts.

But even knowing that Thom loved her, it was so sweet to hear him say so. And to say it in return. "Oh, Thom. I love you, too."

Eyes dark with emotion, he kissed her again. Longer this time. But not as long as Georgiana wished.

Within a few minutes, she was standing at the porthole with the blankets and satchel strapped to her back. Thom had offered to carry them, but had agreed it was more important for him to move as freely as he needed to than to relieve her of a few pounds' burden.

Gripping the cold frame, she leaned out and looked over. Here at the front of the airship, the prow projected forward over the steep slant of the hull, presenting a sheer hundred-foot drop to the moonlit water below.

Oh, dear God. Her heart thundered against her ribs. This had been so easy to imagine before. Just a simple climb to the weather deck.

Craning her neck, she looked up. With the glass blocking the porthole, she hadn't been able to stick her head out like this and see exactly what they'd have to climb. But there was almost ten feet of smooth, polished wood between the porthole and the rail on the upper deck—and all of it at that same steep angle.

She pulled her head back in. "I made a mistake, Thom. I don't think this will work."

"It will." Thom was pushing up his sleeves over his forearms, sliding aside small steel panels in his wrists, breaking the illusion of smooth metal skin and revealing the gears and pistons within. "You've just got to hang on to me. All right?"

His certainty helped. Though her heart still raced, she nodded.

Moving to the porthole, Thom looked up. He swung his arm. A glint of metal caught the moonlight—a thin cable, she realized. He tugged, seemed satisfied.

He gestured her close. "All right, Georgie. I've got this hooked around the bowsprit. We're going to swing out, and I'm going to pull us up. Once we get up to the rail, I'll look over, see where the crew is. The bird screen they've put across the bow will probably keep us from being seen, but if we're spotted, I'm going to go up and over right there. But if they don't see us, you're going to hang on while I go around the hull and get closer to them. You should take off your gloves for a better grip."

She stripped them off and shoved them into her coat.

The steel of his palm chilled by the air outside, he cupped her cheek. "Now, listen. If it all goes to hell when I cut that balloon, if you see any hint of fire, you drop into the water before she explodes. Try to straighten your body and hit feet first—your legs will heal. Can you swim?"

"A little." She couldn't manage more than a whisper.

"I'll come for you. I'll find you." His head lowered, his kiss a fierce promise. "Are you ready?"

She nodded. After another hard kiss, he moved to the porthole. Gripping the frame at the top, he lifted his body through and sat in the opening with his legs hanging over. Georgiana linked her arms around his shoulders, and buried her face against the back of his neck.

"All right," she whispered.

He leaned forward, pulling her with him. The front of her legs scraped past the porthole frame, and then they were falling out into nothing, the bowsprit creaking above them and her scream locked behind clenched teeth. They spun, the hull and the moon in a dizzying whirl around them. Desperately, she wrapped her legs around his waist, then a windowed porthole spun into her view—the porthole on the other side of the stateroom, over the settee instead of the table—and she realized that they weren't falling, but swinging in an arc around the prow like a pendulum.

Before they swung back, Thom began to climb. A soft ratcheting click came from inside his left arm—winding up the slack in the cable. Georgiana clung to him, not daring to close her eyes, too frightened to look anywhere but up. The long bowsprit spar extended like a spear from the point of the bow, and at its base, the heavy iron loop that anchored the balloon's forward tethers was set into the hull.

"As soon as we reach that anchor, you put your foot on that big loop," Thom said softly. "Then grab on to those balloon cables or hold on to the spar. You can hide right there for a bit."

Better than dangling from the rail. Heart thumping wildly, Georgiana watched the anchor loop come closer. Thom slowed, hanging on to the cable with one hand while reaching around behind her with the other. His forearm rotated against her back, his fingers curving around her side as securely as if he'd been holding her from the front.

"I've got you, Georgie. Now step on that loop."

The iron was as thick as her ankle, but even while dangling from a thin cable a hundred feet over the water, the man she clung to seemed more secure. Clenching her teeth against the whimpers building in her chest, she let her leg slide from around his waist and set the toe of her boot on the anchor loop.

"Reach out and grab that spar now."

Held, but still terrifying to let go. With one arm still clinging to his shoulders, she leaned over. The wooden bowsprit pole was smooth and cold, slippery to her sweating hand. She gripped it tight.

"Pull yourself over, now. I've got you."

It seemed almost impossible to make herself move, then she was over all at once, clinging to the heavy tether cables and looking at Thom.

His dark gaze swept her from head to toe. "All right?"

As long as she didn't look down. Chest heaving, she nodded. The rail was just above her head—truly an easy climb now. She would just have to reach up and pull herself over.

Just as Thom did now, lifting himself and glancing over. After lowering himself again, he hung on to the rail with one hand and unhooked his cable from the bowsprit. A grapple dangled from the end. He folded the claws and slipped the contraption into his left biceps.

"There's just two of them amidships, starboard side," he said quietly. "Only three lanterns. There's none at this end, Georgie, so they won't be coming this way to put one out—and they aren't likely to see you when you look over."

And they would be less likely to see him coming. Good. "Be careful, Thom."

He grinned. "That's the opposite of what we're doing, Georgie."

And then he was gone, silently making his way along the rail. Hardly daring to breathe, Georgiana waited. A cold breeze slipped past her cheeks. The airship swayed slightly, the hull creaking.

A shout rang from the deck.

Heart almost bursting in her chest, Georgiana gripped the rail and hauled herself up to look, feet braced against the cables. The soft glow of the lamps at the opposite end of the deck transformed everything in between into shapes and shadows—two men with pistols extended, but they didn't dare shoot, not with Thom so close to the balloon. With the moon behind him, he was silhouetted ten feet above the deck, hanging from a portside tether cable by one arm. From his other arm, the point of a long blade pressed against the envelope.

His deep voice carried across the deck. "You'd best put those lanterns out."

They hesitated, clearly not believing that he would. It was unthinkable to them, too. Without a word, Thom stabbed the blade through the envelope.

Georgiana's heart stopped. The opposite of careful—but if they didn't risk everything, they'd lose everything.

And it was a risk worth taking. Shouting, the men ran for the lanterns, flinging them over the starboard side, away from the hole. Only a tiny leak right now. Thom had only pierced the balloon's skin; his blade was still buried in the envelope, blocking the leak, and despite the pressure the metal fabric wouldn't rip easily.

As soon as the lanterns were gone, Thom jerked the blade upward, slicing open a two-foot tear. He dropped to the deck with a heavy thud, the steel blade at his arm glinting.

The mercenaries ran. They sprinted to the companionway, shouting the fire alert as they disappeared down the ladder.

Georgiana hauled herself over the rail, stumbling into the coils of rope and crates near the bow. Moonlight spilled faintly over the port side of the deck, lighting her way as she hurried toward Thom. He caught her hand, and they raced to the stern, where the boats hung on pulleys.

Out of breath, she stopped at the tie, frantically unfastening the ropes. And Thom . . . didn't have a left hand.

For the space of a second, she stared. He wasn't holding a blade that had been stashed inside his arm, as she'd thought. His arm *was* a blade. And as she watched, he pushed back a small lever at his elbow, and his forearm unfolded as if being turned inside out. Gears clicked. The blade retracted and his fingers snapped into place, one by one.

Mouth open in shock, she met his eyes. "Thom!"

His grin flashed again. "I asked Ivy for it—in case I was ever eaten by a megalodon, I could cut myself out."

Shaking with sudden laughter, she quickly finished unwinding the tie. Thom hauled on the line and lowered the boat to the deck, then grabbed it by the mooring rope tied to the bow.

"To the tether, Georgie. I don't trust that they won't cut the pulley line if we go down this way."

Dragging the boat after him, Thom quickly started down the moonlit port side, toward the center of the ship. Georgiana followed close behind. But they weren't going to be there alone. Ahead of them, footsteps pounded up the ladder. Mercenaries spilled out of the companionway, shadowy shapes peering through the dark toward them.

"I ripped the balloon open portside," Thom called over the scrape of the boat against the deck. "If you shoot, we're all dead."

More mercenaries came up as he spoke. Winch's voice sounded through the dark. "Put your guns away, you fools! Go pull down the other lifeboat. Billy, Leigh—go find Southampton. He'll need help carrying up that gold."

"I'm here, Mrs. Winch."

Thom abruptly stopped and faced the center of the ship. Georgiana scrambled past the boat to his side. He pushed her back against the rail, behind him.

Southampton emerged from the shadows at the center of the deck, wearing a jacket over his nightshirt and a sword in his hand.

A sword. Fear roiled in Georgiana's stomach. Southampton

couldn't shoot, but he could stab—and he held the weapon with the ease of someone long familiar with it.

He stopped, just over the length of his blade away from her husband. A thin smile curled his lips. "Well done, Big Thom."

To her astonishment, instead of forming his own blade again, Thom pulled on his gloves. His voice was flat and hard. "If you have a brain at all, you'll get into that lifeboat with your crew, and then you'll leave us be. We won't put any claim on your gold. We won't say I was the one that brought it up. Those coins don't matter to me."

"You believe I'll take that risk? Only three people know how many coins you found. I've already silenced your salvage dealer. Now you and your wife must be silenced."

"And your mercenaries?" Georgiana said.

"Ah, yes. Well, they will be paid enough to keep silent."

"Or maybe you'll have them killed, too," she said. In the shadows, the mercenaries had quieted. "Or perhaps they'll blackmail you for more money. Or steal the gold and be done with it."

She hoped Mrs. Winch would at least consider it.

"There will be no blackmail or stealing, Mrs. Thomas." Southampton looked away from her and regarded Thom with amusement. "And my crew and I will be the only ones to survive this. You're a fool for thinking this will save you. We're forty leagues from the nearest shore. The two of you alone will have little chance of reaching it alive."

Forty leagues? Oh, dear God. They would have to row a hundred and twenty miles.

But she wouldn't let the dread overwhelm her. They still had a better chance in a small boat than they did on this ship.

Thom obviously thought so, too. "Little chance is better than none."

"I prefer all or nothing. Now you'd do well to say good-bye to your lovely wife while you still can."

"And you'd best get in your boat and go while you can," Thom said, and she'd never heard his voice so hard and cold. "I was raised under the boot of men like you, who use people and toss them away. When that tower came down, I tore apart men like you. We called them the Horde, but they were the same. And if you don't back away, I'll tear you apart, too."

"They put you down with a tower." Southampton took a step, his blade rising. "I'll do it with a sword."

He lunged, jabbing the blade toward Thom's heart—and stayed, as if his blade had embedded in flesh. Screaming, Georgiana flew forward. But it wasn't what she'd thought. Southampton hadn't impaled Thom's chest.

Thom had caught the blade in his fist.

He stood, staring at Southampton as his fist slid farther down the sword toward the hilt—the glove preventing any spark from steel scraping against steel.

Jaw clenched so hard that his face seemed to shake, Southampton tried to pull back on his sword, then tried to shove it forward.

With a twist of his wrist, Thom snapped the blade and tossed it over the side. Stepping forward, he swung his right fist. A terrible wet crack split the air. Southampton flew back into the shadows at the center of the deck—but by the shape of his head, Georgiana could see that half of it was gone.

Stripping off his bloody glove, Thom threw it to the deck and looked into the dark. "Any of you want a go?"

"I don't think we do," Mrs. Winch answered quickly. "We'll consider Southampton's gold your ransom."

"Fair enough." Thom looked to Georgiana. "Now you hang on to me again."

They'd done it. Heart pounding with sudden relief, she leapt up onto his back, winding her arms around his shoulders. He reached the airship tether—five hundred feet below, still connected to *Oriana*—and grabbed on with his gloved left hand. With his right hand, he hauled the boat over the side by its mooring line.

"Ready?"

She buried her face in his neck. "Yes."

He went over, sliding down the cable toward the water. The tether bowed slightly under their weight—the airship was sinking, the cable taking on slack. With their feet just above the sea, Thom lowered the boat to the surface, then carefully slid the rest of the way down.

Standing in the boat, he hugged her fiercely. Georgiana clung to him, refusing to think of the forty leagues. They'd made it this far.

A splash suddenly sounded nearby, followed by a dismayed shout from Mrs. Winch. Thom stiffened against her.

"Those damned fools." Letting her go, Thom dragged up the oars stowed lengthwise beneath the wooden thwarts and moved to the bow. "Sit, Georgie."

Georgiana quickly took a seat on the center thwart, searching for another pair of oars on the bottom boards. "What happened?"

"They threw the body over." He fitted the oars into the rowlocks. "Now hang on."

"But let me—"

Thom surged backward with a mighty pull. The boat shot forward, almost tumbling Georgiana off her bench. A wild laugh broke from her.

"Oh, Thom! Perhaps forty leagues is not much at all!"

He grinned and pulled again, and they sped across the swells. Georgiana faced forward as long as she could, watching him, until the wind and salt spray blinded her. She turned to look behind them.

Lit by the moon, the airship had just settled onto the surface of the water, the balloon sinking in on itself. The mercenaries had begun filling the other boat—across the distance, she made out their dark silhouettes, the items being tossed from the airship to the mercenaries waiting below. Supplies or gold.

She looked around again as Thom suddenly stopped rowing. The expression on his face warned her to silence. Quietly, he tucked the oars inside the boat and moved to her thwart.

"Shh." He gathered her to his chest, his voice a whisper in her ear. "No noise against the bottom of the boat. Stay absolutely quiet, no matter what."

She nodded against his wet coat, not daring to breathe. They waited, rising and falling with the roll of the sea. Minutes passed.

The boat suddenly jolted, rocking deeper into a swell. Moonlight glinted on a blade of steel racing past the stern—a razor-edged dorsal fin taller than Thom would have been standing. Sharp terror jumped through Georgiana's skin, spearing her heart.

A megalodon.

Thom's arms tightened around her. She watched in horror as the monstrous armored shark sped straight toward the airship, the fin slicing through the path of moonlight.

And from the south, another fin. Oh, dear God.

Faint across the distance, shouts rose from the other boat. Water splashed as they began a desperate rowing. Two men jumped out, tried to swim back to the sinking airship, as if seeking safety.

There would be no safety there, either. A frenzy was starting. The giant sharks would batter the airship's hull until they'd torn everything apart.

Nearing the mercenaries' lifeboat, the fin disappeared beneath the surface.

"Don't look, Georgie," Thom breathed into her ear.

But she couldn't look away. The other boat abruptly lifted up out of the water, as if on a huge wave.

And in one bite was gone. Soon the thrashing swimmers in the water were gone, too.

For a long moment, there were no more shouts, no sounds but Georgiana's ragged breath. The bow of the airship suddenly tipped up, wood splintering. Another fin raced toward it. Georgiana clenched her teeth against a scream of warning. On the deck, a familiar silhouette—Mrs. Winch, standing with her feet apart. A gun barrel gleamed in her hand, pointed at the shark coming toward her.

A bullet wouldn't do anything to a megalodon. Shooting a weapon beneath a leaking balloon would.

The fin went under. The airship tipped sharply to port—and Mrs. Winch fired her pistol.

The airship exploded in a bright ball of light. Muffling her cry, Georgiana turned her face against Thom's throat. Heat rushed past her skin.

Then there was just cold again.

And despite Thom's strength and how quickly he could row, with monsters swimming all around them, forty leagues seemed very, very far away.

The burning remains of the airship were nothing but smoking pieces of flotsam when Georgiana finally succumbed to sleep, held securely in Thom's arms.

Only a few minutes seemed to pass before his low "Wake up, Georgie" pulled her back up, but when she blinked her eyes open, the eastern sky had paled, and pink traced the clouds.

The low thrum of an airship jolted her fully awake.

Still cradled in Thom's lap, she sat up. Her gaze searched the air, her heart lifting when she saw the skyrunner coming from the southeast, her lines sleek and beautiful.

Thom pulled her back against his chest and pressed a kiss to her hair. "They must have seen the explosion," he said softly.

And the remains of the airship burning like a beacon through the night. The etiquette of the seas demanded that any passing vessel offer help and rescue. Now the smoke led them here.

"Have the megalodons gone?" she whispered.

"I haven't seen a fin in more than an hour. That doesn't mean we'd be all right to start rowing."

Georgiana didn't want to risk it, either. She watched the airship's approach, silently urging the engines faster. Slowly, Thom's muscles tensed around her.

"Thom? Is it a shark?"

He made a slight choking sound that might have been a laugh. "In a manner of speaking. That skyrunner is Lady Corsair's."

The notorious mercenary. "I thought you were friendly with her?"

"I am. She'll probably still charge us a ransom before she lets us go."

Georgiana supposed it was the principle of the thing. She didn't mind paying for a rescue, though. It seemed more practical than remaining here.

"All right," she said, and felt Thom's smile against her hair.

"You're not afraid?"

"After watching that megalodon swim by our boat, I've become just as impervious to the threat of madmen and mercenaries as you are."

He laughed quietly against her, and a few minutes later, when the airship hovered overhead and a rope ladder unrolled down to their boat, he urged her up the rungs ahead of him.

Above, a man with a wide grin and the loudest orange waistcoat Georgiana had ever seen leaned over the rail, watching them climb.

"Big Thom! We heard rumors that you'd gotten yourself kidnapped! But now I see that you've just been on a pleasure cruise with your wife."

Thom's gruff reply came from just beneath her. "It seemed like good weather for one—"

From the sea below, a rush of water and cracking wood. Gasping, Georgiana looked down just as enormous jaws crushed their boat to splinters. After a second, nothing remained but small floating pieces.

Astonished, she met Thom's eyes, swallowed hard. "Well," she said. "You missed the opportunity to test out your knife."

And his laugh followed Georgiana the rest of the way up.

Within an hour, Georgiana was walking down a passageway toward another stateroom. In another three hours, she would be home, and quite aware that she and Thom would be returning in much the same way they'd left: on an airship, down a cargo platform. Perhaps even returned to the same spot, with her steamcoach still where Thom had abandoned it.

But Georgiana could not bear to return in *exactly* the same way they'd left.

When they'd left, she and Thom had been on their way to the magistrate's to separate. When they'd left, Georgiana had still been keeping the promise to herself that she would never ask him to stay again.

Now she would beg, if necessary. When they'd left, theirs had been a wreck of a marriage. But in the past few days they'd salvaged something incredible from it, a treasure worth more than any gold—and she couldn't let him go.

But it would not be her choice. If Thom didn't see himself as she did, if he still believed himself a failure, he might want to leave. The very thought of it started a desperate ache in her chest. What would she do without him now?

She didn't know. But it would not be the same as before. She'd survived the past four years.

Georgiana didn't know if she could survive his leaving again.

Eyes blurred, throat knotted, she barely saw the cabin as they entered it. As soon as the door closed, she turned to him.

Before she could get a word out, he kissed her—and yes, this needed to come before anything else. Not a task, but a sheer necessity. She melted against him, his warmth easing the ache in her chest and the pain in her throat. Rough stubble scratched her chin and his coat was damp and her fingers were cold, and this was the most wonderful kiss that there'd ever been.

Until it ended, but then he swept her up and carried her to the bed, and that was even more wonderful.

He set her down on the mattress and stepped back to unbuckle his coat. Voice hoarse, as if something within him was hurting, too, he said, "I need to have you again before we reach home, Georgie."

"You already have me, Thom. Always." Gathering every bit of her courage, she rose up on her knees. "*Always*. When we reach home, I want you to stay. No papers, no separation. I want to call you my husband for the rest of my life."

His fingers stilled on his coat buckle. As if not daring to believe, his gaze desperately searched her face. "Tell me again."

"I love you, Thom, and I want you to stay," she said, and fierce joy replaced the pain. Oh, she would tell him again and again. "I loved you before, but I love you so much more now. Before, I'd have let you leave because the hurt was too much. It isn't now. And I couldn't let you go now, even if I was torn apart. If you went, I'd be trailing along behind you—or tying a chain around you to drag you back. So I want you to stay."

With a sharp hitch of his breath, he clutched her against his chest. Tightly he held her, his hands slipping up her back to tangle in her hair. Gently, he tilted her face up, and the aching love in his eyes was a mirror of her own. "You know I wouldn't have ever gone. But I don't know that I'll be any better a husband than I was."

"Will you be with me?"

"Every single night."

"Will you love me?"

"Always, Georgie."

"Then that's all I need." She tugged him down to the bed. When he sank down on the edge, she straddled his thighs. His coat still needed unbuckling. Her fingers started in on the task. "If it's money that worries you, you ought to know it's not a concern. My business is yours, too—at least the profits from it are, since I invested your earnings to start it. And it's done well. I've got a fleet of ten ships, and I'll soon be acquiring more. Maybe airships, too. It's not a chest of gold, but we won't want for anything."

He struggled with that, but finally nodded. "Considering that gold is likely in a shark's belly, I'll trade it."

"It's a good trade. Your share of the profits is a hefty one." She took a deep breath. "If you want a new ship for your salvaging work, you've earned more than enough to buy another one. A new submersible, too."

"I don't want to salvage."

"You're very good at it."

"I was good at hauling fish, too."

He was good at a lot of things. But that wasn't the question she needed to ask—the question she'd never bothered to ask before. "What will make you happy, Thom?"

"Just you, Georgie. And you loving me even half as much as I love you."

"I love you twice as much as that." And her heart was bursting with it. Smiling, she pushed his coat down his arms. "Is there anything you want to do?"

He grinned and rocked up beneath her. "I want to make you my queen."

"Thom!" She laughed, her face hot. "I'm sure we'll do plenty of that."

"Soon." His expression gentling, he softly kissed her. "You're the one person I care about proving myself to, Georgie. And yet you make me feel like I don't have to."

"You don't have to. You already have, over and over."

"And I'm not going to stop now." And he seemed to be thinking her question over again now, his brow creased in a thoughtful frown. "I do like diving. And I enjoyed working with Ivy." His hand smoothed down her suddenly tense back. "I'm not saying I want to go off and do it again. I'm saying that I liked tinkering, and putting that submersible together with her. I could make more of them, test them in local waters, sell them."

"You'd like that?"

"I would."

Then it sounded perfect to her. "We could build a workshop for you next to the house. Or in town, by my offices."

"I'd like that, too. And I'll figure out how to help you take care of our children—and learn to read and write a bit, so that I can send you love notes and make up for all the messages I never sent before."

Her heart swelled. "I'll send some to you, as well."

"And I'll make a better man of myself."

"Oh, Thom. You're the best man I know. You couldn't be any better."

He lowered his lips to hers, said softly against them, "You're wrong, Georgie."

Smiling, she wound her arms around his shoulders. "You'll have to stay around to prove me wrong."

"I will. You wait and see. You'll never be able to get rid of me."

She'd never try. "Is that your new promise? Because my new promise is that I'm never going to be separated from you again."

"It is, Georgie." His voice roughened. "I swear it."

"And is there any chance you'll ever break it?"

"None at all."

"Then I was wrong, Thom," she said, and leaned in for another kiss. "Sometimes, no chance *is* better than some."

ECSTASY UNDER THE MOON

A Children of the Moon Novella

LUCY MONROE

Author's Note

Dear Reader,

This Children of the Moon story occurs in the years between Moon Burning *and* Dragon's Moon. *It's a stand-alone romance, but perhaps it will give you insight into how difficult it is for the Éan to make the transition to the clans you read about in* Dragon's Moon. *Una and Bryant are very dear to my heart and their story was an emotional one for me to write. Enjoy!*

Hugs,
Lucy

PROLOGUE

THE BEGINNING

Millennia ago God created a race of people so fierce even their women were feared in battle. These people were warlike in every way, refusing to submit to the rule of any but their own . . . no matter how large the forces sent to subdue them. Their enemies said they fought like animals. Their vanquished foe said nothing, for they were dead.

They were considered a primitive and barbaric people because they marred their skin with tattoos of blue ink. The designs were simple at first, a single beast depicted in unadorned outline over their hearts. The leaders were marked with bands around their arms with symbols that told of their strength and prowess in battle. Mates were marked to show their bond.

And still, their enemies were never able to discover the meanings of any of the blue-tinted tattoos.

Some surmised they were symbols of their warlike nature, and in that they would be partially right. For the beasts represented a part of themselves these fierce and independent people kept secret at the pain of death. It was a secret they had kept for the centuries of their existence, while most migrated across the European landscape to settle in the inhospitable north of Scotland.

Their Roman enemies called them Picts, a name accepted by the other peoples of their land and lands south . . . they called themselves the Chrechte.

Their animal-like affinity for fighting and conquest came from a part of their nature their fully human counterparts did not enjoy. For these fierce people were shape-changers.

The bluish tattoos on their skin were markings given as a rite of passage when they made their first shift. Some men had control of that change. Some did not, subject to the power of the full moon until participating in the sacred act of sex. The females of all the races both experienced their first shift into animal form and gained control thereafter with the coming of their first menses.

Some shifted into wolves, others big cats of prey and yet others into the larger birds—the eagle, hawk and raven.

The one thing all Chrechte shared in common was that they did not reproduce as quickly or prolifically as their fully human brothers and sisters. Although they were a fearsome race and their cunning enhanced by an understanding of nature most humans could not possess, they were not foolhardy and were not ruled by their animal natures.

One warrior could kill a hundred of his foe, but should she or he die before having offspring, the death would lead to an inevitable shrinking of the race. Some Pictish clans and those recognized by other names in other parts of the world had already died out rather than submit to the inferior, but multitudinous, humans around them.

The Faol of Scotland's Highlands were too smart to face the end of their race rather than blend. These wolf shifters saw the way of the future. In the ninth century AD, Keneth MacAlpin ascended to the Scottish throne. Of Faol Chrechte descent through his mother, nevertheless, his human nature had dominated.

He was not capable of "the change," but that did not stop him from laying claim to the Pictish throne (as it was called then) as well. In order to guarantee his kingship, he betrayed his Chrechte brethren at a dinner, killing all of the remaining royals of their people—and forever entrenched a distrust of humans by their Chrechte counterparts.

Despite this distrust but bitterly aware of the cost of MacAlpin's betrayal, the Faol of the Chrechte realized that they could die out fighting an ever-increasing and encroaching race of humanity, or they could join the Celtic clans.

They joined.

As far as the rest of the world knew, though much existed to attest to their former existence, what had been considered the Pictish people were no more.

Because it was not in their nature to be ruled by any but their own, within two generations, the Celtic clans that had assimilated the Chrechte were ruled by shape-changing clan chiefs who shared their natures with wolves. Though most of the fully human among them did not know it, a sparse few were entrusted with the secrets of their kinsmen. Those that did were aware that to betray the code of silence meant certain and immediate death.

Stories of other shifter races, the Éan and Paindeal, were told around the campfire, or to the little ones before bed. However, since the wolves had not seen a shifter except their own in generations, they began to believe the other races only a myth.

But myths did not take to the sky on black wings glinting an iridescent blue under the sun. Myths did not live as ghosts in the forest, but breathing air just as any other man or animal. The Éan were no myth; they were birds with abilities beyond that of merely changing their shape.

Many could be forgiven for believing tales of their prince nothing more than legend. For who had heard of a man shifting not only into the form of a raven but that of the mystic dragon from ancient tales as well?

ONE

The Forests of the Éan, Highlands of Scotland

1144 AD, Reign of Dabíd mac Maíl Choluim, King of Scots, and the Reign of Prince Eirik Taran Gra Gealach, Ruler of the Éan

Una stood in shock, terror coursing through her like fire in her veins, burning away reason, destroying the façade of peace she had worked so hard to foster for the past five years.

Her eagle screamed to be released. She wanted to take to the skies and fly as far as her wings could carry her until the sun sank over the waters and the moon rose and set again in the sky.

The high priestess, Anya Gra, smiled on the assembled Éan like she had not just made a pronouncement that could well spell their doom.

Faol were coming here? To the forest of the Éan? To their homeland kept secret for generations. For very good reason.

Reason Una had learned to appreciate to the very marrow of her bones five years before.

"No," she whispered into air laden with smoke from the feast's cooking fires. "This cannot be."

Other noises of dissent sounded around her, but her mind could not take them in. It was too busy replaying images she'd tried to bury under years of proper and obedient behavior. Years of not taking chances and staying far away from the human clans that had once intrigued her so.

She'd even avoided Lais, one of the few other eagle shifters among her people. Because he'd come from the outside. From the clan of the Donegal, the clan that spawned devils who called themselves men.

She'd not spoken to him once in the three years he'd lived among their people.

The grumbling around Una grew to such a level, even her own tormented thoughts could not keep it out.

For the first time in her memory, the Éan of their tribe looked on their high priestess with disfavor. Many outright glared at the woman whose face might be lined with age, but maintained a translucent beauty that proclaimed her both princess and spiritual leader.

Others were yelling their displeasure toward the prince of the people, but their monarch let no emotion show on his handsome though young features. He merely looked on, his expression stoic, his thoughts hidden behind his amber gaze.

The dissension grew more heated. This was unheard of. In any other circumstance, Una would have been appalled by the behavior of her fellow Chrechte, but not this day.

She hoped beyond hope that the anger and dissent would sway their leaders toward reason.

"Enough!" The prince's sudden bellow was loud and commanding despite the fact he was only a few summers older than Una.

Silence fell like the blacksmith's anvil.

Emotion showed now, his amber eyes glowing like the sacred stone during a ceremony. "We have had the Faol among us on many occasions these past three years."

Those wolves had only come to visit. Una, and many like her—justifiably frightened by the race that had done so much to eradicate their own, had stayed away from the visitors. She'd avoided all contact and had not even stolen so much as a peek at any of them.

Not like when she was younger and let her curiosity rule her common sense.

But Anya Gra said these ones, these *emissaries* from the Sinclair, Balmoral and Donegal clans, would live among the Éan for the foreseeable future.

Live. Among. Them. With no end in sight.

Una's breath grew shorter as panic clawed at her insides with the sharpness of her eagle's talons.

"It is time the Chrechte brethren are reunited." Prince Eirik's tone brooked no argument. "It has been foretold that this is the only chance for our people to survive as a race. Do you suddenly doubt the visions of your high priestess?"

Many shook their head, but not Una. Because for the first time in her life, she *did* doubt the wisdom of the woman who had led their people spiritually since before Una was born.

"Emissaries are coming to live among us, to learn our ways and teach us the way of the Faol." This time it was another of the royal family who spoke, the head healer. "We will all benefit."

"We know the way of the Faol," one brave soul shouted out. "They kill, maim and destroy the Éan. That is the way of the Faol."

"Not these wolves. The Balmoral, the Sinclair and the Donegal lairds are as committed to keeping our people safe as I am." The prince's tone rang with sincerity.

The man believed his own words. That was clear.

But Una couldn't bring herself to do so. No wolf would ever care for the Éan as a true brother. It was not in their violent, often sadistic and deceitful natures.

"It is only a few among the Faol today who would harm our

people. Far more would see us joined with the clans for our safety and all our advantage."

Join with the clans? Who had conceived of that horrific notion? First they were talking about having wolves come to live among them, and now their leaders were mentioning leaving the forest so the Éan could join the clans?

Una's eagle fought for control, the desperate need to get away growing with each of her rapid heartbeats.

"In the future, we will have no choice," Anya Gra said, as if reading Una's mind. "But for this moment in time, we must only make these few trustworthy wolves welcome among us."

Only? There was no *only* about it. This thing the royal family asked, it was monumental. Beyond terrifying.

It was impossible.

"You ask too much." The sound of Una's father's voice brought a mixture of emotions, as it always did.

Guilt. Grief. Relief. Safety.

Stooped from the grievous wound he had received at the hands of the Faol when rescuing Una from their clutches, he nevertheless made an imposing figure as he pushed his way toward the prince and priestess.

The leather patch covering the eye he'd lost in the same battle gave her father a sinister air she knew to be false. He was the best of men.

And forever marred by wounds that would never allow him to take to the skies again . . . because of her.

"You ask us to make welcome those who did this," he gestured toward himself in a way he would never usually do.

He ignored his disfigurements and expected others to do the same.

"Nay." The prince's arrogant stance was far beyond his years, but entirely fitting his station as the leader of their people. "I *demand* you make welcome wolves who would die to protect you from anything like that happening again."

"Die, for the likes of me?" her father scoffed. "That would be a fine day, indeed, would it not? When a wolf would die to protect a bird."

"Do you doubt *my* desire to protect you and all of my people?" the prince demanded, with a flicker of vulnerability quickly gone from his amber eyes.

"Nay. My prince, you love us as your father did before you, but this? This risk you would take with all our safety, it is foolishness."

Suddenly Anya Gra was standing right in front of Una's father, her expression livid, no desire for conciliation in evidence at all. "Fionn, son of Micael, You dare call *me* foolish?"

Oh, the woman was beyond angry. Even more furious than Una's father had a wont to get.

"Nay, Priestess. Your wisdom has guided our people for many long years."

"Then, it is my visions you doubt," the *celi di* accused with no less fury in her tone.

Una's father shook his head vigorously. "Your visions have always been right and true."

"Then you, and all those who stand before me today," she said, including everyone at the feast with her sharp raven's stare. "All of my people will give these wolves a chance to prove that not every Faol would murder us in our sleep."

"And if you are wrong? If they turn on us?" her father dared to question.

Una's respect for her parent grew. It took great strength to stand up to Anya Gra, spiritual leader and one of the oldest among them.

"Then I will cast my fire and destroy their clans without mercy," the prince promised in a tone no one, not even her stalwart father, could deny.

Her father nodded, though he looked no happier by the assurance. "Aye, that's the right of it then."

Prince Eirik let his gaze encompass the whole of their community, his expression one of unequivocal certainty. "I will always protect my people to the best of my ability. Welcoming these honorable men is part of that."

Una noted how he continued to push forth the message that these wolves were good men, *trustworthy* and *honorable.*

He was her prince and she should believe him.

But she couldn't.

She knew the truth. Not that she hated all wolves. That would make her like the Faol who had taken her and done the horrible things they had done with every intention of killing her in the end, as they would kill any Éan they came across.

No, she would not share the unreasoning prejudices of her enemy and hate an entire race, making no distinctions between individuals.

But she could not trust them, either.

TWO

Bryant and his companions rode into the clearing deep in the forest. Their guide, Circin of the Donegal clan, pulled his horse to a stop without a sound.

The six Faol soldiers also pulled their horses to a stop.

"Now what?" Donnach, the other Balmoral wolf sent by their laird to act as diplomat to the Éan, asked.

"We wait," Circin said, his youth belied by his confidence.

In line to be the next leader of the Donegal clan once the acting laird, Barr, had trained him to his station as both laird and pack alpha, the youth was an extremely rare shifter with two animals. Not that Circin's triple nature was common knowledge, but Bryant and the others, if they were looking, had witnessed the other man shift into his raven the night before.

Since Circin's clan believed him to be wolf, that meant the Chrechte had a dual animal nature: both Faol and Éan.

"Why aren't you one of the emissaries?" Bryant asked him.

He would think a man who shared his nature with both a raven and a wolf would make a better bridge for the gap between the two races than a pure wolf.

"I lived among the Éan for a year after Barr married Sabrine, but I told no one except the prince and Anya Gra of my wolf. We all felt it best at the time."

Considering the shared past between the two races of Chrechte, Bryant had no trouble understanding why that decision had been made. "Just as your clan isn't aware you are a raven?"

"Some in my clan know," Circin admitted easily.

And then something became clear to Bryant. Circin had shifted where Bryant and the others could see him because he trusted them. "You are acting as a bridge even if others do not know it."

A faint blush darkened the laird-in-training's cheeks. "The trust between the Chrechte brethren must start with the individual man."

"And woman," one of the Sinclair warriors added solemnly.

They all nodded. Highland Chrechte understood the value of all their people. Among the clans, human women were often seen as chattel, but the Chrechte were not like that.

Ancient laws dictated that all had their place before the Creator. Man was nothing without woman and woman was nothing without man. Just as the Éan were not complete without the Faol and the Faol were not complete without the Éan.

The different races of Chrechte had been created for a reason and it was not the role of any individual to try to change that. No matter how misguided and downright evil the actions of some of the Faol.

He still found it hard to believe that in only a few generations the memory of the other races of the Chrechte had been taken from the Faol, leaving the wolves to believe they were the only shape-changers in existence.

Now, others besides just Bryant's family knew and *believed* their ancient stories were more than simply that. They were a history of people that had indeed lived and still did live, if in secret deep in the forest for the past centuries.

One day, wolves and the birds would unite with the Paindeal, their cat-shifting brothers and sisters, again as well. It had to be so.

Bryant had not been chosen as emissary by accident. He passionately desired the reconnection of their races.

Had been raised since he was a whelp to believe the time would come when the Éan would be accepted once again among the Faol. Must be accepted.

The desire to make it so was imbedded deep inside him and he *would* see it to its conclusion.

The Éan needed to join the clans as the Faol had done, for all their good and safety.

Tucked against a branch high in her tree, Una watched in her eagle form as the six Faol warriors followed Circin of the Donegal and her own prince on horseback into the village, riding past the base of the trees in which most of the Éan made their dwellings.

Where there had once been a couple of caves prepared for the humans who stumbled upon the Éan's secret homeland to live in, the village now had several huts. They were for the mostly human families that had chosen joining their tribe over death, or had been born into it since an ancestor made that choice. Very few Éan dwelt among them, those mated to a human or who had been injured in some way that prevented flight.

Her father was one such bird. The home he shared with her mother was at the base of the very tree in which Una perched. She had wanted to live with them when they'd been forced to leave their home among the trees, but her parents had both refused.

She would be safer in their old home high above, they said. A bird should not live on the ground, her father claimed. Their home should not be abandoned, her mother insisted. And Una had known that they were right on all points.

So, she had stayed in the humble dwelling built in the giant ancient oak tree by one of her ancestors.

However, the five years since her horror had been lonely ones. Her parents did not know it, but Una never invited others to share the space that echoed with the loss her family had endured because of her curiosity and disobedience.

It was not just wolves she had a difficulty being in close proximity to. There were only a select few she could stand to be nearby, and the children. The little ones caused no panic in her.

Thanks be to the Creator, because Una's one contribution to her tribe hinged on her ability to be near the young ones.

Her thoughts of the children ceased as the warriors drew close enough for her eagle's vision to make out details of the wolves sent by the clans to somehow prove the improbable . . . that a Faol could be trusted by the Éan.

The warriors were huge, appearing even bigger as they got closer. Some few among their people, like Prince Eirik, shared such stature, but it was not so common among the Éan as the Faol to stand head and shoulders above human men.

One wolf in particular caught her sharp eagle's eye. Wearing the blue and green plaid with thin yellow stripes of the Balmoral, this one wore no shirt with his kilt. The muscles on his arms and torso bulged with strength. A triangle of dark hair to match that on his head covered the skin of his chest made golden by its exposure to the sun.

Brown hair brushed his broad shoulders, the hairs on his face neither clean shaven, nor bristly with an unkempt beard. Sheared neatly to his skin, they accentuated the hard angles of his cheeks and strong jaw.

The wolf's feet were bare, the muscles of his legs strong and corded. The only thing he wore besides the plaid was a huge sword and a knife at his waist.

He looked more imposing than the wolf counterpart he could shift into.

And this man was supposed to come in peace, an emissary for the Faol?

Though the others continued on, he stopped his mount near her father's hut. Turning first to the right and then to the left, he seemed to be looking for something. He cocked his head, inhaling, as if sniffing the air.

Why? What had caught his attention?

Una let out a strangled screech when his head snapped up and his piercing grey gaze was directed right toward her.

A wolf, not an eagle, he should not be able to see her amidst the leaves and branches. Only she felt as if his keen grey eyes were looking right into those of her eagle.

One of the soldiers doubled back, stopping next to him. It was the other Balmoral soldier, by the colors of his plaid. He said something to the grey-eyed wolf, but she could not make out the exact words.

She'd perched herself too far up, and unlike the wolves, her sense of hearing was barely better than that of a human.

Petrified by the Faol warrior's presence and yet feeling a wholly inexplicable longing to fly down and get a closer look, she remained still on the branch.

The other soldier said something again, this time his tone sharper. The grey-eyed man finally turned away and kneed his horse into motion. Just as her father came out of the hut.

Collision seemed imminent and Una let out a shriek of distress, her eagle louder than her human woman would ever be.

But her father did not end up in the dirt, his bad leg taken out from under him. The wolf, moving faster than she'd seen even among the Éan, had dismounted and nudged his horse out of her father's path with his own body.

Unable to deny the need to get closer, Una hopped down from branch to branch until she could hear the Balmoral soldier apologizing to her father.

Her father ignored the man's words, turning without acknowledging him and staring up into the tree. As if he, too, could sense her presence, which was far more likely. Considering he did have the vision of an eagle and was her father besides.

Even if he had not seen her eagle among the limbs of the tree, her father would know of Una's need to see the wolves as they entered the village.

"You are not to come to the village for the time being," he called up to her, proving her supposition correct.

She had no intention of coming into the village with the wolves there, but something stirred inside Una that had not stirred in five years.

Curiosity and *aggravation* at the restrictions placed on her. It only took remembering what those feelings had led her into before, and she was taking flight, making her way back up toward her home with a speed she would normally reserve for chasing prey.

Not that she did much hunting. Even in her eagle form, she could not stomach the hunt. Not after being made into prey herself.

An eagle, Una *should* have become a warrior like the princess, Sabrine, and some of the other strong women among their people.

But Una had no stomach for battle and even less for bloodshed. She should be protecting her people, but Una was inept at any but the most basic tactics of fighting.

Her parents had never said so, but they had to be so disappointed that their only child had turned out to be such a poor Éan.

THREE

Bryant watched the older Éan go back into his hut, unsurprised by the surly lack of welcome.

The Faol had a lot to answer for in their past treatment of the Éan. He and the other wolf soldiers were here in the forest of the Éan for a purpose . . . to show that the Faol as a whole no longer held the wrongheaded views of their ancestors.

There were still some out there, acting in secret against their brethren shifters, but they would be dealt with when they were revealed. With more mercy than most deserved. But the eagle shifter Lais was proof that not only could others besides the Faol fall prey to the wrong thinking that led to wanting to eradicate the Éan, but at least some of those so deceived could be convinced of the truth as well.

With the help of information from Lais, Barr was searching the Donegal clan diligently for the old seeds left behind by their former laird, an evil man who had not respected either human or Éan life.

As his horse took him forward, Bryant's wolf howled in protest. The beast inside him wanted to climb that tree and investigate the intriguing scent that had stopped him at its base.

Considering the number of looks of distrust, and some of outright fear, he and the other wolves had received upon their arrival, that was one course of action that could lead to the very opposite result from the one they wanted. Bryant needed to show the Éan he wasn't a threat.

Against the urges of his wolf, he nudged his horse forward to follow Circin and Prince Eirik farther into the village.

Four of the soldiers were placed in homes with human members of the Éan tribe. None with the bird shifters, and two of them, Bryant and Donnach, were given their own small hut to share. Which meant out of all the homes in the village, only four had been willing to have wolves staying with them.

Prince Eirik had explained that after his people had grown used to their presence, Bryant and Donnach would be given the option of living in the treetop dwelling that housed the prince and his grandmother. From there, they would be able to spend more time with the Éan themselves.

Bryant chose to see that as progress rather than further proof the Éan were not ready to integrate with the clans. As his laird had warned him was most likely the case.

According to stories Bryant's grandfather told, the wolves had not liked joining the human clans, either. Especially after MacAlpin's betrayal, but his forefathers had realized that if the Chrechte wanted to survive, the move was a necessary one.

And in some ways, it was easier done after MacAlpin's betrayal, when no easily acknowledged prince among their own people could be identified because MacAlpin had killed them all.

Not like with the Éan. They had Prince Eirik, who all expected to be named king upon his twenty-fifth birthday.

The Éan had their own spiritual leader, too, and a sacred stone, the *Clach Gealach Gra*, used during their Chrechte rituals. The Faol had either never had a stone, or lost it many years ago and had long since given up their *celi di* in favor of the human's priests.

The Éan were also used to living as they did in the forest, like thieves hiding from the magistrate.

Convincing them of the need to rejoin their brethren and become part of the clans, where many of their freedoms would be curtailed even as they enjoyed others, would be no easy task.

And still, Bryant's wolf had more interest in the scent that caught his attention than in their task at hand.

The mists of the spirit world swirled around Una's legs, even as her shift grew damp and clung to her form. Though she slept, this was no dream.

She had heard of this, the ability some Chrechte had to meet on a plane not purely physical. Oh, it felt real enough, but she experienced it on a level that would impact her body, could even leave marks on it if the stories were to be believed, but where her body had not actually come.

She had always believed such was only possible for the *celi di*, those of the royal blood and some very blessed sacred mates. She was none of those and yet she was here. Wherever here was.

The forest around her did not look like her forest, but had trees wider than ten Faol warriors standing shoulder to shoulder, and so tall she could not see their tops standing below them. The green moss growing on the north side of their trunks was a brilliant green, brighter than anything in the forests of her home.

Flowers grew in clumps of vibrant colors, irises standing waist high to peek through the ever-swirling mists. Birds chirped, though she could not see them, and the sound of a brook babbled in the distance.

Though she'd gone to sleep in the night, the moon high in the sky, it was early morning here, the sun still trailing a golden glow on the horizon.

The sound of a rider on a horse approaching had her turning from the sun, only to see the man from the day before galloping on his big brown warhorse. He spied her. There was no question that he'd done so, for he quickly changed direction, pulling his huge beast of a horse to an abrupt halt before her.

The horse tossed its head as the rider looked down at her in confusion. "Who are you?"

"I am Una." None of the panic she usually experienced around strangers came to plague her, and she found the smallest of smiles tilting her lips upward.

There was joy in being able to address this man without fear.

"I do not know you," the grey-eyed man said, his brows drawn together.

"I am aware." Her smile grew. "I have told you my name. Now, tell me yours."

She did not know this boldness in the physical world, but here, she felt safe. This was the Chrechte spirit realm, a place she as Éan could only be called to, and a place where no harm could come to her.

No Faol with intention to harm would be allowed to enter. Of this her eagle was so certain, even her human heart had to accept it.

"I am called Bryant."

"You are Faol."

"You are Éan?" he asked, rather than stated.

"I am."

"Are you *celi di?*" Though the way his storm-cloud gaze roamed over her said spiritual guidance was the last thing on his mind.

"No." Familiar shame that had no place here still assailed her. "I am nothing special."

"I am sure that is not true."

"You would not know." All urge to smile had fled.

Concern darkened his eyes, as if her sadness truly bothered him. "I am drawn to you."

She merely shook her head.

Bryant dismounted with an ease of movement she knew was not simply because they conversed in the spirit realm. His natural grace delighted her here, though were she to see it at home, she would consider it a threat she knew.

"Were you sleeping when you came to this place?" he asked as he came near, seemingly unconcerned with what his horse might get up to without its rider.

"I was."

"So, this is a dream?" he asked.

"No." Even in her dreams, her terror of the Faol would never let her stand so close to him.

"Where are we then?"

"You are so sure I have the answers?"

"I know only that I do not."

"It is the Chrechte spirit realm."

"I have heard stories." He frowned. "But surely this is not real. This is naught but a dream."

She put her hand out, rejoicing in her temerity to do so, and touched his muscular arm. His hand came up seemingly of its own volition to cover hers. Warmth spread between them, though the mists surrounding them were still cool in the early morning air of this place.

"This does not feel like a dream," he said with quiet awe.

"Because it is not."

"But who are you, if not *celi di*, to bring me here?"

"I did not bring you."

"Then I brought you?" he asked, sounding unsure.

"No. Perhaps we are not even here for each other, merely at the same time."

It was his turn to say, "No," but with a great deal more vehemence than she had uttered the denial. "You are here for me."

"You did not even know where you were; how can you be so sure of that?"

"My wolf wants you."

There was no mistaking the heat in his grey eyes.

"Perhaps wolves are not taught they cannot have everything they want, but we of the Éan know differently."

He tugged on her hand, moving her to stand between his feet, so close their bodies touched.

Her heart raced, but it was not in terror. Her breath caught, but not because her lungs refused to work. For the first time in five years, Una found herself wanting to be near another adult, craving a physical closeness she was sure would be denied her always.

"You crave me as well," he claimed, his expression no longer confused, but knowing in a way that made heat pool low in her belly.

"Here, I may feel all that I am denied when I am fully myself."

"What do you mean?" he asked, his head bent as if to listen more closely.

Or kiss her.

Was it possible that she actually hoped for the latter?

"I cannot abide any but my parents and the very young in close proximity."

"Why?"

"It is not something I would speak of here." The ugliness of her past and her ongoing pain did not belong in this beautiful place.

"One day you will tell me."

She laughed then, as she so rarely did—and only then around the children. "You assume we will see one another again."

"I am living among your people now. If I do not see you in this miraculous place again, I will see you in your village."

She simply shook her head, knowing differently. "I do not go to the village."

At least right now. Her father had forbidden her.

"As time goes on, we will be allowed into the trees."

"I doubt that." Some of the humans living among their tribe had never even received an invitation to do so.

His smile was knowing, but he did not argue with her. Instead, he lowered his head further and whispered against her lips. "I wonder."

"What do you wonder?" she asked breathlessly.

"If you taste as delectable as you smell to my wolf."

She would have answered. She might even have denied him, though she did not think so, not when this was the only taste of intimacy she was likely to ever have.

But he gave her no chance to do either. He simply pressed his lips to hers, kissing her.

It was the most amazing sensation Una had ever known. Her lips did not merely tingle against his, they felt so much more. Pleasure. Fire. And the need for more and more and more.

She gasped her shock at the delight of it and felt his tongue tickle her own through her parted lips.

Her entire body pressed to his, an ache growing inside her for something she had no name for. She moved restlessly against him, the damp shift no barrier between his warm skin and her own.

One large warrior's hand moved down to cup her bottom in a gesture so intimate, Una cried out from it.

And then he was gone.

FOUR

Nothing else had changed around her, but Bryant and the big brown horse had disappeared, as if they'd never been.

Una's hand came up to press against kiss-swollen lips. He had been here. He had kissed her.

And then he'd been taken away? To go to whomever he was actually supposed to meet? The thought saddened her so greatly, tears burned her eyes.

"Why am I here?" she called out brokenly to the empty forest.

"This is a place the Chrechte come for answers," a voice said from her left.

Una did not want to turn to face the other woman, but manners dictated she had no choice.

She turned to find a woman with similar features to Anya Gra, only much younger and without the sadness shadowing her cerulean gaze that was so much a part of the Éan's *celi di*. Had she seen Una's shameless display with Bryant?

The other woman shook her head as if answering the unspoken

question. "This is a place of healing for some, a place for answers for others, some come here simply to find peace."

"I see no one else."

"That is often the way."

"But earlier . . ."

"There is always a purpose in the meetings you have with others here. Remember that, little Una, braveheart."

"I am not brave," Una denied. "Not anymore."

"The spirit of the girl still lives in the heart of the woman."

"I do not think so," Una said apologetically, sorry she had to disappoint the beautiful and clearly kind lady.

"I know your heart as you do not."

"But it's my heart?" Somehow the words came out a question rather than the statement Una had intended.

"Is it?"

Before Una could answer, the woman was gone, too, and then Una felt herself falling, air whooshing by as if she'd jumped backward off the highest waterfall in the forest. Not something she was ever likely to do.

She did not land with a jar, or a thump. She didn't actually feel the landing at all, but suddenly she was on her sleeping furs, inside her own humble home and fully awake, the first rays of morning chasing the night shadows from the room.

Una dressed carefully for the feast to welcome the Faol warriors being held in the royal abode among the trees.

She'd been able to miss the last one held in the village immediately after the men's arrival, not least because her father had forbidden her to go. But none who had been invited to the home of Anya Gra and her grandson, Prince of the Éan, were allowed to say nay.

Not without seriously offending the royal family of the Éan.

And that neither Una, nor even her irascible father, was willing to do.

Rope ladders had been dropped to the village below so leaders in the village along with the soldiers could come into the trees. Those who could not climb the ropes, like her father, would be lifted on a pallet hefted with pulley ropes by the strongest among them.

It was no small task and Una could not conceive of ignoring its significance or effort by not attending herself.

And, well . . . she actually *wanted* to go.

A month ago, Una would have said with absolute certainty that the anticipation she felt now at the thought of attending the feast was impossible to contemplate. But that was before four sennights of visits to the Chrechte land of the spirits.

She'd been back on three different occasions and each time he had been there as well. The Faol warrior, Bryant.

He had apologized for leaving her so abruptly the first time and then said he was sorry he'd kissed her without leave. She'd admitted she probably never would have had the courage to give it. So, he'd said perhaps he would have to kiss her again without asking.

She'd replied that might be best.

It hadn't been stilted, or awkward, but funny and light. And he *had* kissed her. Marvelously.

Though he'd never let his hand roam to her bottom again. She wanted to ask why, but never got the gumption to do so. She had so much more temerity in the spirit realm, but still . . . she was herself.

They talked of many things though. His annoyingly protective older brother, and irritatingly spoiled younger sisters. He told her stories of growing up in a big family and she told him of life among the Éan, daughter to one of the tribe's greatest warriors.

She didn't speak of her horror five years past and he didn't mention his purpose in the village.

Their time always ended too quickly and she feared each sojourn into the spirit world would be their last, or on the next occasion she would not see him. For as much as the spirit *celi di* had claimed all meetings were with purpose, Una was convinced she saw Bryant by happenstance when he was there by some other greater motive.

And tonight she would see him in the flesh.

Would he remember visiting with her in the spirit realm? Would he seek out her company?

Or had her sojourns there merely been the conjuring of an excessively lonely mind fixated on a brief glimpse of a man whose very nature sent Una into a panic.

They could not be friends in the physical realm. Could they?

The very idea was absurd. He was Faol and should he approach her in person, in this place, she was most likely to fall in a faint of panic at his feet.

Sighing at her own shortcomings she had no idea how to overcome, though for the first time perhaps she wanted to, Una straightened her long-sleeved shift. The bodice she pulled on over it was made of supple leather her mother had painstakingly tanned for her. Mòrag had also dyed it heather green, the exact shade of the Éan's plaid, and fitted it to Una's figure with careful stitches that would last many years to come.

Una's skirt was made of their tribe's tartan, in the muted colors of the forest, the thin line the heather green that matched her bodice. Many women of the Éan dressed in leather skirts instead of the tartan, or dresses of the same because the leather wore longer. Some wore kilts only slightly longer than the men's. Those were the warrior women, but Una was far from being one.

She wore no shoes, as most among the Éan were wont to do, but she'd taken care to scrub her feet clean and trim both her finger- and toenails.

Una had spent more time than usual brushing her long hair

until it shone in soft brown waves around her shoulders and down her back. Being an eagle, it was several shades lighter than that of a raven, whose hair usually shone black. It was even lighter than either of her parents', but Una didn't mind.

She'd pulled it back from her face and fastened the sides of her hair together at the back of her head with a leather thong.

She looked neat and as civilized as most Éan managed to do. They did not live as the humans among the clans, but clung to their Chrechte roots.

There had been a time when she'd wanted to emulate the humans, but that time was past. She desired now to be fully Éan, but she could not even manage that very well, could she?

Una could be in the sky with her sharp eagle vision, watching for intruders, but none had ever suggested she do so.

Because she had been deemed untrustworthy. Her shameful curiosity was no secret, not after the cost to her family and tribe to rescue her from her own folly.

"You look lovely, daughter." Una's mother's voice thankfully broke into her daughter's morose thoughts.

Una spun and rushed to embrace the other woman. "It's been so long since you have been home."

"My home is with your father in the village now," her mother gently chided. "This place is the same as the day we left it for the village."

Her mother said the same thing each of the few times she'd come into the trees to visit. The two-room dwelling *was* just as Una's parents had left it. They had taken their prize bed with them and the little furniture they'd accumulated.

Being a home that had been passed down through the generations in their family, it was not sparse. Even with her parents' things gone, the dwelling felt lived-in. Cupboards held dishes enough for two, though Una only used one. There was no cooking fire of course, all cooking had to be done at ground level, but dry foods could be and were stored on the few shelves and in the crannies.

Una had moved the furs she'd used to sleep on the floor of the main room since she was a child into the small bedroom, along with her clothing and personal things. The main room had the natural seats created by the branches of the tree integrated into their home and a small table her great-grandfather had made.

"Would you like water?" Una asked her mother with hospitality that was rarely exercised.

"Yes, dear, but I'll get it myself." Her mother moved to the swollen skin, filled from the water-catchers the Éan had placed high in the trees. "You must make this dwelling your own. One day you will share it with a mate."

Una was only nineteen, but she'd long given up hope of finding a mate. Though she never said so to her mother. The thought of trusting another to sleep beside her filled her with a dread she'd never give voice to.

"Is Father already at the royal abode?"

Mòrag grimaced. "He is, giving Prince Eirik an earful about the wolves, if I have my guess."

"What have they done now?"

"Naught, but to hear your father tell it, each one of them is responsible for every bad turn in our village, from the birth of a deformed kid by the neighbor's goat to the deluge of rain we suffered through this past spring."

"They have only been here a month." And summer was well on its way to the solstice.

Mòrag shrugged and then smiled tolerantly. "You know your father."

"Are the wolf soldiers . . . are they . . ."

"Kind?" her mother prompted.

Una could not imagine it, despite the way Bryant behaved when she'd met him in the spirit realm. After all, Una acted with far more boldness there than was her usual wont.

"Violent?" she asked instead.

"Not at all. Oh, they're good hunters and strong warriors, but they *are* kind and rather more polite than our own soldiers."

"They live among the civilized humans." She never said *civilized* the way her father did, with a sneer in his voice.

But Una's mother acknowledged Fionn's attitude with a frown they both understood. "They do, though it has not made them any less fierce. The one they call Bryant smiles more than I've ever seen a warrior smile though. He seems to want to make friends particularly with your father. I cannot imagine why; Fionn has been rude to him at every turn."

Una's breath caught at the mention of the man she'd only met while sleeping.

"The wolves who took me smiled, too." With sneers and cold evil in their compassionless eyes that she would never forget.

"Not all wolves are like the men who took you."

"I know."

"Do you?"

"Of course, I do not put them all in the same school of fish just because they share a wolf nature." As much as she might shy from Bryant were she to meet him in the flesh, she would not think him capable of the cruelty she'd suffered at the hands of his fellow wolves.

Mòrag looked very sad. "Sweeting, I very much fear that you do."

"That would make me like them, Mother, hating an entire race."

"You are nothing like those men, but neither are these clansmen." Mòrag smoothed Una's already shining hair. "You look so lovely this eve."

Una ignored the compliment, choosing to focus instead on her mother's other words. "Father doesn't like them."

"Your father hates all wolves for what those horrible Faol who took you did to you."

"And him." Una turned away, lest her mother see the pain filling hazel eyes just like her own. "They left him too crippled to fly."

"Aye, but these men our prince has given leave to live among us? They were no part of that."

"But they could have been."

"Could they?"

Una was certain of it. All wolves had that viciousness in their nature. Not that all would give in to it. She sincerely hoped Bryant had never done so.

Mòrag sighed, the sound filled with the same old pain that plagued Una. "Daughter, you have suffered greatly, but not at the hands of *these* men. They will not hurt you."

Trust her mother to see the terror Una worked so hard to hide. "I just don't understand why Prince Eirik had to let them enter our homeland."

"Because change must come."

"But why?" Even as Una asked, part of her longed for change. If not among her people, then in her own heart. So she would not live in such fear any longer.

"It has been foretold."

"And that makes it so?" she demanded.

Though, now more than ever, she had reason to trust the visions of the *celi di*.

"You know it does," her mother said in a tone that showed her shock at Una's words. "Our seers have led us since time immemorial. We cannot begin to doubt their guidance now, not if we want your children to have a hope at life as it is meant to be lived."

"As slaves to the Faol?" Una asked, her worst worries coming to the fore.

"In secret," Mòrag emphasized. "Hiding from the peoples who live in this land with us. It is time for the Éan to come out into the sun."

"No," Una said with anguish she could not hide.

"Oh, daughter." Mòrag pulled her into a hug, but Una would not let herself relax. The tears would come then.

And she would not give any more of her tears to the wolves who had done her and her tribe such irreparable harm.

FIVE

Una's mother had been right, Bryant smiled far more than the Éan warriors were wont to do. Especially her father.

He had a cheerful nature when they'd met in the spirit lands of Chrechte, but she'd thought again that it had been because they were in a place out of time. A place where no harm could come to them and the trials of physical life could not assail them.

But it seemed at first glance as if the man she had met while she slept was exactly like himself in the physical realm.

Right down to being more handsome than any soldier had a right to be. Even his scars, those at least he hadn't had in the other realm, only made him look more appealing. He was no perfect man, who had not faced hardship or battle, but a real warrior who had the marks on his body to prove it.

A larger-than-life presence, he seemed every bit as big and a great deal more intimidating with it, in the flesh. The warrior braids in his mahogany hair depicted his life. He'd told her what each one was for on their last spirit-plane visit. The three on his left side commemorated important events in life as a soldier for the Balmoral pack.

The one on his right was in honor of the grandfather who had died ten years past, bequeathing Bryant both his name and his sword. Her brows drew together in confusion as she noted a second thin braid beside the first. It had not been there before. The ends of this braid were wrapped with bits of string.

If her eyes were not deceiving her, and considering her superior eagle sight, that was highly unlikely, those bits of string were the exact shades of green and brown as her hazel eyes.

She stared into eyes dancing with humor and something else she refused to name. The man near took her breath away.

And that had never happened before.

Not in this physical world where the nearness of strangers was more likely to send her into a fit of panic than passion.

"We have not met." He put his hand out to take hers, his storm-cloud gaze telling a very different story. "I am Bryant of the Balmoral."

Her father knocked the hand away with his walking stick before Una could even think to take it. "Do you know no better than to proceed without a proper introduction?"

"Thank you so much for offering, Fionn." Bryant's tone could only be described as smug.

The man liked besting others in cleverness. She'd noted that even in the spirit plane. She'd found it charming there; here in the flesh, it was more likely to cause her father to erupt in an apoplectic fit.

Sure enough, Fionn's face turned red with fury as his eyes snapped a promise of retribution.

"Bryant, may I introduce my daughter, Una?" Moving slightly so she stood between Una and Bryant, Mòrag jumped in to fill the gap, as she had so many times over the years with Una's father's less-than-polite ways. "Una, this is one of the Faol soldiers our prince has welcomed to live among our people."

Even if Una had not been meeting the man these past weeks while they both slept, she had seen him arrive in the village. She understood her mother's move for what it was, an attempt to protect Una from being forced to take the man's hand in greeting.

Oblivious to Mòrag's machinations, Bryant simply shifted so that he was once again standing far too close to Una. He put his now red-marked hand out a second time in offering, not even glancing at her father to see if the other man would object this time, too.

Una saw her mother's telltale wince turn to a look of astonishment as Una's hand came forward of its own volition to be swallowed in the large, masculine paw.

Though she trembled at a wolf's touch, she allowed it, not yanking her hand back with unseemly haste, not pulling away from his clasp at all.

His grey eyes narrowed, his expression turning concerned as he inhaled the scent of her fear. He would learn only too quickly that, unlike him, Una was far different in the physical realm than the spirit one.

He did not immediately release her, and contrary to her past experiences, her fear dissipated rather than grew. It did not leave her completely. That would have taken a miracle, and she'd learned she was fresh out of those that fateful day five years past.

But Una felt no urge to run and that was miracle enough, she supposed. Bryant's hand was warm and strong, just like in the spirit plane. He did not crush her fingers, holding her hand as if she was as delicate as a summer bird.

"I'm an eagle," she blurted out.

His eyes widened. "That is good to know."

Though she'd told him her bird form in the spirit plane. He'd told her he wanted to see it, but she'd refused to shift. She emphatically did not want to see his wolf. Not even on the spirit plane.

When she made no reply, Bryant added, "I understood eagles are uncommon among the Éan."

She'd told him that as well. She *hadn't* told him that she was not a very good eagle.

"We are, the Faol have killed too many of us off." Though his words were anything but, Una's father's tone was almost friendly. "And I'll thank ye to release my daughter's hand now."

Una gasped. Whether from the cessation of contact with the only man who had ever kissed her, or her parent's unexpected reaction to Bryant, she did not know.

"She's quite charming," Bryant said to her mother. "You must be very proud of her."

Mòrag smiled and nodded. "She is. It's a surprise to us both that our daughter is yet unmated at nineteen."

Heat climbed into Una's cheeks as her father made a sound of disgust, apparently as unimpressed with her mother's impossible attempts at matchmaking as Una herself.

"The Chrechte among our clan often mate at a later age than humans marry. It's a matter of finding the bond intended by fate to be ours, isn't it?" Bryant asked with all appearance of sincerity.

Were sacred bonds so common among the Faol then? She'd only ever known of a handful of sacred matings in her life. Éan were encouraged to mate young without consideration to the hope of finding their one true mate. Without offspring, their people would die off.

And there were few enough babies born among their people as it was.

"You believe you will find your sacred mate?" Una asked, still somewhat surprised by her temerity in voluntarily talking to the wolf, no matter their nocturnal visits.

This was not a topic they had spoken about between pleasure-inducing kisses. And this was not the safety of that place out of time.

"I do. Wherever she may be." The look Bryant gave Una was disturbing in its intensity. "Our laird found his in an Englishwoman. Your own princess is mated to the Faol laird of the Donegals."

"She betrayed her people," Fionn stated with categorical certainty.

Both Una and her mother gasped. Prince Eirik would be livid if he overheard such talk. He might even sanction Fionn, but were Anya Gra to hear such a sentiment expressed, the *celi di* might well curse him and his family, refusing them access to the sacred stone.

"You must not say such things," Mòrag said in a tone that said Una's father was headed for the deepest, coldest part of the loch.

"Hmmph." Fionn had the grace to at least look marginally chagrined.

"Do you believe Sabrine claiming her true mate was a betrayal of your people?" Bryant asked Una, as if it was her opinion that mattered, not her father's.

"The ancient teachings of the Chrechte make it clear that a sacred mating bond should be placed above all else." Una swallowed at the sulfuric glare from her father, but she would not recall her words.

She'd worked so hard not to disappoint him further since the debacle five years ago, but in this, her father was very, very wrong.

"You must forgive Fionn." Una's mother had drawn herself away from her husband in a way that said she wasn't sure she had done so though. "But sacred mates are so rare among our people we forget their importance in the face of simple survival."

Bryant nodded his understanding. "You mate to procreate rather than enjoy the sacred bond. Many among the Faol believe they must do the same."

"Which is not to say that our matings are of no importance," Mòrag stated firmly.

"You and Fionn . . ." Bryant prompted.

"We are not sacred mates, but we were still blessed with a child. For that, I will always be grateful." Her mother gave Una a look filled with warmth and love.

"Every child is a gift," Bryant said with that way he had, like he was certain of the truths in his world, and anyone who might disagree could be made to see the error of his or her ways. "My own parents are sacred mates."

"Did they have many children then?" Mòrag asked wistfully.

"Four that lived out of childhood."

"That is a blessing indeed."

"So my father says. Mum isn't so sure when we are tracking dirt on her recently cleaned floors with our big muddy feet."

"You are all male then?"

"Oh, nay. I have an older brother and two younger sisters, both hellions truth be told, and more trouble by far than either of us boys, to hear my mother tell it. Though one has married and is her husband's headache now. Though she's given us my precious niece, who has the entire family trained to her bidding."

Una found a smile coming to her face. "How old is the wee one?"

"Two summers and full of energy beyond us all." Bryant's eyes glowed when he spoke of his family.

"You must miss them terribly."

"Aye."

"And yet you have made your home here." It was beyond her understanding.

"The repatriation of the Éan will not come without sacrifice. It seems only fair those begin with the Faol, considering the cost your people have already paid over the years."

"*Repatriation—*" Fionn began in a tone that said they were all in for a rant of extraordinary proportions.

Mòrag determinedly interrupted without a single blush. "Una cares for the children of our tribe, you know."

"That is a commendable contribution to make to your clan."

"I should be a warrior," Una admitted with the shame she always felt. "I am an eagle."

"You are perfect as you are," her mother staunchly refuted.

But her father remained silent, his expression showing neither approval nor disdain for his only offspring. He was still clearly angry over the concept of the Éan and Faol reuniting.

"Our women are not trained in warfare," Bryant mused. "If they were, I'm not sure our laird would not be a woman."

Mòrag and Una laughed softly at what was clearly meant to be a joke, but her father frowned. "A woman should always be trained to protect herself."

"On that we agree. Balmoral women are taught to hunt small game and most fathers teach their daughters simple defense, but life among the clans is different than it is for you here in the forest."

"*Different,*" her father derided. "That's one word for it."

Bryant didn't look in the least offended, just smiled slightly. "I know you think little of being civilized and I must admit that the Balmoral are far less so than other clans."

"Hmmph." Her father gave his favorite answer when he had nothing to add.

"Do you never come down to the village?" Bryant asked Una. "I have not seen you there."

The slight emphasis he gave to the word *there* appeared unnoticed by her parents, but Una felt it deep inside. They shared a secret, an intimacy easily equal to that of their kisses.

"I usually come down daily." But she'd been afraid to come down with the wolves there.

Besides, her father had forbidden her.

Fionn frowned. "She doesn't need to be down in the village with strange soldiers running amok."

"We are hardly running amok and surely after a month, not nearly so strange to you any longer?"

"You're a wolf. You'll always be strange," her father pronounced, but without his usual heat.

"I've missed my daily visits with my daughter," her mother said with a plaintive look at first Fionn and then Una.

Guilt suffused Una. She'd kept away from her mother because of her own fear, both of the wolves and of upsetting her father when she knew she'd given up all right to do so.

And deep inside, where she never let others see, she had been beyond terrified she *would* meet Bryant only to discover her sojourns on the spirit plane had all been in her imagination.

"I will come to see you tomorrow," Una promised her mother.

Mòrag smiled, patting her arm. "I would like that."

"Hmmph." Her father contributed, but it was not a denial.

Una let a tremulous smile curve her lips.

"Perhaps I will see you as well," Bryant said.

"Why would you want to?" Una blurted out before thinking how the words might sound.

But Bryant didn't laugh, or even smile. His masculine countenance had turned entirely serious. "I believe you know."

"I . . ." But she did not know what to say.

She did not want to tell her parents about the trips to the Chrechte sacred place. They would worry. Besides, had he not realized yet, she was not the same person here as she was there?

"What are you talking about?" her father demanded.

"In this case, I believe the particulars are between your daughter and *me*." Bryant's expression showed no chance of being moved.

"Nonsense. She is mine to protect and care for."

"Until she is mated."

"She's not mated yet," her father said in a tone Una had never heard from him before.

She stared at him, but he was busy glaring at Bryant.

"Una?" her father prompted without looking away from the other man.

"I don't know." The lie tasted sour on her tongue, but the truth would burn worse.

Bryant's frown of disappointment made Una's stomach twist.

She didn't lie. Not anymore. Not so she could sneak out of the safety of their forest, nor for any other reason. And now this man, who knew her better than even her own parents, believed she was a cowardly deceiver.

But he could not possibly understand. She owed her parents not to cause them any further worry or distress. They could not know her Chrechte nature had drawn her into the spirit world, for she knew not what.

"I don't know what you are talking about," she reiterated stubbornly, ignoring the stain the words left behind on her soul.

"You'll figure it out," Bryant promised before taking his leave of her parents, with more polish than the "less civilized" Balmoral should be able to accomplish.

SIX

Bryant watched Fionn's hut surreptitiously while he and Donnach dressed their kill from their early morning hunt.

Una had said she would come to visit her mother today, but he didn't know when that might be. They had not met on the dream plane the night before.

She called it the spiritual plane, was convinced they were not sharing a dream. He hadn't been sure it wasn't merely his own nighttime imaginings right up until he'd met her at the feast the night before.

He'd had to focus hard to hide his shock, first at her appearance beside the irascible Fionn, and then at the difference in her manner from when he'd met her while sleeping.

Donnach nudged Bryant's shoulder. "Stop staring over there. I told you that old man is not going to warm up to us."

"You're wrong. He was almost civil to me last night." Though Fionn had made his disapproval of Bryant's appreciation for his daughter more than obvious.

"Well, he's not going to be civil if he catches you spying on his hut. Why are you watching it so closely anyway?"

"I met his daughter last night."

"He has a daughter?" Donnach asked, like the idea was too farfetched for belief.

"Aye. She's lovely, with her mother's oval face and pretty hazel eyes. Her hair is a soft brown, different from most among the Éan, lighter than most wolves as well, but not blond." Just like the woman in his dreams, which apparently were not simple dreams at all. "It looks like water falling down her back."

Heat climbed up his neck as Bryant realized how he must sound to the other warrior.

Donnach looked at him askance. *"You find her appealing?"*

"Aye." Bryant frowned.

What was so unusual about that? Many men would find Una attractive, but Bryant didn't say so. He was too busy trying to control his wolf, which was not at all happy at the idea that other males might look with favor upon *his* eagle.

Donnach was frowning, too. "No."

"Yes."

"You cannot."

"I can. I do." What was Donnach's problem?

Even if Bryant had a choice, and he did not (his wolf growled *mate* into his mind), he saw no reason to deny the attraction he felt for a woman so timid in person and so bold in their shared dreams.

Donnach shook his head. "This is not good."

"What do you mean? Mating between the Faol and the Éan will bring about our joining together as brethren easier."

"Is that what this is about? You've decided to mate with the Éan to help our cause?" His fellow Balmoral soldier sounded less than impressed by the idea.

Bryant, on the other hand, thought it had great merit, even if his wolf were not so drawn to the woman.

He shrugged his broad shoulders. "The heart goes where it will."

"Now I know you've lost your mind. What warrior says something like that?"

Bryant laughed, not offended in the least. "My father."

"Your father found his true mate when he was barely into his manhood. I suppose he cannot help himself," Donnach grudgingly admitted.

"Aye."

"Well, he's not normal. He calls your mother honey-sweet and the whole clan knows that woman has a tongue that could strip the bark from the trees."

"My mother *is* sweet." In her own way.

"She's a loving termagant." Donnach should know; he'd spent enough time in their home growing up, Bryant's mother called him her third son.

"That she is," Bryant agreed with pride.

"No wonder you don't find Fionn off-putting. You've had a lifetime's experience on the sharp edge of your mother's tongue."

Bryant smacked his friend's shoulder, but there was no heat in it. He didn't bother arguing his mother's kind nature. Donnach knew she masked a soft heart behind sharp words and he didn't mean any offense.

And it was true. Bryant didn't find the old man, Fionn, particularly surly. He was a crabby old man who clearly loved his wife, true mate or not, and his one and only offspring.

"They're eagles," he told Donnach.

"Huh. I wonder if they know Lais."

"I asked the healer about that yestereve. He said Una avoids him like a swarm of wasps and neither of her parents have made much effort to make his acquaintance."

"That is odd, is it not?"

"I thought so."

"And so you asked Lais why, right?"

"I did. He said something happened to Una and it was at the hands of Donegal Faol. Her father ended up injured to the point of not being able to take flight any longer, but no one speaks of it and Lais didn't know any further details."

Bryant thought that whatever *had* happened had turned Una from the confident, engaging woman of his dreams to the timid creature he'd met the night before.

"That is not promising for your budding romance."

"Why? I'm not a Donegal."

"You are a wolf."

"They will have to learn to accept that." The bond of a sacred mating could not be denied.

"You think it will be so simple?"

Bryant shrugged. "I do. If she is my mate, she will accept my wolf."

"I hope you're right. Or wrong about her being your mate." Donnach's tone was filled with foreboding.

"My wolf howls for the chance to claim her, to scent her so that all would know she is ours."

Donnach looked thoughtful. "Mayhap she *is* your sacred mate, but 'tis equally possible this is your way of building bridges between the Éan and the Faol."

"No matter how much I want the races reunited, I cannot fake a sacred mating."

But the expression on Donnach's face said he wasn't so sure.

It was nearly time for latemeal when Una came out of the trees, flying toward her parents' hut in her eagle form.

Bryant's breath caught at the beauty of the bird. He'd tried to get her to shift for him in his *not*-dreams, but she had refused.

His wolf let out a yip of recognition he was unable to keep inside. The eagle's direction of flight changed and she swooped toward them with a cawing reply, but then she flew up high in the sky.

"There is your ladylove now," Donnach teased.

"How do you know it's her?" Bryant was sure of the bird's identity, but his wolf was drawn to the Éan shifter with a primeval connection he made no attempt to deny.

How could his friend be so certain, however?

The other Balmoral soldier rolled his eyes, his expression mocking. "She's an eagle. You just got through telling me so earlier today. Since arriving we've seen few enough of them in bird form. The fact she started off flying toward her parents' hut was a dead giveaway as well, don't you think?"

Bryant could but nod, his attention fixed on the bird of prey swooping through the air, coming closer and closer to his hut with each figure eight she flew. It was as if she was drawn to him, but could not make herself come closer . . . or stay away.

He willed her to give in and come to him, to show his wolf that she recognized the connection between them after denying him last night.

But the bird continued to fly. Perhaps if Bryant took his attention from her, she would feel the confidence she needed to approach.

This Una was so very different from the one in their nighttime visits. That Una had allowed him near without smelling of rank fear; she had even let him kiss her.

He and Donnach had long since finished dressing their kill of the morning. They now worked on tanning leather from a deer Bryant had taken down the week before.

Bryant went back to it.

"Playing hard to get?" Donnach teased.

"Hoping she will come closer if she doesn't think we are watching her."

"You do have it bad," the other soldier opined with something between envy and disgust.

The sound of flapping wings came just before Una landed on the branch sticking out from the hut's wall. All of the huts had them. Bryant hadn't understood what the branches were for when he'd first noticed them. Now he did.

The branches were a place for the Éan to perch when they did not wish to shift back into their human form.

His eagle looked interested in the skin and Bryant smiled up at her. "'Twould make a lovely pair of boots, would it not?"

Una cocked her head to one side, then dipped it as if looking pointedly at his bare feet.

He just shrugged. Like many Chrechte among the Balmoral, and some humans, too, he preferred to go without footwear. Though he had a pair of carefully crafted, snug-fitting boots for winter lined with rabbit fur.

A gift from his father that Bryant would not dream of refusing to honor by wearing, though he did so only on the coldest days of the year.

The leather he tanned now was not for himself, but he did not think he should mention he meant to use it as a courting gift for the reticent Éan woman.

"You have a beautiful bird," he complimented. "I have never seen an eagle so fine."

Her wings opened, spanning and then laying back against her side, but even her bird's eyes reflected the confusion of the woman within. She was not used to receiving compliments and that was a shame.

"You do not think a wolf could find the eagle form lovely?" Donnach guessed, surprising Bryant.

He had not considered that possibility, but he would be the first to admit (if only to himself) that his brain was not the first thing engaged when Una was near.

Even in her eagle form, her scent called to his wolf and to the man who wanted to irrevocably claim her.

She jerked her head up and down, affirming Donnach's assertion.

"You'd be wrong then. The Faol who believe in the ancient laws and ways of the Chrechte can see nothing but beauty in a shifter such as yourself," Bryant assured her. "My family particularly is happy that the Éan have been found again."

Una made a questioning sound from her throat.

"My mother's family has passed down the stories of their Éan brethren for generations. Her grandmother's granddam was a raven shifter, daughter to one who could shift into dragon form."

"I didn't know that," Donnach said.

"We do not share our heritage outside our family, because most Faol believed the Éan to be nothing more than myth. To claim connection to brethren who had mysteriously disappeared would cause others to call us eccentric."

"Well, your father is not the average wolf," Donnach said leadingly.

Bryant smacked the other soldier so hard he fell back a step. Both men smiled, no anger between them, but Una had taken flight.

"Purgatory's fires," Bryant muttered. "She startles so easily."

"She is rather timid, for an eagle. They are the predatory birds, but she acts more like a dove."

Bryant could not disagree with his friend.

Donnach gave him a friendly push before going back to the leather tanning. "Your family is still eccentric if it claims to be related to a dragon."

"You think so?" Bryant asked noncommittally, knowing full well the old stories were true.

And being true, then it stood to reason that another dragon either lived or would be born again to the Éan. They were the protectors of their race.

But perhaps they were gone as the *conriocht* were from among the Faol. None of their race's own protectors had been born for so many generations that again, most believed the true werewolf with a third form to be nothing but myth.

"You claim to be descendant from the royal line of the Éan?" Fionn demanded in the most querulous tone Bryant had heard from him to date as he limped toward the Balmoral soldiers, a fiercer than normal scowl on his features.

Had Bryant's mate flown away not because she feared him, but because she saw her father's approach?

He could hope, could he not?

"I did no such thing," Bryant argued.

"You told my daughter, *who is supposed to be visiting her mother and me*, not Faol soldiers," he said toward the sky, where the bird continued her circling flight, "that your grandmother many generations back was daughter to a dragon shifter."

"Aye."

"Are you so ignorant you do not realize that is to claim to be descendant of the royal lineage?" Fionn asked scathingly.

"Perhaps I am. Our family did their best to preserve our history from generation to generation, but at some point it must have become enough simply to teach our children that the Éan were real and our own family."

Enough of the history of the Chrechte had been lost because of the divisions caused by their own warlike natures and the secret feud some Faol waged against the Éan.

"You are not a bird," Fionn accused.

SEVEN

Una arrived, dressed much as she had been the night before, and only then did Bryant realize she had disappeared from the sky. It shamed him that he had been so busy arguing with her father, he had not noted her departure.

She stood at a slight distance, but her attention was so clearly focused on what was being said, he had no doubts her curiosity had been aroused. His wolf preened at the thought of their mate showing interest in their history.

Bryant spoke to the old man, but gave a warm smile to his eagle. "I never said I was."

"Yet you claim a royal raven in your antecedents." The glare Fionn cast was leveled at Bryant and Una alike.

"I did not realize that being descendant of a dragon meant that," Bryant reiterated.

Though, it would stand to reason then that if any of the Éan *were* dragons, it would be Prince Eirik. However, if that were the case, surely the Éan would not continue to hide like fugitives in the forest.

A dragon could raze entire villages and would be practically impossible to kill in his shifted form.

Bryant focused on what he did know and Fionn could accept it for the truth it was, or not. Regardless, it was family history he wanted to share with Una. Perhaps she would not fear him so if she realized the past's weight on his actions of the present.

"The last bird shifter born in my family was my grandmother's sister. She was raven and so beautiful many Faol and human alike in our clan vied for her hand in mating."

"What happened to her?" Fionn asked in a tone that said he knew it hadn't been good.

The old man was right, but not because of anything a wolf had done. Unless you counted a man impregnating his beloved wife as a sin against her.

"She died in childbirth."

Fionn's expression softened slightly. "And her child?"

"Took after his father as wolf."

"If she was raven, then your clan wolves would know of our existence before this. And Prince Eirik claims that most of the Faol are wholly unaware of our existence any longer."

"The Balmoral have always believed the old stories and remember the ancient ways of the Chrechte with more dedication than other clans."

"So?"

"Each bird shifter in our family kept their nature secret, though the reason why was another knowledge lost over time."

"So, your clan knew nothing of her heritage."

"Some knew, but most did not."

"And her husband."

"Knew and loved her raven. Why wouldn't he? They were sacred mates."

"Bah . . . again with the sacred mates. You talk as if that miracle happens to every Chrechte, when nothing could be further from the truth." Fionn fixed Bryant with a beady stare. "And it is not the panacea you seem to think it is. Not all is made well and right simply because two people's animals have a hankering for each other."

It was far more than that, but Bryant knew from experience with the chronically crabby man that there would be little purpose in calling Fionn out on his gross minimization.

Bryant chose instead to focus on the latter part of the man's statement. "Perhaps if we Chrechte were better at looking outside our immediate circle for mates, we would find our true bonds more often."

"Hmmph."

"It's true." Donnach put the leather aside and began cleansing his hands in the bucket of water beside the door. "Our own laird is mated to an Englishwoman."

"She used to be English," Bryant emphasized. "And I told Fionn of Lachlan and Emily yestereve."

"So, one man mated to a human." Fionn made a dismissive gesture with his hand. "What does that prove?"

"Our lady's own sister, Abigail, is also true mate to the laird of the Sinclairs. *His* blacksmith shares a sacred bond with a sister to our laird's second. And Lachlan's second is mated to the Sinclair's own sister." Bryant listed off the sacred bonds he'd learned of or witnessed in the past few years.

"Hmmph."

Bryant was coming to dislike that noncommittal utterance, but the expression of interest in Una's keen hazel eyes was enough to keep him talking.

"Had they not looked outside their clans, much less their packs, none of these Chrechte would have found their true mate." Couldn't the old man see what this proved? Did the one Bryant's wolf wanted to mate? "The Chrechte were never meant to live apart, but to live with one another *and* the humans."

"That is not the ancient way," Fionn claimed with the air of a man having made an unassailable point.

"Says who? We have lost many of the ancient ways, no matter how hard we have tried to keep true to them."

"That is not the way of the Highlander, either."

Bryant could hardly argue that point. The clans kept to themselves, developing ties with only a few others for the purposes of trade and waging war. But he knew he was right.

"If our people want to find their true mates, they must be open to mating outside their pack," he reiterated.

"A man does not need his true mate to live a life blessed by the Creator."

Bryant opened his mouth to argue, but realized that doing so might be seen as denigrating the life of the man he hoped to make his father-by-marriage. He snapped his mouth shut.

"Aye, what you say is true, but if we are to continue into the future, we must have more children," Donnach inserted. "Too many matings are not blessed by children."

It was Fionn's turn to open his mouth and then close it without uttering a word of argument. For Donnach's words were true as well.

While the clans around them grew, the Chrechte's numbers fluctuated, but did not increase. Some packs had undeniably shrunk. There were rumors that a pack to the south had grown to numbers unprecedented, but none could confirm the MacLeod pack's true size, nor that of their clan in actual fact.

"There must be more children among the Éan than the Faol," Fionn said disagreeably.

Bryant did not believe him and the way Una shook her head said she denied the words as well. "Your numbers are not so great."

"Because we lose our brethren every year to the murderous Faol."

"And we *all* lose to war."

"We are not at war with the Faol."

"I am glad to hear you say that," Bryant said with a smile.

Fionn met the smile with his customary scowl. "Ye are still at war with us and have been for generation after generation."

"*We* are not at war, but there are the murderous among us. I will not deny it."

"Ye hardly can if you would speak the truth."

"But not all wolves are filled with the hate that spurs these men."

"So you say."

"So I say since I am one of the Faol who would die to protect the Éan." Bryant had been raised to believe it was his calling to somehow bring his feathered brethren back into the Chrechte fold.

The discovery of the Éan's tribe had been the confirmation he and his family needed that the time to do so had come.

"Neither I, nor any of the soldiers who traveled here with me, would kill our Chrechte brethren for no more reason than that their animal takes a different form from our own."

"If that is true, you are an exception."

"Nay. These blackguards who work in secret to destroy, they are the anomaly among the Faol."

"You would have me believe your nature is not violent?" Fionn sneered at the deer hide Bryant had continued to work on.

"We are predators. We hunt. As do your people, but we hunt with a purpose, not for sport."

"The purpose of the Faol is to see the eradication of the Éan."

"Nay!" Bryant's usual good nature slipped and the warrior in him came to the fore. "You accuse what you do not know and without cause."

"You dare say I have no cause?" Fionn's fury burned like a lightning fire in the summer's driest forest.

The old man's walking stick came up with speed, and had Bryant not moved just so, it would have struck his head rather than his shoulder. He did not move completely out of the way, because he'd been taught by his father to always preserve the dignity of his elders.

"Papa . . ." Una's soft, horrified tones interrupted, her eyes filled with fear as she insinuated herself between Bryant and Fionn. "You must not!"

Bryant laid a hand on the smaller curve of her feminine shoulder. "Let him speak his piece. If he does not, it will only continue to fester."

Una spun on him, her expression still tinged with fear, but filled with a bigger portion of disbelief. "You do not think my father has spoken his piece? When does he not rail against the wolf, against what happened to him because of me?"

"Daughter . . . 'twas not you. My loss is at the hands of the evil Faol who hurt you so grievously." The brokenness in the old warrior's voice was hard to hear.

"And it is a Faol you need to rail against," Bryant reiterated. "So, do your railing, old man."

Like the blow to his shoulder, Bryant could take it easily.

"Old man? Whom do you call old?" Fionn demanded with genuine affront.

Bryant kept back his humor with effort, but he did it. "You claim to have cause to dye every wolf with the same bubbling vat of vitriol. So, let me hear it."

"Your people took my daughter. They did unspeakable things to her. She has not been the same since we got her back. Her spirit is broken."

Una stood there, her face suffused with color, her expression equal parts horrified embarrassment and remembered pain. But in her eyes?

In that beautiful hazel gaze, Bryant saw nothing but anger. Anger at the Faol? Anger at her father? Anger at Bryant? He did not know, but 'twas not the muted light of a broken spirit.

"She doesn't look broken to me," Donnach observed, agreeing with Bryant's private thoughts.

Bryant let his smile through this time. "Nay, I would say she appears more a woman ready to break something. I've seen the look often enough on my own mother's countenance to know it well."

"I'm not . . . I wouldn't . . ." Una couldn't seem to get out a full thought and in a strangled tone at that.

"What is it, daughter?" Fionn asked with all the appearance of a man who had no thought to how furious his words had just made the woman before him.

"My private business is *mine*," she finally said in a deadly tone, all signs of her timidity hidden beneath the heat of her offense.

"Aye, it is." Fionn's easy agreement surprised Bryant.

Una, for her part, did not look much appeased. "Then you should not have brought it up."

"Aye, but the fool can already see what his brethren did to me with his own two eyes, and yet he denies it."

"I deny no truth, but your words are wrong." Bryant rarely gainsaid his elders. His parents had taught him better, but this he would not bear.

"These men who hurt you and the woman my wolf longs for, they are not *my* brethren any more than they are *yours*. All Chrechte are brethren in spirit, but in the end each man must stand alone before his maker to have his actions judged."

"You are a fool."

Bryant bristled at the blatant insult. "I am a warrior who would see the division between the Éan and the Faol at an end."

"And then see the true end of the Éan. That is your plan, is it not?" The accusation in Fionn's tone sparked doubt in his daughter's gaze.

"No." Bryant was so damn frustrated. "Speaking to you is the same as conversing with a rock."

Una's breath escaped with a shocking sound of amusement, her fear completely in abeyance for the first time that day.

When all three men turned their regard on her in question, she blushed and then shrugged. "It is only that my mother has often said the same."

"Hmmph."

"Is that your answer when you have no words of denial?" Bryant asked with humor-laced annoyance of the older man.

Again that sweetly unexpected sound from Una. Though she merely shook her head when Bryant gave her a questioning look.

She utterly charmed him.

And he terrified her.

If he claimed her, introduced her to his wolf, then she would know all could be well between them. That he would never hurt her as the Donegal wolves had done.

Something of the heat the thought sparked in him must have made itself known to Una, because she blushed and let off a scent that was nothing like the acrid fear he'd come to expect in such a short time.

"Mòrag would have you and this one join us for latemeal. She wishes to know more of your family's history," Fionn said, with a worried look at his daughter, before indicating both Bryant and

Donnach with a sweep of his walking stick, when the silence had stretched for a long moment.

Donnach looked on the irritable Éan with clear disbelief. "This was your attempt at inviting us to dinner?"

"Are ye coming, or not?" Fionn demanded.

Bryant met the lovely Una's eyes when he answered her father. "We'd be pleased to."

"Speak for yourself," Donnach muttered low enough only a wolf would be able to hear.

Or a very cantankerous old man, if the renewed glare Fionn gave the other Balmoral wolf was anything to go by.

EIGHT

Una fluttered like a hummingbird around her parents' hut, helping her mother with final preparations for the latemeal.

One benefit to the ground village was that a family could cook in their own home without grave concern for the spread of fire.

Una couldn't believe her mother had invited the wolves to sup with them, but part of her was fiercely glad Mòrag had. Una had been terribly disappointed when she hadn't been taken to the spirit lands to meet up with Bryant in her sleep the night before.

But perhaps that was because she barely slept for thought of him. She'd spent the day mooning over the impossible and finally flown out of the treetops for her promised visit to her parents only to find her eagle inexorably drawn to the wolf.

"Why have you invited the Balmoral soldiers? Papa isn't happy about it."

"Bah. Your father spends half his life complaining about one thing or another. I know how to handle him." Mòrag stirred the stew pot, adding a sprig of rosemary. "As I told your father, I wish to hear more of the lad Bryant's family."

"But why?" Una could not understand her mother's curiosity about a wolf.

Her own was based on some obscure desire within Una's eagle, but her mother? She should have no reason to want to know more about any of the Faol.

"Because he looks at you as a man intent on claiming a mate."

"What?" Una practically shrieked. "I'm not his mate. I'm an eagle. He's a wolf. We aren't mates."

No matter how he'd listed off a host of improbable sacred matings to her father.

"As you say," Mòrag agreed far too easily and with such calm acceptance Una knew it to be false.

"You are plotting."

Her mother continued to stir stew that needed no further tending, pretending she had not heard.

"I know it is a disappointment for you and Father." Like so many things about their only daughter. "But I will *never* mate, Mother. I cannot. Not after what happened five years ago."

"Nonsense." Mòrag pulled the bricks from the oven opening and carefully drew forth the long baking paddle with two loaves of heavy dark bread from within.

They smelled so good, Una's stomach would have growled if it were not tied firmly in knots by her mother's words. "It isn't nonsense. Surely you've noticed the wide distance the men of our tribe keep from me. I am considered a poor choice for a mate."

"What rot." Her mother slammed the bread paddle down with more force than could possibly be needed. "You would make a fine mate, but our men keep away because you have made it clear that when any man but your father gets within ten paces of you, you panic like a rabbit in a den of wolves."

Funny her mother should put it that way, for it was exactly how Una had felt five years ago.

Mòrag sighed, looking at Una with sadness. "They know you fear them, so they stay away."

"I won't take a mate, I can't." Una couldn't think of a clearer way to say it to her beloved mother. "I don't deserve a mate," she admitted.

"Yes, you do. Oh, my dearest daughter . . ." Mòrag left the bread to pull Una into a hug.

"I am your only daughter."

"And still dearest to my heart."

"Mama . . ." she said, using the diminutive she'd stopped saying those years go, and for once making no effort to spurn the affection offered.

"You deserve a fine strong mate like your father was for me, and children." Mòrag hugged her hard. "Oh, I hope you have many, many children. I shall be such a fine granddam."

"Mother . . ." Una started, not sure how to get through to the other woman.

"Naught but a sacred bond could pull you from your fear, I know that, child."

"So, you understand?" Una pressed as she gently disengaged herself, needing her mother to accept the truth.

"Oh, yes, daughter. I understand. Do you?"

Una had no chance to answer as her father came inside at that moment, the two Balmoral soldiers behind him.

Both greeted her mother with gratitude for the invitation, and proper Chrechte respect.

But Bryant's attention was on Una from the moment he entered the hut, his wolf's storm-grey eyes fixed on her wherever she moved.

Somehow, Una found herself seated beside Bryant on the floor near the single small table the hut boasted, while her parents took the bench and Donnach sat on the only three-legged stool across from them. It was a cozy gathering, not unlike those in Una's past.

Emotion clogged her throat, making it hard to eat and impossible to converse.

The heat from the Balmoral wolf crossed the space between them, warming Una in strange places, to be sure.

"Una said you told her, when she visited you in her *eagle* form, that you have family among the Éan."

Una didn't know why her mother had to make her visiting Bryant as an eagle sound so . . . significant. She found him fascinating, but felt safer as a bird because she could fly away if she needed to. That was all there was to it.

"In the generations that came before, yes."

Even though she'd been there for most of his explanation before, Una listened with rapt fascination as Bryant recounted to her mother what he had said to her father earlier.

"So, you are related to Prince Eirik and Anya Gra. Have you made them aware of this?"

"I did not realize the significance of my family's history until Fionn pointed it out."

"Your family could only keep so many of the stories from one generation to the next. You lost history, just as we all have." Mòrag spoke with sad resignation. "It is ever true and why the Chrechte are charged with assigning parts of their history to each family and sharing those stories at all the major feasts."

"The Faol do not practice this."

Una's father slurped noisily at his food. "Clearly, or all of the wolves would be aware of the Éan's existence, not only those who wanted us dead."

"Our alpha wants the races reunited for just this reason," Bryant said.

The fervor of true belief infused his voice, and Una caught herself wondering how much of his interest was in her personally and how much was on reconnecting their people. Through a mating?

If that was his plan, he'd do well to look for an easier target. Her eagle screeched in denial at the thought, but Una ignored her bird.

"He plans to come live in the forest, does he?" Una's father asked aggressively.

But Bryant did not rise to the bait. He merely took a bite of his stew and complimented Una's mother's cooking.

"I've taught Una all I know of preparing food," her mother said in reply, and apropos of nothing, Una thought. "Not that she has much use for the knowledge living alone as she does in our former home."

"Why does she live alone?" Donnach asked. "A Balmoral daughter would never be allowed to live on her own as Una does."

"She is safer high in the trees than she would be here in the village with us," her father said, voicing a sentiment she knew well.

And agreed with.

"Surely other families keep their children with them." Bryant sounded confused.

"If Una had stayed in the trees, the horror of five years past would never have happened."

Una felt the horrible weight in her stomach that truth always brought.

Bryant looked far from impressed, or convinced. "If coming out of the trees caused such hardship, your entire village would have horror stories."

"They know better than to venture beyond the depths of the forest."

"You went exploring?" Bryant asked her directly.

She liked the way he refused to talk around and about her. Like the heat of his wolf at her side, it warmed her. "I found the humans of the clans and their ways infinitely fascinating. I liked to watch them in my eagle form."

Una hated admitting her failings out loud, but she would not deny them, either. No matter how much she might like to.

"But you were not caught as eagle," Bryant guessed with far too much astuteness.

"No." She'd been in her human form, swimming in the loch and playing in the falls that fed it as she'd seen the clan's children do.

"What happened? Why didn't you shift and fly away?"

Una rubbed at her wrists where the iron spikes had been driven to hold her to the tree.

Bryant noticed the small telltale gesture and put his hand out. "May I see?"

She should tell him no, absolutely not, as she would if anyone else had requested thus. But Una found herself offering her wrists.

He tugged up the sleeves of her blouse, a growl echoing in the otherwise silent hut as his eyes fell on the scars that could not be misinterpreted.

"They did this to you?"

"They found sport in hurting and terrifying me," she admitted, not really understanding why she did so. Only that her eagle insisted on it.

Bryant lifted his head, his grey gaze boring into her father. "And did you kill them?"

"Those we caught, we killed, but not easily and not without cost."

"There were nearly a dozen of them. They performed some strange ritual, not of the Chrechte, I don't think."

"Any women?" Donnach asked, his voice filled with revulsion.

"No. Only men. One of them was being initiated into the group. He drove the spikes in, to prove his commitment to their cause."

"He is not dead," her father said with frustrated venom. "But I have been in no condition to hunt him."

"Would you still recognize his scent?" Bryant asked in a tone that made her shiver.

"We are not wolves, our sense of smell and hearing is only slightly better than a human's."

"You would recognize him."

"I would," Una said with certainty. "Though it is my deepest wish never to lay eyes on him again."

"Describe him."

"Why?" Una asked, unable to understand why he would request such a thing of her.

"That I may find and kill him."

"What? No!"

"He was Donegal," Donnach guessed.

"They wore no plaids. I do not know if all the men were of the same clan, though some were. I'd seen them among the Donegals before that," she admitted in a quiet voice.

Una could not understand it when she found herself pulled into Bryant's lap and was even more shocked when neither of her parents made a complaint.

"Describe this miscreant to me," Bryant urged, his chest rumbling with a wolf's growl.

It should have frightened her, but for the first time in five years, Una felt truly safe. 'Twas a conundrum she had no hope of deciphering, but gave thanks for all the same.

To have even a few moments without fear would be a blessing indeed. If the cost was describing the men who had hurt her, the ones her clansmen had not killed . . . then it was a price she would pay.

Later, Bryant insisted her mother accompany Una back into the treetops to see her safely in her home. She wanted his company, not that of her parent, but no words left her lips to tell him so.

NINE

Una did not see Bryant for five days after the dinner with her parents. Not at night, while she slept. Not each afternoon when she went down to visit her mother in the village. She didn't see the other Balmoral, Donnach, either.

On the second day, she inquired in passing if her mother had seen Bryant, but Mòrag hadn't heard the question. And Una had been too embarrassed to be asking it to repeat her words.

She noted her father was less vocal in his displeasure about the Faol soldiers staying in the village, but he didn't mention Bryant by name.

On the third day, Una's eagle grew restless enough for her to repeat the question to her mother, but received a simple, "I don't know," in reply.

Not at all helpful.

Given Una's reticence in social situations, her mother's astonishment could be forgiven when Una suggested they visit one of the families housing another Faol warrior, this one from the Sinclair clan.

"I did not realize you were on close terms with the daughter of the house."

"We are of an age," Una said noncommittally.

In truth, Una had done little to maintain any of her childhood friendships in the last five years. And for the first time, she realized regret in that.

The visit proved wholly unfruitful in discovering the whereabouts of the Balmoral soldiers, but Una enjoyed reconnecting with her once bosom friend very much.

She was also quite proud of her reaction to the Sinclair soldier. As long as he stayed on the other side of the room, her fear remained controllable and no attack of panicked terror ensued.

By the fourth day, she was desperate enough to ask her father if he had seen the soldiers.

"They've gone hunting," he replied.

She should have considered that possibility. Still . . . "Aren't wolves very good at the hunt? I would not have thought he would be gone this long."

"It depends on the prey they are hunting." When her father did not follow up that statement with a diatribe about how the Faol hunted the Éan, Una was both confused and surprised.

The fifth day showed no more sign of the men's return than the first. She returned to her home in the trees quite late, hoping if she stayed in the village with her parents, she might be there when the men returned from their hunt.

But her mother sent her home after the sun had set, saying she and her father were old people and needed their rest.

Una barely noted her father's umbrage at once again being called old, and flew up to her home in the treetops, determined to seek out her prince the next day and ask him the whereabouts of the two soldiers.

Surely it was his responsibility to know, as he was beholden for their behavior while among the Éan.

She readied herself for bed, brushing out her hair with desultory movements, holding little hope that tonight would see her on another sojourn to the spirit realm.

A sound like claws scratching on the floor came from the other room and Una froze in her movements. While the noise could not possibly be what her senses were telling her it was, it was definitively not the sound of branches rustling in the wind, either.

She knew each nuance of that music with great mastery, as she'd spent her entire life hearing it.

The candle beside her bed cast the room in which she slept in dim golden light, but there was no mistaking the shape of the shadow in the doorway.

Wolf.

She dropped the brush in shock . . . but not fear. She'd been so certain if she ever saw his other form, she'd be terrified out of her mind.

But in that moment, Una realized it was not the wolf that she feared. It was the evil in men's hearts that would allow them to do to her what the ones who had caught her had done.

He whined at her, like asking for permission to enter.

She took a deep breath and letting it out, patted the spot on the furs beside her. "They were not wolves when they hurt me."

She knew she sounded like she'd just made that realization, but then again . . . she had. All this time, she'd been so afraid. Of the Faol that hunted her people. Of the warriors in her own tribe. Of men.

But she had no reason to fear the wolf.

She knew it in her deepest being.

He crept forward slowly, as if not to scare her. She waited with held breath for him to come closer.

He settled on the furs beside her and she let the breath out in a long sigh. “My eagle is certain you are my protector.”

He nodded his canine head and then nuzzled into her lap.

She reached down with tentative fingers and brushed them through the soft wolf’s pelt. “You are a beautiful creature.”

They had no need for words, for she could see the satisfaction her words gave Bryant and his wolf.

“I was afraid to see you like this, but nothing about your wolf frightens me.”

He made a chuffing noise and nuzzled her again, more forcefully, nearly knocking her backward.

She found herself giggling, a sound she hadn’t heard from herself in so long, it momentarily stunned her into immobility.

He shifted so his head rubbed into her neck and she giggled again. Stars above.

But she was ticklish.

“I forgot,” she whispered into his ruff.

He made a whining sound of question.

“That I am ticklish.”

That chuffing sound came again and then he was rubbing the other side of her neck and finally she knew what he was doing.

“You are scenting me.”

It was not as if he could answer in his current form, but his ministrations increased, his wolf rubbing against every bit of exposed skin she had.

Her neck, her face, her hands, her feet and then he was trying to nose under her shift.

She jumped back. “Stop. What are you doing?”

He made a whining sound again, this time more plaintive.

"I will not take off my shift," she assured the wolf.

He took hold of the hem in his teeth and tugged, his intent clear.

"Stop that. You are going to rip it."

The wolf did not appear to care, pulling harder on the fabric.

"You are too forward," she accused and then realized how ridiculous she sounded.

Telling a wolf, of all things, it was too forward.

Oh, she knew that like other Chrechte, Bryant was fully cognizant as a wolf. But she also knew that like herself, when in his animal form, for the most part his animal instincts ruled.

"You can't mean to scent me all over," she said, though she was very much afraid he did.

His only answer was to tug harder on the hem of her shift. The sound of fabric renting filled the air.

She cried out. "Fine. Will you please stop? I'll take it off."

He stopped tugging, but did not let go of the shift.

"I promise," she said, unable to believe her own words, but even more the genuine intent behind them.

She was going to allow the wolf to scent her. His need to do so was so strong, she could not deny him.

She did not understand, but she knew that she'd missed him these past five days and feared never seeing him again.

The ache to be near him had caused her eagle to constantly fight for supremacy . . . she had wanted to take to the skies and find him.

She'd had no thoughts to fly beyond the deepest parts of the forest in five years.

Bryant released her shift and she tugged it over her head, but put her hand up to stop him coming closer. "After you have scented me, you will shift. We will talk."

He gave a short bark of agreement and she dropped her hand.

He marked her body with his scent, making her giggle more

than once as she discovered more ticklish places than she knew she had.

Finally, the wolf seemed satisfied and lay beside her on the furs, a strange rumbling sound much like a purr, but not, coming from deep in his chest.

Mayhap it could be described as a happy growl?

Regardless, 'twas more than apparent the beast was appeased.

She let him bask in his contentment for long minutes before reminding him that he needed to shift.

He gave another bark of acquiescence and she turned her back to give him privacy for it.

"You no longer fear me," he said by way of telling her it was done.

She turned to face him, curiously unashamed of her nudity. "There is naught to fear in you."

He was the only man who would ever see her thus. Of that she was certain.

"Some have reason to refute that statement."

"No doubt, but they are not me."

"Nay, they are not you."

She swallowed, finding it difficult to form the words she wanted to say, but she forced them out. "I missed you."

"And this surprises you?" He did not sound happy by the prospect.

"It does."

"Why?"

"I do not know you."

"You know me too well."

"But . . ."

"In the dreams we shared—"

"They were not dreams; I explained when we were together in the land of Chrechte spirits."

"Call them dreams, or a different place our spirits go, but we shared our time there, aye?"

"Yes."

"You allowed me to kiss you."

"I have courage there I do not usually enjoy."

"You have a sense of safety there you do not feel when you are awake."

"I felt safe when you held me in my parents' hut."

"That is good to know."

"Is it? Why?"

"You know."

She shook her head, even as her eagle whispered a word she'd been sure the bird would never utter. *Mate.*

"Tell me, Una, who shares dreams among our people?"

"*Our* people?" she asked.

"Yes, *our* people. We are all Chrechte. You are an eagle. I am a brown wolf. Others among my clan are white, grey and black . . . some with differing gifts merely because of the color of their fur. In your own tribe you have ravens and eagles."

"And hawks." Though their numbers were even less than the eagles, as both protectors of their people had been hunted near to extinction.

"I did not know."

"They are so few, we protect their numbers by never exposing them, even to the humans in our tribe."

"It is a hard way to live."

She nodded. No use denying the truth.

"But sometimes even a very difficult life comes with blessings."

"Most times, yes."

"Like finding your true mate." The expression in the wolf's eyes filled with meaning.

Una shook her head, not so much in denial as incomprehension.

"Una, sweeting . . ." He moved forward until the heat from his body called out to hers. "What does it mean when two Chrechte share their dreams?"

She opened her mouth to tell him that they hadn't been dreaming.

But he laid his finger against her lips. "Or are called together in the land of the spirits?"

"I don't know," she whispered. "Only those of royal blood, or who are called on a quest can visit the spirit plane."

He was of royal descent, but that didn't explain her being there with him. And in each sojourn, she had only ever seen someone else that first time.

"Or sacred mates."

"It cannot be."

"It is."

"But . . ." She was going to argue that she was afraid of him, that they could not be mates because she could not share intimacy with him.

Only it would have been a lie. Una no longer felt even a trickling of anxiety in Bryant's presence.

"They didn't violate me," she said so quietly, she was not sure he would hear.

"They tortured you."

"I have scars." Faded in five years, but still there.

"I see nothing but marks of strength and courage on a beautiful body."

"I . . ."

"You belong to me. With me. Now and always."

"I can't."

"You do."

Her gaze rose to meet his. "Can a wolf love an eagle?"

"Aye."

Her breath stuttered and she waited for him to say more.

"How could I not love you, Una?"

"But you do not know me."

"I know you in a way none other ever could," he argued.

She shook her head.

"I have killed for you," he claimed.

Her body went rigid with shock. "What?"

"Your father told me you wondered where I had gone. He told you I was hunting."

The import of his words was not lost on her, but it was only secondary in that moment. "You spoke to my father first?"

"It is proper. And he needed to know it was done."

"What? What was done?"

"The men who hurt you. They are dead."

TEN

"How?" She did not doubt his wolf's prowess at the hunt, but how had Bryant found the men whom she had not seen in five years?

"Lais helped me. Based on your descriptions and what he knew of his former clansmen, he was able to guess at the identity of the one who did this." Bryant ran his thumb over the scar on one of her wrists.

"He was Donegal then?"

"Aye. Lais did not participate in the kill, but he helped us to track your tormentors."

"But why?"

"Justice."

"What of mercy?"

"You were not their only victim."

"How do you know?"

"They confessed . . . boasted more like."

"And for that, they had to die?"

"Aye."

She tried to feel shock, or dismay, but all she experienced was a profound relief. "I am glad."

"Aye, because they did not break your spirit."

"My father thinks they did."

"He knows better now."

"Because you told him?"

"Yes."

"Is killing love then?" she asked, not mocking, but trying to understand.

"Let me show you what it means to be mated to the one destiny created just for you and then *you* will tell *me* what love is."

She would have chided him for his arrogance, but could find no breath for words. Not with him standing so close, his sex already hard and kissing her stomach with moisture.

She was a shifter and though she had more modesty than most, she was accustomed to nudity for the shift. But this nakedness with him was different.

It made her feel things her body had not yet experienced, though her eagle told her they were right and true. She wanted to touch, to be touched.

She wanted to join with him as she'd been certain she would never join with another. The thought of her father's reaction to her mating a wolf came forth to bedevil her, but for the first time in five years the thought of disappointing him was less important than the happiness flickering to life inside her.

And yet, she said, "My father—"

"Has given us his blessing, grudging though it is. If I hurt you, he will dismember me. It was a vow."

She nodded, unexpected joy surging through her. "My mother believes us to be true mates."

"She is a wise woman."

"Aye."

"The time for talking is past." His words came out strained and tight and the hardness standing sentinel between them shifted against her skin, leaving a trail of moisture in its wake.

She reached down and ran her fingertip through the viscous fluid. Though her senses were not as sharp as a wolf's in this regard, the scent of him still drove her near to her knees.

Her eagle cried out to be claimed.

She brought her finger to her mouth, tasting his essence with a delicate lick of her tongue.

Bryant's eyes flared with passion and a growl sounded from his throat before he yanked her to him, stealing the salty flavor from her tongue and replacing it with the sweetness that was his mouth. The kiss was incendiary, beyond anything they had shared in the spirit realm.

The sensations in the flesh were more acute, sharp with pleasure so great she moaned against his lips entirely wantonly.

His hands roamed over her body; everywhere the wolf had scented, Bryant now touched, making her his before he ever joined their bodies as one.

Spots that had been ticklish before now buzzed with delight at each caress, enhancing her arousal until even she could smell the scent of her body's preparation for him.

One big hand slid between her legs, masculine fingers delving into flesh that had never been touched. Even by her.

The ecstasy was so immense, her strength gave out. He held her up with no evidence of effort, his muscular arm locked tight around her while his hand touched her most intimate flesh in secret and surely forbidden ways.

It felt too good to be proper behavior.

But then she was an Éan . . . propriety meant little to her people.

This delight, however? It was something too amazing to ever do without again.

Oh, that the Creator would not let her have to do without it again.

The arm holding her up shifted, and suddenly his fingertip was between her nether cheeks, teasing at flesh she never would have suspected had so much feeling.

She tore her mouth from his. "Bryant!"

"Aye, lass?"

"You . . . that . . ."

"Nothing is forbidden between mates."

Her head came forward, her mouth settling against the join of his neck and shoulder. "Mates," she whispered before biting him in a way meant to leave a mark.

His entirely masculine groan of appreciation shivered through her, making her thighs clench. "I thought only wolves bit to mark their mates."

She nuzzled into his neck, kissing and licking where she'd bitten him. "I will scent you, too, though maybe not as thoroughly as you have done me."

Her eagle only needed this kind of cuddling, head to head, to be satisfied. The feminine Chrechte inside her, on the other hand, wanted Bryant to wear marks of her possession just as she was sure to wear his.

He laid her down on the furs. "This is forever, you understand that?"

She looked up at him in confusion. "Isn't it always?"

He shook his head. "But that doesn't matter, because *this* is."

"Yes."

He growled and then devoured her, his mouth following the trail his fingers had blazed earlier.

When he took one of her nipples into his mouth, she arched up off the furs, feeling that right in her core. He continued to caress her body to a higher and higher pitch of pleasure.

She wanted to return the favor, though she had no experience of a man's body.

He didn't seem to care, moaning and growling with every exploration of her fingers. She traced the lines of his muscles down his chest, along the tree trunks he called legs and then to that hot, throbbing erection between them.

It pulsed in her hand, her fingers unable to completely encompass its girth.

She did not ask if he would fit in that place inside her. There was no option. He had to fit, because she must have him inside her.

She spread her legs in invitation and his head came up just like a wolf scenting the wind. "You want me."

Did he need the words? "Yes. Claim me."

Stillness came over them, the moment profound, where only a second before it had been all heated passion.

He shifted until his engorged flesh pressed against her untried opening. "Do you accept me into your body?" he asked in ancient Chrechte.

"Yes," she responded in kind.

"Do you accept me into your life?"

"Yes."

"Does your eagle accept me as her mate?"

"Ye . . ." Una had to swallow back inexplicable and wholly unexpected tears. "Yes."

"Will you accept my protection, my care and my Chrechte honor as yours?"

"I will."

He fell silent.

She stared up at him through the candlelight, taking several calming breaths before she asked. "Do you accept my body as your only succor?"

"I do. I will never lie with another."

Though true mates were not physically capable of doing so, his tone said his promise was deeper than mere physical ability.

"Do you accept me into your life?"

"Now and always," he promised in their ancient tongue.

"Does your wolf accept me as your mate?"

"Oh, yes."

She smiled at his vehemence and then asked the final vow. "Will you accept my care and support, the love my heart will have only for you?"

It was not a necessary promise in the current Chrechte ceremonies, but the ways of the ancients were strong in Una's treetop home this night.

"Always."

Anya Gra would bless their mating later, speaking the ancient words over them in benediction, and they would receive their mating marks, tattoos of blue ink that would show any who cared to look that she and Bryant were mated for life. The prince would proclaim them man and wife before the entire tribe, but these vows spoken tonight were irrevocable.

None could undo them or deny their validity, though none but the Creator witnessed them.

Neither spoke or moved for long seconds and then he breached her, the pain instant and great. She cried out in shock, but he stopped moving even before she made a sound, remaining still while her body adjusted to the foreign intrusion.

Miraculously, the pain brought back no bad memories and soon was transforming to a pleasure so intense, the world outside the joining of their two bodies ceased to exist.

She shifted her hips, sending pleasure zinging through her. He reacted with a curse in their ancient tongue and she found reason to smile even as she moved again.

The wolf could not stand for her to be in control for long and within a moment he was directing their movements, his body thrusting so his big erection pushed and pulled in and out of her body.

Each tiny increment forward and back brought with it a million sparkles of delight throughout her body. She was soon mindless with the ecstasy of his claiming, her body moving of its own volition in ways meant to enhance the already overwhelming pleasure.

"You are mine," he ground out as he bottomed out in her, pressing against something inside that was beyond pleasure and not quite pain.

"You are mine."

"Aye."

"I am yours," she agreed then.

His smile was feral.

And then he swiveled his hips on the next downward thrust and she felt the maelstrom inside of her spiral out of control. She screamed as her body exploded with pleasure too great to bear in silence.

"I give you my child," he promised as his body went rigid and then he cried her name out and spilled his seed inside her.

"You believe we made a child?" she asked in awe, but grave doubt.

Even sacred mates didn't get with child that quickly, did they?

"I know I did."

ELEVEN

And suddenly, they were no longer in her bedroom in the trees, but lay together, joined as one beside the bubbling brook in the land of the Chrechte spirits.

"We are not asleep," Bryant said in awe.

"We were never dreaming."

"You like to be right."

"Mayhap."

He smiled down at her, his hardness inside her not deflating as she'd once been told by her mother to expect.

"Bryant?"

"I will claim you again, here in the place that gave you to me."

She could do naught but nod.

And they made love again. It was love, too . . . as he had promised. He'd shown her the emotion that defied reason, time and circumstance.

This time she spoke her words of love as she found the ultimate pleasure. "My heart beats for you now."

His expression held such a wealth of emotion it brought healing tears to her eyes. "I love you this day and forever, my eagle. My sacred mate."

"You believed."

"And now you do."

She nodded, her throat too choked for more words.

"You will be a bridge between the races." The words spoken by the *celi di* Una had met the first time she'd come to the spirit plane washed over them with a power that sent Una's pleasure spiking again.

"Your children will bless this generation and the ones to come," the *celi di* continued to intone.

And then she was gone.

"That was . . ." For once, Una's Faol warrior appeared lost for words.

"Surprisingly right." Having a *celi di* speak a blessing and prophesy like that over them as they consummated their sacred mating was . . . the ancient way of things.

And really beautiful.

The spirit realm melted around them and they were back in her bedroom, her *mate* still inside her.

He began moving again and she made a sound, not a protest, but perhaps simply shock.

"We have an entire night of joining to look forward to," he said as if reading her expression.

"But . . ."

"We are sacred mates."

"And that makes everything perfect?" she asked, even as her body greedily accepted his.

"We make it perfect, or as near as we can. It is up to us, your eagle, my wolf, our humanity to make this mating all that the *celi di* said it would be."

"I don't want to leave the forest."

"Then I will live here with you."

"I will go to meet your family," she offered, and even as the words left her mouth, she knew that a day would come when she would willingly leave her home in the forest behind.

Not today . . . but the day was coming.

Bryant's smile was blinding, brighter than a thousand candles lit in a single room. "My mother is going to love you."

"So long as her son does, I will be content."

"With all my heart."

"It is a miracle."

"Don't you know, Una? Life is a miracle."

And for the first time in five years, she believed it.

Her agreement was lost in his kiss.

GLOSSARY OF TERMS

bairn—Scottish Gaelic term for baby

beguines—self-running nunnery without vows to the church, not supported by the official church as related to Rome (historically accurate term in the British Isles)

ben—hill

Ben Bristecrann—broken tree hill (a sacred spot to Ciara's family)

brae—hill or slope

Cahir—warriors who fight the Fearghall

celi di—Scottish Highland priest practicing Catholicism with no official ties to the church in Rome (historically accurate term in relation to Scotland and Ireland)

Chrechte—shifters who share their souls with wolves, birds or cats of prey

Clach Gealach Gra—(moon's heart stone) the bird shifter's sacred stone

conriocht—werewolf (protector of the Faol, shifts into giant half wolf/half man–type creature—protector for the Éan is the dragon and Paindeal is the griffin)

Éan—bird shifters (ravens, eagles and hawks)

Faol—wolf shifters

faolán—little wolf (Gaelic term of endearment)

Faolchú Chridhe—(wolf's heart) the wolf shifter's sacred stone

Fearghall—secret society of wolves intent on wiping out/ subjugating other races of the Chrechte

femwolf—female wolf shifter

kelle—warrior priestess (mentioned in Celtic mythology)

Kyle Kirksonas—River of the Healing Church (where the healing caves are on MacLeod land)

loch—lake

mate-link—the special mental bond between true/sacred mates

mindspeak—communicating via a mental link

mo gra—Gaelic for "my love"

Paindeal—cat shifters (large cats of prey)

Paindeal Neart—(panther's strength) the panther shifter's sacred stone

usquebagh—"water of life" (Scotch whiskey)